J M

A NANNY UNDER
THE MISTLETOE
BY
TERESA SOUTHWICK

AND

SINGLE FATHER,
SURPRISE PRINCE!
BY
RAYE MORGAN

D0528321

MILLS &
BOON

Dear Reader,

It's December!

That's exclamation-point-worthy, since I live in Las Vegas and triple-digit heat is just a bad memory. Last year, ten days before Christmas, we actually had snow. Honest. I took pictures, because it felt like a little miracle.

Now the holidays are here again!

This time of year teases our senses with food, decorations, lights, the fragrance of pine. Some of my favourite movies, books and stories are about Christmas. *It's a Wonderful Life*. *Miracle on 34th Street*. Like the themes of Cherish™, love and family are at the heart of these tales. They leave us smiling and possibly reaching for a tissue—in a good way.

So, with 2010 drawing to a close, I hope all of you have a very happy ending to this year. May your December include mistletoe, magic and miracles.

Happy holidays!

Teresa Southwick

A NANNY UNDER THE MISTLETOE

BY
TERESA SOUTHWICK

All the characters in this book have no existence outside the imagination of the author, and have no relation whatsoever to anyone bearing the same name or names. They are not even distantly inspired by any individual known or unknown to the author, and all the incidents are pure invention.

First published in Great Britain 2010
Harlequin Mills & Boon Limited,
Eton House, 18-24 Paradise Road, Richmond, Surrey TW9 1SR

© Teresa Southwick 2009

ISBN: 978 0 263 88846 1

23-1210

Harlequin Mills & Boon policy is to use papers that are natural, renewable and recyclable products and made from wood grown in sustainable forests. The logging and manufacturing processes conform to the legal environmental regulations of the country of origin.

Printed and bound in Spain
by Litografia Rosés S.A., Barcelona

Teresa Southwick lives with her husband in Las Vegas, the city that reinvents itself every day. An avid fan of romance novels, she is delighted to be living out her dream of writing for Mills & Boon.

To my friend Mary Karlik,
a talented writer and extraordinarily strong woman.
You're proof that the best things do come in small
packages. I hope 2010 brings you nothing
but good things.

Chapter One

Until now, Libby Bradford had never understood how it felt to be so angry you couldn't see straight. At least being this furious kept the grief at bay. Or maybe her fear was so big there was no room for the sadness.

She stared across the utilitarian oak desk in her boss's office. "I really need to talk to someone."

Probably it was the thread of desperation in her voice that made Ginger Davis shut off the computer. "Just a guess, but you didn't come to see me just to discuss the newest show at the Hard Rock Hotel. I'm listening."

Humor normally took the edge off Libby's intensity, but not this time. "Jess Donnelly is going to take Morgan Rose away from me."

"*The* Jess Donnelly?"

"Is there another one?" Libby couldn't imagine the world was big enough for two of him. At least not in his world. "I'm talking about Las Vegas's most eligible and obscenely rich bachelor."

It wasn't often Ginger looked surprised, but she did now. An attractive, brown-eyed brunette somewhere near fifty, she could pass for twenty years younger and it would be pathetically easy for her. Maybe because she loved what she did. As president and CEO of The Nanny Network, she placed thoroughly vetted nannies with famous and wealthy families who cherished competence and confidentiality in equal parts. She had also opened Nooks and Nannies, a preschool that included child care as well as parent and caregiver enrichment classes. Libby was a teacher here.

"Now it makes sense."

Huh?

"What makes sense?" Libby asked her boss. "His attorney called and said that when Jess has child care in place he will take custody of Morgan."

"Mr. Donnelly contacted me about hiring a live-in nanny."

"He did?" Fear balled in Libby's belly.

"Yes. I explained that I recently had two of my employees leave the agency to get married." Ginger removed her glasses. "But you didn't come by my office to hear that I'm shorthanded."

"Not really. It's Morgan I'm concerned about."

"Since Mr. Donnelly didn't share details, I had no idea that he was looking for a nanny for *your* Morgan. I had the impression that your friend Charity left her daughter to you."

Hearing her best friend's name brought a fresh wave of sorrow that hurt Libby's heart. Charity and her husband, Ben, had been in Africa for ten months on a humanitarian mission. They'd been killed by a rebel faction in a raid on the village where they were working.

"No one thought they wouldn't come home." Libby's

voice broke and she stopped, trying to manage the unmanageable emotions.

"Apparently someone thought about it. Otherwise Mr. Donnelly wouldn't be making inquiries about child care," Ginger gently reminded her.

If Libby had been less emotional and more rational she would have commended Morgan's parents for taking care of the details. Except she'd fallen in love with the child she was caring for and giving her up to a man like Jess Donnelly seemed wrong on so many levels.

"Jess *was* named Morgan's guardian in her parents' will," she finally admitted.

"I see."

"I don't," Libby said, squeezing her hands together in her lap. She'd always thought this office a warm place, what with its friendly oak desk and orange and yellow wall prints. But today everything felt cold.

"Why do you question their decision?"

Libby slid forward to the edge of her chair. "Because Charity and Ben trusted *me* with their child when they went halfway around the world."

Ginger's voice was full of gentle sympathy when she asked, "Are you angry because they put a humanitarian effort ahead of their daughter's well-being? Or because they died?"

"Both," Libby said without thinking.

Ginger nodded. "You grew up with Charity and were best friends. You told me that her primary goal in life was to make the world a better place."

"And isn't that ironic? Because the world is so much worse for her not being in it."

Libby had spent more time at Charity's house than with her own messed-up family because there wasn't any tension there and everyone was welcomed with open arms, accepted in a way Libby would never be where she lived. Her friend's folks took the girls to nursing homes, hospitals and women's shelters to give back to their community and make a difference.

"Charity was raised to help people. But now my primary concern has to be raising Morgan the way Charity would want. Her child's welfare is the most important thing."

"It seems to me that she'll be well taken care of."

Not by Jess Donnelly. The man was certainly handsome, wealthy and powerful. From firsthand experience Libby knew he was also arrogant, selfish and shallow. She'd met him the first time when Charity and Ben got married. Her attraction to him was instantaneous. The earth moved. Lightning struck. Cupid's arrow nailed her right smack in the heart.

He'd flirted and fixed his intense blue eyes on her. His thick dark hair and Irish good looks had made quite a lasting impression. She'd have been his for the asking. But he'd never asked.

Actually, he'd left with the other blonde bridesmaid, the buxom one Libby still fondly thought of as the wedding slut. In the nearly six years since Morgan's birth, Libby and Jess had occasionally seen each other, at Morgan's christening, birthday parties, Christmas. Every time their paths crossed, she felt the pull of attraction even though Jess would stick out his hand and say he didn't believe they'd met before, then proceed to introduce himself.

The first time Libby gave him the benefit of the doubt, believing a new hairdo and ten-pound weight loss made her look different. After that it became clear that her breasts just weren't big enough to snag his attention, let alone make her name worthy of remembering.

She pushed the humiliating past from her mind and looked at Ginger. "You think he can really take care of Morgan?"

"Mr. Donnelly certainly has the means to provide for her."

"It takes more than money to raise a child."

"I couldn't agree more," Ginger said. "It's too bad the two of you can't co-parent."

"What do you mean?"

"He has the resources, you have the heart. Seems like a partnership made in child-rearing heaven."

Libby's mind started to hum as an idea began to take shape. "I could be her nanny."

Ginger stared at her. "You already work here at the preschool."

"Which will save you time in the vetting process since I'm already a Nanny Network employee."

Her boss frowned. "Since you have a personal history with the client, I'm not sure this would be an ideal situation."

"I respectfully disagree. Personal history isn't how I'd describe what we have. A handful of get-togethers over the years." And none of them had been the least bit personal, she thought with a mixture of annoyance and yearning that annoyed her even more. "He and I both knew and cared about Morgan's parents. She's a child who needs all the love and support she can get right now. The last thing she needs is to be yanked away from what's familiar and plopped into life with a stern guardian she barely knows."

"You make it sound like a wacky version of *Jane Eyre*."

"Not my intention," Libby assured her. "Just the opposite. It seems like a win-win situation. You said yourself that with his money and my maternal skills we'd make the perfect parents."

"That was an off-the-cuff comment."

"But it makes sense," Libby said, warming to the role

of persuader. "You said you're short-handed right now. This is the perfect solution. I can do double duty—take care of her for Jess and continue to teach here at the school. I'll bring Morgan with me, just like I have been. Her routine wouldn't change and that's important right now."

Ginger tapped her lip thoughtfully before saying, "There's a certain logic to the idea that I could run by Mr. Donnelly."

"Of course he needs to make the final decision." Libby didn't think that would be a problem. As long as his personal life wasn't inconvenienced, Jess would be happy.

"This could be a short-term answer for everyone," Ginger said cautiously.

Exactly what Libby was thinking. It was impossible for her to imagine loving Morgan any more even if she'd given birth to her. She couldn't simply turn her over to a guy who had the sensitivity of a robot. She especially couldn't hand vulnerable Morgan Rose to him, then walk out of her life.

If Jess approved this arrangement, it would give Libby time to figure out a long-term solution.

Jess Donnelly had agreed to be guardian of his best friend's daughter, but he'd never thought he'd have to. Maybe he'd agreed *because* he never thought he'd have to. People did that all the time, never seriously entertaining the possibility that either parent would die, let alone both of them at the same time.

But the worst-case scenario had come to pass and now he was waiting for Morgan. In a few minutes the child's current caretaker would deliver her. Negotiations between his lawyer and the Nanny Network relayed through his secretary resulted in him expecting the nanny, Elizabeth Bradford, momentarily.

He'd checked the child-care company's references and

called a random selection of current and former clients, all of whom had nothing but high praise for the professionals Ginger Davis had provided. Since he didn't know the first thing about raising a kid, let alone a five-year-old girl, he was more than happy to defer to the kid experts.

It wasn't that Jess didn't like children, so much as he didn't relish the idea of someone depending on him. He knew from firsthand experience how betrayal and disillusionment felt. It was especially unpleasant coming from the one person on the planet you counted on. This was his best friend's kid. The friend he'd vowed to support. Always. A friend who was the brother he'd never had. Jess had promised Ben, given his word, which put the pledge firmly in sacred territory. When you watched a friend's back, you didn't turn your own on a sacred promise.

He blew out a long breath as the pain of loss squeezed his chest. "What the hell were you thinking, Ben? No way am I prepared for this."

The phone rang, jarring him into action. He picked up the extension from the end table by the cream-colored sofa. "Yes?"

"Peter Sexton, Mr. Donnelly. Building security. There's a Miss Morgan Rose Harrison to see you and Libby—"

"They're expected," he said. "Bring them up."

Jess had fervently hoped the newly hired nanny would get here before Morgan so he'd have an on-site expert who could hit the ground running when he took custody of the little girl. If the nanny didn't show up soon, he'd be calling Ms. Davis and make Nanny Network news as the first dissatisfied client putting a big fat black mark on its pristine reputation.

The doorbell sounded and since he was already standing in the two-story foyer, it took only a second to

answer. A young woman and small girl stood there—
Libby and Morgan.

The taller blonde was slim, blue-eyed and pretty plain.
Or maybe plainly pretty. On the few occasions they'd met,
he'd never been able to decide. Her shiny hair turned under
and barely touched the collar of the white cotton blouse
peeking from the neck of her navy sweater. Dark denim
jeans did remarkable things to her hips and legs, leaving
no mixed feelings about his opinion of her figure, which
was firmly in the approval column.

The little, tiny blonde who clutched an old, beat-up doll
to her chest had curly hair and brown eyes she'd inherited
from her father as well as the hint of an indentation in her
determined chin. Both blondes stared expectantly up at him.

"Hi," he held out his hand. "Jess Donnelly."

"We've met."

"Right. How long has it been?"

"Last Christmas. Almost a year ago."

He remembered seeing her under the mistletoe at Ben
and Charity's holiday party. It would have been so easy to
catch her there and claim the kiss he'd wanted since the
first time he'd seen her, but he'd deliberately let the chance
slip by. Instinct said she wasn't the sort of woman he could
easily walk away from and he didn't get involved with any
other kind.

"You look great." An understatement.

Libby glanced at the little girl for a moment. "We
missed you at the memorial service."

"Yeah." Pain sliced through him at the reminder that his
friend was gone. "I was in Europe on business and there
was a snow storm. The airport was closed for two days."

"I see."

He couldn't tell from her carefully neutral tone whether

she did or not. Either way there was nothing he could do about that. And what really mattered was his friend's child.

He looked down at her. "Hello, Morgan. Do you remember me?"

Her blond curls bounced when she shook her head. "Not really."

"That's okay," he said, guilt twisting in his gut. "Welcome to my home."

"Nice place," Libby said. Something flashed quickly through her eyes before she continued in a pleasant voice, "The security gates are pretty cool and a twenty-four hour guard who used his key card to escort us to the penthouse on the top floor of the building, in the private elevator, no less, is a nice touch."

Did he hear sarcasm in her voice? Or was the edge simply a symptom of the awkward situation? Did it matter?

"I'm glad you like it." He looked at the child. "What did you think, Morgan?"

"It's okay," she whispered, looking uncertain as she stepped closer and slid her small fingers into the woman's hand.

"Are you going to invite us in?" Libby asked.

"Of course." Mentally he smacked his forehead as he stepped back and opened the door wider.

"Don't forget your suitcase, Morgan," Libby cautioned.

The little girl nodded, then took the handle of a princess-pink weekend-size bag and rolled it onto the foyer's beige marble floor where no princess suitcase had gone before. The woman did the same with a plain black bag. For the first time he thought about the little girl's things. Surely she had more than would fit into the two pieces of luggage just wheeled in.

Major awkward silence followed that flurry of activity

as the three of them stood there. He wasn't sure what to do next and wished again that the nanny would show up and bail him out. In the meantime he figured that a tour was in order. It's what he normally did with a first-time female guest. Although nothing about this situation could even remotely be described as normal. And this small female would be a permanent resident, a thought that registered pretty high on his uneasiness meter.

"How about I show you around?" he offered.

"We'd like that," Libby answered, then looked down. "What do you say, Morgan? Would you like to see your new home?"

Still clutching Libby's hand, the little girl nodded apprehensively. The solemn look on her pale face said she liked the idea about as much as a double helping of Brussels sprouts.

"Follow me."

He led them into the living room with its floor-to-ceiling windows that showed the extensive outdoor area. Because the penthouse was on the top floor, he had a private pool and patio with barbecue. "If you want a view of the Las Vegas strip, you've come to the right place."

"I'm sure Morgan is thrilled at the idea of looking at the adult entertainment capital of the world," Libby said wryly.

"Good point." Another mental forehead smack.

"Although she'll like looking at the pretty lights. Right, sweetie?" When Libby smiled at the child the tenderness in her expression was almost palpable.

"It's pretty high up," the little girl answered cautiously, keeping her distance from the windows.

Libby looked around the room with its dark wood tables bearing traces of European design. "The couch and chairs are very beautiful, but they look like they'll show every spot."

"I haven't found it to be a problem." He glanced at the cream-colored furniture with the overstuffed brown pillows, then at the child, the first to set foot in his place. Life as he'd known it was about to change.

Jess led them through the kitchen that included a morning room with a door onto the terrace. The spacious formal dining area held a table for eight, matching buffet and china cabinet. They walked through the large family room, past the leather corner group and plasma TV. After showing them the living room and master bedroom, he walked to the other side of the condo and pointed out Morgan's bedroom.

"You'll have a king-size bed and your own bathroom. What do you think?" He glanced at the little girl who was looking back at him as if he'd just beheaded her favorite doll.

"It's awfully big." Her mouth trembled. "What if I get lost?"

Instantly Libby went down on one knee and pulled her into a hug. The gesture was completely natural and struck him as incredibly maternal and reassuring. The way a mother should be. The way his mother had been until everything changed.

Libby tucked the child's hair behind her ears. "It's scary, I know. Change always is. But in time you'll get used to it and hardly remember anything else," she explained.

"What if I wake up and it's dark and I get scared?"

"I'm sure Mr. Donnelly won't mind if you leave lights on." She looked up at him. "Right?"

"Of course."

She gently brushed her palms up and down Morgan's arms. "That's an awfully big bed for a little girl. Probably he'll get you a smaller one, maybe with a trundle. That's a bed that slides underneath and pulls out so if you're afraid at night someone can stay in your room. A new bed means a bedspread and sheets. Maybe the princess ones you like. Then the walls might have to be painted to match. That would be your favorite color and would help you get used to a new place."

"What's your favorite color, Morgan?" Jess asked, struggling to find something to say. With the ladies he had no problem, but little girls were out of his league.

"Pink." She met his gaze and her own was troubled. "Sometimes purple."

"Lavender," Libby clarified.

Neither was an earth tone as far as he knew, but no one would accuse him of being the interior design police. Among other things, he built hotels and exclusive resorts, then hired people to decorate them. Exclusively.

"We can talk about altering things," he said. "But I think it might be best to hold off on any sweeping changes until getting some feedback from a child-care professional."

"I'm a licensed preschool teacher, Mr. Donnelly. I've spent the last few years with kids of all different ages at Nooks and Nannies." Her full lips compressed into a straight line. "And Morgan has been in my care for quite a few months. I think I'm eminently qualified to express an opinion on her new environment and would be happy to consult with you about what will help her adjust to her new and different surroundings."

He studied the twin spots of color on her cheeks and the way her blue eyes darkened to navy with this show of spirit. She was standing up for the kid who wasn't even hers and he wondered suddenly whether or not there was a man in her life. The two thoughts would have been contradictory except for his history.

After his dad died, his mother had elevated him to man-of-the-house status. It was the two of them against the world until she fell in love and remarried, at which time she couldn't get rid of Jess fast enough. So he couldn't help wondering if Libby had a boyfriend. If so, was she relieved to hand off this child so she could put the guy first? And he had no reason to care since she'd be gone in a few minutes. And where was the nanny he *was* paying for her expertise in regard to Morgan's environment?

"I'm getting the distinct impression that you don't like my place," he said.

She stood to look at him, but kept a hand on the little girl's shoulder. "It's spectacular and quite lovely. I've never been in a more beautiful home."

"And yet you're talking redecorating."

"If you don't mind my asking, how big is it?"

"About sixty-five-hundred square feet, including the pool and patio," he answered, unable to completely suppress the note of satisfaction. His mother's main squeeze hadn't been shy about expressing the opinion that Jess was a screwup who wouldn't amount to anything. So sue him for taking pride in his spectacular success.

Libby absently nodded as she glanced around. "It's very big and one doesn't need to look far to realize it's a very adult environment."

"I'm not sure what you're getting at."

"The decor is dark. Strategically lighted artwork hangs in nearly every room. There's expensive glass and pricey figurines on flat surfaces and in cabinets. What if something gets broken because a child is high-spirited and energetic? Sticky hands and art projects aren't compatible with light-colored fabric and expensive wood. How is a five-year-old supposed to feel comfortable here?"

"I'm almost six, Aunt Libby," Morgan piped up.

"Yes, you are, sweetie, right after Halloween, Thanksgiving and Christmas. I forgot that you're almost a grown-up." A smile turned up the corners of her full mouth, then disappeared when she looked at him again.

"Is there a point to the running commentary?" he asked.

"I'd feel more comfortable if you seemed the slightest bit willing to compromise for Morgan's sake."

Jess rested his hands on his hips as he studied her. There was something in her voice and a look skipping across her face that made him think her critique of his habitat was more personal than professional. He hadn't seen her often but their paths had crossed enough for him to know that she was smart, very smart. But he'd never seen this sassy side of her before and wondered if he'd done something to tick her off.

Regardless of her attitude, he would concede that she had a point. "Is it possible to cut me some slack? I wasn't expecting to have a child dropped—" He glanced at Morgan and tempered his words. "This situation is not something I anticipated."

"I understand." For a split second profound sadness stood out in her eyes, reminding him that she'd also lost a friend.

"Look, Libby, let me rephrase. After consulting with Morgan, I will discuss kid-friendly changes to her environment with her nanny." He looked at his watch again. "If she ever gets here."

"If she—" Libby's expression went from sad to surprised. "Did you talk to Ginger Davis?"

"Yes."

"Personally?"

"I made initial contact. Then my representatives were in negotiations with her regarding the particulars," he admitted.

"So you never actually spoke with her about the final arrangement?"

The final arrangement? Just like that he felt the need to defend himself. "I'm deeply involved in a massive resort project. My secretary and lawyer handled all the details." The look in her eyes made him add, "Both are trusted professionals who have been on my payroll for a number of years. I have complete faith in their ability to handle my affairs."

"So you staffed out the responsibility of child care?"

Her tone was neutral, the question more about information gathering to fully understand the situation. But again his defensive instincts kicked in. "I've done my homework regarding The Nanny Network and fulfilled my fiduciary responsibility as Morgan's guardian. Elizabeth Bradford comes highly recommended and will take exemplary care of Morgan."

"Elizabeth Bradford is the nanny?"

"Yes." Something about the way she said it made him brace himself. "Why? Do you know her?"

"I do. And I'm quite sure that she'll take very good care of Morgan."

He detected a definite "gotcha" tone to her voice. "What's going on?"

"You really don't know, do you?"

He couldn't shake the feeling that there was a joke unfolding at his expense. A surprise was coming and in his opinion that was never a good thing. "Know what?"

She tilted her chin up, just a bit defiantly. "Libby is a nickname for Elizabeth. It probably slipped your mind that my last name is Bradford. That makes me Elizabeth Bradford. Apparently you missed the part in the negotiations where Morgan's current and future child-care professional are one and the same person. I'm your new nanny."

Chapter Two

Libby knew she shouldn't be surprised that Jess had introduced himself again and barely remembered the last time he'd seen her. He'd proved over and over that she was about as memorable as a bus bench. Part of her desperately wanted him to notice her. The practical, street-wise part instinctively knew there was as much chance of that as deleting her past and inserting one that included a home where she felt wanted.

More shocking was that he'd been expecting a stranger named Elizabeth Bradford. When Ginger had told her that it was a go for her to be Morgan's nanny, she'd assumed he knew about and had agreed to the arrangement. Obviously she'd assumed wrong. He'd started the ball rolling then turned everything over to his employees, who didn't have a clue about them being acquainted.

"Aunt Libby?" The small hand gripped tighter.

"What is it, sweetie?" With an effort Libby kept her tone even and friendly. Kids didn't miss much going on around them—good and bad. She didn't want the little girl to sense her concern. If anyone was to blame for this misunderstanding, it was Jess. He'd been too busy to take a personal interest, which was exactly the reason she'd felt the need to stay with Morgan in the first place.

"Is it time for SpongeBob yet?" Morgan asked.

"You're right. I forgot." And the distraction would be good, Libby realized. She recognized confusion on Jess's face. "It's a cartoon."

"I knew that. I think. Do you want to watch television?" When the little girl nodded, he pointed into the family room. "Right this way."

He grabbed the remote from a shelf in the entertainment center then turned on the TV. "What channel?"

Libby wasn't surprised that he didn't know off the top of his head. News, sports or movies were probably more his thing. That wasn't his fault. She told him the numbers that were second nature to her and seconds later the big yellow guy with the quirky smile came on the screen followed by the sound of his squeaky voice.

Wow. It was the most awesomely clear, bright, big picture she'd ever seen up close and personal. Probably it was the best, latest and most expensive technology on the market. A far cry from her small, old, economical set.

Libby touched the little girl. "Look, Morgan. Sponge-Bob has never looked better. What do you think?"

The thin shoulder lifted briefly. "It's fine."

"Why don't you sit on the sofa with your doll?"

Uncertainty glittered in her eyes before she scrambled up onto the big, L-shaped leather corner group. She looked tiny and frightened and Libby hated leaving her by herself, but it was the lesser of two evils. The bigger bad would be this vulnerable child being present for the talk Libby and Jess were obviously going to have.

Ginger was an extraordinarily efficient woman. Because Jess hadn't handled the negotiations personally, obviously something had been lost in translation. Like the fact that he was already acquainted with Elizabeth Bradford.

"We'll just be in the other room, kiddo." She leaned down for a quick hug. "Just a few minutes. Okay?"

Clutching her doll, Morgan stared up with sad brown eyes. "Promise?"

"Cross my heart." She automatically made the gesture over her chest then held up two fingers.

When she glanced at Jess there was an odd expression on his face. Then he angled his head and she followed him into the foyer, where the plain black and princess suitcases still stood, looking very out of place on the marble floor with the fancy crystal chandelier overhead.

Jess, on the other hand, looked right at home. Which he would, since this *was* his home. She'd always wondered what it was like, a part of her curious about the man who couldn't even remember her name. But she remembered everything about him in far too much detail. The flesh-and-blood man was even better than the image she carried around in her head.

Other than the wedding where she'd first seen him in a traditional black tux, the other run-ins had been casual and his clothes reflected that. Formal or informal attire made no difference; he was an extraordinarily handsome man. She thought she'd prepared herself for seeing him face-to-face, but steel girders and cinder blocks wouldn't have been enough to do the job.

It was Saturday and clearly he wasn't dressed for the

office. In his chest-hugging black T-shirt and worn jeans he looked less like the wealthy man she knew he was. His black hair was cut short and the scruff of beard on his cheeks and jaw made his blue eyes look bluer. Her heart hammered, making it hard to think straight, which was darned inconvenient when thinking was important because she had a lot on the line.

He folded his arms over the chest she'd just admired. "So, let me get this straight. You're the nanny?"

"I am." At least she hoped so.

"I don't think so."

"Give me one good reason," she said.

"We know each other—"

"That's not technically true," she interrupted. Best to take the wind out of his sails before he picked up speed with that thought process. "Knowing each other would imply you remember my name. But every time our paths cross you stick out your hand and say 'Hi, I'm Jess Donnelly.'" She slid her own shaking hands into the pockets of her jeans. "That says Teflon brain."

"Excuse me?"

"You know. Teflon. Slippery. Nothing sticks. Like the fact that we've met. In my book, we really don't *know* each other."

"You were Charity's maid of honor. You came to their housewarming barbecue. You're godmother to that child."

"And you're godfather."

"I remember."

"All evidence to the contrary." She bit her tongue but it was too late because the words were already out.

His gaze narrowed on her. "I learned a long time ago not to assume that everyone recalls who I am. I meet a lot of people and always introduce myself." He lifted one broad shoulder in a casual shrug. "It's polite, avoids potential awkwardness and now it's a habit of mine."

"I see." But it wasn't really okay and she didn't know why. "So you're aware that I've been taking care of Morgan for over nine months?"

"Ben mentioned it." A dark look slid into his eyes. "Before he and Charity left—"

"When he asked you to be her legal guardian if anything happened," she finished.

"Yeah."

"Obviously there's been something of a misunderstanding. Just so you know, I'm more than willing to take on the nanny job."

"No."

"Even though I've been caring for her all this time?" She blinked. "Just like that? You don't even want to think about it?"

"There's nothing to think about."

"So you really want to take on a child you hardly know and didn't come to see while her parents were gone? Not even when you found out her mother and father had passed away?"

"I already explained that I was out of the country at the time."

"And I was the one here with her. The one who had to break the news that Ben and Charity weren't coming back."

"I promised my friend that I would raise his child if anything happened to him. I gave my word."

"But they gave Morgan to me," she countered.

"So you want to keep her. I get it." He ran his fingers through his hair. "The thing is they made me her legal guardian."

"Paperwork. It can be changed if you agree."

"I don't."

"Even though you don't really want her?"

"Who said I don't?" he asked sharply.

She raised a hand to indicate his posh penthouse. "There are signs."

"I assured Ben that his daughter would have everything she needed and he shouldn't worry." He looked at her. "So I found the finest child-care service available to provide supervision. Now you're here. How did that happen?"

"Since you were too busy to seal the deal, maybe you should ask your lawyer and secretary."

"I will. And Ginger Davis is on my list, too. Frankly I'm questioning her judgment in sending you."

"She wouldn't have sent me unless you approved," Libby defended. "I'll admit it was my idea—"

"There's a surprise."

She glared at him. "Just think about it and you'll see that this makes sense. Morgan has been with me since her parents left and it could potentially be harmful to leave her in the care of strangers. I'm willing and eager to be her nanny. It's a good plan."

"Define *good*," he said.

"Continuity of care for Morgan at a time when she's especially vulnerable."

"By that you mean yourself." He stared at her. "Why didn't you come to me? Approach me up front and run this scenario by me?"

"I tried."

"Apparently not very hard."

"You're not really like the rest of us, are you? Do you remember what it felt like when the name of gazillionaire Jess Donnelly didn't open doors or grease the wheels in getting you past secretaries, administrative assistants, doormen and security? Right to the top of the food chain?"

"I'll admit there are layers to my organization."

"No kidding." She blew out a breath and struggled for calm. "I didn't set out to campaign for this job. As it happens I already work for Ginger at the preschool. We discussed the arrangement and she decided there was some merit to my suggestion. I assumed that when she said everything had been worked out you'd agreed to it." She folded her arms over her chest. "No one told me negotiations had gone through your minions."

"Look, I've only ever been introduced to you as Libby. I didn't know you and Elizabeth Bradford were one and the same. It seems a conflict of interest since we have a prior relationship."

"What we have isn't a relationship. It's a series of brief encounters, ships passing in the night. Nothing about that is personal enough to prevent me being Morgan's nanny."

He shook his head. "Look, Libby, I don't think this is going to work out—"

"Aunt Libby?"

Jess whirled around and when he moved, Libby saw Morgan behind him. She didn't know how long the little girl had been there. "Hey, sweetie. Is SpongeBob over?"

"No."

"Is something wrong?" Libby asked. Stupid question. Everything was wrong, she realized. But nothing good would come of letting Morgan see her desperation.

"I got scared. You sounded mad."

"I'm sorry. And I'm not mad." Not at you, she wanted to say. She hurried over to the child whose brown eyes were now worried and filling with tears. So much for hiding the highly charged situation from her. "We didn't mean to disturb you."

Morgan brushed a finger beneath her nose and stared uncertainly at Jess. "Is he making you go away?"

"We were just talking about that." She looked at him.

"I don't want you to go. I don't want to stay here by myself. Please, Aunt Libby—"

When Morgan started to cry, Libby gathered her close. "It's going to be okay, baby. It will."

"I d-don't want you to g-go away."

Jess ran his fingers through his hair. "Don't cry, Morgan. Your Aunt Libby isn't going away."

"Really?" Libby said.

Morgan lifted her head and looked at him. "Really?"

"Really. I'm sorry. I didn't handle everything very well. Your Aunt Libby is mad at me." He shrugged when she lifted one eyebrow. Points to him for getting it. "The truth is that you're both going to stay here with me and Aunt Libby is going to be your nanny."

"What changed your mind?"

"You were right," he said. "It wouldn't be a good idea to let a stranger look after her. So I'd appreciate it if you'd stay on. Until she's adjusted to the situation."

"Okay."

"Is that all right with you, Morgan?"

"Yes." She nodded eagerly.

"Then we have a plan for the short term."

That was good enough for Libby. She'd take what she could get and figure out the rest later.

"Seemed like a good idea at the time" was the best way Libby could describe her first week under Jess's roof. Libby had been so sure the living arrangement would take the edge off her attraction, but not so much in the first week. Even when he wasn't there, which was ninety-five percent of the time, the place was all about him.

Pictures of him hiking in Red Rock Canyon. A carelessly discarded expensive silk tie in the family room. The spicy scent of him in *every* room made it feel like having his arms around her. Or was that wishful thinking? Not that it mattered. Or it wouldn't if she could say the idea was unpleasant. Nothing could be further from the truth.

"Aunt Libby?"

"Hmm?" She pulled her thoughts back to tucking Morgan into bed. "Sorry, sweetie. I was thinking about something else."

"That's okay." The little girl pulled the sheet and blanket more securely over her.

"Do you want me to finish the story?"

"No."

Libby studied the serious little face. "Is something on your mind?"

"Yes."

Libby suppressed a smile. When Morgan first came to stay with her this method of communication had taken some getting used to. Instead of blurting out whatever was going through her head, she worked her way to it with a series of questions. It wasn't efficient, but eventually what she needed to discuss got discussed.

"Is everything all right at school? Your kindergarten teacher says you're one of her pet pupils and she's not supposed to have favorites."

Twin dimples flashed on the child's cheeks when she smiled. "Miss Connie is nice."

"She is very nice."

Nooks and Nannies Preschool had a kindergarten class

and Morgan went there while Libby was working with her preschoolers. Charity and Ben had been supposed to come home before first grade to enroll the little girl at the school near their home. Now their child lived in a luxury penthouse condominium, a different home. Fortunately, Jess had agreed with her that changing schools right now wasn't the best plan.

"So if school isn't keeping you up at night, what's bothering you?"

Morgan clutched her doll against her thin chest. "I don't think he likes me."

"Who? A boy at school? Is someone being mean to you?"

"No. That guy."

"Who?" Alarm trickled through Libby.

"My daddy's friend."

"You mean Uncle Jess?"

She nodded. "I don't think he's very happy that we came to live with him."

Libby had hoped Morgan didn't pick up on the signs that he was ignoring them, but no such luck. "Why do you think that, sweetie?"

"He's never here."

"Sure he is," Libby protested. "In the mornings."

Her stomach tightened as she remembered just today he'd come into the kitchen to say goodbye before heading to his office. In his pinstriped navy suit and red tie he'd looked particularly handsome. Freshly shaven, with every hair in place, he'd set her female parts quivering with awareness. Darn him. He'd revved up her hormones, then raced out the door.

"Two times he drank a cup of coffee while I ate cereal. But he doesn't sit down with me. Not like you do, Aunt Libby."

Sometimes a smart and perceptive child could be worrisome and this was one of those times. At least she wasn't perceptive enough to notice Libby's insane crush on Jess, but that probably had more to do with her young age. There was still an ick factor regarding boys.

Libby wished for the good old days because her current plan wasn't coming together very well. Every exposure to Jess was supposed to be like a vaccination and living here should have been the booster. *Should have* being the key words.

"Jess is a busy man, sweetheart. He has lots of people working for him and depending on him."

"Does he eat supper?" Morgan asked.

"I'm sure he does." If he didn't, the impressive muscles that filled out his T-shirt would be fairly nonexistent. And they were definitely existent, positively thriving. In a mouth-watering way. Libby had no ick factor where he was concerned.

"I've never seen him eat supper, Aunt Libby. He doesn't like us."

Libby figured that was true enough for her, but he had no reason to dislike this sweet, innocent child who was right about him not coming home for dinner.

"He doesn't really know us yet," she said. "Give it time. This is new for him. He's not used to us, but that will change. Everything will be all right. You'll see."

"Promise?"

"Cross my heart," she said.

After a big hug and lots of kisses that made Morgan giggle, Libby turned on the world's brightest night light. "Sweet dreams, love bug."

"Okay," Morgan answered sleepily as she rolled to her side.

With a full heart and troubled spirit Libby watched for

several moments, then made up her mind to talk to Jess. It wasn't long before she heard the front door open and close.

Imagine that. We have touchdown right after the kid is in bed. Morgan wasn't the only observant resident of the penthouse. Apparently Jess was aware of her bedtime and how to avoid it and her.

Libby found him in the kitchen, where he was reaching into the refrigerator for a beer and the plate of food saved for him. The angle gave her a chance to admire his excellent butt. That thought was immediately replaced by a mental command for her hormones to back off.

"Hi, Jess."

He straightened and turned to meet her gaze. "Hi."

"How was your day?"

"Fine. Busy." He shrugged. "You?"

"I just put Morgan to bed. You can go in and tell her good-night if you want. I don't think she's asleep yet."

"That's okay. It might upset her routine."

Hers or his? she wondered.

"You must be hungry," she said.

"Why?"

"Besides the plate of food in your hand?"

He glanced at it and a small smile tugged at the corners of his mouth. "I missed dinner."

"We noticed."

"Oh?" He removed the plastic over the meatloaf, mashed potatoes and green beans, then set it in the microwave and pressed the reheat button.

"Yeah, what with your chair at the table being empty and all."

He twisted the top off his beer and took a long swallow, then looked at her. "What's on your mind, Libby?"

"Funny, that's just what I said to Morgan when I tucked

her in bed. I could tell there was something bothering her. She tends to share what's on her mind at bedtime."

"Do I need to know what it is?"

Of course, you nit, she wanted to say. Struggling for patience, she said, "You're her guardian."

"And I pay you to make sure she has everything she needs."

She walked over to the granite-covered island and kept it between them as she met his gaze. "It's also in my job description to make sure you're aware of what's going on with her emotionally. I thought you should know that she's noticed you don't come home for dinner."

"I see."

That's all he could say? Libby rubbed her palms over the black-and-beige granite countertop, but the smooth coolness did little to ease the heat trickling through her. Heat that was part attraction and part annoyance. Just breathing the same air with him raised her pulse when she most needed calm rationality.

In her college speech class there had been discussion of techniques for calming nerves in public speaking. The one about picturing your audience naked came to mind, but with Jess in the same room that only throttled up her quivering nerve endings. Her best bet was to say what she had to and leave.

"Morgan thinks you don't like her."

"That's ridiculous. She's a kid. Of course I like her. How did she get an idea like that?"

"Besides the fact that you work really hard at not being around her?" Libby struggled to keep accusation from her tone.

"I'll cop to the working hard, but it has nothing to do with avoiding her."

"Really?"

"What's this really about?" he asked.

Apparently she'd been unsuccessful in maintaining a neutral expression. She might as well say what had been on her mind.

"Was weather the real reason you couldn't be at Ben and Charity's memorial service? Or was it about dodging the hard stuff? The part where you're Morgan's guardian?"

Stark pain etched itself on his face and looked even darker for the scruff of beard that was three hours past his five o'clock shadow.

"I'll admit to being grateful that weather grounded my plane. But it had nothing to do with the kid and everything to do with the fact that a memorial service meant facing the truth that my friend was gone and he wasn't coming back."

"If anyone knows how you feel, it's me." Missing Charity was still a raw and ragged wound inside her. She was probably the only person on the planet who knew exactly how Jess felt. And she sympathized with him. "I didn't want to go either."

He took another long drink of his beer and pulled the plate out of the microwave. "I'd have been there if weather hadn't shut down the airport."

She believed him and that realization made her feel all gooey inside. Under the circumstances that was the wrong way to feel.

"The fact is," she said, "Ben and Charity made you Morgan's guardian. The designation implies making an effort to be involved with her. Just like Ben would have been if he were here."

A muscle jerked in Jess's jaw as he stared her down. "Define *involved*."

Libby tapped an index finger against her lips as she thought about the question. "Think of her as a resort development. Periodic reports from a project manager. That would be me. Intermittent on-site social interaction with said project. That would be—"

"Dinner?" he guessed.

"Go to the head of the class," she said.

He ran his fingers through his hair, then nodded. "I'll make it a point to be home for dinner tomorrow night."

"Promise?"

"Is that really necessary?"

"I don't want to tell Morgan you'll be here unless it's going to happen," Libby said. Life was full of disappointments and she didn't want more than necessary for a little girl who was dealing with the worst one of all.

"Promise." He made a cross over his heart and held up two fingers.

"Okay, then. It's a date."

Almost instantly she regretted her phrasing. That made it sound too personal, which was so the wrong tone. She wanted him to take an interest in Morgan, not herself. Mostly.

And so she felt the same conflict of smart women throughout time. How could she want him so intensely when she wasn't sure she liked him at all?

Chapter Three

The next night Jess walked into the penthouse and heard Libby's voice, the smoke-and-whiskey huskiness that skipped over his skin and made him hot. Now was no exception. When she stopped talking, a little-girl giggle filled the silence. This was the first time he'd ever heard that sound in his home and it made him smile. Amusement faded fast when he remembered why he was here.

To get involved with Morgan. Libby's words came back to him—like Ben would have been if he'd lived.

"I'm trying, buddy," Jess whispered. "Man, I wish you were here. I'm already screwing this up."

Libby had figured out that he worked late to avoid the situation at home. She'd nailed him and he didn't like it. He also wasn't sure how he felt about her coming up with the idea of being the nanny. On one hand, he was glad to have someone caring for Morgan that she knew and felt comfortable with. Someone who could make her giggle, he thought when the sound came to him again.

On the other hand, Libby had also guessed that he hadn't wanted to go to the memorial service and seemed to share the feeling. She'd gone soft when they discussed it, unlike the harsh way she'd reviewed his home as it related to being kid-friendly. But he could tell that she didn't particularly like him and he didn't particularly care. At least he tried not to because that was a slippery slope straight to hell.

Jess set his briefcase down by the front door, took a deep breath and walked into the kitchen. Every light in the room was on, including the under-the-cabinet fluorescents. Morgan was sitting on one of the six tall, padded wrought-iron stools arranged in a semi-circle around the island. Libby was across from her putting something on a cookie sheet. The glass-topped dinette was set with three woven placemats, plates, eating utensils and glasses. Until the last week, he'd always come home to a dark, silent penthouse. All this light and activity made him feel as if he'd stepped into an alternate universe.

Libby looked up and saw him standing there. "Hi."

"Hi." He lifted a hand when Morgan turned in his direction. "Hey."

"Hi," she said, not quite looking at him.

Until he made his presence known, Libby and Morgan had been talking and laughing. Now it was as if the cone of awkwardness had descended, closing off the giggles. Suddenly the room wasn't quite so bright. Maybe Libby had been wrong about Morgan wanting him there.

He observed Libby, noting how the tailored white cotton blouse and snug jeans set off her curves to perfection. There was uncertainty in her vivid blue eyes. Maybe they took on that extraordinary color because her cheeks were flushed. It didn't matter why, really, because the more he saw her, the more he realized how striking she was.

"So," she said.

"What's for dinner?" He looked at Morgan, who was staring at the beige-and-black design on the granite-covered island.

Libby waited a couple of beats, then answered with exaggerated cheerfulness in her tone. "We're having chicken nuggets and french fries."

He moved beside her and studied the mystery chicken pieces arranged in rows on the cookie sheet. He picked one up and examined it. "I have a number of luxury resorts that employ world-renowned chefs and I don't think one of them has this particular entrée in their repertoire."

"It's Morgan's favorite." Libby gave him a look, although her tone was still relatively good-humored. "She chose this for dinner."

He'd meant the words in a teasing way but the little girl looked worried. Clearly she didn't get his sense of humor, but he'd put his foot in his mouth and needed to salvage the situation somehow.

"I can't wait to try this," he said, wondering if his voice had enough enthusiasm or was over-the-top.

"You're going to love it," Libby promised. "Isn't he, Morgan?"

"I guess." She didn't look up.

"And to balance this meal nutritionally, I've made a salad with various kinds of lettuce, veggies, shaved almonds, croutons for crunch and blue cheese crumbles just because."

"Yuck," Morgan commented, wrinkling her nose.

"You know the rule," Libby said.

The little girl heaved a huge sigh. "I don't have to like it, but I have to try it."

"Seems fair," Jess said.

This brought back memories of his own childhood, before his dad died. Before everything went to hell. He knew the signs well enough to know that Morgan was on the dark side now. He wanted to make it better, but he didn't even know how to carry on a conversation without hurting her feelings.

"Why don't you tell Uncle Jess what you did at school today," Libby suggested, as if she could read minds.

His next thought was the realization that the little girl had never addressed him by his given name, let alone said "Uncle Jess." He'd have remembered that. When he'd dropped in on her parents, they'd run interference and the visits had been scattered, infrequent. Not enough for her to remember him.

Now he was the one in charge of running interference, which made him certain that fate had a sadistic sense of humor. It also made him want to put a fist through the wall, but that wasn't an option.

"What did you do in school, Morgan?" he asked, grateful that Libby had thrown him a bone.

Morgan glanced up at him, then down again. "I made a pumpkin."

"It's there on the refrigerator. For Halloween," Libby explained.

He looked behind him and saw the construction paper creation held to the front of the appliance with a magnet. The little girl had colored it green and he was about to say something about pumpkins being orange when he noticed Libby shake her head slightly in a negative motion. Fortunately he wasn't quite as dense as a rock and got her drift.

"Wow, Morgan. I really like your pumpkin," he said. "You did a great job."

"One of the kids said it's the wrong color," she mumbled.

"What do they know? Maybe this is a pumpkin that's not ripe yet," he suggested.

Morgan lifted one slight shoulder in a shrug.

When he met Libby's gaze, her expression was sympathetic. That wasn't something he was used to seeing. If anyone could sense that it was him. When his mother had brought home a guy two years after his dad's death, Jess had known in seconds that he didn't measure up. He'd always gotten the same hostile vibe from Libby.

He was accustomed to her shooting daggers at him when their paths crossed in a party setting with other people around. He'd always noticed her but managed to find someone safe to take his mind off her. That wasn't the case now. Worse, he kind of liked that she was cutting him some slack for his inexperience.

But there was something else about her that was different, too. Her blond hair was tousled around her face, teasing her pink cheeks. The smile she flashed him was bright and beautiful and made his chest feel weird. Intelligence snapped in her eyes and her mouth made him wonder if it would taste as good as he imagined.

From the first moment he met her, he'd been concerned that she could take his mind and libido to a place he'd always managed to avoid going. And he shouldn't be going there now.

"How long until dinner?" he asked. "I'm going to change clothes."

"About fifteen minutes," she answered.

He nodded and headed out of the room. It wasn't nearly enough time, he thought, feeling cornered in his own home. If he hadn't promised to eat dinner with Morgan, he would leave. But he'd crossed his heart and somehow knew that the gesture was tantamount to sacred between Morgan and Libby.

As if that wasn't enough proof of their attachment, the sound of Libby's voice followed by Morgan's giggle sliced into him and rattled around, echoing off the emptiness there.

The female interlopers in his world had a bond—the two of them against the world. He remembered the feeling from long ago and felt a flash of wanting to be a part of it again. But he'd experienced an alliance like they had and found out it wasn't something he could trust. A unit as tight as Libby and Morgan's had no room for him. Even if he wanted to join, which he didn't.

Sooner or later he'd wind up in the cold anyway, so the cold was where he would stay.

Dinner could have been more awkward, but Libby wasn't sure how. Her cheeks and jaw hurt from smiling too much and her brain was tired after thinking so hard to single-handedly keep up a three-way conversation. Jess had stuffed his face full of nuggets and fries, then excused himself—a polite way of saying he couldn't get away fast enough.

Once he'd vacated the table, Morgan released her inner chatterbox and turned back into the child Libby knew and loved. If Ben and Charity had been able to see their daughter's future, would they still have named Jess her guardian? She wasn't so sure. But there was something she needed to discuss with him and finally found him in the morning room.

Libby hadn't thought to look there because it was evening and there were no lights on, which had made her think the room was empty the first time she'd checked. Now she stood in the doorway. The only illumination came from the lights on the Strip that were visible through the floor-to-ceiling windows. As he'd said on her penthouse tour, it was a fabulous sight.

She felt a stab of guilt for pointing out that a five-year-old girl had no frame of reference to appreciate the adult view. It was true that billboards and taxis flaunted advertisements of scantily-clad women that Morgan shouldn't see, but from here the view was classy and breathtaking. And she didn't just mean the lights. Jess looked pretty fabulous, too. But he always did to her.

"Jess?"

The light on a glass-topped table came on instantly. He was sitting in a rattan chair on a plush, cream-colored cushion.

"Is everything okay?"

That depended on what he meant by *everything* and *okay*. But she figured he probably meant was there a crisis for which his presence was required.

"Fine."

"Okay. Good."

"Do you mind if I sit down?"

There was only a slight hesitation before he said no. That could have been her imagination, but she didn't think so because the look in his eyes said she was marginally more welcome than a global financial crisis.

There was an identical chair beside his and she lowered herself into it. The seat was deep and if she slid back, she felt her feet wouldn't touch the floor. Jess, on the other hand, had no problem, what with his long legs.

Before dinner he'd changed out of his suit into a pair of jeans, a cotton shirt and navy pullover sweater. It was a preppy look that he somehow pulled off as rugged. Her stomach did that quivery thing she recognized as acute attraction—unwelcome, but best acknowledged so it could be dealt with.

Libby folded her hands and settled them in her lap, angling her knees toward him. "So, how did you like dinner?"

"Awesome."

"Really?"

"Best I ever had."

"So, you've eaten chicken nuggets before?"

"It's been a while." Something darkened in his eyes. "But, yes, I have."

"The amount you consumed was pretty amazing."

"Did Morgan notice?"

"That you were shoving record-breaking amounts of food in your mouth to redeem yourself for dumping on her favorite meal?"

"Yeah. That."

"No."

"Just so we're clear, I wasn't dumping on her choice. That was humor."

"She's five." Libby gave him a wry look. "She doesn't know *world-renowned, repertoire* or *chef*."

"I got that." He folded his arms over his chest as he stared out the window.

"Complimenting her artwork was a nice save."

"Oh, please." Now his look was wry. "It was pathetic and you know it."

"What I know," she said, feeling sorry for him in spite of herself, "is that you didn't have a meltdown when you noticed a magnet on the expensive stainless-steel front of your refrigerator."

"Don't think it didn't cross my mind," he answered.

Libby laughed, but it didn't lighten her mood. She wasn't here to worship at the altar of Jess Donnelly and be seduced by his charm and self-deprecating humor.

"But you held back."

"I would have made a joke about it but I was afraid she'd think I wanted her drawn and quartered at dawn."

"You're exaggerating."

"Only a little." He blew out a long breath. "It probably didn't escape your notice that I'm not very good at kid talk."

"No? Really?" she said in mock surprise. "I swear I was planning to get out the duct tape to shut you up."

The corners of his mouth curved up slightly. "In my own defense, it has to be said that I spend my days in meetings about budgets, building materials and stock market shares. Until a week ago I didn't have to know about nightlights, green pumpkins or trying something I don't like."

Libby didn't want to sympathize with what he was going through and worked hard to suppress it. He'd agreed to be Morgan's guardian should anything happen to her parents. The argument that no one expected they wouldn't come home didn't fly with her. For God's sake, they'd gone halfway around the world to a place where bad, life-threatening things happened much more frequently than here in the States.

Jess could have taken the time to get to know Morgan. He could have made the effort to fill his friend's shoes and make the absence of a little girl's father a little easier for her. But he hadn't done that.

He was doing the right thing now and got points for that, but no sympathy for the fact that talking to a little girl, a virtual stranger, wasn't easy. Still, for Morgan's sake, she decided to help him out. Be a bridge.

Libby blew out a breath. "Kid talk takes practice, just like any other language. Ask her questions."

"Like?"

"What's her favorite color?"

"Pink," he answered. "Sometimes purple, better known as lavender."

Would wonders never cease? He'd actually listened that day they'd first arrived. "So ask things you don't know. Such as what she did at school."

"You covered that," he reminded her.

"I found out she made a pumpkin. A good question would be why that, as opposed to a ghost or pirate."

"I just figured it best captured Halloween." He shrugged.

"Of course, but asking shows that you're interested and could get her talking. Which brings to mind an obvious question."

"Obvious to who?"

"Everyone."

"That's where you're wrong, Libby. I have no idea what to say to her next."

"I keep forgetting you don't live in the real world." She sighed. "You do know that Halloween is when kids dress up in costumes and go trick-or-treating for candy?"

It took several moments before the "aha" light came on in his eyes. "So the question is—what does she want to be for Halloween?"

Libby smiled. "Give the man a prize."

"Even though the man doesn't deserve it?"

He sounded sincere. Like he didn't believe getting a clue was anything to be proud of. And she had to agree with him. It wasn't a big deal. But the fact that this being-out-of-his-comfort-zone side to Jess was something that she'd never seen before *did* land squarely in big-deal territory. It could make him sympathy-worthy and she couldn't afford to feel that way. She wasn't here to stroke his ego, but as Morgan's advocate. It was time to bring up the subject she'd come here to discuss with him.

"I just tucked her into bed and we were talking about something—"

Alarm jumped into his eyes. "The fact you're here means she had something on her mind."

"I see you've gone to the bad place where you're expected to eat fish sticks as well as chicken nuggets every night for the rest of your life." She smiled. "Don't worry. It's not about that." His confused male look was so astonishingly cute that there was a definite tug on her heart. "She remembered that you said you would think about making changes to her room."

"Oh." He relaxed. "Okay."

"Letting Morgan put her personality stamp on her own space might help her to niche in with you."

He steepled his fingers and tapped them against his mouth. "I have no objection to that."

"Good. So, let's figure out when you can take her shopping."

He shook his head. "I don't need to approve her taste. Just let her pick out whatever she wants and send the bills to me."

It was like he'd pulled down a shield to hide the vulnerability she'd seen just moments before, when he worried about how to talk to a little girl. What was up with that?

"Shopping with Morgan is a good way to know her and build up a collection of conversational questions," Libby pointed out.

"I'll pass."

"Don't you want to be a part of picking things out?"

"It's not necessary."

"No one said it was. But to continue our discussion of a little while ago, it's a way to break the ice. Which you were just wondering how to do. Because she lives with you now. You're her family."

"No."

"Excuse me, you're her guardian."

"And as such I will make sure she has everything she ever needs, but don't call it family because I don't know how a family is supposed to behave." He met her gaze and there were shadows in his own.

"Ben and Charity believed otherwise or you wouldn't be Morgan's guardian."

"A past like mine makes their judgment questionable."

"What happened to you?" she asked.

"My father died when I was a boy. A little older than Morgan."

"I'm sorry," she said automatically.

"Don't be. It was a long time ago."

"Even so…" She thought for a moment. "It would seem that a loss like that would make you more sympathetic to what Morgan is going through—"

He held up a hand to stop her. "What I know is Ben and Charity meant for me to provide for Morgan's material needs. He was my friend and knew me and my limitations and he still asked me to take her. So I'm prepared to pay the bills." He stood, signaling an end to the discussion. "Is there anything else?"

"I'll let you know."

He nodded. "Then I'll say good night."

When he was gone the chill in the morning room made Libby shiver, a feeling fueled by sympathy she couldn't stop this time. She realized how little she knew about Jess's life. She hadn't been aware that he'd lost his father at such a young age. At a time when he felt the loss destroyed any sense of family for him. What about his mother?

Libby had never known her own. The woman had died before she was old enough to remember her. Her father was still alive, still an opportunist who used people. But she'd grown up watching a family support their own. Even though she'd never felt a part of that family, she understood the dynamic and the love that underscored everything.

Apparently Jess hadn't been as lucky. She'd always thought of him as the golden boy, never touched by tragedy. Obviously there were more layers to him than she'd suspected.

Only time would tell whether that was good or bad.

Chapter Four

Libby pushed the control button and watched the security gates into Jess's luxury condo complex part like the Red Sea. Glancing in the rearview mirror of her practical little compact car, she smiled at Morgan, who was barely awake in her car seat. She'd learned that napping this close to bedtime could vaporize the evening schedule.

"Hey, kiddo. Are you excited about your new princess comforter?"

"Yes," the child answered, then sleepily rubbed her eyes.

"You know, your new bed has to be delivered before you can use the new things."

"When is it coming?" Morgan asked again.

"Saturday." Libby drove into her assigned space next to Jess's. She noted that his car wasn't there yet, which meant he was still working. Or something. She turned off the car's ignition.

"Why can't they bring my bed tomorrow?" Morgan asked.

"Because we're at school all day and no one will be at home to let the delivery men in. They wouldn't know where it goes," she explained.

"What about Uncle Jess?"

Yeah. That was a good question. Libby wanted to warn Morgan not to count on him. The man was unwilling to do the hard work. The answer to what about Jess was as simple as that.

It had to have been hard losing his dad so young, but he was making a deliberate choice to keep this precious little girl at arm's length. No matter what he said about Ben and Charity knowing him, Libby would never believe his passive parenting is what they'd have wanted for their little girl.

But she couldn't say any of that out loud in answer to the question.

"Uncle Jess works, too. Very hard. He can't be here for the delivery." Or anything else, Libby added silently. "So we'll just keep all the bedding stacked in the corner of your room until Saturday."

"Okay." Morgan unhooked herself from the safety seat and opened the rear passenger door.

Libby lifted the twin comforter and the bag with matching sheets and towels from her trunk. The two of them managed to carry the bulky shopping bags to the private elevator, then rode it to the penthouse. She pulled the key from her jeans pocket and turned it in the lock. But when she tried to open the door it didn't budge. After turning the key in the opposite direction, the door opened, which meant she hadn't secured it properly when they'd left earlier.

"That's funny," she said.

"What is, Aunt Libby?" Morgan looked up with big, innocent brown eyes.

"I was sure I locked the door." She always did.

This was a secure building, but leaving an unobstructed way into a luxury penthouse was like an engraved invitation to get ripped off. Her only excuse was that she'd had Jess on her mind a lot. The distraction took a toll and important things like not locking up were the result.

She set the bags down in the foyer and her purse on the circular table.

"I'm thirsty, Aunt Libby."

"How about a gigantic glass of milk?"

The two of them had grabbed a burger at the mall, but before leaving she'd fixed a salad and pasta for Jess, then left it in the fridge.

She smiled down at the little girl. "Soda with your hamburger for dinner was a treat but you still need milk."

"Why?"

"It has calcium to give you shiny hair and strong teeth and bones so you'll grow up big and strong."

Libby walked into the kitchen where the light was already on, which made the hair at her nape prickle with unease. On top of that there was an almost-empty plate of pasta on the counter. One of the bar stools had been pulled out for sitting down on.

"This just keeps getting weirder."

"Uncle Jess ate his dinner," Morgan said.

Libby didn't think so, what with the fact that his car wasn't in its usual space. She didn't think he was home yet. Not only that, there was a half-full wineglass beside the plate. Jess was a beer guy as far as she knew. She picked up the stemware and looked closer.

"Uncle Jess didn't pour this, not unless he's started wearing lipstick."

Libby wondered whether or not she should be afraid.

Should she take Morgan out and call 911? It didn't feel like there was anything bad going on. This had a sensation of familiarity, of being at home and comfortable with the surroundings.

"Aunt Libby—"

"What, sweetie?" she said, preoccupied with what to do.

"It's like that story you read me," Morgan said, excitement humming in her voice. "Remember? The one about the girl and the three bears."

She raced out of the room before Libby could stop her. And she needed to stop her because in that story they found the girl in bed. Hurrying to catch up, Libby went into the family room where she found Morgan standing still, staring down the long hall that led to Jess's bedroom. A beautiful, curvaceous woman was walking toward them wearing a man's black silk robe. Libby was thinking it was probably all she was wearing but couldn't say for sure and didn't really want to confirm. Her next thought was that although she'd never seen him in it, the robe was probably Jess's.

"This is the three bears' story and Goldilocks is a redhead," she mumbled.

The woman tightened the tie at her waist and stopped in front of them. "Who are you?"

"I'm Libby. Who are you?"

"Elena Cavanaugh. I wasn't aware that Jess got married."

"He didn't. How did you get in here?" Libby demanded.

"With the key he gave me. And you?"

Libby settled her hands on Morgan's shoulders. The two of them lived here and shouldn't have to justify their presence. Red, on the other hand, had a lot of explaining to do. "I'm the nanny."

Elena's gaze dropped to Morgan. "I didn't know he had a child."

"A recent development," she explained, giving the small shoulders a reassuring squeeze. "What are you doing here?"

"I'm a flight attendant. Jess gave me a key. We're—" Her gaze dropped to Morgan. "We're *friends*. When my flight schedule brings me to Las Vegas I stop by to say hello."

"Without calling?"

Elena shrugged. "He likes surprises."

"Why are you wearing that robe?" Morgan asked.

"You're a cutie," the woman said with genuine warmth. "I'm Morgan."

"It's nice to meet you, Morgan. I like your name. And to answer your question, I was just going to take a bath."

"To get ready for bed?" the little girl innocently persisted.

"Something like that." Elena looked at Libby. "But I see that Jess has made some changes around here."

"This all happened recently." Libby glanced down at the child in front of her. "For Morgan. Jess isn't actually her uncle. He's her guardian because…"

Elena nodded slightly, letting her know she didn't have to go into detail in front of the little girl. It was a sensitive thing to do and took the starch out of Libby's indignant outrage over this "arrangement." Though she had no right to it, there was probably a little jealousy stuck between indignance and outrage.

"I think I'll just go and get dressed," Elena said.

Morgan stepped away from Libby. "Are you leaving already?"

"It would be best," the woman answered in the same words Libby was thinking.

"You're not going to sleep over?" Morgan persisted.

"That wouldn't be a good idea." Again her response was exactly what Libby would have said. Elena turned and walked back down the hall.

When they were alone Morgan looked up at her. "I wish she would stay. She's nice, Aunt Libby."

"I can see why you feel that way." The kid meant stunning, Libby thought. What in the world was Jess thinking, giving out keys to his place? Didn't he ever see the movie *Fatal Attraction?* She felt like the queen of snark because Elena seemed nice enough under incredibly awkward circumstances.

The front door opened and closed, and speaking of the devil, he walked into the family room looking like he'd just arrived for a magazine fashion shoot. Charcoal suit, white shirt, red tie. Awesomely appealing. How could he look so good at the end of a long, difficult day? Libby felt as if she'd been run over by heavy equipment and it was his fault.

"Hi," he said, smiling at both of them. "I see you did some shopping."

"My new bed is coming on Saturday," Morgan said. "I got a princess comforter and sheets to match. Want to see?"

He looked from her to Libby. "I think that's the most words she's ever strung together in my presence."

"Mall magic," Libby answered, wondering how to diplomatically bring up Elena in front of a child.

"So you guys had fun?" he asked.

"You could say that."

He must have heard something in her tone because he frowned. "Is something wrong?"

"You could say that, too."

"What's going on?"

"Hi, Jess." The flight attendant stopped just inside the doorway and he whirled around to look at her.

After a couple of beats he said, "Elena." Shock mixed with recognition equaled awkward.

"You look great," she said. The crisp white shirt and

navy pants of her flight uniform made her shapely figure look even more curvy.

"Right back at you." He glanced at Morgan. "I'm sorry I wasn't here when you got in."

"No problem."

"The thing is, this isn't a very good time—"

"Yeah. I kind of figured that out on my own." She smiled with genuine regret as she handed him his key. Then she stood on tiptoe and placed a soft kiss on his lips that clearly said goodbye. Looking first at Libby, then Morgan, she said, "It was nice to meet you both. For what it's worth, I think Jess will be a really good dad."

On what planet? Libby wanted to ask. But Elena was gone before she could say the words even if she dared.

Libby blew out a breath. "I can truthfully say that nothing like that has ever happened to me before."

"I bet she drinks lots of milk," Morgan commented.

"Why?" Jess and Libby asked together.

"Because her hair is shiny. She has nice teeth and is big and strong." Morgan looked wistfully toward the front door. "She's pretty. I want that color hair. And when I grow up, I hope my boobs are like hers."

Jess looked as horrified as Libby felt but she was pretty sure it was for a different reason. Libby was already a woman and there was no chance of her growing into the "assets" necessary to get Jess's attention.

Jess wondered which of the gods he'd pissed off and, more important, what sacrifice it would take to get them off his back. While Libby supervised Morgan's bath and bedtime rituals, he was in the morning room downing his second beer.

When this child fell into his lap, he'd known life would

change, but he hadn't counted on parts of the old one creeping in. Elena looked good, no question about that. She was fun, flirty and fantastic in bed. Part of the fun was her showing up without warning. That was exciting, or at least it used to be. Her goodbye said they were over and he would have understood even if she hadn't returned the key.

The thing was, it didn't bother him, which bothered him more than anything. That was just wrong and he blamed a petite, blue-eyed blonde who didn't seem at all intimidated or impressed by his wealth and power.

He blamed her because she had the damnedest way of creeping into his thoughts at inconvenient times. Board meetings. Business lunches. Phone calls. It was difficult to concentrate when a memory of her tart comments made him smile. Or the way she caught her top lip between her teeth sent his thoughts to kissing first that lip and then the bottom one to see for himself how she tasted.

And suddenly he sensed her behind him. Although she didn't make a sound, he knew she was there. The hair at his nape prickled and his skin felt too tight. That happened when normal blood flow was involuntarily diverted to points south. This was the last thing he wanted or needed.

"Jess? Can I talk to you?"

The last time they'd talked in here was chicken-nugget night. Libby had given him a crash course in child-speak. She'd encouraged him to engage Morgan in conversation and complimented him on what was right with his style. Then he'd seen the light in her eyes dim and extinguish because he'd disappointed her. Libby was a grown-up, but Morgan wasn't. What if he let her down? He was pretty sure conversing with the kid didn't include her sharing that she wanted a big bosom and red hair when she grew up. So he'd already failed her.

Libby didn't understand why family was a hot button for him. How could he explain that love had cost him the only family he had? She wouldn't understand that promises made and broken were what destroyed all he thought he knew about love and loyalty. He wanted to say no to the talking, but knew that wasn't an option.

"Why don't you have a seat?" he suggested, turning to meet her gaze.

"No, thanks. This won't take long."

"Okay. Shoot."

The choice of words was unfortunate because he suspected Libby would very much like to do just that. After Elena left and Morgan said what she said, her nanny had glared at him in a way that could reduce a lesser man to a brown stain on the rug.

"Is Morgan settled?" he asked.

"That's a good question."

Here we go, he thought. "What's wrong?"

The look on her face told him what he already knew—stupid question. "Let's start with the naked woman in your bed."

In his obviously flawed judgment, she sounded jealous, and the idea of that had some merit. "If we're going to discuss this rationally, let's get the facts straight. We don't know if she was naked and I have no independent confirmation that she was in my bed."

"You know what I mean."

"I really don't." It wasn't easy to remember innocence, but he put as much as possible into his voice and expression.

Jess was baiting her, plain and simple. He was deliberately agitating her because, as stupid as it sounded, she was beautiful when she was angry. More beautiful, he amended. Not in the classic, statuesque, turn-a-man's-head way

Elena was. But in a down-to-earth way that was more appealing than he would have ever believed.

"Okay." She put her hands on her hips, drawing his attention to curves that made his palms tingle. "Let me put it like this. Morgan could have walked into a scene featuring a naked woman in your bed. It's not something I want to explain to her. Do you?" She paused thoughtfully and tapped a finger to her lips. "Oh, wait, you're the guy who doesn't do kid talk at all which would make explaining sex to a five-year-old—"

"Almost six," he pointed out.

"Right. Because a couple months would solve the problem entirely."

Definitely beautiful, he thought. "The situation was awkward, I'll admit that. But it wasn't as bad as it could have been. So, I guess I'm wondering what you want me to do."

She blew out a breath. "And I guess I'm wondering how many more keys are out there? How many more of your women are going to show up unexpectedly?"

Elena was the only flight attendant he dated. He'd given her a key because it was convenient for both of them. She'd have a place to stay when she was in Las Vegas and he enjoyed her showing up out of the blue.

He could tell Libby there were no more women, but then they'd have nothing left to talk about. For reasons he couldn't explain, he wasn't quite ready for this conversation to be over. Scratching his head he said, "It's hard to put an exact figure on it."

"*Figure* being the operative word." Sarcasm surrounded every syllable.

"No pun intended." Again he let his expression ooze innocence. "So Morgan had some questions?"

"I managed to do damage control. This time."

"How?"

Her eyes narrowed and the expression was sexy as hell. "She's still young and naïve enough to believe that *people* look past a woman's appearance to find her inner beauty."

Her emphasis on the word *people* told him she really meant men. Truthfully, the kid's comment about growing up had freaked him out big time. "I'm glad you were able to smooth things over."

"Is it necessary for me to point out that boobalicious babes arriving without warning is going to be a problem the older Morgan gets?"

"I will take appropriate action to avoid a repeat of the situation," he assured her.

"How?"

"Excuse me?"

"Do you have a master list of who has access to your home?" she grilled him.

"I've never found it to be necessary."

Her stubborn, pointed little chin lifted slightly. "Now it is."

"Would you feel more secure if I had the locks changed?" Even though it's not necessary, he added to himself.

She nodded. "It's a start."

"I'll take care of it."

"Thank you." She stared at him and caught her top lip with her teeth.

Heat shot straight through him as his mind went to a place where he kissed her until both of them were clinging to each other because neither could catch their breath. The next part of the mental picture had her naked in his bed. Before the vision went any further, he looked closer and noticed there was something else on her mind. And he would bet it had nothing whatsoever to do with his bed.

"What?" he asked.

She shook her head. "It's none of my business."

"Since when has that stopped you?" He shrugged. "Go ahead. Tell me what's on your mind."

"You don't really want to know."

Probably not. But now he was too curious. "Yeah, I do want to know."

"Technically you're my boss. I'm your employee. It's not my place to offer an opinion."

Curiouser and curiouser. Now he really needed to hear what she had to say. "Just pretend I'm the company suggestion box. Or better yet, a comment card. The one that says we're really interested in your feedback. Et cetera. Lay it on me."

"Okay. If you insist." She folded her arms over her chest. "I can't help noticing that you don't seem like the type of guy who embraces parenting. The sort who doesn't do the dance of joy at being tied down."

She was right about that. Ties gave people the power to stab you in the back. If someone was going on the offensive, he preferred to see it coming and take appropriate evasive measures in order to defend himself. Maybe that's why he was so drawn to Libby. She had no problem with telling him what was on her mind, whether or not he wanted to hear it.

Jess met her gaze as the defensive part of him locked and loaded. "My energy has been focused on business for a very long time. I put together some cash and parlayed that stake into something of much greater value. With one enormously successful resort open on the Strip and another one in development, not to mention partnerships in properties all over the world, there's not a lot left over for anything else."

Which is why relationships like Elena worked for him. No demands, just rewards.

"I understand what you're saying," she agreed, in a tone that indicated she didn't see at all. "The problem, as I see it, is that when you're raising a child, being tied down comes with the territory."

Okay. She'd nailed him. Mission accomplished. It was a direct hit on the target. What she meant was that Ben and Charity had picked the wrong guy to take care of their kid. Did she really think he wasn't aware of that?

On the day she'd delivered Morgan, she'd accused him of not really wanting the child. He hadn't confirmed or denied but defended himself with a question. *Who says I don't want her?* Libby was dancing around it again now, but the meaning came through loud and clear. He wasn't the go-to guy and his friend had misplaced his trust.

He was more than ready now to end this conversation.

"Okay, Libby. Point taken. I'm well aware of my short-comings and limitations."

"It's not a flaw," she backpedaled. "Some people just aren't cut out to raise kids. Self-awareness is a good thing."

Jess ran his fingers through his hair. "I don't know why Ben chose me to be Morgan's guardian, but he did."

"And what you're doing is admirable, Jess, but—"

He held up a hand to stop her. "I assured my friend that his child would be taken care of if anything happened to him. It was one of the last conversations we had. You're here in my employ to take care of Morgan. I gave my word and I'm doing my duty."

Disappointment was evident in her eyes again and he hated putting it there. One of the perks of living alone was not having anyone to let down. He would have to learn not to let it bother him the way it was now.

Chapter Five

After her students had gone home for the day, Libby had work to do while Morgan was being supervised in the Nooks and Nannies after-school program. She sat behind the flat oak desk in her brightly decorated classroom. The walls were filled with pumpkins colored by her kids, as well as witches, ghosts and other costumed characters to commemorate the upcoming event. When Halloween was over next week, she wanted to go right into projects for Thanksgiving and Christmas.

As she thumbed through material for ideas, several caught her eye. Paper plates and brown construction-paper feathers to fashion a turkey. If everything was cut out and ready, the kids would have fun pasting it all together. There was another one that used small magazines with the pages folded to form the turkey body, then a pattern to cut out the long neck and head.

It would make a great centerpiece for the dinner table on the big day but would require a lot of supervision, a higher adult-to-child ratio than normal. Mental note: ask for parent volunteers. There were enough involved parents this year to make it a fun exercise for everyone.

Christmas would be next, a time rich in project material from trees and ornaments to Santa and presents, as well as the spiritual side of the season. She wanted this holiday to be special for Morgan, the first without her parents.

The thought made Libby's heart heavy. Her own holiday memories were filled with Charity, and then Ben. Some of them included Jess, because he was their friend, too. A vision of him popped into her mind followed by a familiar yearning that lately had turned into an empty ache. Her seeing-him-every-day plan to crush out her crush didn't seem to be working all that well. Not much had changed from the days when their paths crossed because of mutual friends.

In all fairness, it wasn't Jess's fault that she had the hots for him but left him so cold he couldn't remember her name. She knew that and in spite of it, her longing for him was still an issue even though no one would ever accuse him of being a parent, let alone one she could count on.

The intercom on her phone buzzed and she picked up. "This is Libby."

"Hi, Lib, it's Mary in the office."

"Hey." The receptionist's tone was normally upbeat and cheery. It took Libby a couple of seconds to realize that wasn't the case now. "What's wrong?"

"Morgan is here. She had a little accident—"

"I'll be right there."

Libby ran out of her classroom and to the administration offices, which were in another building. There was a small room just off the reception area where the kids went with minor scrapes and bumps, where first aid was handled. The door was open and she heard whimpering. The knot in her chest squeezed against her heart as she braced herself and walked in.

"Hey kiddo. You have a boo-boo?"

The little girl was sitting on a chair, her right hand wrapped in a towel. There was blood on her pink sweater, jeans and white sneakers. It was more shocking because, for some stupid reason, she hadn't expected to see blood.

She looked at Sophia Green, the Nooks and Nannies director, who was sitting beside Morgan, an arm around her shoulders.

"What happened?" Libby asked.

Sophia's gray eyes were serious as she tucked a strand of reddish-brown hair behind her ear. "She cut her hand."

"How?" Libby knew that question bordered on dense because it didn't matter. But in that heart-stopping moment, it was all she could think to say.

"The kids were at outside playtime. Morgan was by herself near the perimeter fence. She reached through and picked up a piece of glass."

Libby dropped to her knees beside the little girl. "Oh, baby—"

"I didn't know it was sharp, Aunt Libby." Tears welled in her brown eyes.

Words of censure fueled by her own fear were on the tip of her tongue, but somehow Libby held back. This wasn't the time for a safety lesson.

"Okay, sweetie. We'll put a Band-Aid on it and fix you right up."

"About that, Libby—"

If she'd been thinking more clearly, she'd have realized there would already be a bandage on the boo-boo and

Morgan would be showing it off. Because that wasn't the case she knew it was more serious.

"What?" she asked Sophia.

"It's a little deep," the other woman said gently. "I think she needs stitches."

"Okay."

Libby was doing her best imitation of calm even though her hand shook as she brushed the hair off Morgan's forehead. "I'll call the pediatrician."

"Lib, it will probably be faster to take her to Mercy Medical Center. The emergency room has a pediatric trauma specialist available twenty-four hours a day."

Libby glanced up at the little girl's pale face and frightened eyes. "You don't think that would be scarier?"

Sophia shook her head. "They're specially trained for things like this. Not that I think it's that serious, but the staff knows how to put their littlest patients at ease in these circumstances."

She trusted implicitly her friend's judgment. Sophia had been with the Clark County department of family services before job burnout sent her to Nooks and Nannies. The woman had seen trauma. If anyone knew how to deal with it, Sophia did.

"Okay. We'll go to Mercy Medical Center."

"I'll drive you."

"Thanks."

That way she could call Jess to meet them there, then she could concentrate on keeping Morgan calm.

A couple of hours later Libby was sitting alone with Morgan in one of the emergency room's trauma bays. When they'd been called back she'd insisted Sophia didn't have to stay. That was before she'd known how long they'd be waiting. She still hadn't spoken to Jess. His cell phone went straight to voice mail, which was now full due to all the messages she'd left. Unable to reach him directly, she'd tried his secretary, who'd informed her he was in a meeting and had left strict orders that he wasn't to be disturbed. The problem was that Morgan couldn't be treated until he authorized it.

That wasn't the only problem, just the most pressing. Somewhere deep down inside, Libby knew she wanted him there for herself. She was scared, too, and could really use his support, a strong shoulder to lean on, someone to talk to. Not just anyone. *Him.*

At that moment the privacy curtain moved and she expected to see the nurse who had been checking in on them whenever possible for the last couple of hours. Instead, Jess stood there. She hated how glad she was to see him, how badly she wanted to throw herself in his arms and have him hold her.

"I got here as soon as I could," he said, stopping on the other side of the bed.

Right. Not soon enough, she thought.

Her resentment and anger were out of proportion to the situation and she wasn't sure why. But this wasn't the time to call him on it any more than scolding Morgan after the fact would have been.

"How is she?"

Why do you care? she wanted to ask. But part of her knew that was just taking all her fear and frustration out on him.

She blew out a long breath. "Worn out. We've been here a long time. You got my messages?"

A muscle jerked in his jaw. "Yeah. I need to give permission for treatment."

She nodded. "You could have done it over the phone."

"I've never handled something like this. It seemed better to show up."

"The pediatric trauma specialist—Dr. Tenney—looked at her hand and said no nerves or tendons or anything that would permanently affect her fine motor coordination were compromised."

"That's good," he said.

"It is, but she needs stitches, because of where she cut herself. Movement in her palm will make healing take a lot longer unless he closes the cut."

His mouth thinned to a grim line. "Something like this never crossed my mind. How did you handle stuff while she was with you, after Charity and Ben left?"

Libby met his troubled gaze. "I had power of attorney. I was authorized to approve routine check-ups, visits to the doctor's office and whatever came up. When they died everything changed. You're her legal guardian and I couldn't sign any of the forms. So we've been waiting—"

Her voice cracked and the weakness shamed her, making her more self-conscious.

"Libby, I'm sorry. I had no idea."

"Your secretary said her orders were that you not be disturbed. She's very good at her job."

"Still—" He ran his fingers through his hair. "This should have been an exception."

He looked sincere, she thought. And in all fairness this was a situation she hadn't foreseen. The fact that she'd had a lot on her mind, including him, was no justification for her not to consider what would happen in a medical emergency. But it also made a certain amount of sense that his employees who worked so closely with him knew him better than anyone. Knew his priorities. If a child who needed medical treatment was an exception-worthy event, the woman would have put Libby through to him. She hadn't. And that didn't speak highly of his attitudes toward parenting.

Morgan stretched and opened her eyes. "Hi, Uncle Jess."

"Hey, Morgan. How are you?"

"Not good." She glanced at her hand. "I got a boo-boo."

"I heard. Does it hurt?"

"Not really," she said. "Want to see it?"

His hesitation wasn't all that obvious, but Libby saw. "Sure." He lifted the small surgical drape covering the little hand and winced, turning a little pale. "It looks like it hurts a lot."

"If I hold really still it's okay." Morgan's eyes filled with tears. "But I've been holding still for a long time. I wanna go home."

"Can't blame you," he said. "I'll go do what I have to do to make that happen."

Libby watched him disappear and aloneness surrounded her again. Wasn't she the perverse one? Jess was damned if he did, damned if he didn't. She didn't trust him with this child, but Libby was desperately drawn to his strength and support.

Not more than a few minutes later Jess returned. "Okay. Everything is taken care of. The doctor will be here in a few minutes to fix you up and pretty soon you can go home."

"Thank you, Uncle Jess."

The small, sad voice brought a pained look to his face. "Morgan, I'm very sorry you had to wait so long."

"That's okay."

"No, it isn't," he said. "I didn't get the message and it's my responsibility to let the doctor know he can do what's necessary to make you better. I was in a meeting."

"Was it important?" Morgan asked.

"Yes. It means lots of people will have jobs."

"That's pretty important," the little girl agreed.

Jess shook his head. "My secretary didn't give me the message."

"Why not?"

"Because I told her not to."

"You made a rule?"

"I guess you could say that." He reached out with one finger and brushed a stray strand of hair from her cheek. "I just want you to know that I'm very sorry you had to hang around here so long."

Libby waited for him to say that nothing like this would ever happen again. He didn't. She knew Jess took a promise very seriously and the flip side of that was not to make a vow you couldn't keep. But this was one that he should move heaven and earth to make and not break.

"So," he said, looking down at Morgan. "Other than this trip to the emergency room, how was your day?"

"Okay." The small smile she'd given him disappeared. "But I'm scared about gettin' stitches."

"I can see where you would be," he said seriously. "But I've had them before."

"Really?" Her eyes widened. "Is it gonna hurt?"

"The doctor is going to give you some medicine that will make you not feel anything." He held up his finger. "But here's the thing. The medicine comes through a needle, a really small one and it will feel like a little pinch. Then it might burn for a couple of seconds. After that, you won't feel anything."

"Promise?"

He made the cross over his heart and held up two fingers. "Swear."

He'd told her the truth, Libby realized. It would have

been easy to lie and tell her it wouldn't hurt, but he hadn't done that. Which made his omission about promising to be accessible to Morgan all the more significant. If he couldn't make that promise, Libby would see to it that nothing like this ever happened again. She'd make sure that if Morgan needed anything she wouldn't have to wait. Maybe it was time to do something she'd been considering for a while— consult a lawyer about her alternatives for obtaining legal custody of Morgan.

He'd cited his sense of duty, but in her opinion love should trump obligation.

She didn't ever want this little girl to wait for what she needed until Jess could find time to be available. She didn't ever want this precious child to feel like an unwanted obligation. Libby knew from firsthand experience how painful growing up that way could be.

Twenty-four hours later things were back to normal, whatever that was. Morgan was in the Nooks and Nannies after-school program, where she was being watched over and pampered so Libby had felt confident in resuming her teaching duties. A lot of parents counted on child care and the kids could be thrown off by a substitute. If Morgan needed her, she was right down the hall, as opposed to Jess, who had meetings and left orders not to be disturbed for any reason.

Still, after he'd arrived at the emergency room and expedited the little girl's treatment, he'd been great, making her laugh, distracting her while the doctor stitched her hand. Then he'd taken them home, with a detour to a toy store where he bought what he'd called her brave-little-girl reward. Libby had experienced the E.R. with and without him and definitely preferred him there. Which was a bummer since he couldn't be counted on to show up when needed.

Her classroom door opened and Sophia Green walked in. "Hi, Lib."

Her stomach clenched. "Is Morgan okay?"

"Fine. I just checked on her." The preschool director sighed. "Are you going to the bad place every time you see me now?"

"No." And that was a big fat lie.

"Give it time." She sat in the chair beside the desk. "Morgan says her hand doesn't hurt. I think that very impressive bandage is helping in that regard."

"Good. She does like her Band-Aids."

"Miss Connie is keeping her quiet. Which isn't really all that difficult." Sophia frowned. "How is Morgan coping with losing her parents?"

Libby thought about the question. "Fine. She seemed to take the news okay and was a trouper at the memorial service." Now Libby frowned as she mulled it over. "But she never asked many questions and now she doesn't talk about them at all."

"I see."

But Libby didn't miss the deepening worry lines. "She's had to cope with moving. Jess is practically a stranger to her. That's a lot for a little kid to deal with."

"How's the arrangement working out?" Sophia asked. "I mean you being her nanny."

"You mean what's *he* like. Admit it."

Sophia shrugged. "I think it's perfectly normal to be curious about an above-average-looking wealthy man that my friend is living with."

Wow, that was an understatement in every way. Jess was drop-dead gorgeous and the penthouse lifestyle didn't happen without a couple extra bucks in the bank. But the "living with" part made the arrangement sound way too personal.

"I'm not *living* with him—"

"So you commute there to fulfill nanny duties?" Sophia's expression was all innocence except for the gleam in her gray eyes.

"No. I'm a live-in nanny."

"So, how is that working for you?"

It was Libby's turn to shrug. "Nice place. Morgan doesn't want for anything that money can buy."

"I hear a *but*."

"Let's just say it's a good thing I'm a live-in nanny," Libby hedged. "For Morgan's sake."

"Are you concerned about her welfare?"

"Yes."

"Why?" Sophia persisted.

"For starters, sexy stewardesses show up with their own key and let themselves into the penthouse."

"Why would they do that?"

"Oh, please." Libby rolled her eyes. "You're a grown-up. Do the math."

"They drop by for…" Sophia thoughtfully tapped her lip. "*Benefits* when they're in town."

"Right in one."

"And you're jealous."

Not a question mark anywhere near that statement. How irritating that she was so easy to read. Instead of outright denial, Libby attempted a flanking maneuver. "Why in the world would I be jealous?"

Sophia linked her fingers and settled her hands in her lap. "Because he's a hot guy and you have a crush on him."

"Give me credit for some maturity." Again not a lie.

"Age has nothing to do with it. Secretaries fall in love

with their bosses all the time. And the nanny falling for the guy she lives with is the stuff of romantic fantasies from *Jane Eyre* to *The Sound of Music*."

Libby thought about confessing that her crush wasn't a recent development and had happened years before she'd moved into the penthouse, then decided a lie was easier. "You couldn't be more wrong."

"It wouldn't be the first time," her friend conceded. "So, you're concerned because a sexy stewardess with a key is bad because there's a child in the house."

"A child who subsequently decided when she grows up, she wants to be a redhead with big boobs."

"Oh, my."

"No kidding."

"That's unfortunate, Lib, but give him the benefit of the doubt. This is a major lifestyle change for him."

"I get that." Libby picked up her pen and rolled it between her fingers. "If that was the only thing, I'd shrug it off. But he's a workaholic. His priorities are budgets and business models. What concerns me is that so far he's shown no inclination to change his lifestyle to accommodate Morgan."

Sophia nodded. "That's a concern."

"Yeah. Charity and Ben took care of all the details before they left. They dotted *I*s and crossed *T*s. Their decisions were made with abundant thought. And it begs the question—why did they trust me with Morgan for the short term, but make Jess her long-term legal guardian?"

"I can't answer that." Sophia studied her. "What are you thinking?"

"I'm just wondering who would be the better parent," Libby admitted.

"As in changing the custodial status quo?"

"It's crossed my mind. I have an appointment with an attorney."

Sophia sat forward, her expression shocked. "You're talking about suing for custody?"

"I haven't really thought about it in those terms or that far ahead."

"Have you talked to Mr. Donnelly? Maybe he would be willing, possibly relieved, to step aside. It's possible you'd be doing him a favor. You might be able to work out a mutually agreeable solution."

Libby clicked the top of the pen, sending the point in and out. "Before moving Morgan, I tried to talk to him and couldn't get access. Rich people have a lot of insulation."

"It's probably because they need it," her friend commented. "There are probably a lot of folks who'd like to separate him from a million or two."

That was a good point and something Libby hadn't considered. "I suppose it's not easy to trust when you're in his position. But I tried to talk to him when I brought Morgan, that very first day. He adamantly refused to even consider altering custody. Said he promised his friend."

"Sounds awfully noble to me."

Libby would have thought so, too. Except Jess had put a finer point on it and called Morgan a duty. But then, in the E.R., he'd been so sweet with her. Probably guilt for not being available to authorize her treatment. And yet his interaction with her had seemed to be completely natural. It was so confusing and she didn't know what the right thing was anymore.

"What I know for sure is that I love that little girl like she's my own. For me, walking away isn't an option. I just want to talk to an attorney and find out what my options are—if any."

Sophia nodded thoughtfully. "If he doesn't voluntarily agree to walk away, you could be talking about a legal battle."

"I know."

"It could get expensive," her friend pointed out. "No *could* about it. We're talking lawyers and protracted legal proceedings. All of that can add up fast."

"I get it."

"He's got unlimited funds and you—"

"Don't," Libby finished for her.

But technically she was working two jobs and saving every penny possible. Just in case.

Sophia studied her for several moments. "I hope it doesn't come to that."

"Yeah. Me, too."

But Libby wouldn't run away from it either. If she decided to go that route, it would be because that's what was best for Morgan.

"I have to go. So much paperwork, so little time." Sophia stood and looked down. "I have just one thing to say."

"Do I want to hear this?"

"Doesn't matter. It's not directly about you." She smiled. "Morgan is a lucky little girl."

That surprised Libby, what with losing her parents and all. "Why do you say that?"

"Two good people care enough to be there for her. You and Mr. Donnelly are ready and willing to make sure she's got everything she needs. He's got the money, you've got the emotional thing going on."

"That's what Ginger said. It's how I came up with the idea to be his nanny in the first place."

"There are an awful lot of children that no one wants." Memories turned Sophia's eyes stormy and sad.

Libby wondered, not for the first time, about Sophia's

past, but when she looked like she did now, bringing up the bad stuff just seemed wrong. "Thanks for stopping in. It really helped to talk."

Libby finished up her work, then left the classroom and locked the door before stopping by the day-care center to pick up Morgan. They were on the way to the car before she realized she'd forgotten the folder for a project that she'd wanted to look over for the next day. When they rounded the corner a man was standing there, peeking into her classroom window. She recognized him immediately and her stomach knotted.

Speaking of people who'd like to dip into the bank account of the wealthy, or the not wealthy. Just anyone he could use for his own selfish reasons. Including his own daughter—especially his daughter.

"What are you doing here, Dad?"

Chapter Six

Libby stared at Bill Bradford's charming smile and the crinkly lines around his pale blue eyes. It seemed wrong that her father's dark hair was sprinkled with gray. That should be earned by hard work and worry, neither of which the man had ever done. This was the first time in months that she'd seen him, not since her younger sister Kelly had graduated from high school.

That meant he was up to something.

"What do you want?" she asked, pulling Morgan close to her.

"How are you, Lib?"

"Fine."

"Who's this?" he asked, looking at the little girl.

"Morgan," she answered. "Charity's child."

He nodded. "I heard. Kelly mentioned it. I'm sorry."

Libby didn't answer. This man didn't give a rat's behind about anyone but himself. "What do you want?" she asked again.

"Can't a father say hello to his kid?"

"Of course. But when *you* do, there's an ulterior motive."

The charming smile disappeared and the crinkly lines just made him look old. "Have you talked to your sister?"

"We e-mail all the time. She loves UCLA."

He nodded. "Now that she's away at college, Cathy's parents have suggested I should make other living arrangements."

A nice way to say *get out,* and about darn time, she thought. The man had mooched off Cathy's family for years, ever since Libby was a little girl. There was nothing that tugged on heartstrings more than a motherless child. About the time her folks had his number, Cathy turned up pregnant. She'd lost a child to a debilitating disease and descended into despair and drugs. She'd been on the street when she'd hooked up with Bill Bradford. All Cathy had ever wanted was her own baby to love and her parents would do anything to give her that, even if they also had to take in the baby-to-be's worthless father and his kid.

"What about Cathy?" Libby asked.

"She's staying."

So they were splitting up, which meant Cathy had finally had enough, too. At least the woman had been smart enough not to marry him.

He slid his fingers into the pockets of his jeans. "They didn't give me any warning, so I haven't had a chance to put together a plan. Other living arrangements take money and I haven't had time to save up."

She didn't say it out loud—that he'd had the last eighteen years to put away money, but that took ambition. "I don't have any cash to spare."

"I understand. Just thought I'd check." He looked at Morgan. "I know how expensive it is to have a kid."

Play the guilt card and fishing for information at the same time. Classic manipulation.

"I'm her nanny," Libby explained. "Just a working girl."

"I live with my Uncle Jess," Morgan added. "He has a big, big apartment in a very high building."

Bill forced a smile. "Sounds really nice."

"It is. And he bought me a new bed, with princess sheets." She held up her bandaged hand. "I didn't cry when I got stitches yesterday and he took me to the toy store and got me lots of stuff."

"Your Uncle Jess did that?" Bill Bradford's eyes gleamed with interest.

"Don't even think about it," Libby warned. "Jess Donnelly isn't someone you can—"

"*The* Jess Donnelly, billionaire resort builder?"

Darn. Darn. Darn.

"Look, we have to go." She took Morgan's uninjured hand and led her away.

From behind she heard him say, "Goodbye, Morgan."

"'Bye."

When the little girl slowed to look back, Libby tugged her along.

"See you later, Lib."

Not if she saw him first.

Libby kicked herself for letting anger squeeze out common sense. She was trying so hard to leave her past in the past and didn't want it to spill over into her present. All she wanted was what every woman wanted—a family, someone to love who would love her back. She didn't want to be associated with the man whose DNA she was trying so hard to overcome.

* * *

At dinner around the kitchen table, Jess had Libby on one side and Morgan on the other. She was eating fish sticks and fries, picking them up with her left hand because her right one was wrapped in white gauze. Because of him, her trauma had stretched out far longer than necessary.

He felt like pond scum. Actually worse. Scum was on top of the water. What he was settled lower, deeper, darker and slimier, at the bottom of the water. Because of him, the experience had been worse for Morgan, and remembering the way Libby's voice cracked and her struggle not to cry ripped him up even now. Fear had been starkly etched on her face and bothered him more than he would have believed possible.

When he stopped beating himself up, Jess noticed that the girls were quieter than usual. No small talk tonight to fill the silence. Normally Libby picked up the slack, but tonight she looked different. The sunshine was gone and he wondered why. It was best not to consider why he noticed at all.

He looked at her, then Morgan. "So, how was your day?"

"I didn't have to go to the hop-spital."

"I'm glad about that," he said, trying to keep his voice light. Obviously she remembered his boneheaded attempt to distract her from the upsetting situation with her hand.

"But I didn't get to play outside," the little girl added. "Why?"

"'Cuz of my hurt hand." She chewed a French fry. "Miss Connie didn't want me to make it worser."

He glanced at Libby, who would normally have corrected the grammar slip, and was surprised when there was no comment. Definitely preoccupied.

"So what did you do inside?" Jess persisted.

"I colored. But not very good."

"How come?"

He directed the question to Morgan, then glanced at Libby, who was passive-aggressively multi-tasking. She was pushing fish stick bites around her plate and brooding at the same time.

"It was hard to hold the crayons in my other hand." She picked up a green bean and popped it in her mouth. "But Miss Connie said it was art stick."

"Is that scholastic terminology? A secret word between students and teachers?" he asked Libby.

"What?" she hadn't been paying attention.

"Her teacher called her coloring 'art stick.'"

"Artistic," she translated.

"Ah. That means it was good," he told Morgan. "Sometimes it's hard to be objective about our own work."

"Huh?"

"It means that we always like what we do so it's not easy to tell whether or not other people will like it, too."

"Oh." But she still looked confused.

"The good news is that while your right hand is getting better, your left got a chance to be a star."

"I guess." Her look was doubtful.

"So you had a quiet day?" He couldn't shake the feeling something had happened.

"Yup." Morgan nodded emphatically. "Then me and Aunt Libby came here."

He noticed she didn't say *home* and on some level it bothered him. "After yesterday, I'm glad everything was peaceful. So, that's all that happened?"

Morgan scrunched her nose thoughtfully. "I forgot. A man came to see Aunt Libby and asked if he could say hello to his kid."

That sent his "uh-oh" radar into on mode. "Who was he? Libby?"

"Hmm?" She glanced at Morgan and the conversation must have registered on some level because she said, "Oh. Just my father."

Jess realized he didn't know anything about her family and suddenly wanted to. "That's nice. Him stopping by, I mean."

"Aunt Libby didn't look happy. She s'plained to him that she's my nanny."

And had been for a while, Jess thought. That meant she wasn't communicating with him regularly.

"I told him I live with you," Morgan continued. "And that you bought me a new bed even before I hurt my hand. But when I didn't cry you took me to the toy store for a 'ward."

"Reward," Libby clarified, tuning in to the conversation now.

"Right," Morgan said. "I told him stuff about you and Aunt Libby said for him not to think about that. But I don't know what that means."

"It was nothing," Libby said. "He just stopped to say hello."

"But you were mad, Aunt Libby."

"I wasn't mad, sweetie." Libby looked startled. "What makes you think I was mad?"

"'Cuz you squeezed my not-hurt hand very, very tight and made me walk away kind of fast. And you didn't even say goodbye to him, which wasn't p'lite."

"I was just in a hurry to get you home," she said. "I'm sorry you thought I was angry."

"That's okay." She slid from her chair. "I hafta go potty."

She raced from the room, the unexpected visitor forgotten. But not to Jess.

When they were alone, he looked at Libby, who wouldn't

make eye contact. "You must have been happy to see your father."

She looked up and there was nothing happy in her expression. "He shows up from time to time."

"You didn't tell him you're working for me?"

"I did today."

Not what he meant and the look on her face told him she knew that. "Does your mother know about this job?"

"She died when I was born."

"I'm sorry," he said automatically.

Before he could ask even one of the million questions that popped into his head, Morgan ran back into the kitchen and Libby was reminding her to slow down and be careful of her hand. After that the routine ritual of table-clearing and bathtime commenced. The fact that it was becoming familiar to him wasn't as disturbing as curiosity about Libby.

He hoped that was because she so obviously didn't want to talk about her father. He figured that was because of a strained relationship, something he understood only too well. He didn't share information about his mother because there was nothing to be gained by telling a story that always managed to piss him off all over again.

He refused to consider that his high curiosity level was due to anything more than Libby's out-of-the-ordinary reserve. Every time their paths had crossed over the years, her smart, sassy sense of humor drew him, among other things that had caught his attention and some that hadn't until she'd moved into his penthouse.

He'd deliberately pretended not to remember her because he couldn't ever completely forget her. He had sensed the moment they met that she could be more to him, which wasn't something he ever wanted. The problem was getting that message where it needed to go. Every day he became more aware that she was bright *and* sexy. Not drop-dead gorgeous, but definitely pretty. And he was damned attracted.

The good news was that Morgan had talked to him more than she ever had and didn't seem to hold the emergency-room fiasco against him. The bad? Every day it was becoming increasingly more difficult to keep himself from kissing the nanny.

And that would be a huge mistake.

Libby expected Jess to work late and miss Halloween, but that hadn't stopped her from hoping she'd be wrong. She wasn't. When he walked into the penthouse, Morgan was already asleep, worn out from trick-or-treating and the excitement of wearing her costume.

He came into the kitchen, where Libby was standing by the island, inspecting the cache of candy the little girl had collected in her plastic pumpkin.

"Sorry I'm late," he said by way of greeting.

"Yeah."

With his jacket slung over his shoulder and held by one finger, he looked every inch a corporate pirate. His tie was loosened and the first button of his white dress shirt undone, with the long sleeves rolled up to mid-forearm. The look was so blatantly male, so incredibly masculine that he quite literally took her breath away. She wasn't prepared for that, but then she never was. There was no way to brace for the overwhelming force of attraction she'd experienced from the moment they'd met.

Jess picked up a chocolate bar and the expression on his face held traces of regret, which was surprising. "Did Morgan have fun?"

"Big time." Libby tossed a small bag of hard candy with

a tear in the package onto the discard pile. "I took her to the District in Green Valley Ranch. The stores surround a big courtyard and were all giving out candy. It had a safe, block-party sort of feel and there were lots of kids. She had a blast."

"I'm sorry I didn't get to see her dressed up."

"It's not too late. She insisted on wearing her princess costume to bed."

One dark eyebrow rose. "You let her?"

"It's a special occasion. Relaxing the rules seemed like a good idea." *Relax* being the operative word since there was something she needed to discuss with him. "You can look in on her if you want."

"I'll do that."

And there was a surprise. Every time she thought she had him figured out he did the unexpected.

He was gone for a while and returned wearing worn jeans and a pale yellow pullover sweater with the neck of his white T-shirt peeking out. Another masculine look that rocked her hormones. She should be used to it by now, but not so much.

"She looks pretty cute," he said. "While I think it's really cool, I have to ask. You don't think the glow-in-the-dark tiara is dangerous?"

Libby laughed. "I tried to talk her out of sleeping in it, but she was willing to take the risk. Then things threatened to get ugly. That wasn't a hill I wanted to die on, since I can take it off when she's sound asleep."

"Sounds like a wise decision." He opened the refrigerator and grabbed a longneck brown beer bottle, then twisted off the metal cap.

"Speaking of wise…"

Libby wasn't anxious to bring up the subject of his father or parental males in general after all the questions he asked about her own. Jess had never shown quite that level of interest in her before and she regretted more than was prudent that it probably wasn't about her at all. For the record, he was smart to be wary of her father.

As much as she didn't want to, she needed to talk—specifically about his feelings after his father died. He might be able to help Morgan more than anyone.

"What?" He took a drink of beer.

"I was hoping you could help with something."

"If I can," he agreed.

"Miss Connie came to see me today."

"Who?"

"Her kindergarten teacher. She was wondering how Morgan's coping with the loss of her parents."

"What do you think?" he asked.

"That's difficult to answer." Absently she twisted the cellophane ends of a candy package. "I had to break the news to her."

Libby remembered that horrible day. Reeling from the news that her best friend wasn't ever coming home. The realization that she'd have to tell Morgan something that no child should have to hear. "She didn't have an immediate reaction except to get very quiet. I figured she was only five and hadn't seen them for months, which is forever to a kid."

"That makes sense." The tone was casual and completely at odds with the hard edges and shadows on his face.

"But the regular phone calls from Charity and Ben stopped. I've sort of been waiting for her to bring up the subject, if she wants to talk about it."

"And?" he prompted.

Libby toed open the stainless-steel trash can, then tossed in the questionable candy before meeting his gaze. "She hasn't mentioned Charity and Ben at all. The thing is, I don't know how a kid would react to something like that."

He leaned a hip on the bar stool beside her. "I'm not sure how I can help."

"You lost your dad when you were just a kid. I was wondering how you handled it."

He'd started to lift the bottle to his mouth and stopped. The expression on his face said he'd rather walk naked in a hail storm than discuss this.

"That was a long time ago. I don't remember anything specific."

Something about his tone made her think he wasn't telling the whole truth about that. For the life of her she couldn't figure out why he wouldn't open up. For all his flaws, shallowness being top of the list, she'd never known him to be deliberately mean. And clearly he was loyal. Maybe she could get him to share.

"Did you talk about how you felt? To a counselor? A teacher? Or some other professional?"

"No." A muscle in his jaw jerked.

"Was there anything your mother did to make it easier?"

He set the beer down with enough force to splash some of the liquid on the counter. "Like I said, it was a long time ago. And I was only a few years older than Morgan."

"Which is why I think you're the best person to consult about how to proceed—"

"That's where you're wrong," he said. "Little girls are way outside my area of expertise."

In essence he was refusing to discuss the issue, which tweaked Libby's temper. "Right. I forgot. Big girls are more your style."

"I like women," he agreed.

Libby remembered. She hadn't meant to say anything

out loud and wasn't sure why she did now. That wasn't exactly true. It was no surprise that he dated, but seeing Elena Cavanaugh had hurt more than she was prepared for. His type was something she would never be, and face-to-face confirmation was tough to reconcile.

"A child is definitely a responsibility," she said, bringing the subject back to the little girl. "Is the obligation cramping your style?"

"Morgan is the daughter of my best friend. He'd have done the same for me."

That wasn't an answer and sounded more like the company line than a reason to raise an orphaned little girl. This time a dash of irritation made her ask, "Did you ever plan to have children?"

"Honestly?"

"Always the best policy," she said.

"Since high school my focus has been on achieving success. I knew business was the best way to do that and concentrated all my energy in college on learning everything I could to get me where I wanted to be. I'm determined to make the name Jess Donnelly as recognizable and synonymous with Las Vegas resorts as Steve Wynn or the Maloof family with their fantasy suites at the Palms Hotel."

"So children aren't now nor have they ever been one of your priorities?"

"No."

"Why doesn't that surprise me?"

His gaze narrowed. "Has anyone ever told you that's quite the talent you've got for lobbing verbal zingers?"

"I'm glad you like it."

"I didn't say that. Just that I noticed."

"That makes two of us." Libby froze, then let out a long breath.

What she noticed reinforced that her recent appointment with the attorney had been the right thing to do. The family law specialist had promised to research the situation and get back to her on options for Morgan's custody—if it became clear that was in the child's best interest. Libby still hadn't made up her mind about that.

Sometimes Jess showed signs of bonding with Morgan, then he pulled back. Like tonight. Missing Halloween.

Or maybe she was painting her perception of him with the rejection brush he used on her. She wasn't proud of the way she yearned for him to become aware of her but couldn't deny the feelings for him that had simmered inside her for so long.

"What did you notice?" he asked.

Like she would actually share her most personal and intimate thoughts with him. "It's not so much that as watching Morgan tonight. She made a couple of comments about kids with the adults around them. Wondering if they were moms and dads."

Jess folded his arms over his chest. "So you're wondering whether or not her teacher is right about a delayed reaction to losing her parents."

"Yeah. It crossed my mind." Among other things, she thought.

"Do you think she needs to see a professional?"

"It's an option," she agreed. "I think it might be best to just observe for a while."

"Okay," he said.

"And I'm thinking it might be a good idea to get out pictures of Charity and Ben. Not only is there a chance she would open up, but we should try and keep their memory alive for their child."

"You're right. Okay."

Okay. There'd been willingness in his voice to do whatever Morgan needed. That was the kind of thing that warmed Libby's heart and fueled her impossible fantasies where Jess was concerned. It's why she wasn't prepared to do anything drastic to uproot Morgan yet again.

As long as Libby was around to keep that little girl from getting hurt, there was no reason things couldn't stay the way they were. And that was the problem. They'd agreed she would stay on as nanny until Morgan adjusted. There was no guarantee he wouldn't decide tomorrow that Morgan was peachy and Libby's services were no longer required.

She didn't think he was there yet. At the moment she was more worried about her secret crush on him. But she'd had a lot of practice in hiding how she felt and would simply keep on not letting Jess see what was in her heart, the feelings that just refused to go away.

Chapter Seven

Libby and Jess had agreed to let the trauma of the E.R. and the sugar rush of Halloween recede before talking to Morgan about her parents. A week after trick-or-treating, the stitches had been removed and the remainder of the candy stash discreetly discarded.

It was Saturday, two weeks before Thanksgiving, a rare cold and rainy day in Las Vegas. Jess had turned on the gas fireplace in the family room where the three of them had watched Morgan's favorite animated movie. A feeling of yearning enveloped Libby just as tangible and encompassing as the cold. She wanted this to be *real*. She wanted a family.

With an effort, she pushed the yearning away even as she dreaded what was coming.

Morgan wiggled on the sofa beside her and looked up. "I'm bored, Aunt Libby."

She met Jess's gaze and gave him a what-do-you-think-about-now? look. He only hesitated a moment before nodding slightly.

Morgan glanced between them and asked, "What did I say?"

Libby fervently wished he would take the lead on this, which was nothing more than classic avoidance. She was the one with a degree in early childhood education, the one with child-care experience. Of the two of them, she could be considered the kid expert, but that was not how she felt in this delicate situation. She loved kids and cared about every single one, but there was a special place in her heart for Morgan. She was emotionally involved, which made knowledge and experience not very useful.

If it was within her power, she would make this child's life perfect and never let anything bad happen. Obviously she was powerless or they wouldn't be here now. And sometimes pain was a necessary therapy to get to a better place. She clung to that with every fiber of her being.

"Aunt Libby? Am I in trouble?"

"No, sweetie." She slid her arm around the child and pulled her close. "Why would you say that? Have you *ever* been in trouble with me?"

"No." She glanced up through her golden lashes to peek at Jess. "But maybe he's mad about somethin'."

Jess studied her, a serious expression on his face. "Did you make the stock prices in my company go down?"

She blinked and shook her head. "I don't know what that means."

"Just tell him no," Libby advised, rolling her eyes at him.

"No," Morgan repeated.

"Then I'm not mad at you," he assured her.

"Morgan, there's something Uncle Jess and I wanted to talk to you about. But if it's not okay with you, we won't."

"What?"

Libby's heart squeezed at the uneasy look on the little girl's face. She'd like nothing better than to blow this off for a rousing session of paper dolls or cutthroat Candyland. Some of it was about Morgan, but another very large part was that it was going to hurt to talk about this. It was another step in the process of realizing that her dearest friend in the world was no longer *in* this world.

Libby took a deep breath and braced herself. "We—Uncle Jess and I—want to talk to you about your mommy and daddy."

Morgan's little body stiffened against her and she looked down at her hands. But not before Libby saw, or maybe it was just a sense, that the little girl had shut down. Pulled an invisible cloak of protection around her. It didn't take a mind reader or kid expert to get that she didn't want to talk about this either. Probably for all the reasons Libby didn't and a whole lot more she couldn't even comprehend.

"What is it, sweetie?" Libby looked at Jess, who was frowning.

"Nothin'."

"Did you know your daddy was my best friend?" he asked.

"Why?" Morgan glanced quickly up at him.

"That's a good question. I'm not sure why he liked me." He thought for a moment. "But I admired him because he was smart. He was funny. And he always had my back."

"Huh?"

Libby could almost see the wheels turning in his mind as he concentrated on finding words to explain an expression that adults generally understood. He really wasn't used to conversing with kids, but he got an A for effort. And major points for looking so darn cute while he did it.

"It means," he finally said, "that he was always there when I needed him."

"Oh."

Libby wondered if Morgan was too young to realize the irony of the fact that she would never experience the quality that Jess had valued so much in her father. And, if she did realize the extent of her loss, was she angry about it? That's part of what this exercise was all about.

She met his gaze, grateful that he'd started the ball rolling, got Morgan talking. Now it was time to follow his lead.

"Morgan," she said, "did you know your mommy was *my* best friend?"

This time the little girl only nodded, giving her nowhere to go conversationally.

"Why?" Jess asked, picking up on that.

She smiled her gratitude. "I respected her because she cared about everyone, including me. She made me laugh. I loved that about her. But one of my favorite things is that she was a girly girl."

Morgan glanced up, the barest spark of interest in her eyes. "Does that mean she liked girl stuff?"

"Not just liked. She *loved* girl stuff more than any girl I know." Libby smiled even though her heart hurt. "She couldn't go into a store without buying lipstick, eyeshadow or blush. Unless the store she was in didn't carry any of those items. She painted my toes the very first time I ever had that done, and spilled nail polish on the rug."

"Did she get in trouble?"

"No. Her parents were cool." More relatives Morgan would never know. Charity's father and mother had died a couple of years ago, within six months of each other. Ben's folks had passed away before the two had met. "She loved earrings and bracelets, too."

"And tiaras?" Morgan asked.

"Probably her favorite—" Libby's voice cracked and she looked up when Jess's fingers touched her shoulder. She appreciated the show of support even though it came with a tingle of awareness. "Your mom would have loved your Halloween costume."

"Really?"

"Really," Jess said. "Your dad, too. He always called you his little princess."

"I'd forgotten that. He said it when you were born." Libby snapped her fingers then reached over to the table beside her and grabbed a stack of photos that she'd gathered together. "Here's a family picture. Your mom's holding you and there's your dad sitting on the hospital bed."

"I remember when they were getting ready to bring you home from the hospital. Your dad and I spent a long time making sure the car seat was hooked up right so you'd be safe." Jess's expression was shadowed with sadness at the memory.

"And on your last birthday you got chalk and drew pictures on the sidewalk outside with your mom and dad. Here's one of the three of you. Remember that, Morgan?"

"No."

Libby felt the force behind the single word, but didn't know whether that was the truth or simply that Morgan was doing her best not to recall.

She tightened her hold on the child. "Why don't you tell Uncle Jess and me something you do remember?"

Morgan was quiet for several moments. "I don't 'member them much."

"What about your dad giving you rides on his shoulders? Or your mom playing boats in the bathtub, with bubbles?" Libby suggested.

"No." Morgan shook her head. "And I don't 'member what they look like anymore."

Libby wasn't surprised. In fact, she'd kind of expected that. As she handed more pictures to the little girl, Jess got up and left the room. She sighed, glad that he'd stayed for the hard part. But she missed his reassuring presence, something else she wished not to feel yet couldn't seem to stop.

"These are pictures of your mom and dad's wedding."

Morgan looked through them, then pointed to one of the maid of honor and best man. "This is you and Uncle Jess."

"That's right." Libby took it from her.

In the photo she was wearing a strapless lavender dress and Jess looked incredibly handsome in a traditional black tuxedo. He had his arm around her and there was a gleam in his eyes as he looked at her. Even now flutters and hormones collided in her belly, sending waves of wanting through her. He'd thoroughly charmed her that day only to profoundly disappoint later, when he left the reception with another bridesmaid.

Jess walked back into the room with his own pile of pictures and Libby's heart pounded as fast and furiously as it had the day she'd met him, during their friends' wedding activities. She hadn't given up on not having a visceral reaction to him. That achievement was still a work in progress.

He sat on the sofa, on Morgan's other side, and handed her a snapshot. "This is your mom and dad in their condo. It was taken at the housewarming party."

"I have some of those, too," Libby said.

Libby found it endearing that in this age of digital photography he'd bothered to have some pictures printed. It was something they had in common. Morgan shuffled through them and pointed out Libby and Jess in every one.

"Here are some taken in the hospital when you were born." Yet again Libby saw herself and Jess.

"These are from her christening." Jess handed them to Libby first.

She was holding Morgan at just a few weeks old and Jess had his arm around both of them. They were her godparents. She met his gaze and saw the sadness she knew was in her own eyes. It was a grief they shared and somehow that made it a little easier to bear.

The last pictures were of Christmas and Morgan's fifth birthday party in January, just before Charity and Ben had left. It was like watching a disaster movie and wanting to beg them not to go because something bad was going to happen, something they couldn't stop. The holidays that were coming up would be Morgan's first without her parents.

She handed the photos back. "Here."

Libby searched for comforting words. Like her parents would always be with her even though she couldn't see them. In the end she was afraid the concept of spirits or ghosts might be more disturbing.

So she only said, "They loved you so much."

Morgan looked up, her big brown eyes sad. "Who's my family now?"

Well, damn, this had backfired. It brought up more questions than comfort and Libby didn't know how to answer. She wanted to say that she and Jess were her family. They were certainly there for her. They were godparents and now the parent figures on the front line of bringing up this child. But family?

The reality was something else.

Libby's path had frequently intersected with Jess's. There had been numerous opportunities to hook up, if he'd been interested in her. Obviously he wasn't. She felt a pain in her heart that had nothing to do with losing her friend and everything to do with big feelings for him that had nowhere to go.

She pulled Morgan into her lap and hugged tight. "Don't worry, sweetie. You're going to be just fine. I'm here. Uncle Jess is here."

Libby swallowed the threatening tears and couldn't look at Jess for fear he'd see. She wanted Morgan's life to be perfect and it never would be. Her best friend wasn't ever coming home again. She squeezed Morgan just a little closer. Charity was gone, but thank goodness a part of her was still here.

Jess sat on the corner group in the family room and tried to concentrate on the football game. It wasn't easy when fragments of yesterday's conversation with Morgan kept popping into his head. He was well aware of his limitations and never planned to have children. Something that Libby had figured out for herself.

Ben had always told him he'd make a great dad and with the right woman Jess would feel differently. This was different, all right, and Libby was the right woman to raise Morgan. But Jess knew he was the weak link, not father material.

Morgan had opened up a little and he hoped she felt better even though he felt like crap. Libby had asked him how he felt when his dad died and he'd felt like crap then, too. He just hadn't known how much worse things could get. His mom had been responsible for the worse part, but at least he'd had her to get him through the first wave of the grief. Morgan didn't have either parent. The poor kid just had him, a bachelor with no idea how to help her. Thank goodness for Libby.

The two of them were doing girly stuff. Stuff that Charity would have done. What would Ben have done? Probably watch football.

On his seventy-inch plasma flatscreen TV, two teams were fighting it out, sweaty and physical. Games were won or lost on a single play. A split-second decision. The Monday-morning quarterbacking didn't come until Monday morning and this was still Sunday night. But Jess was second-guessing his friend. Probably Ben had fully thought out the decision before asking him to be his daughter's guardian. But Jess just couldn't see in himself what Ben had, nothing that would indicate he was capable.

He saw movement from the corner of his eye and looked up to see Morgan standing just inside the entrance to the family room. She was wearing a pink sweater with sneakers to match and jeans.

"Hi," he said.

"Hi," she answered.

They stared at each other for several moments before he asked, "Where's Aunt Libby?"

"Doing stuff."

"I see." And pigs could fly.

"What are you doin'?"

He glanced at the TV, then muted the sound. "I'm watching a football game. The New England Patriots are playing the Seattle Seahawks."

"Oh."

"I'm rooting for the Seahawks," he added.

"'Cuz they're birds?" she asked, moving farther into the room so she could see the screen full-on.

"No, because they're the underdog."

There was confusion in her eyes. "So they're dogs?"

"No." He wanted to laugh at her literal interpretation but she looked so serious he held back. "*Underdog* is just an expression. It means no one thinks they'll win."

"Why do you want them to?"

"Because it would surprise everyone and I like surprises." He looked at her sober little face and in his own mind put a finer point on that statement. He liked *good* surprises, not the kind where friends didn't get to see their kid grow up.

Morgan moved closer, leaning on the end of the corner group. "Are the birds winning?"

"No. But they're only behind by seven points. A touchdown," he explained.

She scratched her nose. "What's that?"

"It's when a team takes the football over the goal line into the end zone to put six points on the scoreboard."

"But you said it was seven."

"It is after they kick the extra point."

"They kick it? Does it hurt?"

"No."

Jess never knew kids took things so literally. He looked at the total confusion on her face and tried to remember a time when he had known absolutely nothing about the game of football. He'd started watching when he was about Morgan's age because he enjoyed spending time with his dad. Because he'd asked questions, his father had patiently explained the basic rules of the game.

After his mother remarried, watching the sport was the only thing he and her husband ever did together without arguing. And every argument was followed by his mom taking a side opposite her own son.

Jess put the remote control on the coffee table. "After a

team scores, they have to kick the ball over the bar between the goal posts for an extra point."

"Six plus one is seven," Morgan said.

"Correct. You're pretty good at math."

"That's what Miss Connie says."

"Your teacher?"

"Uh-huh."

He wasn't sure where to go now. Then Libby's words came back to him. *Kid talk takes practice. Ask things you don't know.*

"Do you like Miss Connie?" It was the next question that popped into his head.

"Uh-huh. She took care of me when I cut my hand."

He tried not to think about how he'd let her down that day. Since then he'd authorized Libby to do whatever might be necessary for Morgan's well-being and instructed his secretary to interrupt him immediately when she called. If that happened, it would be about this child and he wanted to know.

"I'm glad Miss Connie was there for you."

She rubbed a finger on the arm of the furniture. "Aunt Libby told me that my real daddy wishes he could be with me."

"She's right. Your Aunt Libby is a pretty smart lady." And hot. Sharp-witted and sexy. Even when she was calling him on his crap. Maybe he liked her *because* she stood up to him.

Morgan scrambled up onto the sofa and sat with her legs sticking straight out in front of her. "She said that my daddy maked sure I'd be okay with you."

"That's right. He did." And Jess had given a solemn promise to watch over her.

She turned the full force of those big, innocent brown eyes on him. "Does that mean you're my daddy now?"

For a little thing, she carried quite a wallop. The words felt like a sucker punch and he couldn't catch his breath, but the expectant expression on her little face demanded a response.

"I'll make sure you're okay. Your dad asked me to be your guardian and that means I'll take care of you."

"But will you be my daddy?"

Persistence was a good thing, he told himself. He wouldn't be where he was today without it. But right at this particular moment, he wished Morgan had a little bit less.

There was no way he could take Ben's place, but he'd have to be a moron not to see that this little girl needed reassurance. He simply couldn't lie to her.

"I'll always be your Uncle Jess," he assured her.

"But that's different from a daddy," she said.

"How?"

"'Cuz there are things daddies do. I have a list."

"What kind of things?" he asked, feeling dumb as a rock for not instinctively knowing.

She slid off the couch and dug a piece of paper from her jeans pocket. "Stuff like riding a bike."

"Do you have one?"

She shook her head and blond curls danced around her face. "But I'm gonna ask Santa Claus to bring me one."

Note to self, he thought. She was a believer in North Pole lore and wanted a bike for Christmas. He'd have to discuss that with Libby.

"What else is on your list?"

She looked down at the wrinkled paper with uneven printing. "I don't know how to tie my shoes yet. Or swim." Glancing out at the terrace complete with pool, she added, "What if I fall in?"

"If you can't swim that could be a problem. Although your Aunt Libby watches over you pretty carefully." The words were spoken in a calm and reasonable voice. Inside he wasn't quite so Zen. Probably Libby would have brought up the subject of swim lessons when the weather warmed up. Or he might have thought of it himself, but he didn't quite buy that. "Is there anything else?"

"Allowance," she said.

For a couple of beats he didn't have a clue what she meant, then it dawned on him. Weekly earnings for work completed. Chores to be determined by the adult in charge.

"That's a very comprehensive—" He realized the word was too big for her. "A very complete list you've got there. Aunt Libby and I will make sure everything is taken care of."

"Okay." She moved closer and handed the paper to him.

From down the hall Libby called out and Morgan turned her head, indicating she'd heard. "I hafta go."

"Okay. See you later."

"'Bye." She raced out of the room.

When he was alone, Jess let out a long breath. The good news was that their picture presentation featuring Morgan's parents had been successful in bringing up some feelings. The bad news? She wanted Jess to wear the daddy hat. Worse, the look in her big eyes said she trusted him to wear it well, but her belief in him was misplaced.

He'd lived with two sides of the dad thing—the father he'd lost to cancer and the man his widowed mom fell in love with later. His dad had made him promise to be the man of the house. His mom promised that Jess was the most important person in her life. But when she remarried, he'd been caught in the middle and felt like a screwup at everything he touched.

He never wanted to disappoint Morgan the way his mother had him. It's why he never pictured himself with kids. He didn't want to screw up a brand-new life.

Emotional detachment was second nature to him now. It had worked real well because he'd managed to push everyone away except Ben. Now his friend was gone. The good thing about being alone was that there wasn't anyone to let down.

Until now.

Chapter Eight

After putting Morgan to bed, Libby walked into the family room and saw Jess watching TV. But not watching. There was a program on but the sound was muted. He was staring at the big screen with a dark and broody, faraway expression on his face. She'd just come in here to let him know that Morgan was asleep, everything was quiet and to say good-night. She was going to stand in the doorway, not get in close enough for the delicious smell of him to make her hormones dance. It was all about delivering her message, then beat a quick retreat to her room and refuge. It was a plan; it was a *good* plan. Sensible. To the point. In and out before the constant yearning inside her could be whipped into a frenzy of need by prolonged exposure to his potent charm and masculinity.

A closer look at the face that never failed to make her weak in the knees brought out a heavy sigh.

"Jess?"

He looked up. "Hmm?"

"I just wanted to let you know Morgan is asleep."

"Okay."

She cocked her thumb over her shoulder, indicating the area behind her. "I'm going to turn in. Busy day tomorrow."

"Oh?"

"Yeah. The excitement level of the kids really goes up before Thanksgiving. And leading up to Christmas it's a big challenge to keep them under control."

"I bet."

"Right. So I need all the sleep I can get." Or not, as thoughts of him always crept in and disturbed her rest.

"Libby?"

She'd just started to turn away and winced when he said her name. "Hmm?"

He hesitated for a moment. "Speaking of Christmas…could I talk to you for a minute?"

This wasn't part of her plan. It so wasn't what she'd come in here to do and every instinct urged her to come up with an excuse and walk away. But there was something so lost in his expression. Something that tugged at her heart. He didn't look like his usual confident self, which was noteworthy. If she had to guess, she would say he was afraid of something and that wasn't the Jess Donnelly she knew. But, darn, it made him a Jess she wanted very badly to get to know.

She blew out a long breath and moved farther into the room, across the coffee table from him. "What's up?"

Jess hit a button on the remote and light from the TV flickered out behind her. "It's about Morgan."

"I figured." No way would he want to talk about Libby. She wasn't the sort of woman who made a man like Jess look the way he was looking now. "What about her?"

"She talked to me."

Libby wanted to throw her hands in the air and holler *woo-hoo,* but she was pretty sure that wasn't the reaction he was looking for. In fact, his shell-shocked appearance reminded her a lot of the way she'd felt when Morgan asked them yesterday who her family was.

"What did she say?"

He stood and ran his fingers through his dark hair. As usual, her insides liquefied. In his long-sleeved white cotton shirt and jeans worn in all the most interesting places, he was her three-dimensional fantasy guy come to life. The angles of his face were all rugged male and the brooding made him mysterious. The stuff of a romance-novel hero. All she could think about was how it would feel to be in his arms.

"Libby, I am so in over my head."

His words brought her back hard and his unease was contagious. "Oh, my. What did you talk about?"

"I was watching the game. Patriots and Seahawks."

"Okay." That didn't seem relevant, but all right.

"It seemed like there was something on her mind but she didn't come out with anything. I didn't know what to say. The thing is, I'm not into girly girl stuff."

"That's all right." One look at his wide shoulders and the masculine five o'clock shadow darkening his cheeks and jaw would clue anyone in to the fact that he was a manly man who'd recoil in horror at girl stuff.

"So I started talking football," he continued.

"Sticking to your comfort zone is good."

"I explained what a touchdown is. Kicking the extra point and why I root for the underdog."

Libby really liked that about him. "Good for you. But none of that explains why you're upset."

"I'm getting there. Just trying to add context."

"Okay. Didn't mean to interrupt."

"She talked about her teacher a little and I remembered what you said about asking questions."

That was incredibly likable, too. Not only had he listened, but he was trying to apply her advice.

"Then what?" she encouraged.

"She mentioned what you told her, about her dad. That he made sure she'd be okay. With me."

"Right. I did. She needs to feel secure," Libby confirmed.

"That's when she asked if I was her daddy now."

And that explained the brooding look that bordered on panic. "What did you tell her?"

"I explained about being her guardian and taking care of her. But she wanted clarification on the whole daddy thing."

"And?"

He shook his head and stared at a spot over her shoulder. "I can't take Ben's place. I didn't really know what to say so I told her I'd always be her Uncle Jess."

"How did she take that?"

The look on his face said not well, but Libby'd had no indication tucking the little girl in bed that anything was bothering her.

"She gave me a daddy list."

"What?"

He moved closer, until they were nearly touching, and held out his hand with a wrinkled piece of paper. "It's a list of things dads do. Like teaching her how to tie her shoes. Swim. Set an allowance. Ride a bike. By the way, she's going to ask Santa for one for Christmas."

Again, that explained her casual reference to Christmas triggering this confession of the soul. "The good news is that she's opening up."

"The bad news is she's opening up to me. I'm in way over my head," he repeated.

"Don't go to the bad place," she said calmly.

"Give me one good reason why not. I've got no skill set for this. My dad died when I was twelve, and my stepfather—"

"What?"

This was the first time he'd mentioned that. The only time they'd discussed his loss, he'd shut down tighter than a prison during a riot when she mentioned his mother. Libby couldn't help being curious, mostly because this Jess wasn't cocky and confident. This Jess was vulnerable and sensitive. He was someone she could fall for.

"Let's just say he wasn't my idea of a parental role model." Jess set on the coffee table beside him the tattered paper with daddy duties on it, then ran his fingers through his hair. "The point is that nothing in my background has prepared me for this. And I don't want to mess her up."

"That's not going to happen."

"How can you be so sure?"

Good question, but suddenly she needed to reassure him. Putting that into words was tough but his eyes gave away how much he wanted her support.

"I know because you're trying," she said. "You listened to advice and put it to practical use."

"I did?" His clueless expression was so endearing.

"Yes. Granted, your conversation was sports based, but that's irrelevant. You connected with her, Jess. That's the most important thing."

"Talking football is one thing." He rubbed the back of his neck. "Dad talk is something else."

"Sincerity is half the battle." She settled her hand on his arm and felt the heat of his skin through his sleeve.

He met her gaze and something dark and intense heated

in his eyes. "I could *sincerely* screw up that little girl's life without your input. I need *you,* Libby."

The passion of his focus on her face trapped all the air in her chest and she couldn't breathe.

I need you.

The words were deeply personal and became sexually charged, making the blood pound in her ears. Libby swayed toward him but would never be clear on who moved first. In the blink of an eye or the beat of a heart, his mouth was on hers.

One of his arms circled her waist and he pulled her against him. His other hand cupped her cheek and then his fingers tangled in her hair, holding her steady while his lips thoroughly explored hers. He kissed her nose, eyes, cheeks and hair. The contact was so sweet, it felt as if he'd kissed her heart.

They were touching from chest to thigh and his muscular strength in contrast to her feminine curves practically made her hormones weep. Although she'd tried desperately to deny then ignore the yearning for him that had always simmered inside her, she couldn't deny it now. They were so close it was impossible for her not to feel the physical evidence that he wanted her, too.

She could hardly believe that the fantasy she'd harbored from the moment they'd met wasn't a dream. But here he was, holding her and kissing her. She heard his raspy breathing and it was an echo of her own. But doubts crept in. She put her hand on his chest.

"Jess?" Did that wanton, whispery voice really belong to her?

"What?" His lips were on her neck and he stopped kissing her, then blew on the moist place where his mouth had just been.

She shivered and her brain short-circuited, but she managed to say, "This probably isn't a good idea."

"I know."

"There are a lot of reasons why it's not the smartest move," she said, not wanting to leave the shelter of his arms.

"Uh-huh." He cupped her cheek in his palm, then ran his thumb over her kiss-swollen bottom lip. "Can you give me three?"

"Three what?" She couldn't think when he touched her like that.

"Reasons." His gaze lowered to her mouth and heat flared.

"Right this second I can't even name one."

"Then how important are brains and logic?" he asked logically.

For some reason that made perfect sense to her. Probably because the way she felt, she'd implode if she walked away from him now.

"Brains and logic are highly overrated." Her words were almost slurred as the spicy scent of him surrounded and intoxicated her.

He slid his palm down her arm, then let his fingers entwine with hers and led her willingly down the hall, into his bedroom. He picked up a remote control from the nightstand beside the king-size bed and hit a button. Instantly the window covering parted and the glitz of Las Vegas magically lighted the dark room.

She'd been in the master suite before, but never with Jess. The bed was an imposing four-poster oak frame with matching nightstands. An armoire and dresser were arranged around the room's perimeter. A black-and-beige comforter covered the mattress, hiding the sheets beneath.

She looked up and her breath caught at the way outside light caressed the rugged line of Jess's jaw and shadowed the angles of his face. He needed a shave and she knew from minutes ago that the stubble would scrape her face, but she welcomed every tangible experience. It was better than a pinch to make this moment real and scratch it into her consciousness.

"Does that remote control gizmo turn down the bed for you?" she asked.

He shook his head, a sexy, wicked gleam in his eyes. Reaching beside him, he yanked the bedding down, revealing the silky, cream-colored sheets.

"Okay?"

"That works, too."

Jess let his gaze roam over her from head to toe. When it settled on her mouth, heat flared and he groaned. "You are one sexy little schoolteacher."

"Me?"

He nodded. "And just so you know. The innocent thing works for me."

"What innocent thing?"

His only answer was to kiss her, unleashing a sense of urgency. They pulled, tugged and yanked on each other's shirts and jeans, desperate for skin-to-skin contact. With her clothes scattered around her, Libby crawled into the bed and stretched out, the sheets cool to her naked, heated flesh. A moment later, Jess was beside her, kissing, touching, taking her to a level of desire that she'd never known.

He cupped her right breast in his hand, brushing his thumb across the taut nipple. "Beautiful," he breathed.

The approval started a glow deep inside that expanded to every part of her. She settled her palm over his knuckles and heard him suck in a harsh breath. Slipping his hand from beneath hers, he traced a tender touch down over her belly, then slid a finger inside her, teasing her in the most intimate way. Her hips lifted, communicating her sense of need.

He rolled to his side, reached into the nightstand and pulled out a condom. In seconds he opened it and covered himself. Then he was beside her again, kissing, stroking and taunting her with his touch. Her thighs automatically parted in invitation and he settled over her, balancing his weight on his forearms.

He entered her with tender slowness, then sighed with satisfaction, which was quite possibly the sweetest sound she'd ever heard. He stayed still for agonizing seconds before pushing fully into her. His tension was tangible just before he stroked and plunged, again and again.

He took her to the edge and in a blinding flash of light, they both went over. Pleasure poured through her and she held on tight as he shuddered in her arms. They didn't stir for a long time, drenched in satisfaction and too sated to move.

Finally, Jess rolled away. Even with her eyes still closed, some part of her registered that a light went on somewhere. Minutes later it went off, just before she felt the mattress dip beneath his weight.

He gathered her to his side and brushed a kiss on her temple. "Wow."

"Wow, indeed," she murmured.

It was the last thing she remembered before falling asleep in his arms.

Libby felt her bed move and opened one eye, expecting to see Morgan. Instead, the French doors leading to the terrace were a big clue that this wasn't her bed, and she wasn't in her room. She had a very good idea who'd caused the mattress to dip. Glancing behind her, she identified Jess's broad shoulder and muscular back.

"Holy Mother of God—"

She groaned softly as everything came back to her in a rush of heat followed by a dear-Lord-what-have-I-done feeling. If a feeling could be rhetorical this one was because she didn't need an answer spelled out. It was there in every pleasure-saturated muscle in her body. She'd had the best sex of her life with Jess Donnelly, after which she remembered feeling safe and warm and happy.

The dim light peeking through the shutter slats told her that it was morning, but she had no idea of the time. The clock was on the other nightstand and seeing it would require major mattress movement to see over Jess's shoulder. That would risk waking him, the last thing she wanted. Facing him after what they'd done would be awkward enough, but when it happened, she wanted to *not* be stark naked in his bed. Fully clothed, preferably with multiple layers, would be marginally better.

Before sliding out from beneath the protection of the covers, Libby tried to figure out how to cover herself. She had a vague, passion-filled memory of her blouse and sweater flying one way, jeans, panties and bra going another.

What she wouldn't give for that black satin robe, but she had no idea where he kept it. She'd never seen it on him. T-shirts and sweatpants were Jess's early morning ensemble of choice, and were adorably manly at that—other than seeing him without a stitch, of course. The urge to peek under the covers now was almost irresistible, not to mention brash, brazen and downright wanton. She could go through his closet, but that seemed an invasion of privacy. A stupid thought seeing as they'd been as intimate as a man and woman could be just a few hours before.

The indistinct outline of the master-suite bathroom was straight ahead. Maybe she could slip in there and wrap herself in a towel, then make it to her room before Morgan woke up and missed her.

Just then there was a flash of light in the hall and the little girl's voice drifted to her.

"Aunt Libby? Uncle Jess?"

Libby groaned miserably. This was like one of those horrible dreams when for no apparent reason you're in a ladies' restroom naked from the waist up. Do you walk out and suffer the mortification? Or stay put and endure slightly less humiliation? Libby never got the chance to decide.

The little girl walked in and said, "Uncle Jess, I can't find Aunt Libby."

"Morgan, sweetie, I'm here," she whispered, hoping he was an extraordinarily sound sleeper. The bedside light went on, instantly dashing that fantasy.

"Morgan?" His voice was raspy from sleep.

In her pink princess nightgown, she appeared on his side of the bed. "I had a bad dream."

That makes two of us, Libby thought.

"A nightmare?" Jess repeated.

The little girl nodded as her solemn brown eyes assessed the two of them. "How come Aunt Libby is in your bed?"

"That's a very good question. I'm glad you asked." He glanced over at her and arched one dark eyebrow. "I'm thinking you should field this one."

Libby would rather poke herself in the eye with a stick and thought of multiple names to call him, starting with *coward,* then moving on alphabetically. But that wouldn't be helpful.

Stalling for time, she said, "Come over here, Morgan."

While the little girl padded over to the other side of the bed, Libby held the covers tightly to her chest and piled two pillows behind her back, trying to create an illusion of

dignity under the least dignified circumstances imagin-
able. She patted the space beside her, indicating that
Morgan should climb up. When she did, Libby pulled the
comforter over her and snuggled her close.

"Do you want to tell me about the bad dream?" Maybe
a distraction would help.

"I don't 'member. It was just scary."

"I'm sorry you were scared, sweetie." And feeling
terribly guilty for not being close when she was. "But
you're okay now. That's the most important thing. Right?"

"Yup." She nodded. "And it wasn't dark in my room."

"Good. That high-wattage nightlight is doing the trick."
Beside her she felt the bed move as Jess fluffed pillows
behind his back.

"There's enough light in there to illuminate the runway
at McCarran Airport," he said wryly.

Morgan looked at him. "So why is Aunt Libby sleepin'
in your bed, Uncle Jess?"

Libby still didn't have an acceptable G-rated answer fit
for a five-year-old's tender ears. All she could come up
with was, "I didn't mean to fall asleep."

And that was the honest truth. If she could rewind and
have a do-over, she would have walked away before he had
a chance to unleash his vulnerability.

"Are you scared of the dark, too?" Morgan asked.

"You could say that," Jess answered.

But it wouldn't be true, Libby thought, aiming a glare
in his direction. His fleeting grin indicated her look had
been promptly received and instantly ignored.

Was he even the slightest bit bothered by what was happening? The same man who just hours ago was concerned
about messing up this child? If there was any silver lining,
it was that Morgan was too young to understand.

"Are we gonna have a baby?" the little girl asked.

"What?" Libby and Jess said together.

There was very little satisfaction to be had from the fact that the *B* word had gotten his attention in a big way.

"Why would you think that?" Libby asked, trying desperately to keep her tone calm, cool and in control.

"I heard one of the kids at school."

"Carrie?" Libby asked, and the little girl nodded. "Her mother is pregnant."

"What did you hear Carrie say?" Jess asked.

Morgan rubbed her nose. "Her mommy's tummy is gettin' big because there's a baby inside. She's gettin' a little brother 'cuz her mommy and daddy sleep in the same bed."

"I see." So much for Morgan being too young to understand, Libby thought. Although there was some comfort in that it didn't sound like the mechanics of the birds and bees was being shared. "It's true that Carrie's mom is going to have a baby."

"Can we have one, too?" Morgan asked. "I want a baby brother. Or a sister. Is your tummy gonna get big, Aunt Libby? 'Cuz you slept in Uncle Jess's bed."

Libby winced at the heartbreakingly hopeful tone. Disappointing this already wounded child wasn't something she would knowingly do. But if she and Jess had done anything right in the midst of so much wrong, it had been taking precautions against conceiving a child. And if there was a God in heaven, a merciful God, she amended, He wouldn't punish them for a single weak moment.

She was trying to formulate a generic, nonresponsive response when the alarm on Jess's nightstand went off.

"Saved by the bell," he muttered.

That's for sure.

Now she had to figure out how to resolve this situation

to keep everyone's dignity and sensibilities in one piece. "It's time to get ready for school, Morgan. Do you want to wear your new lavender jumper?"

"But you said I shouldn't wear that 'cuz I might get paint on it," the little girl reminded her.

"How about just this once if you promise to be very careful?"

"I will be," the little girl said sincerely. "I promise not to get it dirty."

"Okay then. Why don't you run along to your room and pick out a long-sleeved blouse to go with it?"

"Okay. I can get dressed all by myself." She pushed off the comforter, scrambled down from the bed, then raced out of the room.

As soon as they were alone, Jess reached down to the floor beside him and grabbed his shirt, then tossed it to her.

"Thanks."

"Don't mention it."

Words to live by.

She shrugged into the too-long sleeves with as much modesty as possible. When she slid from the bed, the shirt-tail hit her mid-thigh, which was all the coverage she needed for her escape. Without a backward glance, she left the master suite and hurried to her own room.

She pulled the collar tightly to her and sniffed. The material smelled like Jess, making her stomach shimmy as always when his fragrance surrounded her. That reaction was fraught with problems.

It meant that sleeping with Jess hadn't neutralized her crush. On top of that, Morgan was delighted at the prospect of adding a baby to the mix. Libby was no shrink, but she would bet part of that reaction was about them being a family, which she'd clearly indicated she wanted.

The reality was that Jess had only agreed to this nanny arrangement for the short term. After last night's slide into the personal, he could have major second thoughts. It was quite possible that he'd decide Morgan had adapted and Libby's temporary employment could be permanently over.

What if he told her to go? That her work there was done?

The thought of leaving Morgan broke her heart. She would be out in the cold without the child she loved as her own.

And without Jess.

Chapter Nine

A kid walking in on Jess the morning after he'd had mind-blowing sex with a beautiful, complicated woman was a sitcom scenario that had nothing to do with his life. At least it hadn't until now.

He needed to man up and make adjustments.

It was weird that sleeping with Libby had brought him to that realization. And even after she had annihilated his willpower, he still couldn't decide if she was that beautiful or was just growing on him. Sitting on the brightly colored plastic bench across from her, Jess watched her watching Morgan climb around the play equipment at the fast-food burger place down the street from the complex where he lived.

Complex was the operative word. Had he suggested this kid-friendly dinner outing because he was manning up? Or to avoid talking about what happened that morning?

Even though she'd been naked in his bed, Libby had handled the situation like a seasoned pro. He still couldn't believe the little girl had connected the dots and gone to wanting a baby sibling. He didn't know what to do with one kid, let alone two.

The real question was why he'd slept with Libby in the first place. He'd been attracted to her for years without acting on it. Granted, having her under his roof made it more of a challenge, but he'd been handling it for weeks. Until last night.

He wanted to believe that his control had slipped because the scope of his responsibility was finally sinking in and he'd reached out to her. Nothing more than a moment of weakness. But that didn't explain why he wanted her again.

She looked at him then and something in his expression made her eyes widen and her lips part. "So," she said, releasing a long breath. "Can you believe Thanksgiving is next week?"

"Time flies." *When you're having fun,* he added to himself. Last night could be filed under the heading "too much fun." It was the reason for the tension arcing between them now. The post-sex conversation that needed to happen was like the elephant in the room. Everyone knew it was there, but avoided bringing up the subject.

"Uncle Jess. Aunt Libby, look at me," Morgan called out to them from the top of the climbing apparatus in the playroom where kids were allowed to expend their energy.

"I see you," Libby said. "Be careful up there."

"I'm going to slide down, Uncle Jess. Watch me," she called.

"I'm watching." And checking out the structure for possible risks.

When the little girl slid through the red tube to the rubberized floor, they both watched her go right back up.

Libby glanced at him. "Last year I spent Thanksgiving with Charity and Ben and Morgan."

He'd gone to Aspen with a cover model. Now he couldn't even remember her face. If he never saw Libby again, he knew that her clear blue eyes, bright smile and determined chin would be unforgettable.

"Do you need the holiday off? To have dinner with relatives?" Maybe the father she didn't want to talk about?

"No." Libby tensed and met his gaze. "What about you? If there are family commitments, I can make myself scarce."

"No."

"No commitments? Or no family?"

"It's just my mom. She does her own thing. We're not close." They had been once, before she threw him under the bus one too many times for the guy who'd replaced his dad.

"I'd be happy to cook dinner," Libby suggested.

"Or I could order from a restaurant."

"You don't trust me?" she asked, challenge in her eyes.

"You have to admit that breaded tubular tenders containing questionable meat products are more your thing."

"That's about getting a finicky five-year-old to eat. I'm actually a pretty good cook."

"Do you enjoy it?" he asked.

"Yes. But I can see you're skeptical. I might surprise you."

She already had. And not just because of how responsive she'd been beneath his hands and mouth.

"So you really want to do the turkey-and-a-big-meal thing?" he asked, getting his mind back into the conversation with an effort. "It's a lot of work and not in your job description."

The gleam in her eyes dimmed, but she recovered quickly. "I think a quiet dinner with Morgan would be just right this year."

"Okay, then."

"Look at me climb up," Morgan called to them. Her voice echoed in the big room.

Jess watched her foot slip and said, "Be careful, Morgan."

"I will." The little girl looked over her shoulder and grinned.

"Are you sure she's okay?" he asked Libby.

"I'd be more worried if there were a lot of kids in there with her. But by herself she's fine."

Having been alone for a long time, he could relate to that. "So, back to Thanksgiving."

She nodded thoughtfully. "With my class I try to emphasize that the holiday is about being thankful for our blessings. We can carry that theme over with Morgan." Her mouth pulled tight for a moment. "It's really sad when you think about it."

"What?" He took a sip from the straw in his cup.

"Neither of us has anyone to be with on the holiday. Morgan had family and now they're gone. How do you spin that into something thankful?"

"Good question."

"If I hadn't agreed to keep her, they wouldn't have gone," she said sadly. "They wanted to do it before she started first grade, before she got caught up in sports and other extracurricular activities."

He wondered whether or not she knew about his part in this, then decided to get it off his chest. "There's plenty of guilt to go around."

"What do you mean?"

"There were costs involved in their humanitarian cause.

I gave them the money to make it happen because they were both determined. A fire in the belly."

Jess waited for her anger and recrimination but it never materialized.

She nodded as if understanding exactly what he meant. "I saw that commitment, too. It was something they talked about and planned to do before having children, but Morgan was an accident. Then they adjusted their time frame and tried to do justice to the compassionate cause so emotional to them and the child they loved so much. But if either of us had just said no—"

"Charity and Ben would be alive," he finished for her.

"Yeah."

"For what it's worth, I'm glad not to bear this guilt alone. I'm thankful to share it with you."

She nodded even as a frown marred the smooth skin of her forehead. "What we don't share equally is custody of Morgan."

For reasons he'd never know, they'd asked him to be the legal guardian and he'd made a promise to her parents. The expression on Libby's face told him she didn't understand. "And that bothers you?"

"I love her very much, Jess."

"It shows."

"And I need to know where I stand," she added.

"You're her nanny."

"But for how long?"

"I'm not following," he said.

"The day I brought Morgan to you, we agreed to this arrangement until Morgan adjusted to the situation."

He remembered. Even then he'd realized that Morgan needed someone familiar. He'd agreed Libby should stay even though there was the potential for a conflict of interest because of a personal connection, one that had become even more personal. Now they were getting closer to the elephant in the room.

"I need you, Lib." He hadn't meant for the words to come out with quite so much hunger and hoped she hadn't noticed.

"Define *need*," she said.

"I'd have to be made of stone not to get how right you've been."

She blinked. "I'm sorry. Did you just say I was right?"

"I deserve that," he said, smiling. "But I'm not too proud to admit when I'm wrong. Putting a roof over Morgan's head isn't the beginning and end of my responsibility. Fatherhood isn't about being a placeholder. A guy needs to be proactive in a kid's life and I have no idea how. That's where you come in."

"Oh?"

"I'm counting on your guidance to effectively interface with Morgan."

Libby's look was wry. "For starters you have to talk to her like a regular person, not a computer geek."

"See? That's exactly what I mean."

"I'm not sure I understand," she said.

This was where the conversation got awkward. He wasn't in the habit of sleeping with a member of his staff. It wasn't a company rule, just his own personal code. When you crossed that line, things got weird and upset the work environment.

In this case that involved Morgan. She'd had enough to deal with already and loved Libby, counted on her. He wouldn't be to blame for her losing someone else that she needed in her life. Jess needed her, too, but he was a grown-up and could put his feelings aside.

"Jess?"

"You're a vital *employee,* Libby."

Surprise was evident on her face. "Meaning?"

"What happened last night was my fault." There, he'd said it. Time to drop-kick the elephant into oblivion.

"I see." Her tone said that was a lie.

"I'm counting on you to help navigate this child-rearing situation with Morgan. She has to take priority over everything." Even wanting Libby again. "We need to put last night behind us and move forward. For Morgan's sake it can't happen again."

"You're right, of course. I couldn't agree more. Consider it forgotten."

The words were politically correct, but her face told the truth. It wasn't like him to read feelings, but he could now. Maybe because this was Libby.

He recognized the hurt in her eyes from all the times he'd pretended not to remember her. But what he saw there now was somehow worse.

With a cup of tea, Libby sat alone in the morning room as the lights of Las Vegas stood out in stark relief against encroaching twilight. This six-thousand-square-foot penthouse was a lot of real estate, but without Morgan it really felt enormous and empty. What made her uneasy was that she was getting a preview of what life would be like without Morgan when Jess decided he could navigate the child-rearing waters by himself.

Take today, for instance.

He'd escorted Morgan to the movies and suggested Libby might like the afternoon off to relax after working so hard on Thanksgiving dinner the day before. They'd had such a nice day and the little girl didn't seem to be comparing the holiday to last year's with her parents. Now it was T-day plus one and so much for him *needing* Libby.

A shiver danced down her spine at memories of the intense expression in his eyes when he'd said that. Her female radar had clicked on and cranked up. But that was before he delivered the stunning blow.

He didn't want her.

That declaration had followed his song and dance about finally getting that a father should be proactive. That he'd been disconnected from the situation. *Jess Donnelly was wrong* should be splashed on a billboard and displayed on the 15 freeway for everyone to see that he'd actually said it out loud. But that had just been to grease her goodwill for the real message.

She wasn't an Elena Cavanaugh, who had a free pass to his bed whenever she wanted. Not only that, he'd had to go and be noble about it. Taking the blame. Saying it was his fault. Again he was wrong. Libby had been a willing and eager participant.

And now she was alone. He'd taken an ecstatic Morgan to an IMAX theater to see the latest animated movie. Libby didn't know what to make of his behavior. Based on her own recent experience, he was too capricious and that made him untrustworthy.

Like her father.

With Jess, Morgan would never have to worry about a place to live and food on the table like Libby had. But emotional starvation could be every bit as harmful. Still, there was no reason to take him on regarding his guardianship as long as she could be Morgan's nanny. Unlike the firm stand he'd taken on their personal detour, he hadn't given her an answer on how long she could expect to be in Morgan's life.

She hadn't heard anything from the attorney, which meant he was still researching the options. Hopefully it was a step she would never have to take, but knowledge was power and…

Libby heard the beep from the deactivated security system that signaled the front door opening. She painted a smile on her face and felt like the world's biggest phony when she went to meet them.

"Hi, guys. How was the movie?"

Jess was standing in the foyer holding Morgan, who had her arms around his neck. "Her tummy doesn't feel good."

That sounded like a direct five-year-old quote and Libby hurried over to them. She brushed her hand over the little girl's quilted pink jacket. There was a nasty stomach flu going around. A lot of kids had missed school because of it.

"What's wrong, sweetie?"

"I might hafta throw up again." Morgan didn't lift her head from Jess's shoulder.

Alarmed, Libby looked at him. "Again?"

"The Lexus can be cleaned," he said, choosing his words carefully.

Libby had to like that response and knew she was being bitchy for not wanting to. She looked at Morgan's pale face and pathetic expression as she felt her forehead. "It doesn't feel like you have a fever. I'm so sorry you don't feel well. Do you think you can handle a quick, warm bath?"

"Will you help me?" the little girl asked.

"Of course. Don't I always?"

"Yes." Morgan nodded, still using Jess's broad shoulder for a pillow.

It was enough to make female hearts go "aww," and Libby was no exception. She looked up at him and couldn't decipher the intense expression on his face. "Will you carry her into the bathroom?"

"Of course."

But he didn't add "don't I always?" because he hadn't yet established a pattern of involvement with this child. So far it was only words to the effect that he'd changed.

But as promised, he carried Morgan into the large, luxurious bathroom and set her down on the fluffy pink accent rug beside the beige tub. Backing away, he said, "I'll be right outside if you need me."

"That's okay. I've got her."

He shook his head. "It's the least I can do. Can I get anything?"

Lately he'd done a lot of talking about needing her. Only once had it been about *her,* the night he'd taken her to bed. Otherwise the need was all about her child care skills. If it weren't for Morgan, she'd quit the nanny gig and just teach. It was too hard being around Jess. Then she thought about not being with this little girl she loved so much and knew leaving voluntarily would never happen.

Libby had removed the jacket and was on her knees releasing the pink Velcro sneaker fasteners. She looked up and saw that he sincerely wanted to help. "Okay. Yeah. Her nightgown is in the top right-hand drawer of her dresser. Panties and socks, too."

"Okay. I'm on it."

That was different. She'd let him off the hook, but he hadn't taken the out. Again she had to admire him.

Libby turned on the tub's gold hot and cold fixtures to start the water. When the temperature was warm enough, she put down the stopper. There was a soft knock on the door and Jess stuck his arm in. In his big hand he held all the requested night wear.

"Anything else?" he said.

She went over and took the things from him. "This is great. Thanks."

"It's the least I can do," he said again.

His participation was beginning to sound like penance. Was that guilt she heard in his voice? There was a story and she was getting awfully curious. She quickly removed the rest of Morgan's soiled clothes and lifted her into the tub's warm water.

"Morgan, what did you have at the movies?" she asked as she soaped up a washcloth.

"I don't 'member, Aunt Libby. I'm too tired." She sat quietly.

Normally she was giggly and active at bathtime, so Libby washed, dried and dressed her as fast as possible. She carried her into her room and tucked her into bed. Her eyes closed as she turned onto her side and she fell asleep almost instantly.

After turning on the nightlight, Libby left and went to find Jess.

She found him in the family room at the wet bar, pouring himself a drink. The front of his powder-blue sweater and worn jeans had stains similar to what was on Morgan's clothes. That probably happened when he'd carried her all the way up here.

"Rough day?" she asked.

"You have no idea." He tossed back the contents of the glass in one swallow, then sucked in a breath. "Is she okay?"

"Sleeping."

"That's good."

"I wonder if she has the stomach virus that's been going around school." Libby waited for him to take that and run with it.

"No. It's all my fault."

That sounded familiar. Was he being noble again? "What did you do?"

"I let her have popcorn, soda, red vines and ice cream," he confessed.

"Ooh." She winced at the sheer volume of junk.

"I know. Go ahead. Take your best shot. You can't call me anything worse than I've already said to myself. I can't believe I was that stupid. She's five—"

"Almost six," Libby reminded him.

"She's a little kid and I fed her like she was the Seattle Seahawks' defensive line. I have no idea what I was thinking."

"I didn't say anything."

"Maybe not, but I can almost hear you thinking it," he accused.

"Actually, I hadn't gone there yet. But now that you mention it…what *were* you thinking?" She moved closer and the recessed lighting illuminated the dark, guilt-ridden expression in his eyes.

He ran his fingers through his hair. "I wanted her to be happy. To have a good day. If she asked for it, she got it. I forked over the money without considering the consequences. I practically got her whatever she looked at."

"That's really pretty sweet." Libby didn't have the heart to help him beat himself up. She was peeved at him for brushing her aside, but this wasn't about her. How could she be mad when he was doing exactly what she'd been urging from the beginning?

"Sweet?" He shot her an annoyed look. "Don't even talk about sweet. And don't be nice to me. I'm an idiot who doesn't deserve the consideration."

"You are," she agreed, just to humor him. "But you're an idiot with a good heart."

"That's not making me feel better."

"Okay. How about this? Why in the world would you let her have all that junk food?" Her voice dripped with mock censure.

He paced in front of the floor-to-ceiling windows for several moments then stopped in front of her. "You're making fun of me."

"Just a little."

One corner of his mouth curved up in a most appealing way. "Am I overreacting?"

"You're being a goof."

"And you're being too kind. I made her sick, Lib."

"Just an accessory to the crime," she corrected. "I'd be willing to bet that you didn't personally shove all that sugar into her mouth."

"The thing is, I remember how empty I felt after my dad died. Maybe this was all about preventing her from feeling that way. Giving her twice as much to compensate for losing both of her parents."

Libby put her hand on his arm, an automatic gesture of comfort, but the warmth seeped into her and surrounded her heart, setting up a siege situation. "You're on the right track, Jess. Spending time with her. Doing fun stuff—"

"Like making her sick?" He shook his head. "A shrink would have a field day with me."

"And me. And probably everyone we know or ever hope to know."

"Okay. Point taken. But I guess what I need to know is how to avoid another incident in the future."

"Really?" She couldn't help smiling.

"Of course really. What do I do?"

She tapped her lip thoughtfully. "What would you say

to an employee who wanted a promotion that they weren't qualified for?"

"I'd say no."

"Exactly. *N-O*. Practice it. Next time you're tempted to go to the dark side, just say no."

"Believe it or not, I actually said that to her today."

"All evidence to the contrary," Libby commented wryly.

"Ha-ha." He folded his arms over his chest. "She wanted to go in the bathroom and I couldn't go with her."

"Good call. A man in the ladies' room might have been a problem." She respected his protective instincts, but added, "It would have been okay to let her go in if you stood outside and waited."

"I did better than that."

"Oh?"

"I found a female security officer and she went into the ladies' room with Morgan." He smiled proudly at his problem-solving brilliance.

Libby just stared and somehow stopped herself from saying "aww." If his goal had been to melt her heart, all she could say was mission accomplished. She felt all gooey inside, which didn't make her one bit happy. And she couldn't even say she hadn't been warned.

At the burger place he'd told her that he was ready to take on the responsibility of parenting Morgan. But Libby hadn't really believed he meant what he said. She'd have been wrong and needed her own billboard to that effect on the 15 freeway.

That brought her to the biggest problem. She'd been able to temper her attraction to Jess with disapproval when he behaved in the usual shallow way. But that was happening less and less and made her wonder if she'd been wrong about him all along.

If that was the case, it would make working for him even more difficult. How was she going to protect herself from falling for the man who needed her, but didn't want her?

Chapter Ten

This was his first parent-teacher conference and Jess wondered if Connie Howard, kindergarten teacher, could tell he was a fraud. The fiftyish, blue-eyed brunette obviously was aware of the circumstances that had landed Morgan in his care. But did she realize that not long ago he'd been a carefree bachelor who gave house keys to hot flight attendants and now the little girl wanted red hair and big boobs when she grew up?

Whoever was in charge of fate had a wacky sense of humor if they thought he could raise this child into adulthood with any chance for normal. Then again, fate had also sent him Libby.

He glanced up from Morgan's file on the kindergarten teacher's desk to look at Lib. With her blond hair pulled back, her slender neck was right out there, tempting him to taste her again. Her full lips compressed with concentration, then curved upward in a smile. She was so smart, so witty, and still managed to be sweet and nurturing. These days he actually looked forward to going home and it wasn't about sex. That couldn't happen again because it could cost him Libby and he'd be lost without her. Correction: Morgan would be lost.

"It's a pleasure to finally meet you, Mr. Donnelly."

"Likewise," he said, wondering if that comment was judgment or simply a statement of fact. He could thank his mother's second husband for his inclination to dissect a conversation and separate out the criticism. With his step-father, most of it was negative so there was very little guessing involved.

"Morgan is a delightful child," the teacher continued. "So sweet and eager to be of help and do the right thing."

"I couldn't agree more." Libby glanced at him and smiled.

He returned it, then struggled to return his focus to the teacher. "She's a good kid."

Right. And he'd had so much experience with kids that he'd earned the right to have an opinion.

"So how's she doing?" he asked.

"Academically? Just fine. Morgan is solidly at grade level in everything. In fact she's one of my brightest students," Miss Connie said. "But there is something I'm concerned about."

"What?" he asked, before Libby could.

"Socially she's having a difficult time."

"Is someone being mean to her? A bully?" Libby asked. "I wish you'd said something sooner—"

"It's not that," Connie assured them. "Morgan isolates herself. The children were reaching out, but they've stopped. There's only so much rejection a person can take."

Jess glanced at Libby again and wondered if she'd

reached her quota from him. He remembered every rejection, perceived and real, that he'd ever dumped on her. Yet not long ago, he'd kissed her and she'd kissed him back, loving him until he'd thought his head would explode. And he rejected her yet again. He wouldn't blame her if she said adios, but thank goodness she loved Morgan more than she found his behavior objectionable.

"She doesn't have friends?" Libby asked, surprised and obviously upset.

Connie shook her head. "She's quiet and introspective. She keeps to herself and makes no effort to establish friendships."

"But in preschool there was nothing like this," Libby protested.

"She made friends easily," Connie agreed. "But just after she started kindergarten her best friend moved away."

"Oh—" Libby's tone was part whisper, part groan. "I'd forgotten."

"On top of that she lost her parents," Jess added.

"It doesn't take a mental giant to figure out a trauma like that would change her. Saying goodbye to her friend is a loss, too."

"That's very true." Connie looked at them. "I think her parents' deaths have affected her more deeply than she lets on. Children react according to their personality. Some become rowdy and act out in order to get attention. Others internalize their feelings and become more quiet. It's my opinion that Morgan falls into the latter category. I believe she's reluctant to form attachments for fear of losing anyone else she cares about."

Jess could relate. He'd been doing that since his own dad had died. His mother had promised to be there for him but it only lasted until she fell in love and remarried. Then she couldn't be bothered with him. His fiancée was no better. When he put the ring on her finger, she'd vowed to love him forever. But when he'd brokered a risky business deal, she'd decided forever was only as long as he could afford the life-style to which she'd like to become accustomed. He still had that ring somewhere as a reminder not to form attachments.

Ben was the only one who'd overrun Jess's defenses, through sheer persistence. It worked because the risk had paled in comparison to the reward. Memories of his friend stirred the stockpile of sadness he'd always carry with him.

"What should we do?" Libby anxiously twisted her fingers in her lap.

"Give her time. I know it's a cliché, but time does heal the wounds," Connie said.

"She said something recently." Besides asking if Jess was her daddy now. Besides giving him the list of respon-sibilities that weighed like a stone on his chest. "When Libby and I broached the subject of her folks being gone, she asked if we're her family now."

"That's right." Libby glanced at him, then back at the teacher.

"Probably she's instinctively reaching out to find where she belongs now." Connie leaned her elbows on the desk and settled her chin on folded hands. "She's dealing with an unimaginable loss, and at the same time wanting to fit into a domestic unit."

No one had ever before accused him of being domestic, Jess thought. It was hard to be a unit all by yourself, even though it was the way he'd always wanted things to be. Now he had to rethink that.

"As far as what to do?" Connie sighed. "Make her feel secure."

"Piece of cake," Libby said wryly.

"I know. Just take things one day at a time and be there for her. Encourage her to talk about what's on her mind."

Check that, he thought, thanks to Libby. She was the one who had encouraged him to discuss things. On his own he would have put a great deal of effort into avoiding any conversation about personal feelings.

"She seems to enjoy hanging out with Jess," Libby said.

He felt two pairs of eyes on him and shrugged. "I just explained the basics of football."

"And you took her to the movies," she revealed.

He so didn't want to talk about something that felt a lot like a failing grade in Fatherhood 101.

"That's good. Keep it up—" There was a knock on the door and Connie called out, "One minute."

Libby glanced behind her. "Your next appointment?"

"Yes, I'm sorry. If you'd like, we can schedule a time to speak more about this when parent conferences are over."

"That would be great." Libby slid the strap of her purse onto her shoulder.

Jess stood, too, and held out his hand. "Thank you, Ms. Howard. I appreciate your insight."

"You're welcome." Her look was sympathetic. "Hang in there."

Jess put his hand to the small of Libby's back as he guided her out of the room and past the mom and dad who were next. His palm tingled with the contact and he wanted to slide his arm around her, pull her closer, make the touch more intimate. With a great deal of effort, he kept his hand right where it was until she stopped in the empty hallway outside the classroom.

Libby looked up at him, her blue eyes filled with concern. "Before we pick her up from Sophia's office we need to talk."

About Morgan. Right. He needed to get his mind off the way Libby's body fit so perfectly to his and back on how to help Ben's little girl cope.

"Okay. You first."

"Me?" She held out her hands in a helpless gesture. "I don't have any answers."

"You're the expert. It was you who realized she was forgetting Charity and Ben and organized operation photo retrospective." He resisted the impulse to tuck a stray blond hair behind her ear. "By the way, thanks for the pat on the back in there."

"What?"

"Telling her teacher that I hang out with her," he explained.

"You do."

"So do you," he pointed out. "You're always there for her, even here at school."

"That's all good," she conceded. "We both do stuff with her."

"But she wants a family." He ran his fingers through his hair. "I'm not sure how to do that."

"At least you had one."

Meaning she hadn't, he realized. She'd tried to get him to talk about his feelings about losing his dad, but he'd gone on the defensive. Maybe that had been a boneheaded move. "Things were great in my family before my dad died. Then my mother found a guy and remarried."

"You don't look happy about it," she said, studying him.

He didn't want to talk about that part. "The point is, I remember a time when Mom, Dad and I did stuff. All of us together."

"You think Morgan wants to do that with you and me?" she asked, surprised.

"I'm shooting in the dark here," he conceded. "But I

don't think Ben would want me to let his daughter grow up socially stunted. I've got baggage from my past, but the bright spot was always Ben. How can I not do everything to make sure Morgan has a shot at the best parts of being a kid? How can I not leave any stone unturned so that she can find a best friend? So she can find her Ben?"

"Or Charity," Libby agreed. "So you're saying we should do family activities?"

"What's the harm?"

He winced even as the words came out of his mouth. That meant spending more time with Libby and struggling to keep his feelings in check. The feelings that could jeopardize his commitment to his best friend's child. But if hanging out with Morgan and Libby would help, then he was in. Keeping his distance from a woman had been instinctive until Libby came to live with him. She'd short-circuited all the barriers he kept in place. But somehow he would find a way to maintain an emotion-free zone and not further complicate this already complicated arrangement.

After all, where was the harm in doing the right thing?

"Do I want to know how you got tickets for a sold-out Christmas show on ice at the last minute?" Libby asked.

They were in a luxury box at the Orleans ice arena waiting for the crowd to thin out before leaving.

"I could tell you my secret, but then I'd have to kill you." Jess's smug look disappeared as he glanced at Morgan, peering down at the oval of ice below. "Just kidding."

"She didn't hear and I knew you were joking."

Libby had thought he was being funny earlier when he'd come home and announced he had tickets for the holiday show. Their conference with the teacher had only been two nights ago and he was already taking on the duty of family outings. No, not family. This was simply the three of them out and about. That's all.

"Seriously," she said, "how does one get the best seats in the house at the last minute?"

"You told me once that I'm not like other people."

"I remember."

She hadn't meant it in a good way, so his point was lost on her. She'd meant that he had layers of people between him and opportunists like her father who would try and take advantage of the man who'd recently landed on the list of the world's billionaires. The Internet was a fertile source of information and she only felt the tiniest bit guilty for Googling him.

It wasn't a question of which business had garnered him a place in affluent company, but more about whether or not a business existed that he didn't own. And that was only a slight exaggeration.

"But you're changing the subject." She glanced out the glass and noted that people were still filing out of the arena. Morgan was engrossed in watching the big machine driving around the ice to smooth it. "Exactly how did you snag these tickets?"

"That wasn't changing the subject. I'm explaining that I really am like everyone else. If you cut me I bleed. If you wrong me I hurt."

"Is that Shakespeare?"

"I have no idea, but it sounds like something he would have written. That's not important. My point is that the only way I'm different from the average person is my tax bracket."

"Because the amount you send the Treasury Department could neutralize the national debt?"

"I wouldn't go that far." He thought for a moment as they watched the people below slowly walking up the aisles toward exit signs. "The difference between me and the average person is that when I say money is no object, it's not lip service."

"Or bragging?"

"Never." There was an angelic expression on his face as phony as your average get-rich-quick scheme. "It's not bragging if it's true. Admittedly, some of the assets that put me in wealthy company are in stocks and bonds. It's not all sitting in a bank, or a hidden safe in the penthouse. Or under my mattress."

"Okay. I get it. So, are you saying you greased some palms to get the tickets?"

"I know people who know people who hooked me up. For the right amount of money."

"As easy as that."

Libby slid the strap of her purse more securely on her shoulder as she studied him. Jess Donnelly was better looking than the average guy, so much so that he would probably get some notice in Hollywood. Visually that was all that set him apart. His penthouse was luxurious and pricey, but not unobtainable. Tonight he was wearing jeans and a cream-colored pullover sweater with the collar of his white shirt peeking up from beneath it. The clothes were expensive and came from well-known designers, but labels weren't visible.

The cars he drove weren't cheap, but also were not one-of-a-kind standouts. And suddenly she wondered what a billionaire did with all those billions.

"So, other than getting tickets, where does all that money go that you're not bragging about?" She met his inquisitive gaze without looking away. "It's no secret you've got it, but I can't see where."

"If you've got it, there's no need to flaunt it."

"Humor me. My imagination is limited and I have no idea how one would spend when money is no object."

"Idle curiosity?" he asked.

When she was thinking about Jess Donnelly it never felt idle, but she was definitely curious. "Pretty much."

He thought for a moment. "I have real estate all over the world. Location. Location. Location. It's always a good investment."

"Where, for instance?" She folded her arms over her chest.

"A house in the Hamptons. Another in Aspen. Condo in Hawaii."

"Yeah," she said wryly. "Me, too. What a coincidence."

He grinned at her sarcasm. "Then there's the Gulfstream."

"Jet?" she asked.

"No, the hang glider." Who knew he would see her sarcasm and raise her a bite or two? "Technically the plane is for business, but it gets me from point A to point B faster than commercial airlines." A shadow darkened his eyes when he added, "Unless there's bad weather and everything is grounded."

"Do you have a boat?"

He shook his head. "But I'm looking into buying one."

She figured he was probably talking yacht classification. For her it would be something in the rowboat family. In all the years she'd known him, she'd never once thought in terms of him being wealthy. But he'd told her that since high school he'd focused on achieving success. He'd concentrated on business in college and learned everything that would get him where he wanted to be. The name Jess Donnelly was definitely right up there with the big boys.

Morgan watched the Zamboni drive off the ice, then joined them. "Uncle Jess, you promised me a souvenir."

"I did. Are you ready to go pick something out?" Her

blond curls danced around her face when she nodded enthusiastically and he said, "Okay. Let's do it. I think the crowd has pretty much cleared out."

The three of them left the box with Morgan between them, holding their hands. They rode down in the private elevator that let them off where the merchandise was on display. There were T-shirts, character dolls, stuffed animals and an array of snow globes. While Morgan walked around looking at everything, Jess and Libby followed to keep her in sight.

"It was awfully nice of you to grease palms and bring us here," she said.

He slid his hands into the pockets of his jeans as he watched the little girl gingerly touch a doll with pink net tutu and tiara. "Is Miss Connie a good teacher?"

Funny how she'd never noticed him answering questions in a roundabout way. That made her question how well she'd actually known him. Over the years she'd made a lot of general assumptions and formed an opinion that could be flawed.

This time Libby had a pretty good idea where he was going with his response. "Her reputation as an educator is impeccable. Her insight into kids is legendary."

He nodded. "So it wouldn't be especially smart to ignore advice from a legend."

"Not only did you not ignore her, you set a land-speed record for implementing her suggestion."

Libby figured this outing was about the three of them doing something together. It was homework. Literally. Except it had begun to feel real and that was dangerous, in a very personal way.

"Uncle Jess?" Morgan ran over and looked up at him. "I found something."

"Good for you."

She continued to stare upward. "Maybe more than one thing."

"Show me," he encouraged.

She bit her lip. "I can't decide. There's a princess doll and a whole set that has magic markers and a coloring book with Santa Claus and elves and the North Pole."

"Maybe we should get both."

The little girl's eyes got bigger and the look on her eager face was more magic than the markers. "But I saw some dresses and shoes. Costumes. Like the ice skaters wore. For playing dress-up."

He squatted down to her eye level and without hesitation said, "That sounds too good to pass up. I guess we'll have to get all three if you can't make up your mind."

Morgan smiled, then threw her arms around him. "Thank you, Uncle Jess."

He picked her up and met Libby's gaze. "It's not red vines and ice cream. Probably won't make her sick."

"True. You've mastered saying no to junk food. But princess paraphernalia, not so much."

"You can tutor and lecture till the hereafter won't have it, but it's impossible to say no to that face."

"I see what you mean." Libby's heart squeezed at the carefree smile Morgan was wearing. It had been missing for a while. "A little spoiling can buy a whole lot of security."

After purchasing everything, they headed for the valet stand in front of the resort to retrieve the car. Morgan chattered as they walked.

"I want to be an ice skater when I grow up."

Jess glanced at Libby. "I guess that's a better career choice than hair color and body parts."

She laughed. "You'll get no argument from me."

When they got to the lobby decorated for the holidays with ornaments, garland and a tree, Morgan's happy expression slid away. She stopped and stared longingly at the lights and shiny ornaments on the branches.

"Do you have a Christmas tree, Uncle Jess?"

He guided her out of the flow of people walking in and out of the busy lobby, then went down on one knee in front of her. "Do you want a tree, kiddo?"

One small shoulder lifted in a shrug. "I guess."

"We can do that." But her solemn expression didn't budge and he noticed. "What is it, Morgan?"

"I don't know if Santa knows how to find me."

"What do you mean?" he asked.

"I'm not livin' in the same place and he might not know where to leave my presents."

Libby's heart squeezed again, but this time it wasn't a happy thing. Last year this child's life was carefree and normal. Now it had turned upside down.

Jess rubbed a hand over his neck. "What do you think we should do about that?"

Libby put a hand on the little girl's shoulder and pulled her close. "I bet a visit to Santa would take care of that."

"Really?" Morgan looked up.

"Really. We can go see him and you can give him your new address and tell him what you want for Christmas," she suggested.

"That sounds like a pretty good idea to me," Jess agreed.

Morgan didn't look convinced. "Are you sure?"

"Absolutely." Jess pulled the princess doll from the bag he carried and handed it to her. "And we'll get the best tree ever. Maybe one for your room, too."

That put the smile back on her face. "Promise?"

He crossed his heart and held up two fingers. "I swear."

Libby knew she was there because of how seriously he took his vows. She'd been hired as the nanny for the child he'd sworn to care for. They'd agreed she would stay until Morgan adjusted, which was happening before her eyes. Every holiday and occasion without Ben and Charity would set a precedent for the next one when Morgan wouldn't remember what it had been like before Jess.

But Libby wondered how long before she had to see what it was like without Morgan and him.

He was really stepping up for her. That meant Libby had even more face time with him and that was the last thing she needed. Sex hadn't meant any more to him than it did with a surprise visit from the flight attendant, but it meant quite a lot to Libby.

Lust with a generous helping of respect very well could equal love, but he only wanted her as the nanny. Tonight was a sign that it wouldn't take long for him to get the hang of daddyhood. She knew from growing up with a father who'd tossed her aside when he could use his newest kid to put a roof over his head that personal value had a short shelf life.

Libby wondered how much longer Jess would have any use for her.

Chapter Eleven

The Saturday after the ice show, Jess admired the ten-foot tree in the corner of his family room. You had to love twelve-foot ceilings at Christmastime, especially when trying to impress a little girl. He glanced at the little girl in question and noticed that she'd fallen asleep on the sofa.

He opened his mouth to alert Libby, then closed it again, the better to concentrate on her. Just reaching up to adjust an ornament, she flashed a slice of bare flesh when her sweater slid up. The sight of that smooth skin winking in and out tweaked the ache he'd carried inside since making love to her. If he was being honest, he'd carried it around longer than that. But being with her had made it worse.

Of all the mistakes he'd made in his life, and they were legion, that's the one he wanted back.

Not because it wasn't fantastic. That was the problem. It was better than awesome and he wanted her again, a slippery slide into relationship hell. He sighed as he admired Libby's shapely rear end. Compared to her, flight attendants with keys were simple and uncomplicated.

"This is the most beautiful tree I've ever seen." When she glanced over, he was pretty sure she hadn't caught him staring at her butt. "How did you get all this stuff so fast?"

"Again, I remind you, when you say money is no object, you have to mean it."

"Ah. How could I forget?" She nodded knowingly.

"I made some phone calls. Had stuff delivered. The shopping with Morgan for more ornaments you already know about." He shrugged. "Easy."

"It smells heavenly." Libby breathed in the pungent scent of pine. "And it's truly the most spectacular tree."

"It's the first one I've ever had," he said.

Her hands stilled before she slid him a surprised look. "Ever?"

"Since I've been on my own." It felt like he'd been alone most of his life. Until now.

"Wow." Her gaze dropped to the couch. "Morgan's awfully quiet. Is she asleep?"

"Yeah."

Libby peeked over the high back of the sofa, then came around to stand beside him. She smiled down at the blond pixie. "She's worn out from all the excitement. You sure didn't waste any time following through on your promise."

"I didn't get to be a billionaire by standing back and twiddling my thumbs."

He smiled, remembering that conversation. She'd been sincerely curious about how a guy spent his money. His gold-digger radar didn't pick up any signs of ulterior motive. Unlike the visitor he'd had at his office yesterday.

"Libby, there's something I need to talk to you about."

"Okay," she answered without hesitation. "First let me put Morgan to bed."

When she started to lift the child, he said, "Let me."

"I can do it."

"No doubt. But she's almost six, which means she's pretty heavy."

He didn't wait for a response, but scooped up the little girl and carried her to bed. She was so small, so defenseless. A powerful wave of protectiveness washed over him that was less about his promise and more about a hold on his heart.

In her pink bedroom, a small tree with white lights stood on the dresser. Jess smiled, recalling how shocked, surprised, excited and delighted Morgan had been when he'd kept his promise.

Libby slipped off the small sneakers, then pulled the princess sheet and matching comforter over the little girl. "She can sleep in her sweatpants and T-shirt just this once," she whispered.

He nodded, because nanny knew best.

When they were back in the family room, she began to stack empty ornament boxes. "What did you want to talk about?"

Her blond hair shimmered from the glow of the holiday lights and made his hands ache to touch her. And that wasn't all. His body ached, too, in places he'd never known existed. Then he realized she'd said his name.

"Hmm?"

"You said there was something you needed to talk to me about."

"Right." He slid his fingers into his jeans pockets to keep from making another mistake he couldn't take back. "Your father came to see me yesterday at my office."

It wasn't surprise that stilled her hands this time, but shock. Not in a good way. Jess couldn't tell for sure since she was bathed in multicolored lights, but he'd bet all the color had drained from her face.

"He did?"

"Yup."

"And you talked to him?"

"I did."

"Why?"

"It was only polite since he dropped by," Jess said drily.

She shook her head. "I mean you're insulated from regular folks. How did he get past your people?"

"My staff has instructions to make sure I get every message." After what happened when Morgan got hurt, he wasn't taking any chances. "I was told a Bill Bradford wanted to see me. He said he's your father."

"What else did he say?" She stood, her whole body looking rigid enough to shatter.

"He said that you had a pretty sweet deal working as a nanny for a guy like me. And he feels he's entitled to a piece of it because of all the years he took care of you."

"That sounds like my dad." There was nothing warm or especially proud in the confirmation. It was more like disgust and humiliation. "I'm sorry he bothered you, Jess. I'll make sure it doesn't happen again."

"I offered him a job." He knew she was going to ask him why and that would be tough to answer since it had been purely a knee-jerk reaction.

"Doing what?"

He shrugged. "That's up to the Human Resources department. I instructed the director to find something fitting his qualifications."

"I don't think he has any. And he's not your obligation."

"Funny thing about responsibility. It's a hard habit to break."

She tilted her head and her hair was like a silky, golden curtain. "I get the feeling we're not talking about my father anymore."

"Good catch. I was remembering my mother."

"What about her?"

Jess didn't know why he'd admitted that. Maybe to keep Libby from feeling bad, like she had the only dysfunctional parent on the planet. Maybe it was about erasing the guilty, horror-stricken expression from her beautiful blue eyes, so full of holiday hope moments before. Whatever the reason, the cat was out of the bag now and not going back in without a fight.

He blew out a long breath. "After my dad died, I tried to man up like he'd told me. *Take care of your mother,* he'd said. She was only too happy to let me. She promised it was the two of us against the world and let me have a say in decisions. Because she didn't know what she'd have done by herself."

"That must have made you feel pretty good about yourself," Libby commented.

"Yeah. But the self-esteem was like a house of cards."

"I'm guessing by that remark and the hint of bitterness in your voice that things were bumpy when she remarried."

"Good guess." Even he heard the hard edge in his tone and resolved to work on that. "It's not easy for a guy to go from top dog to go-away-kid-you-bother-me."

"The balance of power shifted?"

"Understatement. On a scale of one to ten, my opinion went from the top into negative territory. It was like that promise never happened. She threw me under the bus every time—"

"Every time what?"

"Something happened at school."

She folded her arms over her chest. "Like what?"

He shifted his feet and resisted the urge to look away, at the same time regretting bringing this up. "Fights."

"And?"

"I started hanging out with a different group."

"By 'different' I'm going to take a leap here and guess this group didn't take the path of least resistance."

"You're implying they were looking for trouble?" He almost smiled. "I'd say it was more about pushing the envelope."

"So you got into trouble. Sounds like that was out of character for you."

"It was more of a growth period."

She frowned. "So how did your mother throw you under the bus?"

Jess hadn't meant a casual remark about responsibility to turn into a cheesy, this-is-your-life moment.

He didn't want to talk about the past because there was no way to change it. Done. Over with. What you couldn't fix you ignored. Move on. But genuine concern and empathy shone in her eyes and he couldn't hold back.

"I was accused of cheating on a test."

"In what subject?" she asked.

"Math, I think." Actually, it had been AP Geometry. A trauma that big wasn't something he'd forget.

"For what it's worth, math is not my thing—"

"I didn't cheat," he said, angry that she seemed to believe the worst.

"I didn't say you did. That was commiseration."

"It was a rumor started by a jerk pissed off at me for stealing his girlfriend."

"And your mother didn't believe you were innocent?"

"Give the lady a gold star." He remembered his rage that she listened to his stepfather paint him with the juvenile delinquent brush and believed everyone but her own son. It was a gut-level betrayal and something he couldn't forgive. "On top of that her husband had had enough of 'the punk.' He gave her a choice—him or me."

"Oh, Jess, she didn't—"

"She did. I ended up in boarding school—more of a military academy. His suggestion." That was bad enough, but what bothered Jess most was that his mother had never looked at his father the way she did the new guy. She'd thrown love under the bus, too.

"That's awful." Libby put her hand on his arm. "I'm so sorry that happened to you."

"Not your fault." That was his standard macho reply, but it was strange how her touch, the connection, somehow made him feel better.

"Kids should feel they have someone in their corner. A support system. But—"

"What?" When she pulled her hand away he missed the warmth.

"I hate to play devil's advocate, but I am a teacher."

"And how many of your little angels do you accuse of cheating on arts and crafts?"

"You're not going to distract me." The corners of her mouth curved up. "This is the scenario as I understand it. You were running with kids who had questionable judgment and that tends to make adults form an opinion that may be unfair. Put yourself in your mother's shoes—"

"Do I have to?"

She ignored that. "What if the educational professionals from Morgan's school told you she'd been fighting, cheating on tests, hanging out with kids who smoke and had sex—"

"Stop right there." He covered his ears and started to hum.

Laughing, she pulled his arms down. "Seriously, what would you do?"

His first instinct would be to talk to Libby and get her advice. All he said was, "I wouldn't dump her in boarding school."

"Because she's a duty?"

"I believe in keeping my word," he said. "Unlike people who make empty promises."

She nodded. "I sympathize. You just described every man I ever dated."

"And I sympathize. My dating history is pretty checkered, too."

"It can't be as bad as mine," she said.

"On the contrary. I made the mistake of asking a woman to marry me."

Her eyes widened. "What happened? Something must have, since I know you're not married now."

"It lasted until I made a business deal that public opinion said was going to ruin me. She bailed."

"That's bad. But you had the last laugh, Mr. Billionaire. At least you took a chance. I never did."

"Because of your dad?"

Her gaze jumped to his. "Probably."

After meeting the guy, he could understand. He also felt protective of her and that wasn't like him. He waited for more, but she didn't say anything. Not even in the spirit of he'd bared his soul and she could, too. He'd never thought her mysterious, but he did now. And damned if she didn't wear it well. But he couldn't help wishing mystery was all she wore right now.

"Since you're probably wondering, I offered your father a job because maybe he needed a second chance."

Her lips pressed tightly together for a moment. "Nice of you. And just maybe he won't let *you* down."

What did that mean?

As if he needed one more reason to not be able to get her out of his mind. If only he could figure out a way to get her back in his bed without upsetting the delicate balance of this life they were making for Morgan. He didn't want to jeopardize it. He just wanted her with every fiber of his being.

But he was doing his damnedest to make the best of this second chance, to do the right thing and not act on those feelings.

Las Vegas was chilly at night in December.

Libby pulled the collar of her coat more snugly around her neck and watched as the carousel turned with Morgan riding one of the horses. Jess stood beside her and every time the two of them came around she waved, and tried to hang on to her heart.

It wasn't easy. Since the teacher conference, Jess had been engaged in making Morgan feel secure. Tonight they were touring the Magical Forest at Opportunity Village. It was the biggest fund-raiser of the year for the organization that provided jobs and assistance to adults who experienced disabilities or traumatic brain injury that had left them physically or intellectually challenged.

The grounds of the facility were transformed into a Christmas village, complete with toy shop at the North Pole. Pathways wound through the displays and lights turned the place into—well—a magical forest. And Morgan was laughing when the carousel brought her around again.

The sight made Libby smile. If he didn't take them somewhere, at home he suggested board games and watching TV together. He was there every night for dinner, a complete turnaround from the guy who thought raising a child was only about writing the checks. This felt like a family.

Whoa. Libby stopped herself right there. In her experience family was just an illusion, like this village. Also in her experience, the things men did were selfish, fraught with ulterior motives. How long could he keep up this front? It wasn't real, and she would be an idiot to let herself get sucked in. Morgan's welfare was her priority and always would be.

The carousel slowed and came to a stop. She watched Jess gently lift the little girl down from the horse and trailed behind as she raced ahead. The ride operator smiled as he said something to Morgan. Then the two of them came through the white wooden gate and joined her at the spectator fence.

Libby dropped to one knee. "Did you have fun, Morgan?"

"I guess."

She looked up at Jess. "How about you?"

"I don't think I ever realized how awesome a carousel is."

"It sure looked like you guys were having a blast."

Libby stood and took the little girl's hand in hers while Jess walked on her other side. The three of them strolled along the pathway oohing and aahing at candy canes, lighted sleighs, Christmas trees and reindeer.

"Look." Libby pointed to a display with elves wearing striped leggings, red pointy hats and green curly-toed shoes. "Santa's helpers are getting the toys ready for delivery on Christmas Eve. Isn't that cool, Morgan?"

"Kind of."

Something was up. She'd been happy and smiling on the

ride, and had been responding to all the togetherness. Now the withdrawn little girl was back. Libby looked up at Jess, who shrugged, indicating that he'd noticed and had no idea why the child's mood had changed.

"Are you warm enough, sweetie?"

"Just fine, cuddles," Jess answered, clearly trying to lighten things up.

"I wasn't talking to you, sweet cheeks," Libby said wryly.

"Oh." He looked at Morgan. "Are *you* warm enough?"

"Uh-huh."

"Does your tummy feel okay after going in circles on the carousel?" Libby asked.

"Yup."

"Hey, kiddo, do you want to go to the gift shop and pick out a toy?" Jess suggested.

Morgan shook her head. "Not really."

That was a stunner. What was bugging her that a little retail therapy couldn't cure?

They were coming up on a wooden bench with a black wrought-iron frame. Libby pulled the little girl over and sat her down. Then she and Jess took up positions on either side.

"Maybe we should rest a minute," Libby suggested.

"Great idea. I don't know about you, Morgan, but I'm tired."

No answer. The short little legs stuck straight out in front of her as she stared down and plucked at the denim on her knee. Libby met Jess's gaze and shrugged. Finally she decided to just come straight out and ask.

"What's wrong, Morgan?"

"Nothin'."

"Come on, kiddo." Jess slid his arm across the bench back. "You were laughing on the ride and now you're not so happy. What happened?"

She looked up. "That man."

"What?" His expression went from concerned to furious in a heartbeat.

"The one at the carousel—"

"Go on," Libby encouraged. There was a knot in her stomach. "Did he do something?"

"No." The little girl shifted. "He said Merry Christmas. Have fun with your mom and dad."

Libby bit back a groan and saw the same reaction on Jess's face. The guy had made an honest mistake. They were trying to be a family and should have expected this to happen. It was good they looked like a bonded unit, but it was supposed to make this child feel secure, not sad.

She forced herself to ask the question even though the answer was clear. "How did that make you feel?"

"Not good." She looked up. "My mommy and daddy aren't coming back. Right?"

"Sweetie, we already talked about this," Libby reminded her.

"I know. But I still kept hopin'."

And now it's beginning to sink in that death means you'll never see someone again, Libby thought sadly. It was a lesson she wished this innocent child never had to learn.

Libby took one of the little hands into her own. "Sweetie, is that why you don't play with the other kids? Because you know how hard it is and how much it hurts to lose people you care about?"

She didn't react for several moments, then finally looked up. "I'm scared that you and Uncle Jess are gonna leave."

Jess went still, as if he'd taken a punch to the gut. "I'm not going anywhere, Morgan. I'll be here for you, kiddo. I promise."

He made the cross over his heart and held up his fingers.

Libby understood now why a promise meant so much to him. The person who should have loved him most had broken a solemn vow and hurt him deeply. The fierce expression on his face said he'd never do that to anyone—especially this innocent child. If he gave his word, you could believe he would keep it.

Libby didn't have any legal standing, but if feelings counted for anything she could promise that, too. She pulled the little girl into her lap and held her tight. "I love you so much, Morgan."

The child held herself stiffly for several moments, then curled into the embrace. "I love you, too."

Libby kissed the top of her head and rocked her gently. "Good."

"And you too, Uncle Jess."

He slid over, eliminating the space as he put his arm around both of them. "Back at you, kid."

Morgan looked at both of them. "Does this mean I should call you Mommy and Daddy?"

Wow, way to reach in and squeeze a heart, Libby thought. She looked at Jess and realized this was how he must have felt when Morgan gave him the daddy list. The night they made love. That memory made her lightheaded when she had to focus.

"Is that what you want to call us?" she asked.

Morgan mulled that over for several moments. "I like calling you Aunt Libby and Uncle Jess."

"Okay, then," he said. "That settles it."

"But—" She scratched her nose. "If I do call you that, can you still keep doin' mommy and daddy stuff anyway?"

Libby nodded, which was the only answer she could make, what with the lump in her throat. She blinked back tears as Jess held out his arms and pulled Morgan to him.

"Kiddo, we're there for you even if you call us Fred and Wilma Flintstone."

Morgan giggled. "Okay."

So just like that he'd fixed her five-year-old world. For Libby? Not so much. Fred and Wilma were married and had equal rights to Pebbles. Libby just worked for Jess and couldn't count on this lasting forever. She did love Morgan, so much. As if this child were her own.

And the man?

She was doing her level best not to fall for him and he was making that awfully hard.

"Uncle Jess?" Morgan put her arms around his neck. "It's kinda cold out here."

"It certainly is. What was I thinking?" He stood with her in his arms.

"You were prob'ly thinkin' that it's warm in the gift shop."

He laughed at her sly hint. "When did you get to be a mind reader? That's almost word for word what I was thinking."

He hefted Morgan onto his strong shoulders and started down the sidewalk. Libby trailed after them, heart heavy as she wondered if this was a glimpse of her future.

Being left behind.

Chapter Twelve

"Do you think she'll be all right?"

Libby and Jess had just returned to the penthouse after dropping Morgan off for Nicole Smith's sixth birthday party. He'd fretted all the way. As much as Libby wanted to join in, she figured one of them had to remain calm and rational. Since she was the nanny and a professional, it was her job not to freak out right along with him.

"Morgan really wanted to go," she reminded him for the umpteenth time. "That's a good thing. It means she's ready to risk making friends."

"Okay," he said, pacing back and forth across the family room. "Then maybe I'm not ready for it."

"I would have said something if I thought she wasn't going to be fine. Even though I'm a little nervous, too," she admitted.

In front of the floor-to-ceiling windows he suddenly

stopped walking and looked ready to spring into action. "Maybe we shouldn't have let her go."

"We talked about this, Jess. The group of girls is small. I know all of them and their parents, all good, responsible people. Sophia is there to help supervise. They're going to the Bellagio to see the Christmas decorations in the conservatory. The ratio of kids to adults is two to one—"

"I'd feel better if it was the other way around."

"That's not completely true," she said.

"Oh?"

"You'd feel better if you were there."

"Are you saying I can't delegate?" He folded his arms over his chest. "Because I can delegate just fine. I do it all the time. Every day, in fact. You can't run multiple companies like I do without trusting other people to do the job they were hired for."

"Exactly."

"What does that mean?"

"It means that Morgan is with Sophia, whom *I* trust because she's in charge of kids every day. The mom of the little birthday girl is a teacher's assistant hired by Sophia. She's worked at Nooks and Nannies for a year and a half."

"But what if Morgan wanders off? Or an adult turns her back and someone grabs her? What if she disappears—"

"What if a meteor levels the hotel?"

His eyes narrowed on her. "What if you're making fun of me?"

"No *if* about it," she said, grinning.

This was a very different man from the one who'd played clueless tour guide in this penthouse on that first day with Morgan. Different from the one who'd told her to buy whatever the little girl needed and send the bills to him. For a man to whom money was no object, worrying was a far cry from signing checks.

Libby couldn't resist teasing him because it was either that or kiss him. He was so darn cute and caring. A little less cute didn't make a difference to her one way or the other. It was the caring part that was getting under her skin in a big way.

"Jess, it's a very public place. There are 'eyes in the sky.'" She was referring to the inconspicuous security cameras installed in all the hotels. "And the limo you hired will chauffeur them back to Nicole's for the sleepover."

"Do you think she'll last the night?"

"The important thing is that she knows she doesn't have to. I think we made it pretty clear to her and every adult in the southern Nevada area that if she wants to come home she can call—no matter what time it is. We'll come and get her. Or she can just call if she wants to chat."

He raked his fingers through his hair. "I can't believe I let you talk me out of going."

"So you can shadow her?" Libby shook her head. "She needs just a little space."

"I wish I'd said no, even though you're right that she needs to do this."

The approval burrowed inside and warmed her heart and soul. He didn't like it, but he'd taken her advice and that made her like him even more than she already did. The shallow Jess would have given permission for the outing and never given it another thought. This guy wanted to trail the group to make sure she was safe.

Libby wished with all her heart that she'd never gotten to know this side of him. It was much easier to deal with this man when she disliked him.

"There was no good reason not to let her go."

"You don't think preventing me from turning gray overnight is good enough?"

"First of all I seriously doubt you'll turn gray that fast." Looking at his thick, dark hair made her want to run her fingers through it. That evoked visions of an unforgettable night in his bed with twisted sheets and hot kisses. "Second, the adults assured you that if she so much as stubs her toe we'll know about it." She felt for the cell phone in her jeans pocket just to make sure it was still there.

He didn't miss the movement. "You're nervous, too."

"I admitted that. What's your point?"

"My point is that I don't understand how you can sound so annoyingly rational when you feel the same way I do."

"Because both of us going off the deep end is too ugly to contemplate."

Jess thought about that for several moments, then nodded. "Okay. I can see the wisdom in that."

"Believe me, I'd like nothing better than to wrap her in a cocoon and make sure nothing bad happens to her ever again. But that's about my peace of mind, not what's in her best interest." Libby took a breath when he moved in front of her. "It was clear that she really wanted to do this. And it's such an important step in the healing process. Feeling secure enough to make friends."

"I know." He sighed. "That doesn't mean I have to like it."

"Who are you and what have you done with Jess Donnelly?"

"*Now* why are you making fun of me?"

"A little while ago I was remembering the day I brought Morgan here for the first time. You were, shall we say, not what I would call embracing your new role."

"That was before I realized that this place is too big and too quiet without Morgan." He glanced around the room and there was a sincerely sad expression in his eyes. There was no question that he missed the little girl.

"I didn't cut you any slack, Jess. I'm very sorry about that."

"It's okay."

"No, it's not. But, for what it's worth, I think Charity and Ben knew exactly what they were doing when they made you Morgan's legal guardian."

He smiled. "It's nice of you to say that. I'm just doing the best I can."

"They'd expect nothing more or less," she assured him.

She'd been so wrong about him. He was having separation anxiety issues just like a real dad and the *aha* light went off in Libby's head. She needed to make a call and tell the attorney to stand down. No way would she initiate any action to take Morgan away from him.

"What?" he asked, noting the way she stared.

"This reaction makes it hard for me to believe you never thought about having children. Especially knowing you were engaged at one point. Which means you were thinking about marriage and settling down."

"And you know how well that turned out. Clearly her agenda was very different from mine."

That comment neither confirmed nor denied what she suspected. In spite of his turbulent childhood, he'd been willing to take a chance on having a family and the woman had turned him against it.

Libby felt the hot blast of anger as it rolled through her. The self-centered witch had hurt him and given him one more reason to avoid commitment. Why would he even think about giving a relationship another shot? That would be stupid and a stupid man wouldn't be smart enough to make billions.

"And you?" he asked.

"What about me?" She knew what was coming and was sorry she'd brought the subject up. Talking about herself, especially to him, wasn't easy.

"Don't you want kids of your own?"

"I have children," she answered. "Every one of my students is one of my kids."

"You're evading the question," he accused, one dark eyebrow lifting.

"The God's honest truth is not an evasion. I genuinely care about every child in my care."

"I don't doubt that. But that kind of nurturing instinct makes me think you'd want the whole experience of pregnancy, birth, baby. The whole nine yards."

"You left out romance," she said.

"So tack it on. Can you honestly say you don't want the package?"

It's exactly what she wanted. But real life never worked in her favor. "I don't expect romance."

"Why?" He looked sincerely interested.

If she'd known talking about herself would take his mind off Morgan, she'd have turned the conversation in that direction a long time ago. Then again, maybe not.

A conversation about a father who manipulated and used his children and other people for his own selfish agenda wasn't something she was especially proud of. Then there was the fact that she shared his DNA. Not that she could ever imagine her and Jess together as a couple, but sharing the reality of her dysfunctional early years wouldn't endear her to him. The truth was that she was too cynical about men to ever let one romance her.

Now he was waiting for her to answer his question about why she didn't expect it. Taking a page from his book to change focus, she asked, "Are you looking for romance?"

"We're not talking about me. Thank goodness. I'm much more interested in you."

Rational thought was no match for the hormones unleashed by that comment. It was incredibly seductive. "Don't be. I'm pretty boring."

"Not to me." He stepped so close their bodies nearly touched. Behind him lights from the Christmas tree bathed the room in a magical glow. Her heart started pounding when a hungry expression darkened his face and jumped into his eyes.

"It would be so damn simple if you were dull and unexciting," he whispered.

Libby knew he was going to kiss her. It wasn't about being psychic, but more about how very badly she'd been wanting him to do just that. At this moment she only knew that simplicity was highly overrated. Complications were so very tempting. She was the moth to his flame and all she could think about was how much she wanted him to burn her.

And how wrong that would be.

She was on borrowed time with Morgan—and Jess. The little girl was at a birthday sleepover now, proof that very soon Libby's services would no longer be needed. This felt like a father, mother, child—a family—but she couldn't afford to hope it was real. Every day Jess was doing the right thing, which made her care about him more. It also brought her closer to losing everything she'd ever wanted after glimpsing how wonderful it all could be.

Jess dipped his head, but before he could make contact, she backed away.

Libby turned, not sure where she was going. Anywhere away from him. She made it to the family-room doorway before his words stopped her.

"Don't go."

She wanted to ignore him and run away, but it was like some force prevented her from moving. Slowly she turned toward him. "I have to."

"Why?"

There was no point in lying because surely he could see in her eyes that she was his for the taking. "Because I want so badly to stay."

"Go with that," he advised.

"It's not that easy."

He moved closer but didn't touch her, not with his hands. But the heat from his body and the spicy scent of his skin wrapped around her and she could feel him everywhere.

"You know I want you, Lib." His voice was deep, low, erotic.

"Why?" For years he'd barely remembered her name. All of a sudden he noticed her and the timing couldn't be worse. She wanted things to go on just as they were, even if not having him became more painful every day. "Never mind. I don't really want to know."

"It's a question for the ages, isn't it?" He smiled, but there was no humor in it. "What combination of hair color, facial features and body type makes just the perfect blend of chemistry to generate attraction?"

"Do you have an answer?" She stared up at his unsmiling face and started to tremble. Whatever chemistry had attracted her the very first time had only grown more potent.

"No." He ran his fingers through his hair. "On paper you're completely wrong for me."

Anger pricked her and she snapped, "Well, you're no prize either, buster."

This time when he grinned it was all amusement. "And then you hit me with a zinger and I don't give a damn about anything else. I guess that means I'm pretty messed up."

Just like that, anger evaporated, leaving nowhere to hide. "Join the club." Still, one of them had to be strong. "We agreed this wasn't a good idea."

"I vaguely remember that conversation. But for the life of me, at this moment I can't recall what the heck I was thinking." Slowly, he reached out and trailed his index finger over her cheek.

Libby shivered and whispered in a strangled voice, "It had something to do with me being a vital employee."

"You are that." Cupping her face in his palm, he added in an achingly soft tone, "Vital. Much more than you know."

"I recall exactly what you said." She was struggling for control here. It was getting more difficult by the second to keep in mind exactly why this was a bad idea because the look in his eyes and the sensation of his touch combined to chip away at her best intentions. Although there was that saying about the road to hell being paved with them.

"What exactly did I say?" The words were laced with amusement.

"That you needed my guidance with Morgan. You're counting on me to navigate the strange and wonderful world of child-rearing."

He frowned. "I don't believe I used the words strange or wonderful."

"I embellished." She shrugged in a so-sue-me gesture.

"What's your point, Lib? I'm sure you have one."

"How can you be so sure?"

"Because you're one of the brightest women I've ever known. On top of being too sexy for my own good, you're quick, witty and sassy. You say what you think regardless of whether or not I want to hear it. Do you have any idea how rare that is in my world?"

She shook her head. "And that's my point. We come

from different worlds. I'm here because of Morgan. What happens when she doesn't need me anymore?"

His expression turned gentle and understanding. He nodded slightly, as if knowing where she was coming from. "She'll always need you. Whatever happens, we'll work it out."

Easy for him to say. He had the law on his side. She wanted him with every fiber of her being and had never quite understood that expression until this moment. But she managed to pull together one last-ditch effort to deflect the desire growing rapidly inside her.

"The best way to work it out is for me to walk away. Right now," she said, regret clear in her voice.

He glanced up, then met her gaze. "Are you willing to risk it?"

"Why? What risk?"

"It seems wrong to waste perfectly good mistletoe."

Heart sinking, she looked upward and remembered him explaining to Morgan about what happens when someone catches you beneath the pesky green sprig. He took half a step closer and wrapped his arm around her waist, pulling her snugly against him. It was like her whole being sighed in surrender as she curled into his warmth. Then he dipped his head again and there was no way she could break the sensuous spell.

His lips met hers and it was instant fire sucking the oxygen from her lungs. *In for a penny, in for a pound,* she thought, wrapping her arms around his neck and sliding deeper into the Donnelly magic. He tasted her slowly, a featherlight touch that tangled her senses and knotted her insides—in a very delicious way.

As he kissed her into oblivion, his hands moved up and down her back, over her waist, then stopped when his palms cupped her tush. Pleasure nipped through her and she made a needy little moany noise that earned a seductive guttural sound from him.

Libby instinctively pressed her lower body against him, feeling the ridge of his arousal that proved the truth of his statement that he wanted her. Lust slammed through her and she couldn't seem to get close enough.

Breathing hard, she mumbled against his mouth, "You have too many clothes on."

He smiled with his lips still on hers. "Funny, I was just thinking the same thing about you."

"Kissing under the mistletoe is carved in stone, but—"

"Anything else is just going to be uncomfortable," he finished for her.

"You're a mind reader," she accused.

"It's a gift."

"'Tis the season," she whispered, reveling in what he was giving her. A priceless night to remember.

"I have an idea." He kissed her neck with a thoroughness that stunned her senses.

"Should I be afraid?" Stupid question. It was way too late to worry about that.

"Never."

In one fluid movement, he bent and settled his broad shoulder at her midsection, then straightened and lifted her off her feet.

"Jess—" His name came out half squeal, half scream. "Put me down."

"Not yet." He purposefully walked down the hall to his room.

"What are you doing?" Besides giving her a different perspective on his excellent butt.

"Not giving you time to think or change your mind."

"I can respect that."

He set her on her feet beside his big bed and grinned. Then he turned, fiercely focused. Reaching out with shaking hands, he slowly unbuttoned her blouse, tugged it over her arms and off. Then he unhooked the closure of her jeans and settled his palms on her hips.

He rubbed a thumb over the bulge in her pocket and pulled out her cell phone. "I think this might be safer here," he said, putting it on the nightstand beside the bed.

Libby undid the holster from his belt and set his phone beside hers. "We wouldn't want to miss a call."

"No." He reached around, unhooked her bra and let it slide off. Then he filled his palms with her breasts. "Perfect."

His sigh of satisfaction made her smile when she remembered her annoyance that she wasn't memorable to him in this area. How things had changed. How perfect it felt to have him touch her this way. She could have stayed like this forever except for the overwhelming yearning to touch him back.

After slowly unbuttoning his shirt, she rested her hands on his chest, savoring the way the coarse dusting of hair tickled her fingers. Leaning forward, she trailed kisses over the contour of muscle until he groaned with sexual frustration.

"You're killing me, Lib."

"I have the power."

Challenge glittered in his eyes before he said, "We'll see about that."

In half a minute he had the rest of their clothes on the floor and her in the middle of his bed. He kissed her neck, then slid his mouth to her breast. A surge of pleasure shot through her and turned her insides liquid with heat. Her thighs quivered as she writhed with the need to have him inside her.

"Jess—you're killing me," she echoed.

With his mouth on her belly he laughed. "Sweet revenge."

"Please—"

Without answering he took protection from the night-stand and covered himself. Then he rolled to his back and with his hands on her waist, settled her over his length. He matched the rhythm of his hips to hers and pressure built inside her. In a flash of light, pleasure exploded through her. A moment later he went still and groaned out his own release.

Revenge had nothing to do with it and when he pulled her into his arms it was simply sweet. Again she felt as if she wanted to stay there forever. Maybe that was possible.

Christmas was the season for hope.

Chapter Thirteen

Jess heard a breathy little female groan just before he felt a smooth, soft, shapely leg thrown over his. He smiled, remembering the intriguing female who was attached to all that sex appeal.

Libby.

Elizabeth Bradford.

The nanny he'd finally caught under the mistletoe who had then proceeded to kiss the living daylights out of him.

He opened his eyes and watched her sleep, full mouth relaxed and soft, blond hair wild around her face. Running his hands through the silky golden strands had been as much of a turn-on as getting her naked. It had been even better than the last time because he knew where to touch and what to do to push her over the edge.

For him following her over was as simple as looking at her, and he wasn't sure when she'd become so important.

Somehow this woman had worked her way inside him. He wasn't sure yet, but he might not mind. He wasn't sure yet, but he might just like waking up to find her in his bed.

He raised up on an elbow and rested his head on his palm. With the other hand, he brushed strands of her hair away to better study the curve of her cheek, the determined line of her jaw, the smooth skin on her forehead.

Looking closer he noticed a small scar that disappeared into her hairline. He'd never noticed it before, probably because her hair was hiding it.

What else did she hide?

A wave of what he could only describe as protective curiosity washed over him. She'd revealed very little about herself and what little he knew had been pried from her with a lot of effort. If it didn't cause her pain, chances were she'd have blabbed freely. What did she keep bottled up inside? He wanted to know everything.

He reached over and gently traced the jagged mark near her hair and her eyes blinked open. She looked startled, which he took to mean that waking up in a man's bed didn't ordinarily happen to her. He kind of liked that.

"I didn't mean to wake you."

"It's okay." Her voice was rusty.

Just a few hours ago it had sounded similar, but for a very different reason. The memory of her passionate response made his body grow tight with the need to have her again.

Shyly, she pulled the sheet more securely over her breasts and the gesture made him smile. The movement contrasted so drastically with her bold and breathless reaction last night.

"I have to go," she said.

"Why?" That was the last thing he wanted.

"I shouldn't be here. What if Morgan—" Her eyes grew wide. "She's still at the sleepover."

"Yeah. There was no call, so she made it all night."

Jess couldn't believe he'd forgotten, but so had Libby. Part of him was glad he'd made her forget. Part of him was appalled that he could. But he wasn't used to thinking about anyone besides himself, and apparently the parental muscles needed more of a workout. Yup, *appalling* pretty much described his feeling of not remembering.

The little girl had become very important to him and forgetting for any reason wouldn't happen again. He'd never realized how empty and lonely his life had become before the female invasion. No way did he want to go back to an estrogen-free zone.

"I miss her," he said.

"Me, too."

"Without her here it feels like something's out of whack." He traced a finger down her neck and across her bare shoulder. "On the plus side, she can't walk in on us."

"We need to pick her up by ten," Libby reminded him. "I have to clean up."

Before he could talk her out of that, she was up and on his side of the bed, grabbing his shirt to throw on. After gathering her clothes, she set a land-speed record in escaping. Faintly he heard the bathroom door close.

A shrill ring interrupted his thoughts and he reached over to retrieve the cell from the nightstand beside him. It wasn't his phone, but he answered in case it was about Morgan.

"Hello?"

"Ms. Bradford, please," said a female voice on the other end of the line.

"I'm sorry. She can't come to the phone. Can I take a message?"

"That would be great. I'm a temp. Mr. Erwin has been swamped and apologizes for the length of time it's taken to respond to Ms. Bradford. He hired me to help his secretary make follow-up calls."

"I see." Too chatty, Jess thought. Not a good quality in a business professional. "What's the message?"

"Mr. Erwin would like Ms. Bradford to call his law office for an appointment to discuss her options in her child custody case."

Jess's blood ran cold as an icy anger pushed through him. He couldn't believe he'd been so stupid yet again. When he realized the person on the other end of the phone was trying to get his attention, he said, "Don't worry. I'll give Ms. Bradford the message."

He slapped the phone closed as anger caught fire inside him.

That call was definitely about Morgan, but not in a way he'd ever expected. And he should have. Letting his guard down had been a big mistake. Suddenly he minded very much that Libby had made him care and he hated that it had been so pathetically easy for her.

After quickly cleaning up, Libby found Jess waiting for her in the kitchen. His hair was still damp from his own shower, making him even more devastatingly handsome than when she'd opened her eyes a little while ago to see him staring tenderly down at her in his bed.

But when she looked closer, the intense expression on his face clued her in that something was terribly wrong. This wasn't the easygoing man who'd gently brushed the hair off her face just a little while ago.

"Jess? What is it? Morgan—"

"Yeah. In a way. You had a call." His voice was chilly and sent a shiver through her.

"Was it Sophia? Is Morgan ready to come home?"

He held out her cell phone, careful not to touch her when she took it. "It was from your attorney. He wants to talk to you about a custody issue."

Libby gasped as if he'd sucker punched her. "I can explain—"

"Of course you can." His voice dripped sarcasm. "But I'm pretty sure there's nothing you can say that I want to hear."

"Jess, please listen—"

"I have to pick up Morgan." He left and the penthouse door slammed moments later.

Libby realized that she had as much chance of stopping him as she did of sticking out her foot to halt a runaway train. Stupid. Stupid. Stupid. She'd meant to contact the lawyer and cancel his services, but dealing with Morgan and Jess had made her forget about everything else. Maybe since he hadn't fired her on the spot, there was a chance that when he cooled down, he'd be willing to hear her out.

Hours later, when he still hadn't returned with Morgan, she didn't know what to think. She was wearing a path on the tile and carpet because six thousand square feet wasn't big enough to pace away her tension. The need to do *something* mushroomed inside her until she couldn't stand it.

Sliding her cell phone out of her jeans pocket, she pushed the speed dial. When a familiar female voice answered, she said, "Sophia, it's Libby."

"Hi. Did Morgan talk your ear off about what a wonderful time she had?" Her friend's voice was normal and upbeat. "It was so great, Lib. I wish you'd seen the way she interacted with the girls. She's making friends. There was one little rough patch and she wanted to call home but I managed to calm her down—"

"I wish you'd let her." It might have prevented what could be an even rougher patch.

"Did you talk to Jess? He told you how well Morgan did last night, right?" Concern replaced the cheerful tone in Sophia's voice.

"I haven't seen him yet," Libby admitted.

"But he picked Morgan up a long time ago." Moments passed before Sophia asked, "What's wrong?"

"He found out I consulted an attorney about custody."

"Oh." There was a long pause before she said, "I can hear it in your voice that he didn't take it well."

"He was so angry, Sophia. I should have listened to you and given him the benefit of the doubt. He wouldn't even let me explain."

"For what it's worth, he didn't show any of that when he picked Morgan up. He's so sweet with her."

"I know." Her stomach twisted at the magnitude of the mess she'd made of everything. "He's not the man I believed he was."

"And you thought he was that man because of your father." Sophia had heard Libby's pathetic story. She was one of those people who'd seen it all, heard it all and far worse, so nothing shocked or surprised her.

"Yeah. And when Jess found out about the lawyer, he went to the bad place because of stuff that happened to him as a kid."

"You two make quite a pair."

"What does that mean?"

"If you weren't in the middle of all this you'd get it." Sophia sighed. "You and Jess are hiding from the bad stuff, just like Morgan. Talk to him, Lib. Tell him what you went through growing up."

"I doubt that it will make a difference to him. If you'd seen the way he looked at me…" She closed her eyes, trying and failing to shut out the dark expression in his eyes. "He'll never forgive me."

"Not for you. Do it for Morgan. You and Jess are grown-ups and it's about time for you to deal with the past if you're going to get Morgan through this."

"What makes you think he'll listen to anything I have to say?"

"Because it's clear that he loves that little girl. Don't you see? The two of you together are best to raise Morgan because of what you've been through. All this time you haven't faced up to the past for yourselves, but I believe you'll get it right for a kid who just doesn't need another challenge in her short life."

"From your mouth to God's ear," Libby said fervently.

She thanked her friend for not saying "I told you so," said goodbye, then resumed pacing. What with hindsight being twenty-twenty, she wished she'd given Jess a fair chance. A couple of times she'd tried to talk to him about her standing in Morgan's life and he'd only said she shouldn't worry, it would be all right. Now? Not so much.

And this mess was all because Sophia had been right about something else. What Libby felt for Jess was more than a crush and thinking the worst of him had been the best way to keep from getting hurt.

Boy, that sure backfired. *Fired* being the operative word. Libby was pretty sure she'd fallen in love with him. Unless she could convince him that her motive had been pure, she was also pretty sure he was going to fire her.

Worried? Oh, yeah. She'd never been more scared in her life.

It was after seven that night when Libby finally heard the front door open. She hurried to the foyer and was breathless when she saw Jess with a sleepy Morgan in his arms.

"Hi," she said.

Jess wouldn't look at her, but the little girl gave her a huge smile. She wiggled until he put her down. Once free she ran over for a hug and Libby dropped to one knee to gather her close.

"Aunt Libby, it was so fun. We slept in the living room on mattresses with air in 'em. And we had pizza. And cake. I didn't eat too much and get sick."

"Good for you." Libby chanced a glance at Jess but there was nothing in his expression that gave a clue about what he was thinking. "What did you do all day?"

"Uncle Jess took me to the park. He pushed me on the swings. Then we went to a movie and shopping. We saw all the Christmas decorations at the mall, but I was too hungry to wait in the big line to talk to Santa."

It wasn't necessary to hear it in so many words. Clearly he'd stayed out all day to avoid her. But the activities had all been kid-friendly and family-oriented, yet more evidence piling up that she had misjudged him terribly.

"Are you hungry, sweetie?" She looked up at Jess, but again he wasn't the one who answered.

"Uncle Jess took me to a real restaurant, Aunt Lib." The little girl's brown eyes grew big and round as her tone turned reverent.

"He did?"

Curls bounced when she nodded. "It was in that big place where the water dances."

"Bellagio?"

Morgan shrugged. "I couldn't read the food on that big thing—"

"The menu?"

"Yeah. That. He read me everything but I didn't know what it was and there were no chicken nuggets. So he got them to make me a hamburger and french fries."

"Money is no object," she mumbled, looking up at him.

It was like he was standing guard, as if he expected her to steal the child away. Just that morning she'd awakened in his bed. The look in his eyes had said he wanted her again, a very different expression from the current one that said he wanted her gone. Cold fear coiled in her belly as she realized that Sophia was right. Libby needed to share her past to explain the unexplainable behavior.

"Aunt Libby, the tables had candles with real fire. And the napkins weren't paper—" A big yawn interrupted the narrative.

It was the opening she'd been waiting for. "You look tired, little girl."

She nodded. "Nicole's mom told us a bunch of times to go to sleep 'cuz we were talking a lot."

That was so blessedly normal and the words squeezed her heart. "Okay, then, let's get you cleaned up and to bed."

Rubbing her eyes, Morgan said, "Okay."

Libby stood and took the child's hand to lead her down the hall to the bathroom. Jess finally spoke.

"I'll be in to kiss you good-night, Morgan."

"Okay." She smiled at him. "Thank you for the beautiful dinner, Uncle Jess."

"You're welcome, Princess." His smile was tender as he looked at the little girl.

Libby desperately wanted to rewind her life, to a place where he didn't despise her. She both wanted and dreaded the talk she needed to have with him. She struggled not to hurry Morgan too much but at the same time, she wished to slow down the bath and bedtime reading ritual. In the end, the child took care of it and simply fell asleep.

Libby turned off the bedside lamp, then put on the night-light. She stood in the doorway for a few heartbreaking moments, watching the sweet child in even sweeter sleep. Somehow she couldn't memorize hard enough the after-bath scent, the blond curls and round cheeks highlighted against the princess-pink pillowcase. Jess had called her Princess, just like her father had, and that brought a lump to Libby's throat.

Libby knew she could wish for a do-over until hell wouldn't have it, but nothing could change what she'd done. It was time to face the music and fix her mistake.

She took a deep breath and went looking for Jess, finding him on the first try in the morning room. His back was to her as he stared out the window at the lights of Las Vegas below. There was a tumbler in his hand.

"She must be exhausted," Libby said. "She fell sound asleep before I was halfway through the story."

He tipped the glass to his mouth and drained the contents. Whiskey. Neat. Unlike this situation. Then he turned and she felt that familiar tickle in her belly when she looked at him. It had always been there but was even more powerful since she'd made love with him. She had a horrible sinking feeling that he was the only man who could do this to her.

She'd hoped the force of his anger had ebbed, but the glare lasering holes through her now made clear how wishful that thinking had been.

"Let me explain, Jess."

"Save your breath. You were scheming to take Morgan away from me. Do I have it right?"

"It's not that simple." She moved farther into the room, leaving a foot of space between them. Maybe proximity would help her get through to him. "I love Morgan as if she were my own child. Her best interests have always been and will always be my first priority."

"Then one would have to presume that you don't think living with me is best for her."

"I didn't at first," she admitted.

"And you came to this conclusion because…" He folded his arms over his chest and fixed the intensity of his gaze on her.

"In my experience, I'd only known you to be self-absorbed."

"I see. And what did I ever do to give you that impression?" The tone was flat, but the dark look grew even darker.

"For starters, at Ben and Charity's wedding you disappeared with one of the bridesmaids."

"And I never remembered your name," he finished. "I should be drawn and quartered in the town square."

Hearing him say the words out loud made *her* feel like the shallow, self-absorbed one. "It goes to environment. Yours didn't seem kid-friendly. I thought she'd be better off with me."

"I gave my word."

"So you said."

"And you manipulated the situation to get the nanny job. Now I see why. To gather information for a custody fight."

"It wasn't like that. I gave my word, too. When they left her in my care I promised to keep her safe. Even from you, if necessary."

Glaring, he set the tumbler down on the table, then met her gaze. "I would never hurt her."

"Not on purpose. But think about it, Jess. Women had keys to your place, let themselves in and got naked. You slept with whoever showed up. Kind of like surprise sex." She blew out a long breath, trying to erase the memory of how sweet sleeping with Jess Donnelly had been. "I'm not saying it was wrong for you. But it is for a child. It seemed obvious to me that being guardian to a little girl would mess up the life you had in place."

"And you didn't believe I was capable of changing?" The words sizzled with resentment.

She hadn't *wanted* to believe it. There was a difference. If she had, there would have been nothing to keep her from falling in love with him. In spite of thinking the worst, she still hadn't prevented that from happening.

"I owe you an explanation for that," she said, neither confirming nor denying. "You wondered about my father and it's about time you knew the truth."

He folded his arms over his chest. "I'm not sure what that has to do with anything now."

Since he didn't refuse to listen, she went on. "My mother died when I was a baby so I have no memory of her, but I do remember living on the streets with Bill. My father. He seemed to be more interested in anything that would take the edge off his reality. Drugs. Liquor."

"And?"

"He found out pretty early on that a little girl, me, would get him the sympathy factor and along with that came help. Either food, or shelter, or both. And he could always use the excuse that he couldn't leave me alone while he worked and couldn't afford child care. There was probably some truth to it at first. I don't remember."

"Go on." There was disapproval in his eyes, but it wasn't clear whether it was directed at her or her father.

"When he was down and out, he met a woman who was in worse shape than him. Cathy." She'd been good to Libby and so had her folks. They'd done their best, but she'd never felt like one of the family. "She'd lost her only child to a degenerative disease and hit bottom, which was where she found my father and hooked up with him. She got pregnant and the baby gave her something to live for. All she ever wanted was a child to love."

"I see."

She shook her head. "The problem was that neither of them was capable of making a living. Her parents wanted to give her a chance at being happy and took her and my father in. Unfortunately it was a package deal and they had to take me, too."

"So you have a sibling?"

"My sister, Kelly. She's in college in California. UCLA."

"Good school."

"Yeah." She tucked a strand of hair behind her ear. "I love her. But I also resented her growing up."

"Why?"

"She was the one everyone wanted. Cathy did—to replace the child she'd lost. Her parents, for the same reason and because a new baby pulled their daughter out of a dark place. They just wanted her to be happy. And my father was thrilled to have another meal ticket."

"Apparently he needs another one," he said. "Because he reached out to me."

"I didn't plan to mention your name when he came to see me. Morgan let it slip," she explained. "I was afraid he'd be a problem because Cathy's parents told him to find another place to live after Kelly went away to school. He was lazy and used all kinds of excuses not to work. He wore out his welcome and their goodwill a long time ago."

"So he came to you," Jess said.

She nodded. It was harder and more humiliating than she'd expected to relate the details of her past and the good-for-nothing man who was her father. But there was a reason, and it was time to get to it.

"The point is that I know how it feels when no one

wants you. You told me Morgan was a duty, just a promise to a friend. I love her so much, Jess. And she'd just lost her parents. I couldn't bear the thought of her feeling unloved and unwanted."

"It was a shock for me." He shifted his weight as the sadness flashed in his eyes. "My best friend was gone."

"And mine."

"You couldn't cut me some slack? You didn't trust that I would come around?"

"My father never did." But Jess had proved he was nothing like her father. "I went to a lawyer just to explore my options. When I saw your heart opening to Morgan, I planned to drop the matter."

"So I guess getting that call was actually a lucky break," he said.

Her heart dropped, not because of what he said, but the cold tone of his voice. "What do you mean?"

"No matter how you slice it, what you did smacks of disloyalty. I've learned loyalty is the most important quality in an employee."

She winced at the emphasis he put on the last word because in his bed that morning she'd felt like so much more. "What are you saying, Jess?"

"I can't trust you, Libby. And that makes working for me impossible."

"You're firing me?"

"Yes."

Chapter Fourteen

"Ow." Morgan put her hands up to hair wet from her bath. "That hurts when you brush it too hard."

"Sorry, Princess." The bathroom mirror revealed the sheen of tears in her brown eyes and he felt like an ax murderer. Although an actual murderer whose weapon of choice was an ax would probably be a sociopath who felt no remorse.

"You forgot to put the conditioner in the bathtub for me to use."

"Yeah."

She'd declared herself a big girl and perfectly capable of bathing herself. If that were true, would Libby have supervised the situation every night? In the end, he'd figured Morgan had been there for the nightly practice and knew more than he did.

"Aunt Libby says conditioner will make my hair not spit."

He frowned, trying to translate the perfectly good English words and make sense of the statement. All day he'd been on his own with Morgan and felt like an equipment-heavy deep-sea diver in the middle of the Mojave Desert. He was not very fluent in five-year-old girl.

He picked up a gadget that looked like a shrimp fork on steroids and braced himself to go at the blond tangles one more time. "So your hair spits when you don't use stuff on it?"

"The ends do." Morgan stood stoic, solemn and brave.

Aha. *Split* ends. "Next time I'll remember to put that stuff in the tub for you."

"Tell me again why Aunt Libby's not here?"

Instead of tears there was fear in her eyes this time and Jess wasn't sure which was worse. He hated both in equal parts.

That morning when he'd told Morgan, he'd known it was a mistake not letting Libby say goodbye face-to-face. Anger was no excuse, but it was the only one he had.

And he'd been angry because she didn't trust him. Furious that she hadn't even given him the chance to screw up first.

Finding out she'd gone to an attorney about custody had released the feelings of not being good enough that he kept carefully locked away. He'd lashed out and it was impossible to make this child understand why Libby was gone.

Not even her explanation had moved him enough to keep him from firing her, though he'd subsequently found out that it was true. He'd made some calls and verified that her father was basically a freeloader who'd used his daughter to manipulate people into feeling sorry for him. How could a man use a child like that?

He was a manipulator; Jess had spotted that instantly. Instead of throwing him out of the office, he'd called the bluff and offered a job—which her father had accepted.

Something in a warehouse. Time would tell whether or not it worked out.

And wasn't that ironic? He employed the father and fired Libby. If he hadn't, she'd be the one using a shrimp fork on Morgan's hair.

"Uncle Jess?"

His head cleared of Libby's image as he met the unnaturally serious childish gaze in the mirror. "Hmm?"

"Why did Aunt Libby go away?"

"She just couldn't stay with us anymore."

It's what happened when you could no longer trust an employee.

Who was he kidding? She was so much more than that. Clearly he was too dysfunctional to claim even a cursory understanding of interpersonal relationships. But the depth of his anger was a big clue. If he didn't care quite a lot, there would have been no reason to be so furious. Annoyed, maybe, at the inconvenience of a child-care interruption, but certainly not this intensity of rage.

Now it was fading and that left him nowhere to hide.

"Why couldn't she stay with us anymore?"

Because he was an ass. How did you translate that into something fit for five-year-old ears?

The worst thing was that Jess recognized something familiar in Morgan's expression. It was the face of a resigned sort of mourning, the way she'd looked when she first came to live with him. Maybe a distraction was in order.

"So what should we do with your hair?" He'd wanted to say WWLD—what would Libby do? But that wasn't exactly changing the subject. "It's kind of wet."

"It's okay like this."

He wasn't especially fond of the martyr tone, either. It was a sign that he was letting her down. "You probably shouldn't go to bed with a wet head. Maybe I should blow it dry."

"That makes more tangles." She didn't add *you bonehead,* but it was implied.

"What about a ponytail?" That should be simple enough, since he'd accomplished one already that day.

She shook her head. "It's all right, Uncle Jess. The pony you did this morning didn't stay in very well. Not like the way Aunt Libby does it."

"Okay." That was a lie. Nothing was okay. "Then how about another cup of cocoa while it dries?"

"No, thank you." She was far too polite and it felt too wrong. "Aunt Libby says it's not a good idea to have drinks too close to bedtime because it'll make me have to go potty."

"I see."

"Besides," she added, "the cup you made at dinner had an awful lot of lumps in it."

So that's why she'd barely touched it.

Intellectually he knew his expertise in cooking cocoa had no direct bearing on what kind of adult she became. But that didn't stop the feeling that he was on the super-highway to father failure.

"Then I guess it's off to bed with damp hair," he said.

She turned and looked up at him. "You could read me a story while it dries."

"An excellent suggestion," he said with way more enthusiasm than he felt.

Mentally he smacked his forehead. Should have thought of that, Donnelly, he told himself. He'd never become involved in the nighttime routine. His bad in a long and ever-growing list of bads.

Jess followed her to her pink bedroom and watched her pile pillows against the white headboard of her trundle bed. Then she climbed onto the princess sheets and pulled the blanket and matching comforter up to her chest. He picked up the new book they'd bought that afternoon and began reading.

"'Twas the night before Christmas and all through the house…"

He said the words out loud and turned the pages without any clue whether or not his performance left anything to be desired. Did Libby add more enthusiasm to her voice? Probably. Everything she did had an eagerness and passion that awed him.

Should he have cut her some slack? How would he have felt in her situation?

When Jess had adjusted his attitude and accepted this little girl into his life, he'd fallen in love with her. He couldn't imagine his life without her in it and would fight anyone who tried to take her from him. Libby had cared for her a lot longer and loved Morgan, too. She'd tried to talk to him about a guarantee of long-term involvement, but he'd blown her off. In Libby's shoes, would he have gone along with that and not consulted a legal professional about his rights?

"Merry Christmas to all and to all a good night," he read.

He closed the book and looked down, hoping Morgan was asleep. Brown eyes stared up at him. "Did you like the story?"

She nodded. "Thank you for getting the book."

"You're welcome." It had seemed like a good idea at their mall outing. Something to take the sting out of the situation. He glanced at her nightstand and the picture of Morgan sitting on Santa's lap. A neutral topic of conversation. Something about her day, which was a technique Libby had taught him. "Did you enjoy talking to Santa Claus?"

She shrugged and tightened her hold on the ragged

doll he'd seen her first day here in the penthouse. "I thought of something I want for Christmas. Even more than a bicycle."

"What?" He'd buy her the moon if it would put the brightness back in her eyes.

"I wish he could bring Aunt Libby back to us."

"I'm not sure that falls into Santa's purview…" When she blinked cluelessly up at him he said, "That's not in the big guy's job description."

"I still wish he could do it."

"It's okay, Princess. Don't worry. I'm here. I'll always take care of you."

She nodded even as tears filled her eyes. "But you don't cut the crust off my sandwich. I'm pretty sure you don't know how to paint fingernails or French-braid hair either. And what if something happens to you?" Her voice caught when she said, "Aunt Libby didn't get to see me sit on Santa's lap. I really miss her—"

His heart cracked in two as she started to cry and gut instinct had him gathering her into his arms. "It's okay, baby."

"No, it's not." Her little body shook from the sobs. "She's never comin' back. Just like my mommy and daddy. I'll never see her again. I miss her so much, Uncle Jess."

He'd seen right from the beginning that Libby and Morgan were a unit. Now he knew there was no win in splitting them up. He hated that he'd been right about ending up in the cold. Outside looking in. Like always.

But if he'd learned anything from his nanny–slash–child-care professional, it was to pay attention. Morgan needed to see for herself that Libby was alive and well.

If he was being honest, he was grateful for the excuse to see her. It hadn't taken long for him to realize he loved her and the feeling wasn't going away just because she had.

"Do you want to visit Libby?" When she nodded against his chest, he said, "Okay."

She sniffled. "Promise?"

"Cross my heart." Instead of actually doing that, he just held her to his heart. "I miss her, too."

"Jess will be here any minute." Libby paced the living room in Sophia's condo. She'd let her own go after accepting the nanny job. Job? "It was more than a job to me," she murmured, as if her friend had been privy to her thoughts.

"You don't have to tell me that." Sophia was sitting on the chocolate-brown sofa.

The night before last, this woman had taken her in when she had no place else to go, and the place was as warm as its owner. In addition to the two bedrooms and baths, there was a dining area adjacent to the kitchen. Reminders of Christmas were everywhere, from the small tree with multicolored lights to the collection of Santas that covered every flat surface.

"I know how much you love Morgan."

"And it bit me in the backside." Libby deciphered the wry expression on the other woman's face. "I know what you're thinking. You told me so. I went to the attorney early on, when I was so worried that he'd make Morgan feel like nothing more than an obligation. But he's changed, Sophia. He's caring and tender. He makes mistakes—"

"Imagine that. The great Jess Donnelly is actually human."

"I know." Just like Libby knew she'd made the mother of all mistakes. "But he learns from what he doesn't get right. He's so not the man I always believed him to be."

"Not shallow and self-centered?"

Libby shook her head. "He's got more layers than a croissant. He's complicated and flawed, but he wouldn't ever deliberately hurt that little girl. He might have agreed to take her in out of duty, but there's no doubt in my mind that he genuinely cares about her now."

"How can you be so sure?" Sophia shifted and tucked her legs up on the sofa cushion.

"The fact that he called me and asked if he could bring Morgan over tonight, for starters."

"How does that prove anything?"

"She had a meltdown because I left. He's bringing her here in spite of the fact that I'm the last person he wants to see."

Libby couldn't blame him, and that was hard to admit since she'd been blaming *him* for stuff almost from the moment they'd met. What she'd done was unforgivable to a man whose own mother hadn't trusted him.

She would never forget the look in his eyes when he'd fired her. Just as she'd never get over the heartbreaking realization that she'd lost everyone she loved. Morgan. And Jess.

Not that he would ever have cared about her the same way she did for him, but at least he'd respected her. And she'd been able to see him every day. It hadn't been clear how much she'd looked forward to that until she couldn't see him every day.

Yesterday she hadn't seen or talked to him and it had been the longest day of her life.

Sophia shook her head. "That little girl has had too much loss. No wonder she had a reaction to losing you, too."

"And that's my point. He's bringing her here in spite of how much he loathes me."

"I'm not so sure loathe is the *L* word I'd use."

"I'm certain enough for both of us. But it didn't have to be this way." Libby wrapped her arms around her waist. "The thing that really makes me kick myself is that I'd already made the decision to call off the attorney."

"So why didn't you?"

"I got busy." To put a finer point on it, she got naked. With Jess. She'd told Sophia all about that and his past, which made her betrayal so personal to him. "What with everything going on, I simply forgot."

Sophia's gray eyes glittered like polished silver. "See, that's the thing. He doesn't strike me as the sort of man who indiscriminately sleeps with someone who works for him."

"He's not."

"It's possible he's falling in love with you," Sophia said.

Libby remembered him taking the blame the first time and knew in her heart he'd sincerely intended that it wouldn't happen again. When he'd taken her to bed a second time, she'd begun to hope that maybe he did care.

Libby shook her head. "He was so angry. So hurt. Even if there's a grain of truth in what you're saying, what I did to him destroyed it."

The death of hope made her life flash before her without a hint of lightness or color and the pain of that stole the breath from her lungs.

"Don't look like that." Sophia swung her legs off the sofa.

"What?"

"Like someone died."

"It feels that way. If I could just go back—"

There was a knock on the door and Libby felt her stomach drop. Her heart pounded painfully in her chest and she struggled for calm. Morgan had already been upset and needed normal in a very big way.

She glanced at Sophia, took a deep breath, then opened the door. "Hi."

"Aunt Libby—" The little girl pulled her hand from Jess's and launched herself forward.

Libby dropped to one knee and gathered the child close. "Love bug—I missed you so much."

"I missed you, too." Small arms squeezed tight around her neck.

Finally, Libby held her at arm's length just to look at her. She took in the child's jeans and pink T-shirt with the matching quilted jacket. Her ponytail was crooked, but other than that she didn't look any the worse for wear.

"How are you, sweetie?"

"Okay. But Uncle Jess makes lumpy cocoa even though he tried real hard. And my hair got all tangled up." Her eyes filled with tragedy. "Why did you leave me and Uncle Jess?"

Libby glanced up but his expression gave nothing away. He apparently hadn't mentioned that he'd terminated her employment. "It's complicated, sweetie."

Confusion swirled in Morgan's eyes. "I was afraid you went away and weren't comin' back forever. Like Mommy and Daddy."

It hadn't been until much later, after the blowup with Jess, that this possibility had occurred to Libby. She glanced up at him again and her heart dropped. Again. In jeans, white shirt and leather jacket he was a sight for sore eyes. Literally. She'd shed quite a few tears since the last time she'd seen him.

She hugged Morgan close one more time. "I'm fine. See? More important, you're fine."

The little girl nodded uncertainly. "But are you comin' home with us?"

"I'd really like to. But that's up to your Uncle Jess." She looked at him and wondered if he could see in her eyes how very much she wanted to.

Morgan turned and said to him, "It's okay with you. Right, Uncle Jess?"

"It's not that easy, Princess."

Sophia walked up behind her. "Morgan, I think your Aunt Libby and Uncle Jess need to talk by themselves."

"Grown-up talk?" the child asked.

"Yes." Sophia held out her hand. "Would you like to help me wrap Christmas presents in the other room?"

"Yeah."

"Some advice, even though it's unsolicited," Sophia said to Jess as she took the little girl's fingers into her own. "Don't punish someone for caring too much just because of people in your past who didn't care enough."

His mouth pulled tight. "I see good news travels fast."

"You're a father now," Sophia said. "That means setting an example to forgive."

Then Libby was alone with him and the words that came out of her mouth were the first that popped into her head. "Morgan wasn't in school today."

"It was best to keep her home. Things were unsettled," he said.

No kidding. Libby had been hoping he would drop her off at kindergarten, but wasn't surprised he hadn't. She'd managed to get through the day, but not being able to see for herself that Morgan was okay had made her anxious and distracted. "I guess you didn't go into the office?"

He nodded, even as accusation darkened his eyes. Defending herself seemed like the best thing to do. Whether he believed her or not.

"I had every intention of discontinuing the lawyer's services," she said.

"Why didn't you?"

She told him the same thing she'd said to Sophia, "I forgot about it." No way would she admit that being with him, thinking about him, had pushed almost everything else from her mind. "I made the original contact before you changed, Jess. I know now that Morgan's in excellent hands."

"Do you expect me to trust you mean that?"

"I understand your skepticism and probably deserve it. But try to understand where I'm coming from." She took a step closer. "I never belonged anywhere. My dad used me to emotionally blackmail people. When he hooked up with Cathy, she wanted him and I was part of the deal. Her parents wanted her and the new baby. But no one wanted me. For me. Not ever. I never really had a family of my own until Morgan." She drew in a breath. "I was so afraid of losing her that I made a mistake."

"Me, too," he said.

That surprised her. "Really?"

"Firing you was a knee-jerk reaction and I never considered what that would do to Morgan. I should have. I didn't think it through."

"That's understandable. And just when she thought it was safe to let people close to her—"

He nodded. "She has to come first."

"I couldn't agree more." She meant that with all her heart, but wasn't sure where he was going. "What does that mean?"

"That I can put aside my feelings. She's a little kid who's just getting her life back together. I won't be responsible for ripping the rug out from under her a second time."

"I can respect that. But I'm still not sure what you're saying."

"If you're willing, I'd like to rehire you as her nanny." He ran his fingers through his hair. "She needs stability and that's what I intend to give her."

Reading between the lines she knew he was telling her he'd do anything for Morgan—including giving Libby back her job, against his better judgment. It was more than she expected and far more than she deserved.

This was so different from their first negotiation about child care for Morgan. She'd been the one preaching stability for this child, which spoke volumes about how far he'd come. There was no mention of a time frame, nothing on the table about the arrangement being in place until Morgan adjusted. He could terminate her in a day, a week, a month or a year. Libby didn't care. She'd take what she could get.

Without hesitation she said, "I'm willing. I'd do anything for that child."

And she meant anything. Including loving Jess and seeing him, even though she could never have him.

His heart was in the right place, but it could never be hers.

Chapter Fifteen

The day before Christmas Eve, Jess drove past the condo complex security gates, waved to the guard on duty, then parked. When he pulled a pile of festively wrapped presents from the tiny trunk of his sporty car, he made a mental note that shopping for a family-friendly vehicle was at the top of his list when the holidays were over.

He was looking forward to Christmas in a way he never had before, thanks to Morgan and Libby. Thank God she'd agreed to come back to him. The short time she'd been gone had given him a grim glimpse of what life without her would be, not unlike the story in *A Christmas Carol*. Just like Scrooge, he'd gotten the message.

He reached into his jacket pocket, making sure the small jewelers box was still there. It was pretty important, since it represented hopes and dreams for happiness that he'd never let himself expect.

Packages filled his arms, making the route to the penthouse more challenging. Second item on his post-holiday list was house shopping. Morgan should grow up in a regular neighborhood and play with regular neighbor kids. He'd pick out a house and surprise Libby, but he needed her input. Everything she'd said that first day she'd brought Morgan to live with him had been right on. This was a grown-up world, and the next environment he purchased would have to be somewhere a child would feel comfortable. Money was no object and he'd make it happen before Morgan's birthday in January.

He remembered what Sophia had said that night a couple weeks ago. *Don't punish Libby for caring too much.* The words resonated with him—so simple, so profound.

After riding the elevator up to the top floor, he managed to get his door opened.

"Libby?" he called.

"In here," she answered.

He followed the sound of her voice into the family room and found her sitting under the Christmas tree with a wineglass in her hand. A bottle of cabernet that looked like it was about three glasses down sat on the counter of the wet bar.

"I'm having wine." Her eyes were a little too bright and her articulation a little too careful.

"I see that." Morgan was at a friend's for a sleepover and he'd given Libby the night off. Probably the first she'd had since becoming his nanny. "It's about time you had an evening to yourself. I'm going to have a long talk with your tyrant boss about that. He's going to get a piece of my mind."

"But you're my boss. And you're not a tyrant." She'd missed the point because of the little wine buzz going on. The nanny couldn't hold her liquor, something he found incredibly sweet, charming and endearing. "Any word from Morgan?"

"She called a little while ago to say good-night. Having a great time with Nicole." Her expression turned wistful and a little sad. "I hope she's found her Charity."

She meant a lifelong friend. Jess knew that he'd always miss Ben, but wouldn't trade the grief for not ever having known him. Their friendship had made it possible for him to be a decent father to Morgan. "I know what you mean."

"What's all that?" she asked, eyeing the packages.

"Ho, ho, ho." He put the pile of presents under the tree. "I've been doing some shopping."

"I thought you were working late."

"Nope. Fighting the crowds at the mall. It was great, but I wish you'd been there—"

"I don't blame you for working so much," she continued as if she hadn't heard him. Her eyes were sad. "If I were you, I wouldn't want to come home to me either."

Someone was having the tiniest little pity party. "It's not that I didn't want to come home, just that with Morgan at a friend's this was a good time to pick up some things to surprise her. That reminds me, we have to hide this stuff and put it out Christmas Eve so she'll buy into the whole Santa thing—"

"I saw the picture of her with Santa. It's too cute. And I missed it…." Her eyes filled with tears.

"Libby, we can take her to see Santa again. She wanted you there and shouldn't have to miss out on anything. I want her to have the best Christmas ever."

"Of course you do. Because you're a good man."

"I'm glad you think so."

"I didn't always," she admitted.

"No. Really?" he said wryly.

"It's all right. You have every right to hate me. All I ever wanted was to make sure Morgan was happy." She drew in a shuddering breath. "Ginger said that you and I were two halves of a parenting whole. It's what gave me the idea to be your nanny in the first place. She said you have the means and I have the mothering."

"She was right. I didn't always think so," he said, echoing her words. "But now I'm convinced that Charity and Ben knew exactly what they were doing when they left her in your care."

"And made you guardian," she said, gesturing with the empty wineglass.

He took it from her and set it on the wet bar. "That's the part I thought they got wrong."

"No. It's the part they got right." She shook her head just a little too enthusiastically and put a hand to her forehead.

"Are you dizzy?"

Without waiting for an answer, he sat down beside her. The smell of cinnamon and pine mixed with the intoxicating scent of her skin and made him want to hold her. But when he started to put his arm around her, she shook her head again.

"Don't be nice to me. I messed up so badly. Charity and Ben trusted you. Who did I think I was to question that?"

"Who you are is the child-care expert in charge of making sure I don't screw it up too badly." He slid his arm around her waist and tugged her into his lap. Holding her felt so good, so right.

"I do love her," she said, resting her head on his shoulder. "More than anything except you."

Maybe he was actually going to get what he wished for this Christmas. "Oh?"

She nodded. "I think I fell in love with you the very first time we met. At Charity and Ben's wedding. I was the maid of honor and you were—"

"Best man." Not. He remembered that day and thinking, no, *feeling,* that Libby was someone who could really matter to him. He hadn't wanted that and deliberately pushed her away. He would never forget the hurt in her eyes or what an ass he'd been.

"I was a jerk that day."

"Yeah. But you're obviously a trustworthy jerk or Ben and Charity wouldn't have put you in charge of their child. I was so stupid. Someone as stupid as me doesn't deserve to be happy."

"You're wrong, Lib." He laced his fingers with hers. "I admire the depth of your love, your capacity for caring. Not just anyone would have been willing to take on a man with my considerable resources, but you didn't hesitate to go to the mat on this one. I have no doubt you'd do that for anyone you love."

He prayed that she truly meant what she'd said about loving him and it wasn't the cabernet talking.

"Mmm-hmm," she murmured.

"I have a confession to make." He kissed her hair and breathed in the sweet fragrance that clung to it. "I tried very hard not to fall in love with you. And that was before I found out that you'd been let down over and over by the one person who should have protected you. That really made me take a step back, because I didn't want to make a wrong move and hurt you more than you'd already been hurt. But I can't stand on the sidelines anymore. I hope you can understand—"

"Mmm," she whispered, snuggling closer.

"My life was pretty empty before you and Morgan. This

might shock you, but surprise sex isn't all that great. If you'll give me a chance, I swear that I'll always be the kind of man you can count on. Of all people, you know how sacred I hold a promise."

Jess held his breath, waiting for a response to his heartfelt, sincere declaration. But there was only silence before he heard a soft, ladylike snore. He looked down and realized Libby hadn't heard the good part because she was sound asleep.

He kissed her forehead, hoping that would get through somehow. She wasn't the only one who'd go to the mat for love and he wasn't letting her get away that easily. Lifting her in his arms, he carried her down the hall and gently put her to bed.

His bed.

"Aunt Libby, I'm home. Uncle Jess came and got me. Are you okay? Wake up."

Morgan's voice cut through the pounding in Libby's head and she opened one eye. It took several seconds to register that this wasn't her room. Or her bed. Not Morgan's trundle bed either. Her stomach dropped, which did nothing good for the nausea that threatened dire consequences if she moved.

"I'm fine, Morgan," she lied.

"Why are you sleepin' in Uncle Jess's bed?"

Good question. Libby wished she had an answer. She opened the other eye and tried to remember what happened last night. She'd been feeling sorry for herself. She was pretty sure Jess had come home looking like Santa Claus, with his arms full of presents. They'd talked, although the content of the conversation was fuzzy. After that, everything went as blank as a TV screen with no disk in the DVD player.

"Aunt Libby, are you and Uncle Jess going to give me a baby sister for Christmas?"

Good Lord, she hoped not. Sitting up she held in the groan and said, "No, Morgan."

"Uncle Jess said you probably weren't feeling well and that's why you're still in bed. I had to come and make sure you were okay."

"I'm fine, sweetie."

So not true. She felt crappy. Note to self, she thought, never, ever drink on an empty stomach again. Things were starting to come back. Like the fact that Morgan had been at a sleepover last night.

"How did you get home?"

"I told you. Uncle Jess came and got me. Nicole's mom said she needed some quiet time."

Libby could relate to that. "Did you have fun?"

The little girl nodded. "Me and Nicole played dolls and watched movies and ate popcorn. She's my best friend."

"I'm glad." Charity would have liked the little girl, Libby thought.

"Knock, knock." Jess walked in with a tray and set it on the nightstand.

"I have to get up."

Jess stopped her with a hand on her shoulder when she threw the covers aside. "I don't recommend moving around too much yet."

"Aunt Libby, how come you slept in Uncle Jess's shirt?" Morgan's big brown eyes were bigger than ever and puzzled.

She looked down with something close to horror at the white cotton that covered her to mid-thigh.

"Aunt Libby was too tired to put on her pajamas so I let her borrow it," he said. "Looks better on her than me, anyway. Don't you think so, Princess?"

"Yes." The little girl giggled. "Can I go watch TV?"

"That's a good idea." Jess nodded his approval. "But under no circumstances are you to look at any of those presents under the Christmas tree."

"Okay." The gleam of excitement in her eyes was a pretty good indication that the temptation would be too much for her.

Libby tried to glare. "That wasn't fair. In fact, it bordered on mean. You know she's going to check out everything."

He nodded, clearly unrepentant. "Figured it would keep her busy for a while. And give you a break."

"Diabolical," she said.

"It's a gift. No pun intended."

The only gift she wanted right now was information. She had three pressing questions. Why was she in his bed? How did she get out of her clothes and into his shirt? And what happened in between those two things?

"Speaking of gifts, I brought some for you—in a manner of speaking. I suggest starting with two aspirin and a glass of water." Jess handed them to her.

"Thanks," she said after swallowing the caplets.

"Drink it all up like a good girl."

"I don't think that's such a good idea." She put a hand on her traitorous stomach.

"On the contrary. Hydration is the best remedy for a hangover."

"Yeah, about that…" She circled the rim of the glass with her index finger. "So, I guess what with all the wine, I got kind of turned around on the way to my room last night?"

"That's one way of putting it." The bed dipped when he sat on the mattress. Their thighs brushed and in spite of how awful she felt, heat trickled through her. "But I'm not sure what you mean."

"I meant that must be how I ended up here. It was very nice of you to let me sleep in your bed." There was the tiniest questioning tone in her statement.

"Trust me." The gleam in his eyes said just the opposite. "I'm not that swell a guy. It was a night to remember."

Then why couldn't she remember it? Her stomach lurched. "Should I be packing up my things again?"

"You think I'm firing you? After last night?" He shook his head as a very satisfied expression settled on his handsome face. "Not on your life. It will go down in the history books as an epic event."

Epic? Lasting, ageless, unforgettable? Not so much after a couple glasses of very fine cabernet. "I don't know what to say."

"You were amazing and that gives you a pass on saying anything. Here." He handed her a plate and took the glass from her fingers. "Have some toast. It will settle your stomach."

"It will take more than crusty bread," she grumbled. But after a nibble, she realized he was right and chowed down two pieces.

"One of these days you'll learn not to question everything," he said, taking the plate that was now empty except for a few stray crumbs.

"I guess I'm cynical by nature."

"No, by environment." His deep voice went soft and gentle with sympathy. "In time you'll realize that you don't have to be that way with me."

Libby stared at him. Who was this man and what had he done with Jess Donnelly?

"Okay, I give up." She sighed. "I don't remember what happened last night. I don't recall being amazing. And I especially don't understand why you're being so nice to me."

"Ouch," he said, wincing. "Amnesia after such a memorable experience isn't especially good for a man's fragile ego."

She managed a full-on glare. "You've got an ego for sure, but there's nothing the least bit fragile about it."

"Now that's the Libby I've come to know." He grinned.

"Tell me the truth. Did we… Um…" She tried to figure out how to phrase it diplomatically, then threw in the towel along with any dignity she ever hoped to have. "Where are my clothes? Did we sleep together? I'd appreciate it if you'd tell me the truth."

"I wouldn't lie," he said seriously.

"Just a figure of speech. It never occurred to me that you would." He was probably the most honorable man she'd ever known. If he weren't, she wouldn't care about him so much.

"We slept together in the same bed, but nothing happened. Not because I didn't want it to," he added.

"What?"

"I wanted more than anything to make love with you." He was dead serious. "But in your condition that would have been taking advantage. And I love you too much to do that."

The words took several moments to sink in. "I'm sorry. I think my hearing has a hangover, too. I could have sworn you said that you love me."

"You heard right. And I have every reason to believe that you love me, too."

"Oh?" Her heart started to pound.

"You told me so last night." He reached out and tucked a strand of hair behind her ear, then brushed the back of his hand softly down her cheek. "It was right after your remark about being too stupid to deserve happiness."

She winced. "Apparently I have more to apologize for than I thought."

"Not to me." A darkly intense look slid into his eyes. "If you hadn't said what you did it might have taken me a lot longer to say something that's been on my mind for a while now."

"What? Since when?"

"Since I fired you," he said. "Big mistake, by the way. But it could be the best one I ever made."

"I don't get it."

"Something Sophia said got past my stubborn streak, although you had me with your speech. I understand how bad things were for you growing up. In spite of that, you have more decency and integrity than any woman I've ever met."

"What did Sophia say?"

"That I was taking out my past on you. Punishing you for caring too much. She was right. I cared—care—about you and that scared me because I know how easy it is to mess that up."

"Oh?" Libby stared at him, afraid if she looked away this momentous moment would disappear.

"If I hadn't sent you away, I might never have realized that I can't live without you." He raked his hand through his hair. "It wasn't very long, thank God. But as soon as you walked out the door I missed you like crazy. I love you, Libby."

"Really?"

He reached behind him and picked up something from the tray he'd brought in. In the palm of his hand was a black velvet jewelry box. A very small box. Just about the perfect size for a ring.

She could feel her eyes widen as her gaze jumped to his. "Is that what I think it is?"

"I'd been thinking about doing this in a more romantic way, some grand gesture in front of a roaring fire and the magic of the Christmas tree. Partly because after I fired you, it crossed my mind that you wouldn't believe me. Then, last night, you said what you said and I had reason to hope. I'm not a man who lets opportunity pass by and I'm not willing to risk something this important by waiting for a perfect moment. Life isn't perfect. It's messy and wonderful and—"

"Jess? Focus—" Please, please say it, she thought.

Being a man of action, he reached out and pulled her into his arms. Then he stared into her eyes, looking unsure and serious and too cute for words. "My love is as real as your hangover and far more enduring."

She had to admit he was pretty darn good with words, too. "Funny thing. I'm not feeling the hangover so much."

He smiled and flipped open the box to reveal a big, square-cut diamond ring. "Would you do me the honor of becoming my wife?"

"Yes." She threw her arms around his neck. "Yes. Yes."

"You're sure?" he asked, laughter in his voice. "Take your time."

"The heck with that." She drew back and cupped his much-loved face in her hands. "I've been in love with you for a long time."

"Since we met at Charity and Ben's wedding." It wasn't a question.

"How did you know that?"

"You told me last night," he said.

She sighed. "Some day you're going to have to tell me word for word what went down under the Christmas tree."

"It was all good. Or it is now." He slid his arms around her. "I want to be a family with you, Lib."

"We already are. You. Me. Morgan. Family is where you find it and how you make it."

"I hope you don't mind, but I called my mother."

"Mind?" He was a man of surprises, her fiancé. Making even more family. "Of course I don't mind. That's wonderful news. And?"

"She asked us to stop by on Christmas. If that's okay with you," he added.

"More than okay. She's the only mom you've got. It's time to put the bad stuff behind you."

"Yeah," he said. "This will be the best Christmas ever."

She felt a shiver as something brushed over her skin. "Has it crossed your mind that Charity and Ben might have been matchmaking when they left Morgan to us?"

"How do you mean?"

"It's silly, I guess. But I can't help thinking that we have two guardian angels who brought us together in order to make us admit what they've known all along."

"And that would be?"

"That we're soul mates. Stubborn ones, I'll admit. But we were meant to be together and needed a nudge in that direction."

He shrugged. "You could be right."

She refused to be sad when she said, "I think it's their Christmas gift to us."

"Saving the best for last," he agreed softly.

"Speaking of gifts, we should go check on our daughter and make sure she hasn't opened everything under the tree."

He stood with her in his arms. "If so, we'll start a new Donnelly family tradition."

"But there won't be anything under the tree Christmas morning," she protested.

"We'll just buy more. None of that matters as long as I get my nanny under the mistletoe."

"Who needs mistletoe?" she asked, settling her mouth on his.

She was starting a tradition of her own, one she planned on repeating every day for the rest of their lives.

* * * * *

SINGLE FATHER, SURPRISE PRINCE!

BY
RAYE MORGAN

All the characters in this book have no existence outside the imagination of the author, and have no relation whatsoever to anyone bearing the same name or names. They are not even distantly inspired by any individual known or unknown to the author, and all the incidents are pure invention.

First published in Great Britain 2010
Harlequin Mills & Boon Limited,
Eton House, 18-24 Paradise Road, Richmond, Surrey TW9 1SR

© Raye Morgan 2010

ISBN: 978 0 263 88846 1

23-1210

Harlequin Mills & Boon policy is to use papers that are natural, renewable and recyclable products and made from wood grown in sustainable forests. The logging and manufacturing processes conform to the legal environmental regulations of the country of origin.

Printed and bound in Spain
by Litografia Rosés S.A., Barcelona

Dear Reader,

When I think of San Diego, I think of rainbows and pastel colours, contrasted with the deep blue of the sea and the bright gold of the sun. Boats and beaches and suntanned bodies. It's a city of dreams and transitions. Cultures don't clash here—they meet and blend together in a magic way. For some, dreams do come true.

Kelly Vrosis comes to San Diego aching for validation. She not only earns that, but ends up finding an honest-to-goodness Prince Charming and losing her heart. But what good does it do a normal, ordinary girl from the Heartland to fall in love with a prince—especially one who is just beginning to test his royal prerogatives? Sounds like a blueprint for heartbreak, doesn't it?

Ah, but there is another factor involved—a tiny little girl with huge dark eyes, a big gaping need for a mommy and a daddy, and a heart damaged by the past. Will she accept Kelly and learn to trust her daddy, the Prince? If only she can, all their dreams might come true.

I have faith! How about you?

Raye Morgan

Raye Morgan has been a nursery school teacher, a travel agent, a clerk and a business editor, but her best job ever has been writing romances—and fostering romance in her own family at the same time. Current score: two boys married, two more to go. Raye has published over seventy romances, and claims to have many more waiting in the wings. She lives in Southern California, with her husband and whichever son happens to be staying at home at the moment.

This book is dedicated to Julie in San Diego

CHAPTER ONE

SOMEONE WAS WATCHING him. Joe Tanner swore softly,
tilted his face into the California sun and closed his eyes.
A stalker. He could feel the eyes focused on the sun-
baked skin right between his bare shoulder blades.

He'd spent enough time as an Army Ranger in the
jungles of Southeast Asia avoiding contact with snipers
to know when someone had him in his sites. When you'd
developed a sixth sense like that just to keep yourself
alive, you didn't forget how to use it.

"Just like riding a bicycle," he muttered to himself,
opening his eyes and turning to see if he could filter out
where the person was watching from.

He'd first noticed the interest he was getting from
someone—someone possibly hostile—the day before,
but he hadn't paid a lot of attention. Joe knew he was
tall and tanned and reasonably good-looking, with thick
brown hair tipped blond by the sun, and he seldom
passed unnoticed by onlookers wherever he went. He'd
assumed it was basically a casual surveillance. Living
half his day wearing nothing but board shorts, he was
used to having his half-naked body studied by strangers.
He knew he had interesting scars.

Besides, he had other things on his mind. Someone was arriving tonight—someone from his old life, although he'd never met her. He was nervous. So he'd been thinking about important changes that were coming, and he'd ignored the lurker.

It wasn't until today that he began to get that creepy shiver of caution down his spine. When the hair on the back of his neck started to rise, he knew it was time to give this situation due diligence. Better safe than sorry, after all.

His gaze swept the San Diego beach. Though there was a fog bank threatening to come ashore, it was a fairly warm day and the usual suspects were flocking in for the waves and the atmosphere—the surfers, the moms chasing little children across the sand, the hobos hoping for a handout. The flirty beach girls were also out in full force—a curvaceous threesome of that variety were lingering close right now, giggling and smiling at him hopefully. There'd been a time when he would have smiled right back, but those days were long gone.

You could at least be friendly, a little voice inside his head complained. He ignored it. What was the point? It only encouraged them. And he had nothing for them, nothing at all.

He gave them a curt nod, but moved his attention on, searching the storefronts, the frozen-banana stand, the tourist shop with the slightly risqué T-shirts, the parking lot where a young, swimsuit-clad couple stood leaning against a sports car, wrapped in each other's fervent embrace, looking as though the world were about to end and they had to get a lifetime's worth of kissing in before it did.

Young love. He had a sudden urge to warn them, to tell them not to count on each other or anything else in this life. Everyone had to make it on his own. There were no promises, no guidelines to depend on. There was only Murphy's Law—anything that can go wrong will go wrong. You could count on that, at least. Be prepared.

But he wisely passed up the chance to give them the advantage of his unhappy experiences. Nobody ever listened, anyway. Everybody seemed to have to learn the hard way.

So who was it that was causing the hair on the back of his neck to bristle? The blind beggar in the faded Hawaiian shirt, sitting out in the sun on a little wooden stool next to his wise old collie? That hardly seemed likely. The cop making lazy passes down the meandering concrete walkway on his bicycle? No, he was watching everyone in a thoroughly professional manner, as he always did. The bag lady throwing out bread crusts to the raucous and ravenous sea gulls? The teenager practicing acrobatic tricks on his skateboard?

No. None of these.

As time ticked by, he began to settle on one lonely figure, and as he zeroed in, the way his pulse quickened told him he was right.

The person was lurking alongside the wall that separated the walkway from the sand. Joe pulled his sunglasses off the belt of his swim shorts and jammed them in front of his eyes so that he could watch the watcher without seeming to be looking in that direction. The culprit was wearing a thick sweatshirt with the hood pulled low, baggy jeans caked with wet sand around the feet, so it was difficult at first glance to see the gender he was dealing with. But it took only seconds of focused attention to realize the truth—this was a woman pretending to be a boy.

That only sharpened his sense of danger. His military experience had taught him that the most lethal threats often came wrapped in the most benign-looking packages. Never trust pretty women or adorable kids.

Turning as though scoping out the activity at the nearby marina, he watched from the corner of his eye as the woman slipped down to sit on the low wall, pulling a small notebook out of the front pocket of the sweatshirt and jotting something in it before stowing it away again.

Yup. It was her all right. And she was keeping notes. So what now?

He considered his alternatives. Direct confrontation was usually counterproductive. She would just deny that she had any interest in him at all, and slink away.

And then what? Very likely, whoever had sent her would just send someone else. Another case of treating the symptom instead of the cause. His curiosity had been aroused now. He wanted to know who was behind this and why.

The only way to make a real attempt at getting to the bottom of the situation would be to get to her some-how—earn her trust, maybe. Get her to talk. But first he would have to draw her out, force her into making a move that would prove her intent.

And why not? He had nothing better to do for the next hour or so of his life.

With a shrug, Joe leaned down to pick up his surfboard, and started toward the next pier. It was undergoing renovation and there were signs posted warning people to stay away. Nice and out of the way, with most of the beach crowd focused in another direction, it would be perfect.

He trudged through the sand, letting his natural inclination exaggerate the slight limp he still had from the leg that was only beginning to fully heal after almost a year of recuperation.

He didn't even turn to see if she was following. He just assumed she would be. The type who tried to mess with his life always followed the script to the letter, and he had no doubt she would do the same.

Kelly Vrosis bit her lip as she watched the man who called himself Joe Tanner start walking. She saw where he was headed—way off the beaten path. Her heart began to thump in her chest. Should she follow him? She was going to have to if she was going to do this thing right, wasn't she?

She only had one week, and she'd already wasted a day and a half not daring to get close enough to really do anything observant. Either she was going to document all Joe Tanner's activities and figure out if he was who she thought he was, or she wasn't, and she'd wasted a lot of time and credibility on a wild-goose chase. Taking a deep breath, she fingered the little digital camera hidden in her pocket, and rose slowly to her feet, ready to do what had to be done.

"Here goes," she muttered to herself, and then started off down the beach, staying higher, closer to the storefronts, trying to be as invisible as possible, but still keep the tall, muscular figure of the man she was following in sight.

She was pretty sure he hadn't noticed her. She wasn't the sort who usually got noticed in crowds, and she'd worked hard on an outfit that would keep her anonymous.

Yesterday, after she'd driven out from the airport and checked into a motel room close to the address she'd found for Joe, she'd walked by his little beach house twice, so nervous she'd thought she couldn't breathe as she went quickly past his gate. She had no idea what she would do when she finally came face-to-face with the man she'd been researching for months now. The whole thing had become ridiculously emotional for her. Oh Lord, what if she passed out?

She didn't really expect that to happen, but it was true that there was something about him that sent her pulse racing—though she would never have admitted it to her coworkers, who had tried to talk her out of coming.

She worked as an analyst at a bureau in Cleveland, Ohio, the Ambrian News Agency. A child of Ambrian parents herself, she was fast becoming an expert in all things Ambrian. The little island nation of her ancestry wasn't well-known, especially under the current xenophobic regime. She'd taken as her special area of expertise the children of the monarchy that had been overthrown twenty-five years before.

It was recorded that they all had been killed that night of the coup, along with their parents, the king and queen. But now there was some question as to whether a few may have survived. And when she'd opened the national newsmagazine almost a year ago now and caught sight of a picture of Joe Tanner, returning war hero, she'd gasped in immediate recognition.

"Ohmigosh! He looks just like… Oh, it can't be! But he sure does look like…"

She knew it was nuts right from the beginning, and everyone she worked with agreed.

So she'd dug into the life of Joe Tanner and used all the resources available to her at the agency to find out all she could. Meanwhile, she became one of the top experts on the royal children. She knew everything about them that was to be known. And a few things that weren't. And she became more and more obsessed.

Now here she was, testing out her theory in real time. And scared to death to actually talk to the man.

It wasn't like her to be such a ninny. She'd grown up with two brothers and usually had an easy time dealing with men on the whole, but ever since she'd caught sight of Joe's face in that magazine article, she'd put him in a special category. She knew he was an extraordinary man, from what she'd read about him. He'd done things—and survived things—that no one she knew had ever done. What was he going to do when he realized that she was prying into his life?

"Kelly, you can't do this," Jim Hawker, the older man

who was her boss and office mate, had warned when she confided her plan to him. "You're letting a wacky obsession take over your common sense. You took one look at that picture and your overactive imagination created a huge conspiracy around it."

"But what if I'm right?" she'd insisted passionately. "I have to go to California and see what I can find out. I've got two weeks of vacation. I've got to see for myself."

Jim had grimaced. "Kelly, you're going to be annoying a man who has done things to people with his bare hands that you couldn't imagine in your worst nightmares. If he really is who you think he is, what makes you think he's going to be happy that you figured it out? Let it go. It's a crazy theory anyway."

"It's not crazy. It's way out, I'll admit. But it's not crazy. Just think how important it could be to the Ambrian community if I'm right."

"Even if you're right, you'll be poking a tiger with a stick. Without the blessings of the agency, you'll be all alone. No backup." He shook his head firmly. "No, Kelly. Don't do it. Go to Bermuda. Take a cruise. Just stay away from California."

But she couldn't stay away from California. She had to find out if she was right. She'd promised Jim she would be very careful. And she wouldn't approach the man himself until she was sure of how she would be received.

Of course, once she'd arrived it had all turned out to be a lot harder than she'd bargained for. She'd picked him out of a crowd right away, but she'd begun to realize she wasn't going to find out much just by observing him.

She needed more—and time was short. That morning she'd spent an hour watching him surf, all the while trying to map out a plan. She was going to have to interrogate people who knew him.

Well, maybe not "interrogate." More like "chat with." She'd already begun to make a list of likely contacts, including the man who ran the little produce store on the corner of his block. The two had seemed quite friendly as she'd caught sight of Joe buying a bag of fruit there on his way home the night before. Then there was the model-pretty girl who lived in the tiny beach cottage next door to his. She'd positioned herself to say hello to him twice already, and though he didn't seem to respond with a lot of enthusiasm, he did smile. She might know something. He didn't seem to throw those smiles around too freely.

And what a smile he had. It made Kelly shiver a little just to remember it, and it hadn't even been aimed at her.

There were also the neighbors on the other side of his house—two college students who shared an apartment in the two-story building. She'd seen him talking to them as they got their racing bikes out that morning, so they might know something. She'd worn shorts and a T-shirt and jogged slowly up and down his street early enough to be rewarded with that glimpse of his day. Then she'd watched as he walked off toward the beach, surfboard tucked under his arm, and she'd quickly donned her current baggy outfit to keep him from noticing that he might have seen her before.

This had been a lot of work, and so far, she'd reaped

very little in the way of rewards. Despite her trepidation, she was feeling a little grumpy. She'd hoped for more.

Kelly kept her distance, continuing to skirt the beach by staying up near the buildings. But she noticed they were mostly boarded up now. The stores had petered out into a semi-industrial area, and it looked as though this whole section of shore had been condemned for demolition and renovation. She glanced around, noting that no one seemed to be about.

And then she looked back at where Joe had been walking.

Wait a minute. She froze. She'd lost him.

She hesitated, realizing she'd last sighted him just before he'd gone behind an old fishing boat someone had hauled up onto the sand. She'd spent a moment of inattention gazing out at the ocean, then at the old buildings.

So where was he? He couldn't have stopped there.

Had he gone under the closed pier? There was more beach on the other side and she waited a moment, searching for him, expecting him to pop out and continue walking on across the empty sand, but he didn't.

There was no one on that side of the pier. The shore turned rocky there, and a fog was rolling in—a bad combination for surfers. Why was he carrying his board if he didn't plan to surf? To keep it safe, she supposed, but it seemed a long way around. Where was he going, anyway?

Glancing back at where she'd begun, she frowned. The sun still shone and people still swarmed the sidewalks, but they looked faraway now. The scene ahead seemed still and eerie.

What should she do now?

Kelly pressed her lips together. She had to keep going. She didn't want to have to waste a lot of time staking out his house again and hoping he'd appear, as she had the day before. Too boring and very little payoff. Now that she had a fix on him, it would be better to keep on the trail right here and now.

Except he'd disappeared behind a boat or under a pier.

With a sigh, she started off. She was going to have to find out which.

The wet sand felt cold against her bare feet. The fog was rolling in fast, and there was no longer any evidence that a sun existed at all. She walked quickly around the old boat, eyeing the peeling paint and barnacles. No sign of Joe. She was going to have to walk under the pier.

She wrinkled her nose. The place was hardly inviting. Dark and dank and creaking, it smelled bad and looked worse. Shadows hid too many angles from view. Crabs scurried from one piling to another. Even the water had a scummy look.

Kelly paused, peering toward the beach, wondering where he could have gone. The fog was too thick to see far. She was going to have to walk through to the other side to really see anything. An eerie foghorn sounded off the shore, completing the strange ocean feel.

Wasn't this the way most murder mysteries began?

She hesitated a moment longer. Did she really have to do this? Couldn't she just go back the way she'd come?

Anyone with any sense would be on her way already. But Kelly was still going. This was what she'd come for....

With another sigh, she stepped under the crumbling supports of the pier, walking quickly to get it over with. Each step took her farther from the light and sank her more deeply into the cold and clammy gloom. She tried to keep her attention on the hints of daylight ahead. Just a few more steps and she would be out....

When the hand came shooting out of nowhere and yanked her hood off her head, she gasped and stumbled in surprise.

"So you *are* a girl," a rough voice said. "What the hell do you want?"

The shock sent her reeling. She couldn't scream, and her legs weren't working right. She looked up frantically, her heart in her throat, trying to see who this was.

Joe Tanner, the man she'd been following? Or someone else, someone more sinister?

This wasn't how she'd planned it. She wasn't ready. She could hardly make him out in the gloom, and wasn't sure if this was the man she had spun her theories about or not. Whoever he was, he was just too big and too overwhelming. Everything in her rebelled, and mindlessly, Kelly turned and ran toward daylight.

Although she felt as if she was screaming, she didn't hear a sound. Only the crunch of sand under her feet, her breath coming fast, and finally, the grunt as he tackled her and threw her to the beach, his hard body coming down on top of hers.

A part of her felt complete outrage. How dare he do this to her?

Yet another part felt nothing but fear. The way the fog had closed in around them, she knew no one had seen what he'd done. She couldn't hope for help from a passerby—not even a cell phone call to the police. It was as though they were in their own world. Jim's warning flashed in her head: *You don't want to be alone with this guy when he realizes you're studying him.*

Her mind frantically searched for all the lost details of that women's survival course she'd taken three years ago. Where were those pressure points again?

"Who are you?" His hand was bunched in the fabric of her sweatshirt. "Why are you tailing me?"

She sighed and closed her eyes for a few seconds, catching her breath. At least he hadn't hurt her. For now, he wanted to talk, not wrestle. Straining to turn her head so that she could see around the edge of her hood, she looked at the man who had her pinned to the ground with the weight of his body, and she saw what she'd been hoping to see.

Yes, this was Joe Tanner. Relief flooded her and she began to relax, but then she remembered Jim's warning again. Kelly was in an odd situation. She knew Joe had no right to treat her like this—but what was she going to do about it?

"Could you let me up?" she asked hopefully.

"Not until I know why you've got me staked out."

"I don't," she protested, but her cheeks were flaming.

"Liar."

He hadn't hurt her and something told her he wasn't going to. She began to calm down. Now the major emotion she was feeling was embarrassment. She should have handled this in a more professional manner. Here she was, lying on the beach with the subject of her investigation. Not cool. She hoped Jim and the others at the office never found out about it.

"You see, Kelly," she could almost hear Jim saying, *"I told you to leave these things to people who know what they're doing."*

Of course, she always made the obvious argument. "How am I ever going to learn how to do this right if you never let me try?" But no one took her seriously.

So here she was, trying, and learning—and messing up a little bit. But she would get better. She gritted her teeth and promised herself that was what was happening here. She was getting better at this.

But she had to admit it wasn't easy to keep her mind on business with this man's incredible body pressed against hers, sending her pulse on a race. He was hard and smooth and golden—all things the perfect prince should be. Good thing she was covered from head to foot in sweatshirt material and denim, because he wasn't covered with much at all.

"Come on," he was saying now. "I want to know who put you up to this." He sounded cold and angry and forceful enough to wipe out any thoughts of sensuality she might be dreaming up. "Who are you working for?"

"N-nobody."

Which was technically true. Her office hadn't authorized this investigation. She was strictly on her own.

"Liar," he said again.

Reaching out, he pulled the hood all the way off
her head, exposing her matted blonde curls. She turned
her pretty face and large dark eyes his way and he
frowned.

"What the hell?"

This young woman was hardly the battle-hardened
little tough he'd expected. She was a greenhorn, no
doubt about it. No one in his right mind would have
sent her up against him.

A little alarm bell went off in the back of Joe's mind,
reminding him about lowering guards and being lulled
into complacency. But even that seemed ridiculous in
this case. She was too soft, too cute, too…amateur. His
quick survey of her nicely rounded body as he'd brought
her down had told him she wasn't carrying a weapon,
though she did have a couple of small, light objects in
the front pockets of her sweatshirt.

He'd had plenty of experience in fighting off threats.
He'd fought off hired guns, martial arts experts, Mata
Hari types with vials of poison hidden in their bras.
This little cutie didn't fit into any of those categories.
He would have staked his life on her being from outside
that world of intrigue he'd swum in for years. So what
the hell was she doing here?

"I'm not 'tailing' you and I don't have you 'staked
out,'" she insisted breathlessly.

He raised one sleek eyebrow, looking her over.

"Then it must be love," he said sarcastically. "Why

else would you be mooning around after me for days at a time?"

Shocked at the very suggestion, even though she knew he was just making fun of her, she opened her mouth to respond, but all that came out was a strangled sound.

"Never mind," he said in a kindly manner, though he was obviously still mocking her, and his mockery stung. "We'll just stay here this way until you remember what the answer is."

"To what?" she managed to choke out.

She tried to wriggle out from under him, but soon realized it was probably a mistake. She could see him better, but that only sent her nerves skittering like jumping beans on a hot plate.

He had hold of her sweatshirt and one strong leg was still thrown over hers. It was pretty clear he didn't like being followed. He was angry and he wanted the truth. Nothing amorous about it.

Still, he was just a little too gorgeous for comfort. She wasn't usually one to be tongue-tied, but being this close to him sent every sensible thought flying right out of her head. His huge blue eyes were gazing at her as though her skin were transparent and he could see everything—every thought, every feeling. She stared at him, spellbound, unable to move.

He began to look impatient.

"Let's cut to the chase," he said shortly. "I gave you your options. Pick one."

She licked her dry lips and had to try twice before she got out an actual word or two. "I…I can't."

"Why not?" he demanded. "I want the truth."

She shook her head, trying to clear it. What could she possibly say that he would understand at this point? All her explanations needed too much background. Despair began to creep into her thought processes.

"I have to get up," she told him. "If you don't release me, I'm going to get hysterical."

"Be serious," he scoffed. But then he looked at her a bit closer and what he saw seemed to convince him. Reluctantly, he rolled away.

"Women," he muttered darkly, but he let her get up, and he rose as well.

She took a deep breath and steadied herself. At least they were out from under that awful pier. The fog hid the sun, but the sand was still warm here and that was a bit comforting.

She looked up at him. He was all tanned skin and muscles, with sand sprinkled everywhere, even on his golden eyelashes. For a moment she was dazzled, but she quickly frowned and brought herself back down to earth. This was no time to let attraction take over. She had work to do.

"What's your name?" he demanded.

"Kelly Vrosis," she responded.

He almost smiled. That answer had been so quick, so automatic, he had no doubt it really was her name. What was going on here? Didn't she know she was supposed to lie about these things?

"Okay," he said. "I was nice to you. Your turn."

She opened her eyes wide, playing dumb. "What?"

she asked, shaking her head as though she didn't have a clue what he wanted from her.

He gave her a long-suffering look. "Okay, Kelly Vrosis. No more messing around. There are only three reasons people follow me. Some want information. Some want to stop me from doing something. But most want me dead." He pinned her with a direct stare. "So which is it?"

CHAPTER TWO

KELLY SHOOK HER HEAD, feeling a touch of panic. "None of those. Honest."

Joe's hard face looked almost contemptuous. "Then what?"

She glanced up at him and swallowed hard. She'd had a cover story ready when she'd started this. It had seemed a good one at the time—something about thinking he was her college roommate's brother—but now it just seemed lame. She had to admit this had turned out to be very different from what she'd expected or planned. Serious consequences loomed. This was scary.

"Uh, well…" she said, trying to buy time while she thought up something better. But then she stopped herself. There was no point in filling the air with nonsense just to give the impression she had something to say. He wasn't going to buy it, anyway.

Things were happening too quickly. She needed a moment to reflect, to stand back and look at this man and make a judgment call. Was he or was he not the man she theorized he had to be?

She'd put all of her credibility on the line, coming to

California and looking him up. Had she done something stupid? Or was she a genius?

Of course, she'd been crazy to get this close to him this early. She was on her own. If she got into trouble there would be no one to call.

Was she in trouble right now? Hard to tell. But it sure felt like it.

She looked him over. His blond-tipped hair was too long and sticking out at all angles. His skin was too tan. His body was too beautiful—and also too scarred to look at without wincing. He was barefoot and covered with sand. He didn't look like any prince she'd ever seen before.

Was she crazy? What if she was completely wrong? How could she have put herself and her career out on a limb like this? Maybe she should just pull back and rethink this whole thing.

"I saw you writing in a notebook," he said, moving toward her in a deliberate way that made her take a step backward. "It was about me, wasn't it?"

"What? No…" But she knew her face revealed the truth.

His clear blue eyes challenged her. "I want to see it."

Taking a deep breath, she tried for a bit of professionalism. She couldn't just roll over for this man.

"You have no right to see it. It's private property. My property."

"If it's about me, I think I have every right."

"No, you don't!"

"Hand it over."

"No."

"Never mind," he said impatiently, reaching for her. "We'll do it this way."

She wasn't certain what he had in mind, but was pretty sure she wasn't going to like it. She took another quick step backward.

"Wait." She put her hand to her mouth. "I think you chipped my tooth."

His first reaction was skepticism and she didn't blame him. It was a ploy, but she was desperate at this point.

"When?"

"When you tackled me."

To her surprise, he actually began to look concerned. "Here, let me see."

Moving forward and not giving her any room to maneuver, he took her face in his hands and looked down. This was a bit more than she'd bargained for. She wanted to protest, but after all, she'd set this up herself, hadn't she? And she really did feel a sharp edge on one of her upper fronts. Now she had to go through with it to prove her point. Tentatively, she opened her mouth.

"Here." She pointed at the place that felt sharp.

He leaned close, staring down. His hands were warm on her cheeks. His maleness overwhelmed her for a moment and she felt a bit light-headed. But his inspection didn't last long. He touched the tooth, then pulled back.

"As far as I can see, no tooth was injured during my expertly executed preemptive strike."

She gave him a look. "Cute," she said, exploring again with her tongue. "It feels chipped to me."

But while she was distracted, he was reaching to pull down the zipper of her sweatshirt, and that was another matter altogether.

"Hey," she cried, trying to jump away from his reach. "What do you think you're doing?"

"Checking," he said with calm confidence.

"Checking what?" She bristled with outrage.

"Don't worry. I've seen it all before." He gave her a sudden grin that just about knocked her backward on its own. "Just checking to see if you have a recorder on you. A bug. A mic."

She moved quickly to protect the little microcassette recorder tucked in the front pocket of her sweatshirt, but his hand was already sliding in there.

"Ah-hah." He pulled it out and waved it at her. "Just as I thought."

"Hey," she cried, truly indignant now, trying without success to snatch it back. "You can't do this."

He grinned again, eyes mocking as he dangled it just out of her reach. "Sue me."

And while she stretched to try to claim it, his other hand shot forward into her other pocket and snagged her notebook and her tiny digital camera.

"Give me back my things," she said, glaring at him, hands on her hips. A part of her was wincing, reminding her that she was reacting like any woman might, instead of like the intelligence agent she wanted to be. But she didn't have time to consider that. She couldn't let him do this!

"Okay now, this is just not fair."

"Not fair?" He set her items on a rock and stood in

front of them, so she knew she didn't have a chance to grab them unless he let her. "Life ain't fair, baby. Ya gotta learn to turn your lemons into lemonade."

Despite his obviously experience based advice, she wasn't ready to sign on to that attitude. She stuck her chin out and shot daggers at him with her eyes.

"You're bigger than I am. You're stronger than I am. You've got an unfair advantage. This isn't a fair fight."

He shrugged and took hold of the hood of her sweatshirt on either side of her face so she couldn't escape, pulling her closer and gazing down into her eyes. Strangely, his look went from mocking to dreamy in less time than it took to think it. As she gazed into his blue eyes, he grazed her cheek with one palm, touching her as though he liked the feel of her skin.

"Who says we're fighting?" he said, his voice suddenly low and sensual.

As humiliating as it was to know that he could turn her reactions on and off like a switch, she couldn't seem to stop them. The seduction in his voice washed over her like a wave, turning her outrage into a sense of longing she'd never known before. All the blood seemed to drain from her head, and for a moment, she actually thought she was going to faint.

Kelly closed her eyes and summoned all her strength. Whatever was going on, she wouldn't let it happen.

"Oh, no, you don't," she said, trying to make her shaky voice firm as she looked at Joe again. "You think you can manipulate me like a puppy dog, don't you?"

He dropped his hand from her face and gave her a

pained look. "I see," he said, turning from her. "What we've got here is a drama queen."

She took a step after him. "Look, you've taken everything I brought with me. You proved you could do it." She put out her hand. "So can I have them back now?"

He shook his head. "Not yet." He hesitated, gazing at her speculatively. He'd already been through her sweatshirt pockets. All that was left were the pockets in her jeans. "What I'd like to see is some ID. Where's your wallet?"

"Oh, no, you don't," she repeated, backing away again. "You're not coming anywhere near these pockets."

His mouth twisted. "I suppose that would be going a step too far," he said with obvious regret.

"Even for you," she added. "Besides, you have no right to do any of this."

He shrugged. "Okay. Come on back here and sit down." He gestured toward the rock. "Let's take a look at what you've found out about me."

He was going to look through her research notes. She frowned, not sure what to do. If she didn't have a real need to get along with him, she would certainly be treating this invasion of her space quite differently. In fact, she might be willing to swear out a warrant right now.

"Sit down," he said again.

"Sorry," she said crisply. "I don't have time. I have to go find a policeman to have you arrested."

He looked at her for a moment, then rubbed his eyes tiredly. "Kelly, sit down."

She gazed at him defiantly. "No."

He gave her a world-weary, heavy-lidded look. "Do I have to tackle you again?"

She hesitated, watching as he sat on the long black rock and began to go through her things.

"Hey, you can't look at that," she said, stepping closer.

"I thought you were going to see if you could find a cop to stop me," he noted casually as he flipped through the pages of her notebook. "This is quite a little document of my life for the last two days," he noted. "But pretty boring."

"The truth hurts," she quipped.

His mouth twisted. That wasn't the only thing that hurt. The leg that had taken a bullet almost a year ago still wasn't totally healed. It ached right now. He'd been standing on it for too long.

And yet he was probably better off than he'd had any reason to hope he would be when he'd returned from overseas. He'd been torn and wounded, in soul as well as in body, and the bitterness over what had happened that last day in the Philippines still consumed him. That had always been worse than the physical pain. The bullets that had torn through the jungle that day had shattered his life, but the woman he loved had died in his arms.

Was that it? Was that what Kelly was after? Was she just another writer looking for a story? He eyed her speculatively.

At first he'd thought she must have worse things in mind. There were plenty of people from his past who might want to take him out. But he was pretty sure that wasn't what she'd come for. She wasn't the right type. And all this note taking suggested she was looking for information, not trying to do him actual harm. At least not at the moment.

In the VA hospital, there'd been a reporter who had hung around, wanting to know details, fishing for angles. He'd seen the article about the "returning heroes" that had featured Joe as well as a group of other men, and he'd sensed there was something more there. He'd wanted to write up Joe's story, wanted to use his life as fodder for a piece of sensational journalism. He hadn't actually known about Angie, but he'd known there had to be something.

Joe hadn't cooperated. In fact, things had gotten downright nasty there for awhile. There was no way he would allow Angie to be grist for anyone's mill. And anyway, the last thing guys like him needed was publicity. Something like that could destroy your usefulness, wipe out your career. If people knew who you were and what your game was, you were dead. Incognito was the way to go.

He was confronting this issue right now. His body was pretty much healed, but his mind? Not hardly. Was he going to be able to go back to work?

That was the question haunting him. He wasn't in the military any longer, but there were plenty of contractors who were ready to pay him a lot of money to do what he was doing before, only privately. And—let's face it—he didn't know much of anything else. But did he still have the heart for it? Had losing the woman he loved destroyed all that?

It hardly mattered. In just a few hours, his little girl—a little girl he'd never met—was arriving on a flight from the Philippines. He should be preparing for that. Once Mei was here, Joe had no idea what his life was going to be like. Everything had been on hold for months. Now he was about to see the future.

He still had no answers. But he knew one thing: he wasn't going to let anyone write about him. No way.

"So it *was* information you were aiming for after all," he said, paging through the notebook and feeling his annoyance begin to simmer into something else.

"Well, not really," she began, but he went on as though she hadn't spoken.

"Too bad you weren't around when I was smuggling contraband across the border," he said sardonically, looking up to where she was standing. "Or when I was inviting underaged girls over to my place for an orgy. Or hiding deserters in my rec room."

She finally slipped down to sit beside him in the rock. "I don't believe you ever did any of those things."

He winced. "Damn. I just can't get any respect anymore, can I?"

She gave him a baleful look. "You're wrong about me," she said calmly. "I'm not trying to dig up dirt on you."

His eyes were hooded and there was a hard line around his mouth. "No? Then what *are* you trying to do?"

She hesitated. What should she tell him? How much could she get away with and not let him know the truth? It was too soon to tell him everything. Much too soon.

And once he knew what she was here for, she had every reason to think that he would like her even less than he did now.

He was waving her notebook at her, his knuckles white. "This is me," he said, and to her surprise, his voice was throbbing with real anger. "You've taken a piece of me and you have no right to it."

She blinked, disconcerted that he was taking this so seriously. "But it's me, too. My writing."

"I don't care." He flipped the notebook open again and ripped the relevant pages out. Looking at her defiantly, he tore them into tiny pieces.

Her heart jumped but she held back her natural reaction. Something in the strength of his backlash warned her to let it be for now. Besides, she knew she hadn't written down anything very interesting as yet. It didn't really matter.

He dropped the scraps into her hand. "Let's see you try to put that back together again."

"Don't worry," she said brightly. "I don't need it. I can remember what I wrote."

"Really. Without this?" He held up her microcassette recorder. "And without this?" He added her tiny digital camera to the collection.

She bit her lip. Once again he was threatening to go too far. Tearing up some notes was one thing. Tampering with her electronics was another.

With a reluctant growl, he handed her back her things.

"Whatever," he said dismissively. "Do your thing. But just stay out of my way, okay?" He turned, running fingers through his thick hair and looking for his surf-board.

She quickly stashed her things away in her front pockets again, watching him anxiously. This seemed a lot like disaster in the making. He now knew who she was, so she couldn't very well follow him. If he found out she was questioning his neighbors, she wasn't sure what he would do, but she knew it wouldn't be pretty.

So she was stuck. Kelly couldn't do anything surreptitiously. Any new research would have to be done right out in the open and to his face. And for that she needed to have a civil relationship with him. That didn't seem to be in the cards, the way things were working out.

Without looking her way again, he began to stride off through the sand, his board under his arm.

She watched him go for a moment, watched the fog begin to swallow him up, her heart sinking. This couldn't be all there was. This couldn't be the end of her research. She might never know the truth now. Was he the prince or wasn't he? She had to find out. Gathering herself together, she ran after him.

"Wait!" she called. "Joe, wait a minute. I…I'll tell you everything."

He kept walking.

"Wait."

She caught up with him and managed to get him to glance at her again. "Have you ever heard of a little island country named Ambria?" she asked, searching his eyes for his reaction to her words.

He stopped in his tracks and turned, looking at her. And then he went very still. Everything about him seemed to be poised and waiting, like a cat in the jungle, preparing to strike.

"Ambria," he said slowly. Then he nodded, his eyes hooded. "Sure. I've heard of the place. What about it?"

There was something there. He'd reacted. She couldn't tell much, but there was a thread of interest in his gaze. Should she tell him what she thought she knew? She was trembling on the brink, but held back. The time wasn't right.

"Nothing," she said quickly, flushing and looking away to hide it. "I just…I'm Ambrian. Or I should say, my parents were. And I work for the Ambrian News Agency in Ohio."

He was searching her eyes, his own dark and clouded. "So?"

"I saw that article about the returning heroes six months ago where you were one of the soldiers featured."

He nodded, waiting.

"And…well, I got some information…. I'm following a lead that you might be Ambrian yourself. I'd like to talk to you about it and…"

He frowned. "Sorry." He turned from her again. "I'm not Ambrian. I'm American. You've got the wrong guy."

No. She didn't believe that. She'd seen the flicker behind his eyes.

"Wait," she said, hurrying after him again. "I really need your help."

She paused, realizing there was absolutely no reason

he should want to help her. She had to add something, something that would give him an excuse to get involved.

"You see, what I'm doing is researching people who were forced to leave Ambria by the revolution twenty-five years ago. A lot of people were killed. A lot of the royal family was killed."

He looked cynical. "Well, there you go. I wasn't killed. And neither was my mother."

Kelly glanced up in surprise. "Who was your mother?"

If he had a mother—a real mother—that could change everything. Her entire investigation was riding on a theory snatched out of thin air. At least that was what they'd told her at headquarters.

Her mouth felt very dry. What if she'd come all the way out here for nothing? Could she stand the ribbing she would take when she went back to her office? Could she hold her head up in meetings, or would she know they were always thinking, *Don't pay any attention to Kelly. She's the one who went on that wild-goose chase after a lost prince who turned out to be not lost and not a prince. Crazy woman.*

She cringed inside. But only for a moment.

Backbone, Kelly, she told herself silently. *Don't give up without a fight.*

Holding her head high, she went back into attack mode.

"Who was your mother?" she asked again, this time almost accusingly, as though she was sure he was making it up.

His mouth twisted and he looked at her as though he was beginning to wonder the same thing herself. "You know, I don't get it. What does this have to do with anything? It's all ancient history."

"Exactly. That's why I'm researching it. I'm trying to illuminate that ancient history and get some people reconnected with the background they've lost."

Meaning you, mister!

He was shaking his head. "I don't need any lost family. Family isn't really that important to me. It hasn't done me all that much good so far."

"But—"

Joe turned on her angrily. "Leave me alone, Kelly Vrosis. This is an important day for me and you've already wasted too much of it. Stay out of my way. I've got no time for this."

"Wow," she said, controlling herself, but letting her growing anger show. "And here I thought you were a good guy. The article I read made you sound like a hero."

He stared at her, his face dark and moody. "I'm no hero, Kelly. Believe me." He worked the muscles in his shoulders and grimaced painfully. "But I'm not a villain, either. As long as I'm not provoked."

"Oh, brother." She gave him a scathing look. "You can't call someone who's never been tempted a saint, can you?"

He studied her, his eyes cold. "I'm not really interested in your philosophy of life. And I still don't know who sent you here."

"I came on my own," she insisted.

He stared at her, then slowly shook his head. "I don't believe that."

He was striding off again, but this time she stayed where she was, blinking back the tears that threatened. There was no doubt about it, no tiny glimmer of hope. He'd closed the door. This investigation was over. There wasn't much more she could do.

CHAPTER THREE

JOE GLANCED AT his watch. It looked as if he still had a couple of hours to kill before heading to the airport. He knew he should be home preparing the place for the arrival of his little girl, and preparing his own psyche for how he was going to deal with her, but he was too rattled, too restless to stay in one place for long. He turned into his favorite coffee bar a couple blocks from his house and got into the line at the counter.

Yeah, coffee. Just the thing to settle his jangled nerves. What was he thinking? A good stiff shot of whiskey would have been better.

But he wasn't going to be drinking the hard stuff anymore, not while he had his daughter living with him. Everything was going to be different.

It had been hard enough just getting her here. Angie's mother, Coreline, had been against their marriage from the beginning, and she'd done all she could to keep Joe from bringing his baby home after Angie died. He'd been prepared, now that he was mostly healed, to go to the Philippines and fight for custody, but word had come suddenly that Coreline had died, and that baby

Mei would be sent to him right away, along with her nanny.

Thank God for the nanny! Without her, Joe would be in a panic right now. But luckily, she would stay for six months to help him adjust. In the meantime, he would make arrangements for the future.

His baby was coming to be with him. It was all he could think about.

The only thing that had threatened to distract him had been his strange encounter with Kelly Vrosis earlier that morning. Hopefully, his demeanor had discouraged her enough that he wouldn't see her again.

He took his drink from the counter and turned, sweeping his gaze through the crowded café, and there she was, sitting in the shadowy back corner. She'd cleaned up pretty well. Instead of the baggy clothes, she was wearing a snug yellow tank top and dark green cropped pants with tiny pink lizards embroidered all over them. His own crisp button-up shirt and nicely creased slacks added to the contrast of the way they had both looked that morning.

As his gaze met hers, she smiled and raised her hand in a friendly salute.

"Hi," she said as he came closer. Her smile looked a little shaky, but determined.

He grimaced and went over to her table, slumping down into the seat across from her.

"What are you having?" she asked, just to be polite. "A nice latte?"

He held up his cardboard cup. "A Kona blend, black. Extra bold."

She raised her eyebrows. "I should have known."

He didn't smile. "You're doing it again," he said wearily.

She looked as innocent as possible, under the circumstances. "Doing what?"

"Following me."

She pretended shock. "Of all the egos in the world! I was here first."

He gave her a look. "Come on, you know you are."

"Hey, I'm allowed to inhabit all the public spaces you inhabit until you get a court order to stop me."

He groaned. "Is it really going to take that?"

She stared at him frankly, pretending to be all confidence, but inside she was trembling. She'd almost given up a bit earlier, but it hadn't taken long to talk herself into giving it another try. Now here she was, trying hard, but it seemed he still wasn't buying.

"Kelly, don't make me get tough on you."

Was that a threat? She supposed it was, but she was ready to let that go as long as she had a chance to turn his mind around. She leaned forward earnestly. "You know how you could take care of this? Make it all go away like magic?"

He looked skeptical. "Maybe I could have you kidnapped and dropped off on an uninhabited South Pacific island," he suggested.

"No. All you have to do is sit down for an interview and let me ask you a few questions."

That hard line was back around his mouth and dark clouds filled his blue eyes. "So you *are* a writer."

"No, I'm not." She was aching with the need to find

a way to convince him. "I'm not interested in writing about you. I *wouldn't* write about you. I know it would be dangerous for you if I did, and I would never do anything to hurt you."

He studied her, uncertain what the hell she was talking about. She was pretty and utterly appealing, and he wasn't used to being mean to pretty girls. But did he have any choice? He needed to be rid of her.

"Listen, I came all the way from Ohio to find you. Let me talk to you for, say…one hour," she suggested quickly. "Just one."

He frowned at her suspiciously. "What about? What is it that you want to know?"

She brightened. "About you. About where you come from. Your background."

He shook his head. This didn't make any sense at all. "Why? What do you care about those things? I thought you were finding places for refugees from your island to go or something. What does all that have to do with me?"

"Because I think…" She took a deep breath. "Because there's plenty of evidence that you might be…"

"What?"

She coughed roughly and he resisted the urge to give her a good pat on the back. When she stopped, she still looked as though she didn't know what to say to him.

"What could it be?" he said, half teasing, half sarcastic. "Maybe Elvis's love child?"

"No." She licked her dry lips and forced herself onward. "Have you…have you ever heard of…the lost royals of Ambria?"

That damn island again. This was the second time she'd mentioned Ambria and she was the second person this week to bring up that little country. What the heck was going on? He stared at her for a long moment, then shrugged. "What about them?"

"I think you're one of them."

His brows came together for a second. "No kidding? Which one?" he added, though he didn't really know a thing about any of them, not even their names.

She took a deep breath. "I don't know that for sure. But I think Prince Cassius would be the right age."

Joe shook his head, an incredulous look on his face. "I want to understand this. You came to California just so you could follow me around and decide if you thought I was this prince?"

"Yes."

"Do you know how nutty that sounds?"

"Yes, I know exactly how nutty it sounds. Everyone I know has been telling me that ever since I got the idea."

He stared at her for a few seconds longer, and then he threw back his head and laughed aloud. "You're insane," he said, still laughing.

"No. I'm serious."

He shook his head again, rising and grabbing his cup. "I should have known better than to stop and talk to you," he muttered as he turned to go. Looking back, he laughed again.

"Now that I know you're unstable, I feel vindicated in not wanting to have anything to do with you and your crazy theories." He raised a hand in warning. "Stay out of my way, Kelly Vrosis. I mean it. Don't waste any more of my time."

She sat very still as she watched him walk away, and the realization hit her hard: he didn't know.

How amazing was that? If he really was one of the princes, he didn't know about it. It seemed almost unbelievable, and yet, somehow it fit with the way he'd been living his life. No one would have thought he was a prince.

No one but her.

She'd lived with the story of the lost royals for months now. Twenty-five years ago, the mysterious little country of Ambria had been invaded by the Granvilli clan. The king and queen were killed, the castle was burned and the royal children—five sons and two daughters—had disappeared. For years it was assumed they had been murdered, too. But lately a new theory had surfaced. What if some of them had been spirited away and hidden all these years? What if the lost royal children of Ambria still existed?

That was the question that had filled her ever since she'd read about them. And once she saw the pictures of Joe in the magazine article, she'd been sure he was one of them.

And was she right? Could this ex-Army Ranger, this California surfer boy, really be one of the lost royals of Ambria? Could he really be a prince? He didn't act like it. But then, if he hadn't been raised to know how a prince was supposed to act, why would he?

Despite all that, the more she saw of him, the more confident she was in her instincts. The DeAngelis family that had ruled Ambria for over five hundred years had the reputation of being the most attractive royals ever. Her opinion? He fit right in.

"Mr. Tanner? This is Gayle Hannon at the customer service desk at the airport. There's been some sort of mix-up. A little girl has arrived designated for your reception, but—"

Joe gripped the receiver tightly. "She's here already? She wasn't supposed to arrive until tonight."

"As I say, there's been a mix-up. She was diverted to a different flight, and it seems the required child caretaker has disappeared. She's…" The woman's voice deepened with new emotion. "Mr. Tanner, she's all alone. Poor little thing. I think you had better come quickly."

"She's hardly more than one year old," he said, stunned. How had she ended up arriving alone on an international flight? "I'll be right there."

All alone. The words echoed in his mind as he searched for his keys and dashed for his car. This wasn't good. He had to get there, fast.

Kelly was out on the sidewalk in front of Joe's house, waiting for him. She'd spent the last few minutes giving herself a pep talk, and she was ready to hang tough this time. As he started his car out, she bent forward and knocked on the half-open passenger side window.

"Joe, listen. I've really got to talk to you. There is something you should know."

He looked at her blankly. "Huh?" he said. "What?"

She hesitated, sensing an opening. "Where are you going?"

"The airport," he said distractedly.

"Can I come with you? I just need to…"

He shook his head, not even listening. "Whatever," he muttered, pulling on his seat belt.

"Oh."

She took that as pure encouragement. Reaching out, she tugged on the door handle. Miraculously, it sprang right open and she jumped in.

"Great."

"Hey." He glared at her, finally seeming to realize who she was and why she was sitting beside him in his car. "Listen, I don't have time for this."

She smiled. "Okay," she said agreeably. "Let's go then."

He hesitated only a moment, then shook his head and swore. "What the hell." He grunted, stepping on the accelerator. "Hang on and keep quiet," he told her firmly. "I'm in a hurry."

She did as he said. He took the city streets too fast and then turned onto the freeway. Once he'd settled into a place in the flow of traffic, she turned and smiled brightly at him.

"So, the airport?" she said. "Are you meeting someone?"

He didn't even glance her way. "Yeah," he said, concentrating on his driving. Then he shook his head and muttered, "She's all alone in the middle of the airport and she's hardly more than one year old."

Kelly waited for a moment, and when he didn't elaborate, she asked, "Who is?"

He glanced at her sideways. "My little girl."

Kelly's jaw dropped. In all her time researching Joe Tanner, she'd never seen a shred of evidence that he had a child.

"Your little girl? What's her name?"

"Mei. Her mother named her. I wasn't there to help with it." He swore softly, shaking his head. "I was never there. Damn it. Some husband, huh?"

This was all news to Kelly. "You're married?" she asked, stunned.

He took in a deep breath and let it out. "I was married. Angie died in a firefight in the Luzon jungle a year ago. And now I'm finally going to meet our baby."

Kelly sat staring out at the landscape as they raced along. The enormity of what she'd thrown herself into finally registered, and it was like hitting a brick wall. She thought she knew so much, and now to find out she knew so little... Had she made a terrible mistake? All those months of researching this man and she didn't have a clue. He'd been married and had a baby? Stunning.

What else didn't she know? If she was so clueless about so much, could she possibly be right about his royal background? It didn't seem very likely at the moment. Heat filled her cheeks and she scrunched down in the seat, wishing she was somewhere else.

Traffic slowed to a crawl. Joe drummed his fingers on the steering wheel, mumbling to himself and looking pained. "What am I going to do with her?"

Kelly sat up straighter. He was obviously talking about his daughter. Why did he sound so lost, so troubled?

"Didn't you have a plan when you sent for her?" she asked.

He raised a hand and gestured in frustration. "There was supposed to be a nursemaid with her. Someone who knows her and can help take care of her."

There was anger in his voice, but also so much more. Kelly heard anxiety she would never have expected from such a strong personality. He'd obviously come up against something he didn't really understand, something he wasn't sure he could deal with. Despite everything, her heart went out to him.

"What happened?" she asked.

He shook his head. "I don't know. They called and said Mei had come in early and she was all alone." He turned and glanced at Kelly, and swore softly, obviously regretting that he'd let her into the car in a distracted moment.

"Why are you here?" he demanded, looking very annoyed. "This has nothing to do with you. And if you think you're going to write about this… Listen, I'm going to drop you off at a pay phone as soon as we get off this freeway."

"No." All thoughts of disappearing from the scene had flown right out of her mind. His dilemma had touched her. She wanted to help. "I swear to God, Joe, I will not write anything about you and your baby. I'm not a journalist. I'm not a writer." She took a deep breath. "And I'm coming with you."

"The hell you are!"

"Joe, don't you see? You need help. You can't handle a baby all by yourself."

"Sure I can. I bought a car seat." He nodded toward the back, and she turned and saw a state-of-the-art monstrosity sitting there, ready to go. Evidently he was ready to buy anything necessary for his child and pay for the best. That should be a good sign, she supposed. Still, he didn't seem to understand what taking care of a young child entailed.

"By handling a baby, I mean more than just putting her body someplace and telling her everything is okay." Kelly bit her lip and then appealed to his common sense. "She's going to be scared. You'll be driving. She'll need more attention than you can give her on the ride home. Face it. You're going to need help."

Kelly took his sullen silence to mean he saw her point, and she breathed in relief. As she studied his profile, her confidence began to creep back. Maybe she hadn't been so wrong about everything, after all. He was so handsome. Handsome and quite royal looking, if she did say so herself.

Joe spotted Mei as soon as he walked into the building. Just seeing her hit him like a thunderbolt.

She was sitting on a chair behind the airline check-in counter, her little legs out straight, her feet in their white socks and black Mary Janes barely reaching the edge. Her dark hair was cut off at ear length, with a thick fringe of bangs that almost covered her almond-shaped eyes. His heart flipped in his chest and suddenly he was out of breath.

Once he'd caught sight of her, he didn't see anything else. The rest of the world faded into a bothersome mist. There were people talking all around him, but he didn't hear a thing. She sat there as though there was a spotlight shining down on her, and he went straight for her.

Joe stopped in front of her, and for a moment he couldn't speak. His heart was full. He hadn't expected this. He was always the tough guy, the one who didn't get caught up in emotions. But from the moment he'd seen this little girl, he knew he was in love. She was so gorgeous, so adorable, he could hardly stand it.

"Mei?" he said at last, his voice rough.

She looked up and stared into his eyes, her little round face expressionless.

"Hi, Mei," he said. "I'm…I'm your daddy."

There was no change, no response. For a second, he wondered if she hadn't heard him.

"I'm taking you home," Joe said. His voice broke on that last word.

Gazing up at him, she shook her head. "No," she said, looking worried.

He stared at her, hardly hearing her or noticing her mood. For so long she'd been a dream in his heart, and now she was here.

And suddenly, the past came flooding in on him. He saw his beautiful Angie again, saw her trembling smile. Saw the love in her eyes as she greeted him, the delight as she told him of the new baby he'd never seen, the fear as their hiding place was discovered by the rebels…the gunfire... Saw the peace and acceptance on her lovely face as she died in his arms. He remembered the agonizing cry ripped from his chest as he'd realized he'd lost her forever, remembered the gut-wrenching fury as he'd taken off through the jungle after her murderers. Felt again the searing pain as their bullets hit his flesh, the aching frustration as he fell to the ground, helpless.

It all came back in a flash, and Joe tried to shake it away just as quickly. He couldn't let this precious child, this gift of love between him and Angie, be hurt by the ugly past.

Still, the past was what it was. He couldn't change it. It had made him into the bitter recluse he was today. But he wasn't going to inflict that on the child. Looking at her now, he knew he was going to do everything he could for her in every way. His heart seemed to swell in his chest. She would be his life from now on. But why did it hurt so much?

"For you, Angie," he murmured softly, his voice choking, his vision blurring with tears.

Kelly looked at Joe in surprise. All she'd seen so far was his tough side, the sarcasm, the arrogance, the disdain. She'd never dreamed such a very small girl could bring a man like this to tears.

Kelly had come in right behind him, but was trying to stay to the side and out of the way. She didn't want to intrude, didn't want to push in where she didn't belong, but he was just standing there, paralyzed with emotion. If she didn't do something, he was going to scare the poor kid to death. There was really no choice. She stepped forward.

"Hi, sweetie," she said with a cheery smile, bending down. "My name's Kelly. I'm your daddy's friend. I'm going to help take you home. Okay?"

The huge dark eyes stared at her solemnly. For a moment, Kelly thought there would be no response. The child's gaze seemed flat, emotionless. Her little features didn't move at all.

Kelly glanced at Joe for guidance, but the look on his face told her he wouldn't even hear her right now.

"Mei?" Kelly said, smiling hopefully. "You want to come with me?"

As though a veil was lifted, Mei's eyes lit with interest and her little head nodded.

Flooded with relief, Kelly put out her arms and Mei went to her willingly, then clung to her. And that was that. Mei seemed to think she belonged with Kelly. No room for other options.

They waited for a required interview with a supervisor, then Joe began to make his way through the paperwork, while Kelly tried to keep the baby entertained as best she could. The bustle of people all around them helped. Whenever Mei felt anxious, Kelly was there to soothe away her fears. At the same time she kept one ear open to the questions Joe was answering, hoping to glean something that would help with her identification. She didn't get much there, but she did hear the name Angie repeated often enough to realize that had to be Mei's mother, and Joe's wife. One look at his face was all she needed to understand the tragedy involved in his losing her.

Kelly noticed that Joe was very carefully avoiding

glancing at Mei. She thought she knew why. He was protecting himself, just getting through the bureaucratic formalities with all due speed. This child had power over him, and he had to wait until they were out of here before he could begin learning how to deal with it.

They were almost done when Joe visibly steeled himself and turned to smile at his daughter.

"Okay, Mei," he said, holding out his arms. "Why don't you let me carry you for awhile?"

The baby shrank away, and as his hands touched her, she let out a shriek that could probably be heard all the way back to Manila. Joe jerked back, his face like stone. He glanced at Kelly, who was at a loss as to how to fix this situation, and then he turned and walked back to the airline counter, where he had a bit more business to complete.

Kelly held Mei closely, knowing this was not good, and feeling a surge of compassion for Joe that almost brought her to tears. But what could she do?

Once all the paperwork was done and they were heading for the parking lot, little Mei's arms went around Kelly's neck and she snuggled in tightly. But whenever Joe turned to look at her, she stiffened, and Kelly began to realize there might be more problems ahead than he had ever anticipated.

CHAPTER FOUR

JOE WAS SILENT on the drive home from the airport. He was the sort of man who liked to be in command of every situation, understanding what was needed, hitting all the bases. The problem was, right now he didn't have a clue. He felt like a swimmer who couldn't touch bottom and had lost sight of the beach. What was he supposed to do now?

The idea of a baby daughter had seemed vaguely pleasant. A little girl to call his own. A miniature version of Angie, maybe—sweet, pretty, a blessing in his life. She was his child and his responsibility.

He'd pictured a friendly meeting at the airport. The nanny would be in charge. After all, he'd been told the woman had been taking care of Mei ever since she was born. He would drive them home, and that would be that. A child in his life—but a child with a caretaker, someone who knew what she was doing.

That was the plan. Reality had caught him unprepared and hit him like a blow to the gut.

No nanny. No caretaker. No safety net.

That wasn't going to work. He didn't know the first

thing about taking care of a kid this age. Or any age, really.

But even worse had been his own emotional reaction to seeing little Mei in the flesh for the first time. He hadn't expected to have the pain flood in that way. His stomach turned again just thinking about it. If he'd known that was going to happen…

Traffic was light, but his headlights bounced against the fog and he had to pay close attention, peering into the darkness as though he might find some answers there. Kelly was sitting next to Mei in the back, talking to her softly, helping her play with a toy attached to the car seat.

He listened for a moment, craning to hear, as though she were speaking in a foreign language he didn't understand. And he didn't. What was he doing here? What was he going to do with this child?

"Did you find out what happened to the nanny?" Kelly asked him as he turned off the freeway and stopped at a red light.

He hesitated, reluctant to tell her anything. She shouldn't even be here. Still, if she wasn't, he would be in even bigger trouble. He supposed he owed her a bit of civility, if nothing else.

"They said she was seen with Mei right up until they went through customs here at the airport, and then she disappeared." He shook his head in disbelief. "They found her sitting there in one of those plastic chairs. She had a tag around her neck with her papers and my name and all that. They gave me the address the nanny used as a contact point, but something tells me that's going to be useless."

He glanced in the rearview mirror. He couldn't see Mei, but that was okay. Right now he didn't want to.

"They said it happens all the time. She'll probably blend right into the immigrant community and it will be hard to ever find her."

Kelly nodded. "That's what I was afraid of."

He frowned and didn't speak again as he turned onto his street and pulled into the driveway.

"You're lucky," Kelly said softly. "She's asleep. I'll bet you can carry her in without waking her."

"Good."

"Do you have a bed for her?"

He turned off the engine and looked back. "Of course I have a bed for her. I've got a whole room ready."

"Oh. Good."

He got out and held the rear door open. He was still avoiding taking a look at Mei. Instead, he studied Kelly, noting that she'd pulled her curly blonde hair back and tied it with a band, though strands were escaping and making a halo effect around her face. She had a sweet, pretty face. She looked nice. His baby needed somebody nice. What if he asked her to stay and…

Grimacing, he turned and looked into the fog that surrounded his house. What was he thinking? He didn't need a woman like this hanging around, distracting him from the work he had to do creating a family for this baby. He should tell Kelly to take a hike. She had no business being here with them. He didn't know her. And she was all wrong for this job. The last thing he wanted for a nanny was a woman this appealing to the senses. She had to go.

Still, the thought of being alone with Mei struck a certain level of terror in his heart. He needed help. Who was he going to get to come at this time of night?

"What are you going to do?" Kelly asked softly, standing in front of him.

He shrugged. "Try to hire a nanny, I guess," he said gruffly.

"You won't be able to do that until morning."

He nodded.

"I'll stay," she said. It was less an offer than a firm statement of intent.

"You?" He looked at her with a scowl. Suspicions flooded back. He may have just been considering asking her to stay, but why was she offering? "Why would you do that? You're not going to get a story out of me."

She threw up her hands in exasperation. "I told you, I'm not looking for a story. I'm not a writer."

She'd said that again and again. But if she wasn't trying to get a story, what was her angle? Everybody had one.

"Then what *do* you want, Kelly?" he asked.

She gazed up into his troubled eyes. She wasn't sure why this was all so upsetting to him, but she could see that it was. He was fairly bristling with tension. Was it just that he didn't know how to take care of a baby and was nervous about it?

No, she was pretty sure it was something more. Something deeper and more painful. Everything in her yearned to help him, human to human. This had nothing to do with her quest for his real identity.

"What I want is to help you. To help the baby."

She saw the doubt in his face, and reached out and touched his arm. "Seriously, Joe. Right now that's all I care about."

He searched her eyes. "I'm telling you straight out, I don't trust you," he said gruffly. "But at the moment, I feel I don't really have a choice. With the nanny gone…" He shrugged, not needing to complete the sentence. His blue eyes were clouded. "You've seen the way Mei reacts to me."

Kelly bit her lip and nodded. She'd been wondering if he'd really noticed, wondering if that was what was hurting him. An unexpected feeling of tenderness toward him flooded her. There was no way she was going to leave him alone with his baby until…well, she didn't know. But not yet.

He looked at her and saw the softening in her face. Suddenly he was breathless. That halo effect her hair had was working again. She looked like an angel.

He didn't want to need her. He wanted to pick up his little girl and carry her into the house and live happily ever after, without Kelly Vrosis being involved in any way. But that wasn't going to happen.

He didn't want to need this woman, but he did.

"Do you have any real experience?" he asked, as though interviewing her for the job. "Any children?"

She shook her head. "I'm not married," she told him. "But I do have two brothers, and they both have kids. I've spent plenty of time caring for my nieces and nephews. I'll be okay."

He stared at her a moment longer, then shrugged.

"You want to bring in her stuff?" he asked shortly, nodding toward the baggage that had come across the Pacific with Mei as he leaned in to unbuckle the baby seat from the car.

"Sure," Kelly said, working hard on looking non-threatening, efficient and cheerful as she gathered the things together. "Lead the way."

He took her through a nice, ordinary living room, down a hallway and into an enchanting little girl's paradise. Kelly gazed around in wonder. The carpet was like walking on marshmallows and it was shiny clean. A beautiful wooden crib stood against one wall, an elaborate changing table beside it. A large, overstuffed recliner sat in one corner. The closet doors opened to reveal exquisitely organized baby clothes on shelves and hangers, along with row upon row of adorable toys.

"Joe, this is perfect. I can't believe you did this on your own."

"I didn't. I hired a consultant to help me."

She almost laughed at the thought. "A consultant?"

"From Dory's Baby Boutique in the village. The woman who runs it knows someone who does these things, and she set me up with a meeting." He put the car seat down and picked up a business card left on top of the changing table. "Sonja Smith, Baby Decorator," he read.

Kelly looked around the room in admiration, her gaze

caught by the framed pictures of cartoon elephants in tutus and walruses in tights. "She does a great job."

Standing in the middle of the room, looming over a sleeping Mei in her car seat, he raised one dark eyebrow and looked at Kelly speculatively. "Maybe you know her?"

She glanced at him in surprise. "No. Why would I know her?"

He shrugged again. "She was sort of pushing me about this whole Ambrian thing, too."

Kelly's eyes widened and her heart lurched in her chest. "What?"

"So you thought you were my first?" he said, showing amusement at her reaction.

Kelly's imagination began to churn out crisis scenarios like ravioli out of a pasta machine, but she held back. She knew better than to pursue it now. The focus had to be on Mei.

Joe moved the car seat closer to the bed, obviously wondering how he was going to make the transfer to the crib without waking his little girl. Kelly started to give him some suggestions, but he did a great job on his own, laying her gently on the mattress. Kelly pulled a soft blanket over her and they both stood looking down at her.

"She's adorable," Kelly said softly.

He closed his eyes and leaned on the rail, his knuckles white. His reaction worried her.

"Joe, what is it?"

He turned toward her, his eyes dark and haunted. He stared at her for a moment, then shook his head.

"Nothing," he said gruffly. "But listen, I really appreciate that you offered to stay. I'm going to need the help."

"Of course you are."

And then she realized he didn't only mean with the care and feeding of a small girl. There was something else tearing him apart. For a man like this, one usually so strong and so confident, to admit he needed help was a big step. She wasn't even thinking about the whole prince thing any longer. She was thinking about the man standing here, looking so lost, racked with some kind of pain that she couldn't begin to analyze.

"I'll sleep right here in the room," Kelly said quickly.

He looked around. "There's no bed."

"The chair reclines. With a pillow and a blanket, I'll be fine."

He frowned. "You won't be comfortable there."

"Sure I will. And I want to be right here in case she wakes up. She'll be scared. She'll need someone at least a little bit familiar."

He moved restlessly, then looked at Kelly sideways. "Okay. I don't have any women's clothes hanging around, but I can give you a T-shirt to sleep in."

She smiled at him. Despite everything, he looked very appealing with his hair tousled and falling over his forehead, and his eyes heavy and sleepy and his mouth so wide and inviting….

Whoa. She pulled herself up short. Where the heck did she think she was going with that thought?

"Uh...a T-shirt would be perfect," she said quickly, her cheeks heating as she turned away.

"Okay."

He didn't seem to notice her embarrassment. Without another word, he left the room.

She let her breath out slowly, fanning her cheeks. She had to remember who he was. Or at least, who she thought he was. She wasn't getting very far on that project—but there would be time. Hopefully.

Joe returned with pillows, a comforter and a bright blue T-shirt that looked big enough to be a small dress on Kelly. She began to set up the chair for sleeping.

He frowned, watching her. "I should be the one to do that. I should sleep in here tonight."

"No," she said firmly. "If she wakes up, you might scare her."

For just a moment, he looked stricken, and Kelly regretted her quick words.

"This is ridiculous," he said, his voice gravelly with emotion. "She's my baby. I've got to find a way..."

"Joe." Kelly felt the ache in him and could hardly stand it. Reaching out, she took his hand, as though to convey by touch what her words couldn't really express. "Joe, it's not time yet. Don't you see? She's probably been raised by only women so far, and to her, you're big and male and scary. She's not sure what to do with you yet. You've barely met at this point. You've got to give her a little time."

"Time," he echoed softly, staring down at Kelly, his gaze hooded. He didn't seem receptive, but he wasn't pulling away from her grip on his hand.

"Yes. She's clueless right now. The one person she depended on, the nanny, deserted her. Mei doesn't know what you might do. Let her get to know you gradually."

"You're probably right." He said it reluctantly, but turned the tables so that he was holding *her* hand, and slowly raised it to his lips, kissing her fingers softly.

Kelly held her breath. She hadn't expected anything like that. But he didn't look into her eyes as he did it, and he didn't say anything more, so when he dropped her hand again, she felt almost as though he'd done it anonymously. Or maybe it was a sort of thank-you for her assistance.

Maybe she'd imagined the whole thing. Or maybe he was just distracted. He was definitely confusing her.

"Uh...thanks, Kelly," Joe said as he turned to go. "Thanks for staying."

She sent a radiant smile his way. "No problem. See you in the morning."

He stared back at her for a long moment, then nodded and left the room.

She shivered. What was it about haunted handsome men that was so compelling?

Sighing, she turned back to the crib. Looking down at the sleeping child, she wanted to brush the hair off her forehead, but was afraid that would waken her. What a beautiful little girl!

"Well," Kelly murmured to herself, "what have you gotten yourself involved in now?"

And then she remembered what he'd said about the designer and Ambria. Alarm bells were still ringing in her head over that one. She wanted to know more. She *had* to know more. But right now he wasn't going to be interested in anything that had to do with the obscure island nation, not until things were a bit more settled in his life.

Kelly only hoped they had the time to wait.

Sleeping in a recliner quickly lost its charm, but she got in a few dozing sessions before Mei stirred. When she heard her, she got up quickly and went to the crib, talking to the baby softly and patting her back until she fell asleep again.

By then Kelly was wide awake and thinking about what she might need the next time Mei woke up. Moving quietly, she opened the door and went silently through the darkened house to the kitchen, to see what Joe had done with the baby bottles and other supplies they had brought from the airport.

The layout of the house was simple, but she'd never been there before, so she was feeling her way when a movement caught her eye, stopping her cold. Someone was on the deck. She could see a dark form through the French doors. Her heart jumped into her throat and she shrank back against the wall, where she wouldn't be seen.

But even as she did so, she realized it had to be Joe. Kelly breathed a sigh of relief and went to the doors. Yes, there he was, leaning on the railing and gazing out toward the ocean—and looking like a man going through hell. Compassion flooded her and she sighed, wishing she knew what she could do to help him.

* * *

Joe tried to pull himself together. "Hell" had been watching the woman he loved die. This wasn't fun, but it was a piece of cake compared to that.

Not to say that it was easy. Seeing Mei reminded him of losing Angie, and that had opened up the past in a bad way. He had earned his agony, but he didn't have a right to take it out on anyone else. He'd gone through a lot a year ago. He'd hated life for awhile, hated his fate, his luck and everything else he could think of. But that was over.

He thought he'd mostly taken care of this already, during all the hours of therapy in the veterans hospital, the long nights of soul searching. He'd finally come to terms with what had happened, and said goodbye to Angie. Hadn't he?

But that was before he'd seen Mei.

That same old deadly agony was lurking. If he let it all flood back over him, he was going to drown. He couldn't go through that again. His eyes were stinging, and suddenly he realized why. Tears. What the hell? He never cried. This was ridiculous. Now, twice in one night… Leaning against the railing, he swore at himself, softly and obscenely. No more tears.

His head jerked up as he heard the door to the deck open. There Kelly stood, lighting up the gloom with her wild golden hair. How could this be hell if he had his own personal angel?

"Hi," she said. "You can't sleep, either?"

He turned slowly to face her, and she peered at him. It was too dark for her to see if his expression was welcoming, or if he wished she'd just go away. That wouldn't be so unusual. He usually seemed to want her gone.

But she wasn't going to go. She had a feeling he was out here brooding, and she didn't think that was a good thing.

"Are you okay?" she asked as she approached.

He didn't answer. He was dressed in jeans and a huge, baggy dark blue sweatshirt with a hood pulled up over his head, while she stood before him in nothing but his bright blue T-shirt. A cool breeze brought in a touch of chill, reminding her of her skimpy nightgown, and she hugged herself, giving thanks that the slip of a moon wasn't giving much light.

Looking up at him for a moment, she still couldn't read his eyes. In fact, she could barely make out the features of his face, hiding there in the shadows of his hoodie. Her heart was beginning to thump again. Why didn't he say anything? Was he angry? Did he think she was meddling? She couldn't tell and she was getting nervous.

She stepped past him and leaned on the rail next to him, looking out at what moonlight there was shimmering on the distant ocean. She could hear the waves, but couldn't see them. Too many houses blocked the view.

"I can tell you're upset," she said tentatively. "Do you want to talk about it?"

"Talk about it!" He coughed and cleared his throat. "You like guys who spill their guts, do you?"

Kelly was glad he'd finally spoken. Still, she could tell that something was bothering him. She could see it, feel it. And if talking it out could soften that sense of turmoil in him, it would be best to do it.

And not just for his sake. If he wasn't careful, his vibes were going to scare the baby. He needed to grapple with it, get rid of it, before he attempted to deal with the new little girl in his life. Kelly sighed, hardly believing what she was thinking. What made her so sure of these things, anyway? She didn't usually walk around claiming to have all the answers, and she knew very well she was groping in the dark as much as anyone.

But there was a child at stake here. For the sake of the baby, she had to do what she could.

"I know you don't really know me," she told him earnestly, "but that might make it easier. In a few days, I'll be gone and you'll never see me again." She gave him an apologetic smile. "Honest. I don't plan to stay in California any longer than that. So if you want to...I don't know...vent or something, feel free."

He looked at her and didn't know whether to laugh or hang his head. So this was what he'd come to—women volunteering to let him cry on their shoulders. How pathetic was that?

Well, he wasn't ready to open his heart to her, probably never would be. But he wouldn't mind another perspective on what he was torturing himself with at the moment. For some unknown reason, he felt as though he could talk to Kelly in ways he seldom did with other women.

Maybe, he thought cynically, it was the same quality in her that made Mei think she was a safe harbor in a scary world. Whatever it was, he supposed it wouldn't hurt to try.

"Okay, Kelly, you asked for it." He turned toward her. "Here's what I'm thinking." He hesitated, taking a deep breath before going on. "I'm thinking this whole thing was a very bad idea."

Just hearing that said out loud made him cringe inside.

She frowned at him, confused. "What was a bad idea?"

"To bring Mei here."

She gasped. "What are you talking about? She's your baby."

"Yeah." He turned and leaned on the railing. "But it was selfish. I was thinking about having an adorable little girl of my own, like she was a doll or something." He looked at her, despising himself a little. "A pet. A kitten."

"Oh, Joe."

"I know better, of course. She's a real human being." He shook his head. Thinking of Mei and her cute little face, he couldn't help but smile. "A beautiful, perfect little human being. And she…she deserves the best of everything."

Turning from Kelly, he began to pace the wooden deck, his hands shoved deep into his pockets. "I didn't think…I didn't realize… I can't really give her what she deserves. Maybe I should have left her with Angie's family. Maybe she would have been better off."

Kelly stepped forward and blocked his way, grabbing

handfuls of sweatshirt fabric at chest level to stop him in his tracks.

"No," she told him forcefully, her eyes blazing.

He stopped and looked down at her in surprise. "No?"

"No. You're wrong."

He bit back the grin that threatened to take over his face. She looked so fierce. And then it came to him—she really did care about this.

"What makes you so sure about that?" he asked her.

"Common sense." She tried to shake him with the grip she had on his sweatshirt. She didn't manage to move his body, but got her point across. "She's your responsibility."

He winced, his gaze traveling over the planes of Kelly's pretty face. She had good cheekbones and beautiful eyelashes. But her mouth was where his attention settled. Nice lips. White teeth. And a sexy pout that could start to get to him if he let it.

"You're right," he told her at last. "You're absolutely right." Then he added softly, "How'd you get to be so right about things?"

She released his shirt, pretty sure she'd convinced him, then lifted her chin and gazed into his eyes. He was so handsome and so troubled, and she wanted so badly to help him, but she couldn't resist teasing him a little.

"I'm an objective observer. You should take my advice on everything."

"Fat chance." He chucked her under the chin and

made a face. "You're the one who wants me to start chasing royal moonbeams, aren't you?"

She caught her breath, wanting to argue, wanting to tell him he was going to be surprised once she'd really explained things. But she stopped herself. It still wasn't time.

She needed more information before she jumped in with both feet. She wouldn't want to raise false hopes. She shivered, as much with that thought as with the cold.

"I'm no prince. Look at me." His voice took on a bitter edge. "My baby's even scared of me."

"That won't last. Give her time."

He nodded, a distant look in his eyes. "My head says you're right, but my heart…" He shrugged. "Like Shakespeare wrote, 'there's the rub.'"

She smiled. A man who quoted Shakespeare. "Where did you get so literary?" she asked him. "I didn't think you went to university."

"I didn't. I signed up for the army as soon as I graduated from high school. But I read a lot."

"In the army?" That didn't fit her preconception.

"Sure. Once you get deployed overseas you have a lot of downtime."

"I thought army guys usually filled that with wine, women and song."

He nodded. "Okay, you got me there. I did my share of blowing off steam. But that gets old pretty fast, and our base had a great library. Plus, the master sergeant was a real scholar, and he introduced me to what I should be reading."

Joe frowned when he saw her shivering. "You're cold."

She nodded. "I should go in."

"Here, this will take care of it."

In one swoop, he loosened the neck of his sweatshirt, then lifted the hem, capturing her under it. Before she knew what was happening, he'd pulled her in to join him.

"What are you doing?" she cried, shocked.

"Shhh." His arms came around her, holding her close, and he whispered next to her ear,"You're going to wake up the neighbors."

The thought of anyone seeing them this way sent her into giggles. "Joe, this is crazy."

Was he just close so that he could whisper to her, or was he snuggling in behind her ear?

"Warm enough?" he asked.

"Oh, yes. Definitely warm."

Though she had to admit *hot* might be a better word. The darkness and the fact that her face was half hidden in the neck of the shirt saved her from having him see how red her cheeks had turned. His skin was bare under the sweatshirt, and now she was pressed against his fantastic, muscular chest. If it hadn't been for her thick T-shirt…

It doesn't mean a thing, she warned herself, and knew that was right. But how could she resist the warmth and the wonderful smoothness of his rounded muscles against her face? She closed her eyes, just for a moment. His arms held her loosely, and since they were out-side, wrapped in fabric, it was okay. She knew he was purposely trying to keep this nonthreatening, and she appreciated it. But no matter how casual he tried to make this, she was trapped in an enclosed space against his bare upper body. Her heart was beating like a drum and her head was feeling light. If she'd been a Victorian miss, she would be crying out for the smelling salts about now.

But she wasn't Victorian. She was up-to-date and full of contemporary attitudes. Wasn't she? She'd had sex and provocative bodies and scandalous talk thrown at her by the media all her life. She could handle this. Never mind that her knees seemed to be buckling and her pulse was racing so fast she couldn't catch her breath. This was worth it. This was heavenly. It was a moment she would never forget.

And then she remembered that he was supposed to be a prince of Ambria. She had no right to trifle with him this way. That thought made her laugh again.

"Joe, let me go," she said, pushing away. "I've got to go in and check on Mei."

"And leave me out here all alone in this sweat-shirt?"

"I think you'll be able to manage it." She wriggled free, then shook her head in mock despair as she looked at him. "I feel like I was highjacked by the moon-light bandit," she grumbled, straightening her T-shirt nightdress.

His grin was crooked. "Think of me as the prince of dreams," he said, and then his mouth twisted. "Bad dreams," he added cynically.

"Stop agonizing out here in the dark and go get some sleep," she advised as she turned to leave. "Mei is going to need you in the morning."

CHAPTER FIVE

KELLY SLEPT LATER than she'd planned, and when she opened her eyes, sunlight was streaming into the room. She turned her head and found a pair of gorgeous dark eyes considering her from the crib. Mei was standing at the railing, surveying the situation.

"Good morning, beautiful," Kelly said, stretching. "Did you have a good sleep?"

The cute little face didn't change, but the baby reached down to pick up a stuffed monkey that had been in her bed, and threw it over the nail as though it were a gift. Kelly laughed, but wondered how long she'd been awake, just standing there, looking around the unfamiliar room, wondering where she was and who was going to take care of her. Poor little thing.

Rising quickly, Kelly went to her. "I'll bet you need a change, don't you?"

She didn't wait for an answer, and Mei didn't resist, going willingly into her arms. Kelly held her for a moment, feeling the life that beat in her, feeling her sweetness. There was no way Joe was sending her back. No way at all.

* * *

Joe was waiting for them when they came into the kitchen. He had coffee brewed and cinnamon buns warmed and sitting on the table. He'd set two places and poured out two little glasses of orange juice. Kelly was carrying Mei and she smiled at how inviting everything looked. Including Joe, who'd made the effort to dress in fresh slacks and a baby-blue polo shirt just snug enough to show off his muscular chest and bulging biceps.

He caught her assessing look and smiled. She quickly glanced away, but in doing so, her gaze fell on where he'd tossed the big blue sweatshirt over the back of a chair. Memories of how it had felt inside that shirt the night before crashed in on her like a wave, and suddenly her cheeks were hot again. She glanced at him. His smile had turned into a full grin.

He was just too darn aware of things.

"Here's your baby," she said, presenting his child for inspection. "Isn't she beautiful in her little corduroy dress?"

"She is indeed," he said brightly, looking warmly at his child. "Good morning, Mei. Can you give me a smile today?"

Evidently not. His daughter shrank back, hiding her face in Kelly's hair and wrapping her chubby arms tightly around her neck.

Kelly sent Joe an anxious glance, wishing she knew what to do to make this better. His smile hadn't faded, though his eyes showed some strain. She approved of the effort he was making. He met her gaze and nodded cheerfully.

"New attitude," he told her.

"Oh. Good." She managed to smile back. "I guess."

"I'm going to take your advice and learn to roll with the punches."

"Did I advise that?" she murmured, gratified that he was at least thinking about what she'd said.

He moved into position so that Mei couldn't avoid looking at him.

"Tell me," he asked her, "what does a little girl your age like to eat?"

Mei scrunched up her face as though she'd just tasted spinach for the first time.

Kelly sighed, but decided to try ignoring the baby's reactions for awhile and hope they faded on their own. Chastising her would do no good. She was a little young for a heart-to-heart talk, so that pretty much left patience. Kelly just hoped she didn't run out of it.

"I know when my niece was this age, she was all about finger food. She loved cut up bananas and avocados, and for awhile she seemed to live on cheese cut up into little squares."

He nodded. "I'll have to make a store run. I'd pretty much counted on the nanny to be the expert in this sort of thing."

"We can wing it for now," Kelly assured him. "And for the moment, I'll bet she would like one of those yogurts I saw in the refrigerator."

"You think so?" He pulled one out and held it up. "How about it, Mei? Ready for some yummy yogurt?"

Her gaze was tracking the yogurt cup as though she

hadn't eaten in days, but when he moved close with it, she hid her face again.

"I guess you'll have to give it to her," he said drily. "She's pretty sure I'm the serpent with the apple at this point."

Mei went into the high chair willingly enough after Kelly let her toddle around on her little chubby legs for a few minutes, but she kept her eye on Joe, reacting when he came too close.

"Don't worry," Kelly told him, smiling as they sat down at the table and she began to feed Mei from her yogurt cup with a plastic spoon shaped like a dolphin. "She'll come around."

He smiled back, but it wasn't easy. They talked inconsequentially for a few moments. Mei ate her yogurt lustily, then played with some cheese Kelly cut up for her. Joe offered Mei a bite of cinnamon roll, but she shook her head and looked at him suspiciously.

"You've gotten over those doubts you had last night, haven't you?" Kelly asked at one point, needing reassurance.

"Sure," he said, dismissing it with a shrug. "Funny how the middle of the night makes everything look so impossible." He gave her a sideways smile. "And yet makes doing things like snuggling in a sweatshirt suddenly seem utterly rational."

"You dreamer," she murmured, holding back her smile and giving Mei her last bite of yogurt. Then Kelly looked at him sharply. "But you aren't still thinking of…" She couldn't finish that sentence without saying things she didn't want to say in front of the child.

He shrugged again. "I know what I have to do. I think I understand my responsibilities."

She frowned. She would have been happier if he'd sounded more enthusiastic, but she had to admit she understood. In the face of so much rejection, it was pretty hard to get very excited. She wanted to tell him not to worry, that surely things would get better soon. There was no way he could stand a lifetime like this—no one could. But he wouldn't have to.

And you know this...how? her inner voice mocked her.

Kelly wasn't sure about that, but knew it had to be true.

"Are you going to be calling an agency to find a new nanny?" It was sad to think of someone else coming in and taking over, but it had to be done. She couldn't stay forever.

"I already have."

"Already? You're fast."

"Well, I called and left a message on a machine. They weren't open yet. But I have no doubt we'll get someone out here by this afternoon at the latest."

"Well, there's no hurry," Kelly told him. "I'll stay until you get someone else."

His eyes darkened and he gazed at her for a moment as though trying to figure out what made her tick.

"Don't you have someplace you need to be?" he asked at last.

"Not at all. My week is wide open."

He looked as though he didn't get her at all. "So you really did come here to California just to find me?"

She nodded.

He shook his head as though she must be crazy. She braced herself for questions, but he didn't seem to want to deal with it yet. Rising from his place, he took his plate to the sink.

Watching him in profile, she was struck once again by how much he looked like a member of the royal family of Ambria. She was going to have to bring that up again soon. But in the meantime, there was another issue to deal with.

"Joe, tell me something," she said as he put the orange juice in the refrigerator. "This designer person who brought up Ambria…"

He turned to face her, then sank back into his chair at the table. "Sonja Smith? What about her?"

Kelly wasn't sure how to go about this delicately, so she just jumped in. "What exactly did she say to you?"

He thought for a second. "She didn't say anything much. She said that Dory at the Baby Boutique had told her she thought I might be from Ambria. That's all."

"Why did the Baby Boutique person think you were Ambrian?"

He shook his head. "I don't know. I went in a week ago and talked to her about needing some advice on stocking a baby's room, and she told me about Sonja and had her call me." He grimaced. "I don't know where she got the idea for the Ambrian connection. I never said anything to Dory about that. I'm sure Ambria never came up. In fact, the existence of Ambria hadn't entered my mind in…oh, I'd say a year or two. As far as countries go, it's not high on my list." He shrugged. "The point is, Ambria isn't a favorite of mine. And I have no idea why anyone would think I was interested."

"Hmm." Kelly gazed at him thoughtfully.

"Sonja came over, did a great job, and that was it. End of story."

"That's all?"

He made a face. "Well, not really. She wasn't just a designer decorator. Turns out she also tries to rustle up customers for tours she arranges. She works at a travel agency and was putting together a tour to Europe, including Ambria, in the summer. She said if I was interested I should give her a call. She thought I'd enjoy it."

Kelly didn't know what to think about that. It seemed a bit strange. Of course, there could be any number of reasons someone of Ambrian heritage might find his face appealing—and familiar, just as she had. It might be completely innocent, just a businesswoman trying to drum up sales for her tour.

On the other hand, it might be someone allied with the usurper Ambrian regime, the Granvillis. And from everything she'd learned lately, if the Granvillis were after you, you were in big trouble. Joe was taking all this lightly, but she was afraid he didn't know the background the way she did. If he had, he might have been more on guard.

That meant she'd better tell him soon. It was only fair to warn him. The fact that she knew he would scoff at her warnings didn't encourage her, but she knew it had to be done. And that somehow she was going to have to convince him.

"Well? Are you interested in the tour?"

He gave her an amused look, then rose to take the rest of the plates to the sink. "No. I've never had a yen to travel to a place like that. In fact, I've done enough foreign travel for awhile. I think I'll stay put."

She nodded. "Are you going to see her again?"

"Maybe. She might come by to meet Mei. I suggested it. I thought she might like to see what the child she did all this for looked like in the midst of it." He frowned, turning to face Kelly. "Listen, what's with the third degree? Does this somehow impinge upon your royal dreams?"

She shook her head. He was teasing her, but she wasn't in a teasing mood. Until she found out what this designer person was up to, she was going to be very uneasy. "Not a bit," she claimed cheerfully. Glancing up, she saw that he was looking at Mei, his face set and unhappy. It broke her heart, and she immediately had the urge to do something about it.

Rising and moving to stand close to him at the sink, she leaned in so she could speak softly and not be overheard by Mei. She'd been thinking about different schemes for getting the child to accept Joe. She could hardly stand to see the obvious pain in his face when his little girl rejected him.

"Here's a thought," Kelly said, very near his ear. "Why don't you just go over and sit by Mei and talk. Don't even talk to her at first, just near her. You could talk about your past with her mother. Maybe tell her how you met. Or anything else you can think of. Her name was Angie, right?"

He turned on her as though she'd suggested he sing an aria from La Bohème. "What? Why would I do any of that?"

Kelly blinked up at him, surprised at his vehemence. "Okay, if you don't want to do it directly, why don't you tell *me* about Angie in front of Mei. About where you met her, what your wedding was like, things like that."

His complete rejection of her idea was written all over his face. In fact, he was very close to anger.

"Why would I be telling you about Angie? Who *are* you?"

Kelly stared at him, her first impulse being to take offense at what he'd said. But she stopped herself. This was an agonizing situation. That was why she was trying to fix things. Didn't he see that? But maybe not. Maybe she was intruding and she ought to back off. Still...

She sighed, wishing she knew how to defuse the emotion he was feeling.

"I'm your friend, Joe. I care." Shaking her head, she looked into his eyes. "And I'd like to hear about it." She put a hand on his forearm, trying to calm him. "Just talk about it. I don't have to be there at all. Let her hear you."

The look on his face was stubborn and not at all friendly. "She's too young to understand what the heck I'd be talking about."

"That doesn't matter. And you never know how much children absorb."

He backed away, not accepting her touch. "No, Kelly. It's just not a good idea."

She searched his eyes. Anger was simmering in him just below the surface. She really wasn't sure why this should make him angry. He'd loved Angie. Angie was Mei's mother. What could be more natural than to tell her what her mother was like?

"It's your call, of course, but it just seems to me that talking about her mother, talking with open affection, would help draw her in, help make her feel like this is part of a continuum and not such a strange place, after all."

He shook his head, eyes stormy. "I think you're nuts."

"But Joe…"

"I'm not going to…to talk about…Angie," he said, his voice rough. "I can't."

Kelly's heart twisted and she licked her dry lips. He couldn't? She felt a surge of compassion, but still, that didn't seem right. He was the sort of man who could do anything. Was there more here than she knew? Obviously.

But there was also more at stake. Mei came first.

Still, Kelly couldn't ignore his outrage. What was she doing here? The last thing she wanted to do was torture him more. And yet she couldn't help feeling that he was going at this all wrong. Avoiding pain was often the best way to bring it on at the worst possible time. Her instinct was to try to nudge him out of the self-indulgence of his grief.

Wow, had she really thought that? Pretty tough stuff.

And yet she stood by it. After all, his comfort wasn't what was important anymore. He had a child to think of. He had to do what was best for Mei.

"Okay." Kelly turned back toward the high chair. "As I said, it's your call. If you can't get beyond the pain, there's no point, I guess."

He didn't answer and he didn't meet her gaze. She spent the next few minutes cleaning up Mei's tray and taking her out of the chair, talking softly to her all the time. He stood with his back against the counter, arms folded, looking out through the French doors toward the sliver of ocean visible in the distance. As she walked out, holding Mei's hand while she toddled alongside her, he didn't say a word.

He knew he'd hurt Kelly by his abrupt response, but it couldn't be helped. He felt angry, though not at her. He was pretty damn bitter at life in general. Self-pity wasn't his usual mode, but sometimes the enormity of it all came down on him and he couldn't shake it until it had worked its way through his system. This was one of those times.

Of course, Kelly had no way of knowing that every time he looked at Mei, he saw Angie. And right now, every time he saw Angie in his mind, he saw her dying right in front of him. He knew he had to get over it. He had to wipe the pain and shock and ugliness from his soul so that he could deal with this bright, new, wonderful child.

Kelly thought Mei's obvious rejection of him hurt. And of course, it wasn't fun to be rebuffed by a sweet little child like that. But he didn't blame Mei at all. She sensed his ambivalence, the way he felt torn and twisted inside, the way he almost winced every time he looked at her, and she reacted to it, as any sensitive, intelligent child would. It was going to take time for both of them.

Meanwhile he had Kelly's strange little project of convincing him that he was a prince of a funny little country he couldn't care less about to deal with. The whole thing could have been genuinely annoying if she weren't such a sweetheart. He had to admit, she wasn't exactly hard to look at, either. In fact, he was learning to like her quite a lot.

Moving restlessly, he gave himself a quick lecture on his attitude, ending with a resolution to be nicer to Kelly. Funny thing was, he knew right away it wouldn't be hard at all.

Kelly played with the little girl in her room for the next hour, helping her try out all the toys, and reading to her from a couple of the soft, padded books. Every few minutes, Mei would get up and run around the room, whooping to her own little tune, as though she had untapped energy that needed using up. She was bright, quick and interested in everything. So far she wasn't saying much, but Kelly had a feeling once the floodgates opened, words would come pouring out, even if they weren't understandable to anyone but the child herself.

Kelly spent some time reorganizing the shelves and finding interesting things packed away there, including some pictures and souvenirs that told a story better than Joe had been doing so far.

When Mei fell asleep over her book, Kelly wasn't surprised. She was still very tired from her long trip the day before. Kelly tucked her into bed, picked up a couple of items and went back out.

Joe was taking care of some bills on the Internet, and she waited until he logged off.

"What's up?" he asked, and she was pleased to see his eyes had lost the sheen of vague hostility they'd had when she'd seen him last.

"Mei fell asleep, but she won't be out long. I thought this would be a good time to plan a walk down to the beach."

"Do you think she's ready for that?"

"Sure. I think it would be really exciting for her." She gave him a smile. "Just think of your first time seeing the ocean."

"Kelly, she just came in on a plane over the Pacific," he reminded her.

"But that's not the same as up close and personal."

"No. You're right." He frowned, looking at her. "Will you be able to carry her? You know she still won't let me do it."

"Why would I carry her," she asked with an impish look, "when you've got that huge baby stroller?" She'd seen it standing in the hallway. "It would be a crime to let it go to waste. Like having a Porsche and letting it sit in the driveway."

"Oh." He grinned at the analogy. "That's right. I forgot all about it." His blue eyes softened as he looked at her, his gaze traveling over her face and taking in the whole of her. "Did anybody ever tell you that you brighten a room just by being in it?" he asked softly.

"No," she said, but felt a certain glow at that.

He shook his head, obviously liking what he saw. "I wonder why not."

She liked this man. How could she not? But liking him too much would be fraught with all sorts of dangers, she knew. She had to be very careful to keep things light and impersonal as much as possible.

"Probably because the whole concept is pure fantasy on your part," she said, trying to stick to her intentions with a little good-natured teasing.

But for once, he wasn't really cooperating. Instead of joining in the mockery, his look became more intense.

"No, it's not." Reaching out, he touched her curly hair, and his smile was wistful for a moment. "Tell me why you came looking for me, Kelly. Why you spent so much time watching me. I still don't understand it."

She looked up into his eyes. How could she explain? Did he really want to hear about her work at the Ambrian News Agency, about how her parents had raised her with a love of Ambria, how she'd studied the royal family for over a year before she saw his picture and knew instantly that he looked remarkably like one of the missing Ambrian princes would at this age? About how she'd fought everyone in her agency for this assignment, and then finally decided to come out on her own time, on her own money, to see for herself if what her intuition had told her was really true?

She might as well cut right to the chase.

"I work for an agency that gathers intelligence."

"What kind of intelligence?"

"Information. Things of interest to the exiled Ambrian community."

He frowned. "Why are they exiled?"

"Because of the people who took over Ambria twenty-five years ago. The coup was pretty bloody, but a lot of people escaped. There's a rather large group of us living in this country. More are scattered all over Europe."

He nodded, seeming to think that over. "So these folks who took over—are they some sort of oppressive regime?"

"Absolutely."

"Hmm. So what do you do at this agency? Don't tell me you're a secret agent—an undercover operative, perhaps?"

She glared at him. "What if I am?"

He grinned. "Well, there's really nothing I can say that wouldn't get me into trouble on that one. So I'll just keep my thoughts to myself."

"Don't worry. I'm not an agent. I'm an analyst."

"That's a relief." He paused. "So what does an analyst do?"

"I pretty much sit in a room and read articles in newspapers and magazines, and try to figure out what is actually going on in Ambria. I analyze information and write reports for policy makers."

"Sounds like a great job. But what does this have to do with me?"

She gave him a wise look. "Over time, I've developed a theory about you."

"You're not the first."

She hid her smile. "I'm sure I'm not."

He looked at her quizzically. "How about a short wrap-up on this theory thing? I've got to get going on some more paperwork, and I don't have time for anything long and involved."

She shook her head. "Never mind. You'll just laugh. Again."

"Laugh at you? Never."

Enough people had already laughed about her theory. For some reason, Kelly couldn't stand mockery from him right now. She had to be on firmer ground with her ideas of his being Ambrian royalty before she told him the whole story. He'd already told her she was crazy to think he might be an Ambrian prince. She wasn't going to go into that again right now. But she could try to get him to understand why she wanted so much to unravel this mystery.

"Do you ever do crossword puzzles?" she asked him.

He nodded. "There was a period of time during my recuperation when I felt like I was a prisoner in that hospital bed. But I had my crossword puzzles, and that was all I did, night and day."

She smiled. "So you know what it's like when you're almost finished with a puzzle, all except for one block of words. You look the hints up, you try different things, nothing works right. You try to put it aside and forget it, but you can't. No matter what you do or where you go that day, you keep fooling with that puzzle, trying different answers out in your mind. And then, suddenly, a piece of the tangle becomes clear and you think you have the key to the whole thing." She looked at him expectantly. "Has that ever happened to you?"

"Sure. All the time."

"You're so certain you have the correct answer," she went on, driving home her point, "but you can't prove it until you go back and find the puzzle and write in the words and see for yourself. Right?"

"Sure."

She threw out her hands. "That's what I'm doing here. I'm trying to prove I found the right answer to the puzzle."

He nodded, frowning thoughtfully at the same time. "So tell me, am I the answer or the puzzle?"

She grinned at him. "Both right now."

Their gazes met and held, and she felt her pulse begin to race in her veins. There was something between them. She could feel it. All her stern warnings to herself about not getting involved melted away. She wanted to kiss him. That desire grew in her quickly and was stronger than she'd ever felt it. Every part of her wanted to reach out to him, to come closer, to hold on and feel the heat. Attraction was evolving into compulsion. Her brain was closing off and her senses were sharpening. His warm, beautiful mouth was becoming her only focus.

Joe looked down at her eyes, her skin, her lips, and he was suddenly overwhelmed with the urge to kiss her. Would she stop him? It wouldn't be that unusual if he were to try to lose this lingering unhappiness in a woman's love.

Well, "love" would be asking a bit much at this stage.

How about losing it in a woman's warm, soft body? Not unusual—it happened all the time. What if he took her in his arms and held her close and let his male instincts come back to life…?

He looked into her eyes again and saw the questions there, but also saw the hint of acceptance. Reaching out, he slipped his hand behind her head, his fingers in her hair, and began to pull her toward him. Her eyes widened, but she didn't resist. His gaze settled on her mouth, and he felt a quick, strong pulse of desire, taking his breath away.

For the moment, she was his for the asking. But what gave him the right to be asking? This wasn't the way it should be. She deserved better. She deserved real love, and that was something he couldn't give her.

What the hell was he doing? Had he lost all sense of decency and self-control? He pulled his hand back and, instead of kissing her, turned away without a word. He felt nothing but self-loathing.

Kelly stood very still, watching him go, feeling such a deep, empty sense of loss that she ached with it. He'd been about to kiss her. What had stopped him? She knew very well what ought to keep *her* from kissing *him*. But what was his excuse?

Taking a deep, cleansing breath, she turned back toward Mei's room and tried to calm her emotions, settle her jumping nerves. If kissing was out, she might as well start preparing for their walk.

CHAPTER SIX

THE SUN SHONE on everything. There wasn't a hint of fog. The sky was blue and the ocean was even bluer. It was a beautiful day.

"I see why they call it the Golden State," Kelly noted. "Everything seems to shimmer with gold on a day like this."

Joe nodded, gazing out to sea and pulling fresh sea air deep into his lungs. He loved the beach. Turning, he glanced at Kelly. She looked good here, as if she belonged.

"I called Angie's family in the Philippines," he told her. "They say they have no idea what happened to the nanny. I got the impression that they couldn't care less."

"You'd think they would want to know Mei was okay."

He sighed. "It's a long story, Kelly. Angie's family didn't ever like me much, and they act like they've written Mei off now that she's with me." He shrugged. "But that's a problem for another time."

Kelly couldn't imagine how anyone could see Mei

and want to forget her. But she quickly pushed that aside. Mei took up all her attention at the moment.

As they strolled down the promenade, Mei sat like a little princess, watching everything with huge eyes. She didn't cringe when Joe came near anymore, but she definitely wanted Kelly to be in her range of vision at all times, and would call out if she lost sight of her. She loved the ocean. When they took her close enough to see the waves, she bounced up and down with excitement and clapped her hands.

Mei was a treat to watch, and Kelly glanced at Joe every so often to make sure he was enjoying it, too. He gave every indication of growing pride in his adorable child.

"Look at how smart she is," he kept saying. "See how she knows what that is? See how she called the dog over? See how she stops and thinks before she calls you?"

She did all those things. The trouble was, she didn't call *him*. And Kelly knew that was breaking his heart.

They bought tacos at a food stand for lunch, then stopped by a viewing platform to sit down and eat them. Kelly had brought along some baby food in a jar for Mei. The child took the food willingly enough, but then would forget to swallow. There was just too much to look at. She didn't have time for the distractions.

They finished eating, and when they weren't staring at the wild and beautiful surf, they sat back and watched Mei watch the people strolling by.

"I've never been to Ambria," Kelly told Joe. "But

from the pictures I've seen, the beaches look a lot like this."

He turned to glance at her, then sighed and leaned back as though getting ready for a long ordeal.

"Okay, Kelly," he said, as if giving in on something he'd been fighting. "Lay it on me. Tell me all about Ambria. I'm going to need the basics. I really don't know a thing."

She gazed at him, suddenly hit by the awesome responsibility he'd given her. If he really was the prince and she was going to be the person who introduced him to his country, she'd better get this right.

Clearing her throat, she searched her memory wildly, trying to think of the best way to approach this.

"Nothing fancy," he warned. "And don't take forever. Just the facts, ma'am."

She took a deep breath and decided to start at the beginning. "Okay. Here goes." She put on a serious face. "You know where Ambria is located. And you know it's a relatively isolated island nation. The DeAngelis family ruled the country for hundreds of years, starting in the days of the Holy Roman Empire, when the Crusades were just beginning. Their monarchy was one of the longest standing ever. Until twenty-five years ago, when it ended."

"And why did it end?" he asked, sounding interested despite himself.

"The vicious Granvilli clan had been their rivals for years and years. Most of their plots had failed, but finally, they got lucky. They invaded under the guise of popular liberation, gained a foothold and burned the castle. The royal family had to flee for their lives."

"Yikes," he murmured, frowning.

"Yikes, indeed," she responded, leaning forward. "They sent their children into hiding with other families sworn to secrecy. The king and queen..." She paused, realizing she might be talking about his parents. "They were killed, but only after having arranged for it to be widely believed that all their children had been killed, as well."

"So as to keep them safe from the Granvillis," he said softly, absorbing it all.

"Yes. If the Granvillis knew they were still alive, they would have tried to find them and kill them, to wipe out any natural opposition to their rule. That's why the children are called the lost princes."

"How many are there?"

"There were five sons and two daughters, but no one knows how many might have survived."

"If any did," he reminded her.

"Of course. Remnants of the old ruling order do exist, but none of them know for sure what happened to the royal children. There are refugee communities of Ambrians in many parts of Europe and the U.S.A. Reunions are held periodically in the old Roman town of Piasa, high in the northern mountains, where they say the oldsters talk and drink and dream about what might have been." She paused for a moment, her eyes dreamy as she pictured the scene. "Meanwhile, most of the younger generation have gone on with their lives and are modern, integrated Europeans and Americans, many quite successful in international trade and commerce."

He nodded, taking it all in with a faraway look in his eyes, just as she had—almost as though he was sharing her vision.

"So what about these lost princes?" he ventured. "What's happened to them?"

"Lately, rumors have surfaced that some of them did survive. These rumors have become all the rage. They've really ignited the memories of the oldsters and put a spark in the speculative ideas of the younger generation. Ambria has been a dark place, shrouded in mystery and set apart from modern life, for twenty-five years. It's a tragedy for history and for our people. Ambrians burn to get their nation back."

He laughed shortly. "Sure, the older ones want a return to the old ways, no doubt, and the younger ones want the romance of a revolution. Human nature."

She frowned. She didn't much like his reducing it to something so ordinary.

"Every Ambrian I know is passionately devoted to getting rid of the usurper regime," she said stoutly.

He grunted. "Mainly the oldsters, I'll bet."

"Sure. Don't they count?"

He shrugged. "Go on."

"Different factions have been vying for power and followers, each with their own ideas of how an invasion might be launched. The conviction has grown that this can only happen if we can find one of the lost royals still alive. Believe me, the ex-pat community is buzzing with speculation."

"Like honeybees," he murmured.

That put her back up a little. "You can make fun of it if you want to, but people are ready to move. The Granvillis have ruled the country badly. They're really considered terrible despots. They've got to go."

Her voice rose a bit as she tried to convince him, and he turned and grinned. "A regular Joan of Arc, aren't you?" he commented.

She colored. "No, of course not. But I don't think you understand how passionate a lot of exiled Ambrians are about this."

He sat up straighter and looked cynical. "Yeah, sure. People are totally passionate in the talking and threatening phase. It's when you put a gun in their hand and say, 'Okay, go do it,' that they suddenly remember something they have to take care of at home."

She swallowed back her first response. After all, he'd actually been one of the ones doing the fighting. He knew a whole heck of a lot more about that than she did.

"Maybe so," she said. "But something has happened that is threatening to put a lot of Ambrians in one place at one time, and if one of the princes shows up…" She shrugged.

He looked up at that, curious in spite of himself. "What are you talking about?"

"Here's what's going on." She leaned forward almost conspiratorially. "The old duke, Nathanilius, has died. He was the brother of the king who was killed during the invasion, and was considered the titular head of the family. The funeral is being planned in Piasa, and it threatens to be chaotic—no one knows who will show up, but they expect a lot of people who haven't been seen in years." Kelly gazed at Joe significantly. "The question is, who will try to seize the mantle of the old regime? Will the Granvillis try to disrupt the ceremony or even assassinate any of the DeAngelis loyaltists who will come out of hiding for the event? It's a pretty exciting time." She smiled. "Dangerous, too."

Some of his cynicism melted away. "Wow. Interesting."

"Yes."

He frowned, thinking. "Twenty-five years ago."

"You would have been about four, right?"

He merely nodded, looking out at the ocean. Memories—yeah, he had a few. He wasn't about to tell her, but he did have some pictures in his head from when he was very young. He remembered a fire. He remembered fear. He remembered being in a boat in the dark. The sound of oars splashing in inky water.

But were they really his own memories? That was the trouble with these things. How much was from tales he'd been told and how much from stories he'd made up himself when he was a boy? He had a feeling he knew what she would say about them. But he wasn't ready to surrender to her royal dreams.

He wasn't sure he wanted to be a prince.

Besides, he had other things on his mind, the most important of which was finding a way to get his daughter to like him. He was getting better at looking at her without feeling Angie's tragic presence. That should help.

He had no doubt she'd sensed that from the beginning, and that had helped fuel her reaction to him.

In some ways he was torn. Anything that reminded him of Angie should be good, shouldn't it? And yet it didn't quite work out that way. He'd loved her so much. Losing her had been hard. But that was hardly Mei's problem.

When you came right down to it, he himself was probably the roadblock to happiness there. He was pretty sure Kelly thought so. The baby was getting vibes from him, a sense of his pain, and she didn't like it. Who could blame her? The thing was, how to get it to stop before it became a habit she wouldn't ever shake? She couldn't distrust him forever.

They walked slowly home, enjoying the adorable things Mei did. People stopped them to say how cute she was. Dogs came up wagging their tails. Even the seagulls that swooped overhead seemed to be screaming her name. When one came especially close, then wheeled and almost lost its balance, Joe and Kelly looked at each other and laughed.

This was real life. This was pretty good.

But Joe's smile faded as he thought of Angie and how she'd never had a chance to live this way with her baby. On impulse, he reached for Mei's hand, hoping she would curl it around his finger. For just a second, she seemed about to try.

But then she realized it was his, and she pulled back and began to cry. Huge, rolling tears sprang instantly into her eyes. Kelly bent over to quiet her, but nothing was going to work this time.

"She's tired." Kelly looked up at Joe apologetically as she lifted Mei out of the stroller. "Don't take it to heart."

"Don't take it to heart?" Had she really said that? A dark sense of despair filled him and he turned away. How could he not take it to heart?

"Joe, I need to give her a bath. Then I'll read her a book and let her play before I put her down for a nap. Maybe you could come in and watch her play? Or maybe even read to her?"

"Yeah, sure," he said. "Maybe."

Kelly watched Joe walk away, and knew he had no intention of doing either of those things. Her heart ached for him, but she went ahead with her plans. Mei loved her bath and liked pointing out the animals in her books while Kelly read to her. She was ready for sleep by the time Kelly put her down. And just as she'd foreseen, Joe never showed up.

She searched until she found him in the garage, waxing down his surfboard.

"You didn't come in to see Mei playing," she said, trying not to make it come out like an accusation, but failing utterly.

He glanced up at her with haunted eyes and looked completely guilty. "I know. What's she doing right now?"

"She's asleep."

He threw down his cloth. "Okay. I'll go in and watch her for awhile a bit later."

Kelly frowned, not convinced he really meant it. This did not bode well. But she had no hold over him. She couldn't make him do something he didn't want to do, could she?

"I'm going to take this opportunity, while she's asleep, to run over to my motel and get a few things. Okay?"

"Sure." He took another swipe at his board. "Do you need my car?"

"No. It's only a couple of blocks away. And anyway, I've got my rental car there. I guess I might as well drive back in it."

Kelly hesitated for a moment, then pulled one of the items she'd found in the room out of a shopping bag she'd brought along. It was the framed photograph of a lovely young woman.

"Is this Angie?" she asked bluntly, holding up the picture.

His head snapped back and his eyes narrowed. "Where did you find that?" he demanded gruffly.

"In Mei's room, packed away on a shelf."

He stared at it, nodding slowly. "Yes. That's Angie."

"I thought so. When I showed it to Mei, she said, 'Mama.' And she smiled. So she obviously knew who it was."

Joe grunted. He didn't have to ask what her point was. He knew.

"She's lovely," Kelly said, looking at the photo. "She looks like a wonderful person."

He nodded. "She was," he said softly.

Kelly looked into his face with real determination. "She deserves to be talked about and treated like a real woman, not an icon on a pedestal. Can't you see that, Joe?"

He nodded again, clearly a little surprised by her vehemence. "Of course."

She drew in a deep breath, then stepped closer.

"You know, Joe, I've had bad things happen. I've had periods of unhappiness when I wondered 'Why me?' I've spent some time drowning in depression."

She looked up to see if he was listening. He seemed to be.

"But I began to read about a psychologist who has a theory that we very much make our own happiness and our own unhappiness. One thing he suggests doing is to act like you're happy, even when you're not. Go through the motions. Pretend. It can seem awkward at first, but the more you do it, the more it begins to come true. Reality follows the form. In a way, you're teaching yourself happiness. And if you work hard enough at it, it can become a part of you, a part of your being."

He was looking skeptical, but he was listening.

"I'm sure it doesn't always work, but it worked pretty well for me."

He peered into her eyes for a moment, then went back to rubbing the surface of his board. "That sounds like a lot of new age garbage."

"Fine. Call it names if it makes you feel better. But it made a real difference in my life." Kelly started toward the door and said flippantly, over her shoulder, "Just sayin'."

Joe kept pretending to work until he heard her go out the front door, then he slumped against the wall and closed his eyes. Why the hell had he let this woman into his life to challenge all his attitudes and assumptions? He'd been thinking about almost nothing else since she'd made her crazy suggestion that morning in the kitchen that he talk about Angie.

He'd been angry with Kelly at first, but deep down, he knew it was inevitable that he do it at some point. After all, he had Angie's baby here. Someday she would want to know all about her mother. Was he going to be able to tell her everything?

Kelly wanted him to get started right away, but she didn't know about what had happened in that jungle. How did you explain to a little girl about how her mother had died and why? Would Mei learn to blame him?

He blamed himself, so why not?

But of course Kelly was right. What was he thinking? It wasn't all about death. It wasn't all about pain and unhappy endings. He'd had many full, rich, happy experiences with Angie that had had nothing to do with the painful part. There'd been love and affection and music and flowers and boat rides on the lake and swimming to the waterfall. It was way past time he let himself dwell on that part of the past, not the horror at the end.

He finished up his work on the surfboard whistling a tune he didn't recognize at first. He knew it was an old song, but where had it come from? And then the words spilled out in his head. "Pretend you're happy when you're blue," it began. Then something about it not being hard to do. He groaned. Even his own brain was against him.

* * *

Kelly wasn't gone long, though she stopped at the market for some baby supplies. But when she got back, something felt wrong. She stopped and listened. Nothing. At least Mei wasn't awake and crying.

She started toward the bedroom, but something stopped her. There was a rustling. There, she heard it again. The sound was coming from a room she assumed was a den, and something about it seemed downright furtive.

Setting down the bags she'd brought, Kelly walked toward the room as quietly as she could and gave the unlatched door a little push. It opened without a creak, and she saw a tall, curvaceous, platinum-blonde woman with a superstar tan going through a large wooden file cabinet. She had her cell phone to her ear at the same time and was talking softly.

"I'm telling you, there's not even a picture book about Ambria around here. Nothing. I can't find one little hint that he even knows what the country is."

Suddenly the woman realized someone was in the doorway, and she whirled to face Kelly, staring into her astonished eyes.

"Uh, talk to you later," she said into the phone. "I've gotta go." She snapped it shut.

"What are you doing?" Kelly demanded.

"Well, hello." The woman said with a smile. She was quite attractive in a tight-bodiced, bleached-blonde, fire-engine-red lipstick sort of way. But somehow, Kelly missed the appeal.

"Why are you going through Joe's things?" she demanded. She was pretty sure she already knew who this was, but it would be nice to have confirmation.

"Oh!" The woman looked stunned that she might be suspected of doing anything wrong. Her eyes widened in faux innocence. "I'm not. Not really. I just wanted to see how Joe had his files set up, because I'm going to be giving him a bid on renovating this den, doing a little decorating, and I wanted to see—" she waved a hand majestically "—I wanted to see how he works."

Kelly didn't buy it for a minute. Frowning, she balanced on the balls of her feet, feeling fierce and protective. "You were going through his files."

The woman was beginning to lose some of that overweening self-confidence she exuded. She actually looked a little worried.

"No. Oh no. I was checking things over so that…"

"Hey, Kelly. You made it back."

It was probably a good thing that Joe appeared at this point. Kelly was not in a forgiving mood. He came into the room carrying a large screwdriver and looking from one woman to the other.

"I was just putting up a growth chart for Mei in the bathroom," he explained, then frowned. "What's the problem?"

Kelly pointed accusingly in the woman's direction. "She was going through your files."

Joe appeared bemused. "Was she? But Kelly, I basically told her to." He gave her an indulgent smile, as though she were a little kid who just didn't get it. "This is Sonja. The woman who did such a great job on Mei's room. She's just looking around, trying to get the lay of the land in case I hire her to redecorate my living areas."

Oh no, she wasn't. Joe hadn't seen what Kelly had seen, heard what she'd heard. She had caught Sonja going through the files, and now she wanted to know exactly what she'd been looking for.

"This was a lot more than merely surveying the work space," she began.

He didn't want to hear it. "Listen, I'm sure it's a misunderstanding. She's okay. I knew she was going to be snooping around, getting ideas."

Sonja sensed victory and she smiled like the Cheshire cat. Kelly bit her lip in frustration. She couldn't understand why Joe didn't see that.

"Sonja, this is Kelly," he was saying, as though introducing two women he was sure would be fast friends. "She's helping me out with Mei, since the nanny didn't show up."

"I'm so glad you got someone." The tall, beautiful woman tossed her hair back and turned her dazzling smile on Joe. "I'd volunteer myself, but you know how it is. I'm good at kiddy decorating but I don't know a thing about actually taking care of the little darlings." She glanced Kelly's way. "I leave that to nannies like your friend here."

"I'm not a nanny," Kelly stated.

"Well, you're doing nanny work, aren't you?" she noted, never taking her eyes off Joe.

"What's wrong with child care?" Kelly asked, at a loss as to why the woman would be saying that with just a hint of disdain. "Every mother on earth does it."

Sonja had obviously grown bored with the conversation. She rolled her eyes in Joe's direction, then sighed. "Well, I'm going to have to get going. Places to go, promises to keep. You know how it is." Her slick smile was all for Joe. "But don't forget, we need to get together and go over my ideas. And talk about my tour plans—plans I'm hoping to rope you into." She gave him a flirtatious smile. "In the meantime, don't forget you owe me a dinner." She tapped her index finger on his chest. "You promised."

Joe was grinning back, basking in all this obvious admiration. It made Kelly's blood boil to see how easily he seemed to fall for it.

"Sure," he said happily. "We'll have to see what we can do to keep that promise."

"I'm looking forward to it."

To Kelly's shock, the woman leaned close and gave Joe a kiss on the cheek, then turned and winked insolently in Kelly's direction. Her attitude very plainly said, *Don't think you've got this one on the line yet, sister. I've got skills you can only dream of.*

She started out, and Joe gave Kelly a happy shrug, then turned back to his carpentry job in the bathroom. Kelly hesitated a moment, then decided to go after Sonja. That woman had some explaining to do.

CHAPTER SEVEN

"WAIT A MINUTE," Kelly said from the curb as Sonja reached for her car door.

The woman turned back with a frown, and Kelly hesitated again. She wanted to accuse her, wanted to question her, but didn't want to do anything that would make Sonja think she was right to suspect Joe had a connection to Ambria. Kelly had to be very careful here.

"No matter what Joe thinks, you and I both know you were searching for information in his files."

She shrugged, putting on her huge dark sunglasses. "Like he said, you misunderstood."

"No. I heard you on the phone, talking about some sort of evidence of a connection you were looking for. If you want to know something about Joe, why can't you just ask him to his face?"

"My dear, once again, you've misunderstood."

"Have I?"

"Yes. Don't you worry your little head about all this. Just take good care of that baby." And she slipped into the car and drove off.

Kelly drew a deep breath. This wasn't good. She was sure of what she'd heard when she'd entered into that room. If Sonja wasn't after Joe because she thought he was Ambrian, she was after him for something else. At any rate, he had to be prepared for whatever was going to be coming down the pike.

Kelly went back into the house and slipped into Mei's room to check on her. The precious child was sound asleep, and Kelly watched her for a moment, wondering what her life would be like. Surely she would warm to Joe soon. He would hire a good nanny and their life together would develop over time. Something inside Kelly yearned to know the outcome, but she knew she probably never would. That was all in the future, however. She was more concerned with keeping them both—Joe and Mei—safe right now. And that was really beginning to worry her.

She had to convince Joe that his friend Sonja was not on the up and up. Slipping back out of Mei's room, Kelly searched for Joe and finally found him just finishing up.

Not giving him time to distract her with jokes, she quickly told him about what she'd heard Sonja say on the phone, and when she'd confronted her a few minutes later. He listened, nodding and looking interested, but he didn't act like a man ready to jump in the car and head for higher ground.

"She was sent here for a reason. I'm sure of it, Joe. She suspects something. She was hunting for evidence of an Ambrian connection."

He was picking up his tools and looking rather proud of the new wooden measuring chart he'd affixed to the wall. Instead of being concerned about what she was saying, he stood back and admired it.

"Well, since I don't have any evidence of an Ambrian connection," he said casually, making a tiny adjustment to the way the chart was hanging, "she's out of luck, isn't she?"

"But don't you see? Just the fact that there are suspicions shows the danger you're in."

He raised one dark eyebrow as he gazed at her cynically. "As a matter of fact, Kelly, the only evidence of an Ambrian connection around here is you."

She opened her mouth but no words came out. What could she say to that? In a way, he was right.

"I hope you were discreet," he added with a hint of laughter in his blue eyes.

"Yes, Joe. I was very discreet." She shook her head as she thought of the last person who had warned her of that. "So discreet, Jim would have been proud of me."

He frowned. "Who's Jim?"

She sighed. "My boss. The one who told me not to come looking for you."

His flash of a grin was electric. "I'm glad you're such a disobedient worker."

She looked up in surprise and her gaze met his and held. That electricity was still there and it sparked between them for just a second, making her nerves tingle and her heart beat a little faster.

She turned away. She didn't want to feel this sort of spicy provocation. This wasn't why she was here.

But she needed to make some things clear to him, and she wasn't sure how she was going to do it. She had to explain more firmly to Joe what this was all about—that he might just have that elusive Ambrian connection, and if he did, he had to face the consequences of that fact. Because those consequences could be lethal.

Turning back, she steeled herself and looked at him sternly. "Joe, you need to listen to me, and you need to take what I say seriously. No kidding around."

The humor drained from his eyes and he waited, poised. She blinked at him in wonder. He was actually receptive to what she had to say. She felt a rush of affection for him and that only made it all so much harder.

Kelly sucked in a deep breath. "I think you have to get out of here. I think you have to go."

His face hardened. "What are you talking about?"

"They've found you," she said earnestly, trying to convince him. "These people—Sonja and whoever she was talking to on the phone—must be either representatives of the Granvilli clan or someone in sympathy with them. Joe, you can't stay here. You can't risk it."

He was frowning. "Risk what? Kelly, I'm not your prince. I'm not *their* prince, either."

"But you see…" She stopped, tortured and not sure how she was going to convince him. "It doesn't even matter if you are or you aren't. If the Granvillis think you're one of the princes, it's the same as if you are. And they'll probably try to kill you."

There. The words were out. She gazed at him, hardly believing she'd actually said it. He stared back, his eyes cold as ice. She couldn't tell what he was thinking, but he took his time giving her an answer, so she knew he had to be considering what she'd said.

"Listen, Kelly," he replied at last, "I've got a few skills in the hopper. I think I can take care of any threat of that kind." He smiled, but there was no humor in it. "I'm not exactly a sitting duck."

She shook her head. She had no doubt he could hold his own in a fair fight. She knew he was a trained warrior. But that didn't mean he could guard against everything. Why did he refuse to understand?

"You can't fight off the secret service of a whole country on your own," she told him ardently.

He looked pained. "Now you're being melodramatic. Slow down. Take it easy. I'm not going anywhere."

"You can't just think of yourself now, you know," she added, trying to drive her fears home to him. "You have Mei to consider."

"Of course." A slight frown wrinkled the skin between his brows. "I'm very aware of that."

"Are you?" She felt tears prickling her eyelids. Why wasn't she better at expressing just how serious this was?

Joe took her by the shoulders and looked down into her face. "You want me to run off and hide somewhere because a woman I hired to decorate my baby's room looks at me and thinks of Ambria." He shook his head as though he just couldn't buy it. "How do you know she isn't one of the good guys? Why are you so sure she didn't emigrate as a refugee, just like your parents and you? How do you know she doesn't want to recruit me into fighting the Granvillis just like you do?"

He had her there. Kelly had no idea, no evidence at all. But she had a very strong feeling. Still, held here in his grip, she could only look up at his beautiful face and wonder why he wouldn't let her save him.

"I'm not getting into anyone else's wars," he told her, searching her eyes as though he thought he might find something to reassure him there. "I've had enough of that. Enough for a lifetime."

"Joe, I…I understand…I…" She was babbling. What else could she do? He was so close Kelly could feel the heat from his body. Her head was full of his clean, masculine scent and her heart was beating like a drum. She couldn't think straight, couldn't manage a coherent sentence. All she could do was stare at the beautiful smooth and tanned skin revealed by the opening in his shirt. Her head felt light and she was afraid she was going to pass out.

Suddenly, as though he'd realized he was holding her shoulders and wasn't sure why, he pulled his hands away and she swayed before him, blinking rapidly and trying to catch her breath.

"Are you okay?" he asked.

She nodded, embarrassed beyond belief. "Yes," she managed to say. "I'm okay. Really."

"I'm sorry to be so adamant about this, Kelly," he told her, his brow still furrowed. "I've got my own problems, and I'm not in the mood for more."

"Of course not," she murmured, but he was already turning away. She watched him go, and slowly began to regain equilibrium, glad he had been too wrapped up in their argument to notice what a fool she was making of herself. She'd never realized she could be such an easy mark for a sexy man. She was going to have to be more careful.

Inhaling another deep breath, she got back with the program. Something had to be done to convince Joe to take the threat of harm more seriously. Kelly thought for a moment, then nodded and went straight for her cell phone. Time to call in the cavalry on this one.

When her boss answered, she smiled, glad to hear his voice again.

"So, Kelly, how's it going, anyway? Found any more princes out there in sunny California?" He chuckled.

She had to bite her lip to keep from reacting sharply. She was so tired of being the focus of all their joking at the agency. "Princes, princesses, earls, dukes. They're a dime a dozen out here, Jim. You ought to come out and find one for yourself."

"Hey, I thought you were going to San Diego. Not Hollywood."

"Cute." She sighed. "Actually, I think Joe is the real deal. I just haven't been able to convince him of it yet."

There was a pause, then Jim said, "You mean he doesn't know if he is or isn't?"

"Nope."

"Wow. That's a new one."

"Yes, it is. And pretty frustrating."

"Hmm." Jim seemed to agree. "But tell me this. If he doesn't know the truth, who does?"

"I do. And apparently someone else suspects as well. Jim, can you do a little research for me? I need some background on a woman calling herself Sonja Smith."

She heard him choke on his cup of coffee, and sighed. "Yes, I know. It's not likely to be her real name. But she's affiliated with a baby boutique here in San Diego." She gave him the rest of what she knew, and he agreed, reluctantly, to look into it for her.

"Don't expect too much," he said in his droll way. "In my experience, every Madame Smith tends to evaporate as soon as you shine a light on her."

"I know. But she's been prodding Joe about Ambria. Now how many people without ulterior motives are likely to be doing that?"

"Not many," he agreed. "Of course, there's you."

She groaned. "Spare me the lecture. I've already heard it."

He snickered and Kelly felt her face go hot. How she would love to prove all the naysayers she worked with wrong!

"Okay, now here's a question for you," Jim said. "When are you coming back?"

"Back?" Her hand tightened on her phone. "I'll be in on Monday. Why?"

"Because it turns out half the office will be going to the funeral in Piasa. We're going to need you here to cover."

Kelly frowned. "What's going on?"

"It looks like one of your lost princes really has shown up."

"What?" Her heart leaped.

"There are rumors that Prince Darius has been seen."

"No!"

"Seems he was living with a family in Holland for many years, then he was a businessman in London."

This was fantastic news. All these months, ever since she'd presented the people she worked for with an outline of her theory on what might have happened to the lost princes, she'd had nothing but doubt and ridicule thrown her way. If they began to show up, her vindication would be sweet.

"And all the time, no one knew."

"That seems to be the case." Jim cleared his throat. "And now he's on his way to Piasa, as is just about everyone in the Ambrian universe."

"Except me." She knew she had no hope of getting the assignment. She was the lowest level employee there, and would be left behind to cover for everyone else. That went without saying. But she could dream, couldn't she?

"I'm not going, either. We'll be here analyzing the dispatches. You know the drill."

"Indeed."

"So, when can you get back?"

"Saturday is the very soonest I can manage."

"Make it early on Saturday. This isn't a joke, Kelly. We're really going to need you."

This news was so exciting, Kelly wanted to dance all the way back to Mei's room. She wanted to tell Joe, but she stopped herself. Not yet. First, she had to show him that there was really a reason he should care.

Mei was still asleep, so Kelly went out to the entryway to pick up some of the packages she'd brought. First she changed out of the clothes she'd worn for two days now, and put on a pair of snug jeans and a cropped seersucker top that showed off a bit of belly button. She spent a few minutes putting baby food into a cupboard, then went out on the deck, where Joe was reading a newspaper.

"What have you heard about the nanny?" Kelly asked him.

He turned and smiled in a way that let her know he liked how she looked out here in the late afternoon sun.

"She'll be here tomorrow afternoon."

"Oh. Good. I hope I'll have time to train her on what Mei likes."

He gave her a lopsided grin. "You've already become an expert on that, have you?"

She answered with a jaunty tilt of her chin. "Sort of."

The truth was, she was falling in love with the child. But since doing so was crazy and would only lead to more heartbreak, she kept quiet about it. Why tell him, anyway?

"Mrs. Gomez is her name. A good friend of mine runs this agency. She'll make sure she's completely vetted. I trust her judgment."

Kelly nodded, biting her lower lip. If she was really honest, she would admit that she didn't relish the prospect of someone else taking over Mei's care.

"The first thing to notice is if she starts asking any questions about Ambria," she pointed out as she made her way to the railing and leaned against it, looking toward the ocean.

"You got it. We don't trust those Ambria-asking people."

She turned her head to glare at him. "This is serious, Joe. Your friend Sonja might just use her influence to stick a ringer in, someone who would spy for the regime. You never know."

"Ah, come on," he said, rising to join her at the railing. The sun was low in the sky and a beautiful sunset was promising to develop. "Even Sonja has her good points."

From the thread of amusement in his voice, Kelly knew he was goading her just for the fun of it. She could either challenge him or play along. She gave him a sideways look and impulsively decided on the latter.

"Wow, you were bowled over by her beauty, weren't you?" she said accusingly.

He shrugged, his eyelids heavy as he looked at her. "You've got to admit she's pretty nice to look at."

"Right." Kelly made a face. "No wonder the Mata Hari types succeed so well with the dopey gender. Men are totally blinded by beauty. To the point where they ignore danger."

He managed to look innocent as the driven snow. "Well, yes. What's wrong with that?"

If only he was as innocent as he looked. She forced back a smile. "Men are just clueless. Babes in the woods. Easy prey for the machinations of the fairer sex."

"Is that how you see me?"

She threw out her hands. "If the shoe fits…"

His eyes narrowed cynically. "Well, Kelly, my dear,

look who's talking. I mean, you've clearly got a crush on me."

Her mouth dropped at that outrageous statement. "I do not!"

"Really? Why not?"

His expression was endearingly surprised and woe-begone, and she had to laugh, knowing he was teasing her.

"You're crazy," she told him. "I'm just trying to warn you to beware of Sonja."

"Sure. That comes through loud and clear." He moved a little closer so that their shoulders were touching. "Are you sure you're not jealous?" he asked softly, as though it was a secret he was sharing with her.

"Jealous?" she practically squealed. "Why would I be jealous?"

He looked at her for a long moment, smiling, then shrugged. "You got me there."

She cleared her throat, a bit relieved. "Exactly."

They stayed there for a few minutes, side by side, neither speaking. The sun touched to the ocean, turning the water red and painting the sky in peaches and crimson. Kelly had a wild fantasy of turning to look into Joe's eyes and curling into his arms. The thought almost stopped her heart cold. She bit her lip and wished it away.

Whether he believed it or not, he was a prince of the Ambrian realm. He wasn't for the taking. She had to keep her thoughts away from such things.

Finding out the truth about his heritage and making sure he knew how to make the most of it—that was what she was really here for. The fact that he was about the handsomest man she'd ever seen beyond the silver screen had nothing to do with it. Nothing at all.

She sighed and turned to go in and check on Mei, but he stopped her with a hand on her upper arm.

"Kelly, tell me why," he said, and as she looked into his eyes, it seemed to her they were haunted by some lingering emotion she couldn't quite identify.

"Why what?" she asked, though she knew.

He swept his arm in a wide arch. "Why all this? Why you're here. Why you want to do this." He shook his head, his gaze searching hers. "But most of all, why you're so intent on putting me up as royalty on a tiny little godforsaken island no one goes to."

She licked her dry lips and searched for the words to explain, words that would convince him what he had to do.

"I told you I'm an analyst for the Ambrian News Agency. I'm the newest, youngest employee, even though I've been there almost two years now. Everybody treats me like a kid."

He pulled back his hand and she returned to leaning on the rail next to him.

"Everything interesting goes to one of the men. Every time a juicy assignment comes up, it's the usual, 'Sorry, dear, we need someone with experience for this one.' And when I ask how I'm supposed to get experience if no one lets me try, all I get are blank stares."

He nodded. "The old Catch 22."

"Exactly. So I decided to pick something no one else was working on, and make it my special field of expertise." She turned to look directly into his eyes. "I picked you."

He laughed and shook his head.

"I'd already been reading a lot about Ambria, and when I picked up a book about the possibility that there were lost children from the old regime who might still be alive, I knew right away this was it. I started finding out everything I could about them. About you."

He looked skeptical. "Did you find any evidence that they really exist?"

She hesitated. "Well, nothing solid. Not then. But I've read everything I could find on the speculation and the rumors. And I've interviewed a few people who think it's possible. And…"

She stopped. She wasn't ready to tell him about his brother Darius being sighted yet.

"But no one who's actually seen one?" Joe asked when she paused.

She winced. It was a sore point, she had to admit. "No."

"And then you saw my picture in that article last year?"

"Yes." She perked up as she remembered her excitement that day. "I'd been working on a montage of photos from the old monarchy, and I'd gotten so familiar with the faces. When I saw yours, it was like a bolt of lightning hit me. I just knew."

"Whoa. Not so fast." He held up a hand as though he were stopping a train. "You still don't really know anything."

"But I strongly suspect. Don't you?"

He didn't seem happy with that question. "I don't know," he muttered.

"There are ways to find out."

He looked uncomfortable and turned his gaze out toward the ocean.

"What if I don't want to find out?" he asked softly, then he swung back and faced her. "Tell me, how is being one of these royal guys who everyone wants to kill going to enhance my life?"

CHAPTER EIGHT

KELLY BLINKED AT Joe. This was quite a revelation. It had never occurred to her that anyone would want to pass up a chance to be a prince, especially of Ambria. It was an honor. Why didn't he get that?

"Do it for history," she suggested.

"For history?" He raised one eyebrow and looked amused.

"Why not? What have you done for history lately?"

He thought about that for a few seconds, and then started to laugh. "What's history done for me?" he countered.

"We don't know yet." She hesitated, then admitted, "Let's put it this way. In all honesty, if you are one of them, it could do a lot for me."

He nodded. "Your reputation?"

"Yes. I'd finally get a little respect at the agency."

He smiled, admiring the light of ambition in her eyes. She had spirit. He liked a woman with spirit. "Does your work mean that much to you?"

"Sure."

The sound of Mei's voice cut off anything else she

might have been about to say. Once Kelly knew the baby was awake, that was her first priority.

"Want to come help me change her?" she asked him hopefully.

He paused a moment, then shook his head. "I'll get dinner ready."

Disappointed, she went in by herself. Mei was standing at the crib railing and calling out, not crying yet, just letting people know she was ready to get out and join the world again. Kelly laughed and held out her arms. Mei threw out her own arms and laughed, too. Kelly held her tightly, murmuring loving words, and wished with all her heart that she would see this sort of interaction between Mei and her daddy soon. Very, very soon.

What they'd been doing so far wasn't working, and there wasn't much time left. She had to start training Mei to deal with Joe in a good, loving way. In another forty-eight hours, she wasn't going to be here for this little girl. Or for Joe, either.

Having Mei acting this way toward Joe complicated things as far as getting him to accept his place as a prince of Ambria. But in some ways, it was all part of the same challenge. Mei had to accept Joe, Joe had to accept his heritage. And what did Kelly have to accept? The fact that she was starting to fall for him in a big way?

No! Where had that thought come from? Nothing of the sort. She was okay. She'd be leaving soon. This was nothing but an assignment, even if she had assigned it to herself. It was a job she had to do. Falling for Joe was not part of the plan.

The main problem wasn't romance, however. The main problem was getting him to realize how important his position was. She had to back off, calm down and think this through. Why wasn't it working? Why wasn't he sharing her concerns? What was she doing wrong in the way she was presenting it to him? Most of all, why didn't he believe that he was the prince?

Quickly, she went back over what had happened since she'd come face-to-face with him. Of course, at first she'd assumed he knew. She'd never dreamed that he would think she was crazy when she brought up the subject. He had no idea who he really was, and at first he'd taken it as a joke.

But what had she really done to convince him? Why should he believe it? She hadn't presented any evidence to him. That was what was missing. She had to lay the foundation or it wasn't going to work.

Kelly changed Mei, played with her for a few minutes, then got her ready for her dinner. She brought her out and put her in the high chair, then got down a jar of baby food and a long plastic spoon. Meanwhile, she chatted with Joe, who was serving up a frozen lasagna he'd warmed in the oven. He'd also whipped up a couple of delicious salads to go with it.

"Hey," she said in admiration. "This looks great. You can cook for me anytime."

"Is that a promise?" he teased.

But when she met his gaze, she stopped smiling. There was something serious lurking behind his humor. What did it mean? She looked away again.

They sat down and ate, laughing companionably

together over things Mei did. The baby didn't seem to pay much attention to her father now, but at least she wasn't screaming every time he came near her.

"She's getting better, don't you think?" Joe asked hopefully, after he'd handed Mei a sippy cup of milk and she'd hesitated only a moment before taking it and drinking.

"Oh yes. I'm sure of it."

Kelly wasn't sure at all, but she wanted to keep his spirits up.

He looked at her and smiled, and she wondered if he could read her mind.

"So when do you think they'll invade?" Joe asked innocently as they leaned back from their meal.

"Who?" Kelly asked blankly.

"The nefarious Granvilli clan, of course. Tell me, what's their modus operandi? Do they like to sneak in at night when their targets are sleeping? Or do they prefer a full frontal confrontation in broad daylight?"

She groaned. "Now you're just making fun of me." Her eyes flashed. "You'll see. Something very bad will happen and then you'll find I was right."

He tossed down his napkin and laughed. "That's reassuring."

"Sorry," she said, rising to take Mei from her high chair. "I'm trying to be pragmatic and realistic. Too much optimism leaves you unprepared for whatever might be coming next."

Joe stayed where he was while she took Mei off to clean her up and change her. He wasn't sure what he thought about this royalty business. It seemed like a red herring to him. If Kelly wasn't so cute and fun to have around, he would be dismissing the whole thing out of hand. But the longer she helped him with Mei and the more she tried to get him to understand how important she thought this all was, the more he understood just how adorable and sweet *she* was, and the more he wanted to do whatever it took to make her happy. So here he sat, contemplating being a prince.

What the hell?

She came back, baby in tow, and he got up to clear the table and wash the dishes. She didn't say anything, but she had a portfolio with her and she took Mei into the living room. He knew she was up to something. He went on cleaning up from dinner, then went out to the living room to join her.

Kelly stood holding Mei on one hip. As he entered the room, she turned and gave him a tremulous smile. She'd arranged eight-by-ten-inch photographs in groups over every flat surface in the room.

"Meet the royal family," she told him with a flourish.

Joe stared at the pictures, and his heart began to beat faster.

"Where did you get these?" he asked her.

"This is my area of research. I brought them along to show to you."

Taking a deep breath, he began to walk the length of the room, looking at them all, one by one. His mouth was dry and he could tell his hands were shaking. He could tell right away that there was something about these people that he connected with, something familiar that resonated in the core of his being. These pictures were going to change his life.

"Well, what do you think?" Kelly asked, after he'd had a good long time to soak it all in.

He turned and looked at her with troubled eyes. "Tell me exactly who these people are," he said.

She pursed her lips. "I warn you, I'm going to talk about them as though they were your family."

He nodded impatiently. "Whatever. Let's just do this. Let's get it done."

She stopped before the first picture, of a very handsome couple dressed quite formally. "This is King Grandor and Queen Elineas, your father and your mother," she said quietly. "This is their official portrait."

She picked up two enlarged snapshots, one of them just after a tennis game, another of them sitting before a fire, both showing an engaging, happy pair. "And here are pictures of them in more casual settings."

He nodded again. His throat was too tight to speak.

"Here is your uncle Lord Gustav. Your uncle the Archduke Nathanilius—the one who just died. Your aunt, Lady Henrika. Your grandmother, also named Henrika."

Kelly paused, giving Joe time to take it all in. He went over each picture slowly as she named the subject, examining the eyes, studying the faces. She put Mei down in her play chair with all its attached toys and turned back to him. As she watched, she could see that his emotions were calming.

"Are you okay?" she asked him at last.

He looked up, his eyes hooded, as though he wasn't comfortable letting her see just how moving this was to him. "Yes. Why wouldn't I be?"

She shrugged. "For a minute there I thought you were freaking out."

He gave her a smile that was quickly gone. "Not me," he said, going on to the next. "Who are these charming children?"

"These are pictures of your sisters and a couple of your brothers. They were taken just a few weeks before the coup."

Joe lingered, studying each face as if trying to learn as much as he could about that individual. His expression had gone from shock and pure reaction to great interest. The pictures might even be said to be doing what she'd wanted them to.

She pointed to the last one. "And here is a picture of you as a four-year-old."

He stared at that one a long, long time. Did he see himself in it? She wasn't sure. She knew darn well *she* saw him in the adorable little blond boy playing with a pail and shovel in the sand.

Joe felt like a man riding a hang glider over a storm. A part of him was clinging hard to the reality that had been his all his life. The other part was catching a thrilling ride on a rainbow. Which one would he end up with? Was he even allowed to choose, or had these things already been chosen for him?

He'd grown up in a working-class family, learning working-class behavior. His goals had been those of the salt-of-the-earth types he saw around him. He'd always known he had a bright, inquiring mind that wanted to go a bit further than most of those around him cared to venture. He'd certainly taken enough ribbing for it in his past. But once he'd become an adult, he'd lived his own life and followed his own dreams. Still, they'd had nothing to do with royalty.

Royalty only happened in fairy tales. He wasn't a fairy-tale sort of guy. Everything in him wanted to reject this crazy idea. It just wasn't him.

And yet, as he looked at this picture of a little prince playing in the sand, something deep inside him resonated with it just a little. As he stared into the faces of the royals Kelly had put around the room, something in each one caught at a place in his emotional makeup that he wouldn't have dreamed of before she had dropped into his life. But he couldn't admit it to her, not yet.

Finally he looked up and smiled at her. "Thanks, Kelly," he said calmly. "This really does help me get a fix on what this is all about."

She waited, hoping to hear more, but he wasn't forthcoming so she shrugged and went on to the next subject.

"I called my office a few hours ago," she told him significantly. "There's news."

He frowned. "What sort of news?"

"There are rumors that one of your brothers has been sighted on his way to the funeral in Piasa."

Joe's mouth quirked. He didn't bother to remind her there was no proof that any of these were his brothers. Not yet. "Which one?"

"Prince Darius." She pointed to his picture. "He would be almost two years older than you."

Joe nodded, looking at the picture and frowning uncertainly. "More rumors," he murmured. "I'd like to hear some substantiated eyewitness reports."

"Of course. We all would." She searched his face. "So what do you think?" she asked again. "Does seeing these pictures stir any memories? Do you feel a connection to these people on any sort of visceral level?"

She was so eager, so hopeful. He turned away and didn't answer for a long time, gazing at the pictures of his brothers. Finally he gave her a lopsided smile.

"Sure, Kelly. They look like a great bunch. Who wouldn't want to be related to people like this?" Joe raked his fingers through his hair, making it stand up in crazy patches like it did right after surfing. "But just because they and their lifestyle of the time are very attractive, that doesn't mean anything, does it?"

"But what if you are related to them? Wouldn't that be wonderful?"

He gave her a glance that said *Not so fast*. "How can I ever know for sure?"

"DNA testing," she answered quickly. "It will take a while to get the results, but it will be worth it. You'll have the facts."

He stared at her for a long moment in a way that made her think he wasn't really seeing her at all. He was seeing something else—something in the past, something in his future.

"But do I really want them?" He looked tortured as he turned away. "Would knowing mean I would suddenly have a whole new area of responsibility? What would I have to do? And what the hell do I care, anyway?"

She swallowed, surprised and somewhat dismayed at his reaction. "Are you saying you really *don't* care? That you don't want to know?"

"Kelly…" He turned and stared at her again. Then his expression softened and he took her face in his hands and tilted it up. "Kelly, I know you care so much. You've been living with this, trying to get the answer to this puzzle, for so long. You have your own life invested in it. But I don't. Until I see more than this…"

She was breathless, not sure why he was holding her face this way, as though she was someone he treasured. But she liked it—she really liked it. Her body felt as though it were made of liquid, as if she could float away on a magical stream of happiness if she let herself. He was so close and his touch felt so good.

He seemed to be studying her face, but she hardly noticed. She was caught up in a wave of feeling—feeling his hands on her face, feeling his breath on her lips, feeling his affection, even his desire. Was that right? Wasn't that the flicker of something hot and raw that she saw in the depths of his eyes? Was she imagining it?

As if to answer that question, he dropped a quick, soft kiss on her lips, and then reluctantly—she could swear it was reluctantly—drew away.

"I've already got a life planned out, Kelly," he told her. "I don't need a major change. I'm not sure I could handle it."

Her face felt cool where his palms had been, and now her heart was chilled by what he was saying.

"I…I think you could handle just about anything," she said, working to regain her equilibrium. "I've seen you surf."

His quick flash of a grin reassured her, but he still looked as though he wanted to go. Maybe he needed to. Maybe he needed to assimilate the information he'd taken in here. Still, *she* needed more from *him*. She had only a short time left and she had to get all she could from it.

"Wait," she said, afraid he would leave the room entirely. "Please, Joe. Do one more thing for me."

He looked into her eyes with a tenderness that confused her. "Anything," he replied.

She took in a deep breath. "Sit down here on the couch with me for a few minutes. Tell me about what you remember of your childhood. Help me fill in some of the blanks."

"Sure." He shrugged, then glanced at Mei. "Is she going to last?"

Kelly hesitated. "I think so. She's still tired from her flight, I think. Baby jet lag. So she'll probably go down soon. But we'll hope for the best."

Kelly sat and so did he.

"The information I have on your background is really sketchy," she began. "I know you spent your early years in London. The woman listed as your mother died, and you were adopted by your aunt and uncle, and they brought you to New York. By the time you were a teenager, the family had moved here to San Diego."

He gazed at her in wonder. "How do you know all this stuff?"

She shrugged. "I know where to look. It's all in public records, and not that hard to get when you know what to ask for." She gave him a quick smile. "It's my job, remember?"

He began to look at her as though he wasn't sure if she was the same Kelly he thought he knew. "Are you some kind of private eye?"

"I've told you all about it before. I'm an analyst. An investigator of sorts. But really just an analyst."

He was still looking at her as though he wasn't too sure, but she was ready to move on.

"Listen, I know about your service with the Army Rangers in Southeast Asia. And I know a little bit about what you went through in the Philippines."

He glanced at her and bit his tongue. There were things he could say, but he wasn't going to say them. She might think she knew, but there was no way she could know the half of it.

"I know about how you were wounded. In fact, it was that article in a local newspaper I just happened to see, all about your wounds and how you were recuperating. That's how I first found out about you. What I don't know is all the connections in between. Tell me why you went into the army instead of going to college. Tell me how you ended up being adopted by those people." She put her hands out, palms up. "Tell me the story from your point of view."

He watched Mei playing with a stuffed clown for a moment, then took a deep breath. "Okay, here goes. Here's what the woman I called 'Mum' always told me."

"Your, uh, mother?"

"No. My mother was a maid who actually did work for the royal family of some country. Mum never seemed to be sure what one, but it could have been Ambria, I suppose. My mother's name was Sally Tanner. She wasn't married and no one knows who my father was. She brought me back to England when I was four, but she died when I was five. I actually remember her a bit. Just a little bit."

He paused for a moment, recalling it all. Yes, he remembered her. But he didn't remember loving her. And that had bothered him all his life.

"I got passed around from one relative to another for a few years and finally got adopted by a sister of Sally's. Martha and Ned Tanner. Martha is the one I called Mum. They brought me along when they emigrated to New York, and we moved to California when I was twelve."

"So you have a family," she noted, relieved to hear it.

He shrugged. "I *had* a family," he corrected. "A family of sorts. I never felt like I was any more than an afterthought, though. I never knew why they decided to adopt me. There was never any real closeness."

He stopped. What the hell was he doing, opening up old wounds to a woman he'd only just met? A woman he knew was fishing for exactly this type of information. Was he crazy? This was the sort of garbage that stirred up old resentments and made them fester. He never told anyone this stuff. Why was he telling her? He was going to stop. Let her find out what she wanted to know by going to these sources she seemed to be so good at finding.

Incredibly, despite his determination, he heard himself talking again. He was telling her more. Unbelievable.

"I grew up pretty much like any other American kid, playing baseball and football and living a typical suburban American life. Ned and Martha got divorced and things got a lot worse financially after that. My so-called brother and sister both began to get into trouble. Things just generally fell apart. So when I graduated high school, I wanted to get as far away from them all as possible. I joined the army. And I guess you know most of the rest."

She nodded, touched and saddened by what he'd gone through as a child. She was so sure he was royal, and yet he'd grown up in hard circumstances, the hardest being not having anyone to really love him. She wanted to put her arms around him and tell him it was okay, but she knew he wouldn't welcome something like that. Besides, what could she promise him? That life would be better from now on? That was something she really couldn't manipulate for him. Better to keep quiet.

By now, Mei was fussing and needed attention. Kelly rose, put a hand on his shoulder and said softly, "Thank you for telling me that, Joe. I know it's an intrusion to even ask you, so I really do appreciate it."

He caught her hand and brought it to his lips, kissing the palm in a way that startled her.

"Isn't it obvious I'll do just about anything for you?" he said, pretending to be teasing, but coming across as serious as she'd ever seen him. He let her go tend to the baby, but her heart was thumping.

She'd spent a lifetime finding all the men she met and dated completely inadequate. And now she'd turned around and fallen in love with a prince.

Mei, who had been so good for the last two days, fell apart when Kelly took her to her room. She cried and she wailed and she sobbed, and nothing could console her. Kelly rocked her and walked her and tried every trick she'd seen her sister-in-law employ. Nothing worked.

Joe looked in on them. "Anything I can do?" he asked.

Kelly shook her head. "She's just so tired, but she can't fall asleep," she told him. "I may have to put her down and let her cry herself to sleep, but I hate to do it. That can take hours."

He groaned. "Oh, well. You're a better man than I am, Gunga Din," he said as he walked back to the other room.

Kelly wasn't sure what that meant, but she knew it was a compliment, so took it in good spirits. But she was getting desperate as far as this baby was concerned.

She held Mei and rocked her and hummed a tune or two, trying to think of something she could sing besides "Rock-a-bye Baby," which she'd already done to death.

And suddenly one came to her. She hummed it for a moment and then began to sing. It was in a foreign tongue, but the words came naturally to her, and she realized after a moment that it was in Ambrian.

She didn't remember ever singing this song before, and yet she seemed to know all the words. She sang it more softly, again and again, and Mei finally began to quiet. It was the only thing that seemed to please the child. In a few minutes, she was asleep.

Kelly kept singing. She knew how easily babies came awake again and she was going to make sure this one was out. At the same time, she was marveling at the mind's ability to pull things from the past, things one didn't even know one possessed. She was singing a song in Ambrian that she was sure her mother must have sung to her when she was a baby. It was all there, sounds more than words, but nevertheless, complete. It felt like a miracle.

Joe heard the whole thing. He sat in the living room and listened to Kelly singing a song in a language he didn't understand, and suddenly he found he had tears streaming down his cheeks. He knew that song. Not consciously, not overtly, but his heart knew it. His soul had been nurtured by it years ago. It was a part of his heritage. He could never lose it.

And now he knew the truth. He was Ambrian. There was no denying it any longer.

CHAPTER NINE

RISING SLOWLY FROM his chair, Joe went to the garage and rummaged around until he found his old army duffel bag. Deep inside, down at the bottom, he found an old cigar box wrapped in rubber bands, and pulled it out. Most of the bands disintegrated as he tried to remove them, and the box opened easily. Inside were artifacts of a life he didn't really remember, and a place he didn't really know. He'd never understood what they were. Maybe Kelly would be able to interpret them for him. He tucked the box under his arm and went back into the house.

She had just put Mei down and was coming out of the room when she met Joe in the hall. He showed her the box.

"Come on into the living room. I want you to take a look at this," he said.

He spread the items out on the coffee table, under the light, and the two of them looked at them. Kelly's heart was beating out of her chest. There were three gold buttons with lion heads carved in them, such as might have been on a little boy's dress jacket. There was a small child's prayer book, a small signet ring, and a brightly colored ribbon with a tin medal dangling from it.

Kelly picked up the prayer book. There was an inscription in the front, written in Ambrian. She wasn't great at the language, but she knew enough to translate, "To my most adorable little son. Say your prayers! Your Mama."

Kelly could hardly breathe. She looked at Joe. "Where did you get these things?"

He shook his head. "I don't know. I've always had them. I assumed my mother, Sally Tanner, had collected them for me. I've never really paid any attention to them. I'm not sure why I've even kept them."

Kelly nodded, her eyes shining. "You understand what this means, don't you?"

He groaned and tipped his head back. "Probably."

"You are almost certainly…" she swallowed hard and forced herself to say it "…Prince Cassius."

"But what if I don't want to be?" he asked.

"Joe…"

He put up a hand to stop her and give himself space to explain his current thinking. "What I'm going to say now may sound like blasphemy to you. I'm a simple guy. I was raised by simple people. I've lived a simple life."

She was shaking her head. "I don't think what you've done with your life is simple at all."

"But it's not an upper-class, royal life. Kelly, once you get to my age, I don't think there's any turning back. I am what I am and what I'll always be."

She pressed her lips together, thinking. She understood

his argument, but didn't believe it was valid, and she was trying to figure out how to counter it successfully.

"I think you have a skewed idea of what royalty is really like," she said at last. "As people, they're not necessarily all that special. These days a lot of them seem pretty much like everyone else."

Joe made a face. "You mean like that prince of that little country I saw on the news the other day—the one who photographers caught with about twenty naked ladies running around on his yacht with him?"

Kelly laughed. "Those were not ladies."

"Probably not." He rubbed his head and grimaced. "Now, I'm not going to claim that such a thing wouldn't appeal to the male animal in me, but they said this prince had a wife and a baby at home. What normal man would think it was okay to do that?"

She sighed. "Sure, there are some royalty who take advantage of their opportunities in a rotten way. But there are plenty that don't."

"Name one."

She hesitated. "I don't have to name one," she said evasively. "And anyway, if there weren't any, you could be the first." Her smile was triumphant. "You haven't grown up being overindulged. You've got your own brand of honesty and integrity. You won't go bad."

His own smile was crooked but his eyes were still sad. "Your faith in me is touching," he said.

"Why not? You deserve it." She picked up the little gold buttons. "I'll bet these were on the jacket you wore the night you escaped."

He gave her a startled look. "What makes you so sure I escaped?"

She put them down and sat back. "Okay, here's what I see as what probably happened—based on a lot of research I've done on the subject and a lot of memoirs I've read. The castle was attacked. Your parents had already set up an elaborate set of instructions to certain servants, each of whom was assigned a different royal child, to smuggle you out if the worst happened."

"And you know this how?"

She shrugged. "People who knew about it wrote explanations later. Anyway, the worst did happen. The Granvillis began to burn the castle. Your mother's favorite lady-in-waiting was supposed to take care of you—she wrote about that in her book on the coup. But something went wrong and you ended up being whisked away by one of the kitchen maids instead, an English girl named Sally Tanner. Here's what I think happened after that. Sally catches a ride to the mainland in a rowboat. The trip takes most of the night, and it becomes impossible to hide you from the others escaping as well. She doesn't want them to know you are one of the royals, so she claims you as her own secret love child, and as no one else on the boat actually knows her, this is accepted."

His face was white. She stopped. "Joe, what is it?"

"I remember that boat ride," he said hoarsely. "The feeling of terror on that trip has stayed with me ever since."

Reaching out, she took his hand in hers. "Now Sally has you and doesn't know what to do with you. She didn't get the special instructions the others are following. She just grabbed a kid she saw needed help, and saved him. Now what?"

Joe laced fingers with Kelly's. "This is all sounding so right to me," he told her. "I can't believe you know this much."

"It's partly speculation, but speculation built on facts," she said. "Anyway, she doesn't know what to do. Should she try to contact someone? But that might be certain death for you. She knows, by now, what happened to your parents. She can't see any alternative. She might as well take you with her and hope something happens that makes it possible to find out what to do with you. She takes you to London to stay with her family, who aren't really sure who you are or what to make of you. They suspect you really are Sally's, a secret child she hadn't told them about. She tells them your name is Joe. Before Sally can contact anyone to find out what to do with you, she dies in an accident."

He nodded. "And that's why they tell me she's my mother." His half smile was sad. "And that's why I can't remember loving her the way a son should. When she died, I was probably still waiting for my real mom to show up and take me home."

"There you go."

He sat brooding for a few minutes. Kelly was still holding his hand, and she smiled at him.

"Joe, I'm sure this is all hard to hear, but you needed to know. Not only so you can decide if you want to take your rightful place in Ambrian society, but also so you can protect yourself. You need to be careful of people like Sonja. Or anyone who might come from the current regime."

He frowned, still trying to assimilate it all. "Tell me again what is so bad about the current regime?"

"They killed your parents."

His eyebrows rose. "There is that." He thought of those beautiful people in the photographs. To think of his parents as a king and queen still seemed utterly ridiculous. But that couple had looked right to him. He liked them. He had to admit there was a crack in his heart when he thought of what might have been—if only the coup hadn't happened.

Joe looked at Kelly, enjoying the way her blonde curls were rioting around her pretty face. She was so gracious and decent and caring. And basically happy. How was he going to make sure that Mei turned out that way?

"Kelly, you said something earlier about some bad things that had happened in your life. I feel like I'm hogging all the emotion around here. Let's hear your story."

"Oh gosh, it was nothing like what happened to you. I'm embarrassed to even bring it up. It's nothing at all. It's just everyday life disappointments. You know how that is…."

"Come on." He tugged on her hand. "I told you about myself. Your turn. Don't hold out on me."

"Joe…"

"You told me about your family, and that there was a time when you were all very close."

"Yes." She went still. "That's true. Actually, I had a wonderful childhood. I tend to forget that sometimes."

"You see, that's what I want for Mei. Somehow I want to create that warm, safe, nurturing ideal, like the Norman Rockwell pictures, for her. Everything's got to be perfect."

Unspoken were the words *like I never had* and she heard them loud and clear. She often felt the same way.

"So come on. What about your family?"

"What about it? I've had one. It's pretty much gone now."

Funny, but this was an area where they had some things in common. No real family around. Not anymore.

"But your brothers and those nieces and nephews."

She nodded. "I see them at Thanksgiving and Christmas. The rest of the year they forget I exist."

Joe looked surprised and somewhat shocked. "Kelly, I didn't realize…"

"Oh, I don't mean to sound bitter. Really. But they're young professionals with young families, and they have very full lives, lives I don't fit into very easily."

He looked puzzled. "What happened to your parents?"

"My mother died when I was eighteen. When she was alive, I definitely had a family. She was the glue that kept us all together. And she was my biggest booster, my best friend. So her death was a major blow to me. It really threw me for a loop for months." And it still gave her a horrible, hollow feeling in the pit of her stomach whenever she thought of it.

"And your father?"

"My father." She took a deep breath and thought about him. A tall, handsome man with distinguished gray hair at his temples, he'd been a prime target for hungry females of a certain age as soon as her mother had died. They'd swarmed around him like bees, and he didn't last long. Kelly remembered with chagrin how she'd vowed to dedicate her life to taking care of the man, only to turn around and find him carrying on with a woman in tight T-shirts and short shorts, the sort of floozy her mother wouldn't have given the time of day to.

"My sixty-five-year-old father married a woman in her late thirties who wanted to pretend I didn't exist," she said, not even trying to hide the bitterness she felt this time. "They live in Florida. I never see them."

"Wow. I'm sorry."

He was looking at her as though he wasn't sure who she was. From the beginning, she'd fit his image of the perfect daughter in the perfect family full of people who loved each other and made sure things went right. Lots of presents at birthdays. A huge turkey at Thanksgiving. All the things he'd never had. And now to find out she was as lonely as he was... What a revelation. Joe had a hard time dealing with it.

Where, after all, was happiness in the world? Maybe you just had to make your own.

"So you see, we're alike," she said with a wistful smile. "We both had great families, and then we blew it."

"We didn't blow it," he countered. "Somebody blew it for us."

"Regardless, it was blown."

"So that's the goal," he said, holding her hand in his and moving in closer. "Don't blow it for the next generation."

She smiled at him. He was going to kiss her soon and she was ready for it. In fact, she could hardly wait. "You got it."

"We need to concentrate on finding good people to marry," he said, his brow furrowed as he thought about this. At the same time, he was cupping her cheek with his hand and studying her lips. Anticipation—what a sweet thing it was.

She nodded, feeling breathless. "Of course, that won't be any problem for you," she noted drily.

"What are you talking about?" he asked as he widened his hand and raked his fingers into the hair behind her head, taking her into his temporary possession.

She made a sound of derision. "You are the type of beautiful man that women swoon over all the time," she said, swooning a little bit herself.

He frowned. "So?" He pulled her closer.

She pushed his hand away. "I refuse to swoon," she claimed, but her words were a little slurred. His attentions were already having their effect.

A smile began to form in his eyes. "So you're an anti-swooner, huh?"

"You could say that. I'm anti feeding your oversize ego any more than absolutely necessary."

He dropped a soft kiss on her lips, then drew back so that he could look at her. "At least you admit my ego deserves a bit of nutrition."

"Hah!" She rolled her eyes. "Not really. I think it needs a strict diet." She smiled, checking out his reaction. "And maybe a few hard truths to help it get over itself."

"Hard truths, huh?" He began to pull her into his arms. "And you're just the person to give them to me. Right?"

She pretended to be challenging him at every turn. "Why not?"

He gave her that helpless look he put on when he was teasing. "Can I help it if women love me?"

"Yes." Kelly tried to pull out of his embrace and failed miserably. "Yes, you can. You cannot be quite so accessible. You walk around so free and easy with that lascivious grin…."

He stopped and looked thoroughly insulted. "What lascivious grin?"

"The one you've got on." She tapped his lips with her forefinger. "Right there on your face."

"You mean this one?" He leaned over her, finding the way to her mouth and kissing her with passion and conviction. "See?" he murmured against her cheek. "Women can't help but kiss me."

Kelly didn't answer. She was too busy doing exactly that.

The morning dawned brilliantly. The sun was shining in glorious celebration and the ocean gleamed like a trove of diamonds. They ate breakfast on the deck, watching the day begin. Joe had made a trayful of scrambled eggs and a pile of English muffins and honey, and Kelly fed

Mei from a small jar of baby oatmeal, then gave her some of the eggs as well. They talked and laughed as the seagulls swooped around, hoping for a handout. Kelly couldn't remember a more wonderful breakfast at any time in her life. This was the best.

A little later, after changing Mei and cleaning up from breakfast, she carried the baby out to find Joe sitting on the deck, looking a bit forlorn.

He'd decided to ignore all this royalty talk for now. He needed time to let it sink in. Today, he was all about Mei and doing what he could to change her mind about him.

"Hi," Kelly said. "What are you doing?"

"Sitting here feeling sorry for myself."

Reality was a bummer. He thought back to the dreams he used to have about what it was going to be like once Mei arrived. Father and daughter. He was already running little clips in his head of himself teaching her how to throw a ball. When he explained that to Kelly, she laughed at him.

"She's a girl. She might not be into sports."

"What are you, some kind of chauvinist?"

"No." Kelly looked lovingly into Mei's small cute face. "What about it, little girl? Want to play ball? Or take ballet lessons?"

Joe shook his head, enjoying how the two of them interacted. Mei was such a darling child. If only she liked him.

"Whatever she wants to do, we'll do," he said firmly. "She's in the driver's seat on that one. It's just that…" He sighed. It didn't pay to get your hopes up.

"I've got an idea," he said, smiling at Mei, who studiously looked away without reciprocating. "I want to take her on a boat ride before the nanny gets here this afternoon."

"You think she's ready for that?" Kelly asked anxiously.

"Sure. There are some boats that go out from the pier. Just small, one hour trips. I think she'll like it."

Actually, it sounded like fun. "Let's go," Kelly said.

A few preparations had to be made. Joe went out shopping to find a little sweat suit for Mei, as her supplies from the Philippines had included nothing for cool weather.

"It will get cold out there on the bay, and this way we'll know she's warm as toast," Joe explained.

Kelly had to admit he was thinking ahead better than she was.

As they stood in line at the dock, Kelly noticed their reflection in the glass at the ticket office. They looked like a beautiful family. It warmed her heart, until she stopped herself.

Now, why had she thought that? What a crazy idea. They could never be a family. Joe was a true image of the prince she was convinced he was, and Mei looked like a little princess. But Kelly looked like an ordinary person. A nice, fairly pretty, ordinary person. There wasn't a hint of royalty in her demeanor.

The boat ride started out well. The captain was full of odd stories and funny anecdotes, and he kept up a running dialogue that had them in stitches half the time.

He showed them where huge sea lions had taken over a small boat dock, yelling like crazy when anyone came near. Then he drove on to an area where sea otters infested a kelp bed, some lying on their backs and opening oysters against rocks held on their bellies. There was a seabird rookery and an island made of an old buoy and a lot of barnacles that housed a family of pelicans. And then they headed toward open sea to find dolphins and possibly a whale or two.

They caught sight of a dolphin scampering through the water, but were out of luck with the whales, despite the fact that Kelly kept urging Mei to "look for whales, sweetie. Keep looking!"

Mei looked very hard, but there was no sign of a whale. She seemed disappointed, so it was time for Joe to pull out his surprise.

He'd gone into the shop at the dock and picked up a present for her, and now he took it from his jacket pocket and held it out. It was a stuffed killer whale, just the right size for a toddler.

"Here you are, honey," he said to his beloved daughter. "I bought you a present. Here's your whale."

Mei looked at him and looked at the whale, then held out her hand to take it. He gave it to her, and without a second of hesitation, she threw it overboard, right into the water. It tumbled in the wake for a second or two, then sank like a stone.

They sat for a moment, staring after it, stunned. Kelly couldn't believe Mei had actually done that. This was too much, a step too far. It couldn't be allowed. To overlook such shenanigans would be no good for Mei, and criminal toward Joe. Kelly glanced at the child, who looked pleased as punch.

"Mei," she said tersely, "No! Your daddy gave you that whale as a gift. You don't treat people that way. You don't throw away presents that people give you out of love."

Joe felt as though someone had just hit him in the head with a brick. It was no use. None of this was going to work. His little girl hated him. In a way, it almost felt as though a small part of Angie had just rejected him for good. How did he come back from that one? What more could he do about it? He really didn't have a clue.

All this garbage about being a prince didn't mean a thing to him. All he really wanted was for his little girl to accept him. Was that never going to happen?

"Mei, you hurt your daddy's feelings," Kelly was saying, keeping her voice calm but firm. "Tell your daddy that you're sorry."

Kelly knew very well that Mei couldn't even say the word *sorry*, but she wanted to get the emotional injury through to her at least. The concept was in that little brain, somewhere. She just wanted Mei to know that people had taken notice.

Mei's huge dark eyes were unreadable, but Kelly could tell her strong words were having an effect, so she stopped. She didn't want to overwhelm her with emotions. Pulling her close, she hugged her tightly and whispered in her ear, "Daddy loves you. And you love your daddy. You just don't know it yet."

The walk home wasn't as filled with fun as the walk to the pier had been, but they returned in time to greet the new nanny. Mrs. Gomez was a warm and lovely older woman, and Kelly could tell right away she was going to work out fine. It was a relief to have someone else to help with the burden of caring for Mei every day. That couldn't go on forever. But for now, it was the way things had to be.

Once Kelly had met Mrs. Gomez, she had no more doubts about her possibly being a spy sent by Sonja. The woman was an open book, a wonderful lady who loved children. But after a couple of hours, Kelly began to wonder what her own purpose here was.

She said as much to Joe. "I guess I could go back to my hotel," she offered, as she helped him wash dishes after lunch.

He looked at her in horror. "What are you talking about?

"I...well, with Mrs. Gomez here, I thought..."

It hit him like a thunderbolt—Kelly might leave. For some reason he'd just assumed she was going to be around as long as he needed her. That was foolish, wasn't it?

He frowned, his gaze traveling over every inch of her, really seeing her, really feeling how empty it would be around here without her. He liked her. He liked her a lot. Maybe too much.

Now why would he think a thing like that? Because of Angie?

He waited a second or two for the pain to grip his heart. There it was, but not quite as sharp as usual. And not quite as anguished.

He turned away, disturbed. A tiny thread of panic

hit him for a moment. Was he losing his feelings about Angie? Were they going to fade?

He remembered when they had racked him with such torture he'd almost thought about ending it all. Life hadn't seemed worth living without her. He didn't think he could go on with such pain wrapped around him like a straitjacket. And then, little by little, the pain had become a part of him.

Was it going to fade if he let himself fall for Kelly? Without it, would he still be the man he thought he was?

He looked at her again and knew it didn't matter. He liked her. He wanted her around. She made him happy in a totally different way than Angie had. But happy was happy. He didn't want Kelly to leave.

"You thought you wouldn't have anything to do here?" he challenged with a smile. "You're nuts." He gave a one-shouldered shrug. "There's always me to satisfy."

She couldn't keep from smiling at that one. "You want me to stay?"

"Heck, yes."

"Are you sure?"

He turned and held her by the shoulders. "Let's put it this way—you're not going anywhere."

She shivered with a feeling very close to delight. His hands felt warm and protective, and he was leaning closer, looking at her mouth. He just might kiss her.

"I'm going somewhere on Saturday," she reminded him. "I have to go home."

"Not if we think of a way to keep you here," he said

huskily, and his mouth took hers gently, and then with more urgency, kissing her again and again, until her lips parted and she invited him in. His arms came around her and she arched into his embrace.

"Kelly, Kelly," he murmured against her ear. "You've got to stay. I can't do without you."

Mrs. Gomez was coming down the hall with Mei, and they pulled apart, but Kelly carried the warmth of his words and the thrill of his kiss with her for the rest of the afternoon. It didn't mean a thing, she knew, but it sure was nice. While it lasted.

Despite the teasing and the kissing, it was quite evident that Joe was troubled by all the changes in his life. When he announced he was taking some time off to go surfing, Kelly knew he really needed space alone to think. She watched him walk away in his cutoff shorts, with his board under his arm and his wet suit over his shoulder and sighed. He was so gorgeous. But he had so much on his mind, and she hoped he found some peace in the cold California waters.

She called her office to see if there was any news, or if Jim had found out anything about Sonja Smith. She hadn't expected much on that score, and sure enough, he hadn't found anything.

"I did find that there are a number of small enclaves of Ambrian exiles we didn't have in the database before, all centered around the San Diego area. So she is probably a member of one of those."

"But you don't know much about them."

"Nope. Still working on that."

"Okay, Jim. Here goes. I got a pretty good confirmation. Joe is almost certainly Prince Cassius."

"So you think he's the real deal."

"Yes, I do."

"Only DNA testing can prove it. Is he willing?"

"He will be. Can you work on getting him a liaison to the current wise men involved? I think someone ought to contact him about going to the funeral."

"You got it. I know who to call."

"Thanks."

"Shall I have him phone you?"

She sighed. "No. I won't be here much longer. Better call Joe directly."

"Okay. And Kelly?"

"Yes?"

"Good work."

She smiled. "Thanks, Jim." And as she hung up she realized he hadn't made one joke at her expense.

CHAPTER TEN

KELLY TOOK MEI down to the strand where the best surfing was, looking for Joe. They found him just as he was coming out of the water. He was wearing his wet suit now and at first Mei looked at this monster in black neoprene coming toward them in horror. When he got close she realized who it was, and Kelly noticed that although she didn't react in a friendly manner, she wasn't stiff with resentment as she'd been before. And when he shook his head, spraying water all over her, Mei actually laughed and clapped her hands together. And then she turned away when he smiled at her.

Joe didn't care right now. The moment was too good to let little things spoil it. He'd had a good workout and thought some things through, and he'd seen his two favorite women in the world standing in the sand, waiting for him as he came out of the ocean.

Good times. His heart was full.

They walked back to the house, enjoying the afternoon sun as it slanted against the neighborhood windows. It wasn't until they were back at the house that Joe told her he was going out in a half hour.

"I've got an appointment, believe it or not. I need a shower and then I'll be gone for about an hour or so."

"Oh," she said. "Okay. Well, I have some things to do. I guess I'll see you later."

He looked at her quizzically. "So you're not going to ask me who the appointment is with?" he teased, as she started to turn away.

She gazed at him, wide eyed. "It's really none of my business. But if you want to tell me…"

He shook his head and waved his hand dismissively. "No, not really. It'll just get you all riled up."

Now, of course, she had to know.

"Okay, Joe. You're dying to tell me. So tell me already. Who's your appointment with?"

He grinned at her. "Sonja. I'm meeting her at the coffee place."

Kelly put one hand on her hip and glared at him. "What?"

"I saw her this morning when I went to the Baby Boutique to find the sweatsuit for Mei. She wants to go over some of her ideas with me."

"What sort of ideas?" Kelly asked suspiciously.

"I guess I'll find out when we meet," he said cheerfully. "I'd ask you to come along, but something tells me we wouldn't get much accomplished that way."

He was right about that. Kelly fumed a bit, then told him, "Joe, you have to be very careful what you say around her. I really think she could be trouble."

"Really?"

"Don't let your guard down. And especially don't tell her about last night."

He pretended to look innocent. "You mean about how you were all over me on the couch?" he said, looking dreamy. "Frankly, I don't think she'd be interested."

"No, you know what I mean. About the things from your childhood. About our new determination about you. Things like that. It would be better if she didn't know."

He nodded, basically agreeing with her. "Despite the way I kid around, Kelly, I do understand where you're coming from. I'll be careful."

"I wish you wouldn't go at all," she fretted as the time came. "What if she—?"

"Hush." Joe put a finger to her lips. "I'll be back in an hour. You stay here and keep the home fires burning. Okay?"

Joe left for the coffee shop and Kelly began to pace. Every "what if?" possible was tumbling through her brain. Sonja was up to something. Kelly didn't trust her an inch. Why was he so easily taken in by her flirtatious act? He thought he was invincible, didn't he? He was going to get blindsided. If only Kelly was there to help him!

That was it. She *had* to be there to help him. Why hadn't she thought of that before? But she couldn't just walk in and stomp up to their table and flop down and join them. Though it would be fun to start needling Sonja, that wouldn't work out well.

No. She had to go incognito.

Racing to the room where she was storing her clothes, she pulled out the baggy sweatpants and hoodie sweatshirt she'd worn the day she first came face-to-face with Joe. It was the only disguise she had, so it would have to do. She asked Mrs. Gomez to listen for Mei, who was taking her nap, and she set off for the coffee shop.

She saw them right away, but they didn't even look up, so she wasn't afraid of being spotted. She ordered her drink, then took a table on the other side of the room and slipped into the chair, keeping her hood down over her eyes.

She could see them quite well, but couldn't hear a word. They were talking animatedly. Sonja seemed to be trying to convince him of something. He was shaking his head and generally doing what Joe did best—resisting joining in with female plans.

Sonja begged. Sonja pleaded. Sonja flirted and tried to persuade. Her body language told it all. And Joe deflected every bit of her proposal with humor and a shrug.

Which was all very well. But what else did Sonja have on her agenda for later? What was she planning to do to Joe? That was what was worrying Kelly.

For a moment, he seemed to get angry. He was making his own points rather forcefully. Kelly strained her ears, but she still couldn't hear a thing.

Then Sonja grabbed his hand and leaned toward him, pleading for something. Joe was looking long-suffering. He shifted away from Sonja. She leaned in closer. He turned his head away—and his eyes met Kelly's. He went completely still.

It was as though an electric charge ignited the air

between them. Kelly glanced around quickly, sure others must have seen it. He stared at her and she stared back. And slowly, a grin began to spread across his handsome face.

What was he going to do? She tensed, ready to run if she had to. He was still talking to Sonja, but he was looking at Kelly. In fact, he was making faces at her! She pretended to sip on the straw in her frappuccino, but her cheeks were flaming, she knew. No matter how much she pulled her hoodie down, she couldn't cover that up.

Finally Joe seemed to tell one too many jokes, and Sonja got up and left in a huff, leaving him behind at the table. He rose slowly and walked across the room to where Kelly was sitting, stopping at her table and waiting. Finally she couldn't stand it anymore and looked up into his face.

"What do you think you're doing here?" he demanded.

"I…I came to get a drink, of course." She straightened and tried to look cool, calm and collected. But he didn't buy it for a moment.

"Kelly."

"Well, I had to make sure. I don't trust her and I kept thinking about all the horrible things she might do."

"Uh-huh." He sank down into the chair across the table. "You thought she might get me into a hammerlock and force me into her car?"

Kelly pretended to consider it. "She's a big lady," she pointed out.

"Kelly." Reaching out, he took her hand in his.

"Listen, I think you take these people much too lightly," she told him earnestly. "They're dangerous." She searched his eyes. "So what did she do? Did she try to find out if you *are* Prince Cassius?"

"Yes. She did."

"I knew it!"

"Actually, she and Dory had pretty much decided I must be one of the princes, but they didn't know which one. They made the association from pictures just like you did."

Kelly snapped her fingers and murmured, "Shazam," under her breath.

"But she's not trying to get me to go back and sign up for my patriotic duty like you are. She wants me to help her make money. In fact, she offered me a job, paying twice as much if I really could prove I was the prince."

Kelly's mouth dropped open in reluctant admiration. "Oh, wow. Good move on her part."

"Yes, I thought so. Clever way to get me to confess." He grinned. "And nonviolent."

Kelly made a face at him. "You can never be too careful," she reminded him.

"Did you really think you were going to defend me from harm?" he asked, with laughter in his eyes and in his voice. "What were you going to do if she started to threaten me?"

"I assumed she really wouldn't do anything like that, at least not in public. But if she had a weapon…"

"You were prepared to throw yourself in front of me? Guard my life with your body?"

Kelly shook her head, all sweet innocence. "Whatever it takes."

"Hmm." He pursed his lips. "What about seduction?"

She frowned. "What about it?"

"If she'd tried it, would you be ready to guard me from that, too?"

She met his gaze and couldn't help but smile. "Maybe."

He held both her hands in his and looked at her across the table with so much affection she had to turn away.

"Don't worry, Kelly. I'll always be true. True to you."

That made her heart turn over in her chest. He might even mean that in the moment. But he didn't mean it the way she wished he would.

"Oh, Joe, stop it."

"You don't think I'm serious?"

She looked at him, loving him, regretting him. Didn't he get it yet? He was no longer free to decide whom he wanted to be true to. He was a prince of the realm. All his romances now belonged to the royal order. He didn't get to pick and choose.

Joe thought he was still in charge of his own destiny. He was a tough guy used to making his own decisions, fighting his own wars, making his own compromises when he chose to. He thought he could decide whether to go along with this royal gig or not, as his mood dictated. He was wrong.

And in some ways, it was all her fault. If she'd left him alone…

But no. That wouldn't have saved him. The Sonjas of the world were already seeking him out. If Kelly hadn't found him, someone else would have. The best, safest path would be for him to join his brothers and be a part of the fight for his homeland. She was convinced of that. Joe was going to have to come to that conclusion himself, though.

"Come on," she said to him, smiling with tears in her eyes. "Let's go back."

Mrs. Gomez went home at six in the evening, but first she made them a set of delicious quesadillas and a huge green salad to go with it. They had an intimate dinner after she left, talking softly, laughing a lot. Mei woke as they finished up, and Kelly brought her out and put her in the high chair to eat while Joe cleaned up the dishes.

He was thinking while he worked, remembering what Kelly had done for him the night before, with the pictures of the royal family, and it gave him an idea. He finished up and went to his room, opening a drawer where he kept most of his pictures of Angie. Just seeing her beloved face again made him smile, and that stopped him in his tracks. A smile instead of agony? Maybe things really were changing.

He took the pictures with him to the living room and invited Kelly to bring Mei to join him.

"What's up?" she asked curiously.

"I'm going to try it your way," he said. "I'm going to tell her about how I met her mother."

Kelly's dark eyes widened. "Oh, Joe," she said, and

a smile brightened her face. "I'll bring her in right away."

Joe set up pictures all around the room, and when Kelly came in, she put Mei down to play, and came over to sit by Joe on the couch. Joe looked at the little girl and felt his heart swell. He loved her so much and he was desperate to have at least a bit of that love returned.

"Mei, I want you to listen to me," he began, hoping this wasn't all for nothing. He was trying to keep his voice low and pleasant so as not to put her off, but so far, he might as well have been speaking pig latin. She made no sign that she heard a thing. This wasn't going to be easy.

"I'm not sure why you decided you had to make me pay like this. I think it probably has something to do with the fact that it was my fault you don't have your mother. I don't know how you could know that on a conscious level, but you feel it. Somehow, you feel it. And I accept it. I can't bring your mother back in the flesh. But I'm going to do as much as I can to show you what she was like. And how much she loved you. How much she still loves you. And how you came to be."

He rose from the couch and began to hold up photographs so that Mei might notice.

"These are pictures of your mother, Angie."

Mei seemed to be playing with her ring of plastic keys and completely ignoring everything Joe was saying and doing, but that didn't stop him. He began putting the pictures of Angie in more prominent places, not laying them on flat surfaces as Kelly had with the royals, but propping them up where Mei couldn't help but see them anytime she looked up from her toys.

"Here is the way your mother looked when I first met her. And now I'll tell you all about that."

He paused, and Mei glanced up as though she couldn't help herself. Joe smiled. Mei looked away quickly, but he met Kelly's gaze and they shared a grin. Mei could pretend all she wanted, but it was clear she was listening. How much she understood was another story, but at least she seemed to have some sense of what was going on here.

"I met Angie at a fiesta," he said softly. "I was stationed in the Philippines. We were out doing some cleanup work about a day's ride from Manila."

He held up some pictures and Kelly nodded. She was so impressed with Joe, so glad he'd decided to try this, although it didn't seem to be having much effect yet. So impressed that he could take advice, change his mind, do something because it might work. He was adaptable. You had to admire that in a guy.

Leaning forward, she asked, "By 'cleanup,' I assume you mean taking care of the bad guys?"

He favored her with a lopsided grin. "You catch on fast." He showed her a picture of himself and some of his army buddies riding in a Jeep. "Anyway, it was one of those huge Philippines parties that last for days. Everybody comes. There's singing and dancing and karaoke. And food—tables set up everywhere overflowing with food. Pancit and lumpia and roast pig."

Mei looked up at the familiar words. Joe smiled at her. She quickly looked down again.

"I caught sight of her right away. She was wearing a long skirt and a Philippines blouse with those high starched, gauzy sleeves. She looked like a butterfly about to take off over the trees. So pretty." He sighed. "Her mother didn't like me from the start. But Angie did, and for the moment, that was all that mattered. We got married and everyone had a wonderful time at our wedding. We didn't have a lot of time together, though. I had to go back to Manila and then, suddenly, I got shipped out to Thailand. She had you, Mei, while I was gone. By the time I finally got back there, rebels had taken over the whole area, killing most of the men."

Kelly gave a start, glancing at Mei. "Joe, do you really think you should…"

He took her hand and held it tightly. "Kelly, she lived with this all around her. She's seen things you wouldn't want a baby to see. And it wouldn't be honest to leave out the ugly parts." He gave Kelly a bittersweet smile. "The truth will set you free," he said almost mockingly.

"I'm not so sure that's always true," she retorted, but she saw his point. "Just don't get too graphic, okay?"

"Don't worry." He took a deep breath and continued. "The family was on the run. They had to leave their beautiful plantation behind and hide in the jungle, finding relatives who would take them in. I searched for Angie for days. When I finally found her, we only had a few minutes before—"

His voice caught and he didn't go on, but Kelly thought she understood. She'd read about how he'd been shot. Angie must have been killed at the same time. Kelly's heart broke for him.

"The rebels were pushed out and Angie's family got their plantation back. But Angie's mother blamed me for her daughter's death. I suppose she was right. It was my fault. If she hadn't come out to meet me that day…" Tears filled his eyes.

"Joe."

Kelly reached out to comfort him, but before her hand could grasp his, she realized Mei had come over, too. Toddling on her little chubby legs, she looked at him for a moment, then leaned forward and patted his leg with her hand. Two pats, and she turned and went back to her toys.

Kelly and Joe looked at each other in astonishment, hardly believing what she'd just done. Joe moved as though to go to her, but Kelly held him back.

"Later," she whispered. "Give her time to get used to this."

He nodded, took a deep breath and went on, talking about things he and Angie had done, about what life was like in the Philippines. As he talked, Mei played with her toys, then lay down on the floor and closed her eyes.

"Do you really think any of this is getting through to her?" Joe asked softly.

"Not the way it would to an adult." Kelly sighed. "But I think it's done a lot of good. It's all in the vibes."

He rose and walked over to where his daughter was lying. "There you go, I bored her to death. She's out cold."

"She's asleep." Kelly smiled. "And with babies, that's

usually a good thing." She rose as well. "Come on. Help me put her down in her crib."

"I'll do it," he said, and he bent down and slipped his hands under her neck and her legs. She woke as he lifted her, and her first reaction was to scrunch up her face and try to wrestle free. But Joe didn't let her. He pulled her against his chest and held her tenderly, rocking her and murmuring sweet words. In a moment, she stilled, and then her eyes closed again and she was limp as a noodle. Joe looked at Kelly and grinned.

Kelly was dancing with happiness—but very quietly. Together, they put the baby in her crib and pulled the blanket over her.

"It's going to be okay," Kelly whispered as they tiptoed out of the room. "You'll see. You've done it. Congrats."

"No, you've done it." He stopped, closed the door to the room and pulled her into his arms. "Thank God for you," he said, his voice low and husky. And then he kissed her.

She'd heard of kisses that took you to heaven, and she'd always scorned such talk.

But that was then. This was now.

And now was very different. Maybe it was the powerful maleness of him that did it. Suddenly everything was all senses—touch and smell and taste—and her brain seemed to go to sleep. His mouth on hers felt as hot and lush as black velvet looked, and it wasn't just touching—it was stroking and coaxing and plunging and drawing her out as she'd never been before. She seemed to be floating, and she couldn't feel her legs anymore.

Everything was focused on the kiss. She was living in this incredible sensation, and she never wanted it to stop.

His body was hard and lean and delicious, and she pressed herself against him, hungry to feel him against her breasts, wanting more of him and wanting it harder.

Vaguely, she realized he was saying something, and then he was drawing back. She didn't want him to go. She clung to him with an urgency she didn't know she had in her.

"Whoa, hold on," he said softly, taking her head in his hands and laughing down into her face. "Kelly, Kelly, if we keep this up, we'll be sorry, sweetheart. Let's take it easy for now. Okay?"

"Oh!" Her face turned bright red. "Oh, Joe, I've never...I mean I didn't..."

"Darling, it's quite obvious 'you've never.' And I don't think you're ready yet, either. No matter what that eager body of yours tells you."

She put her hand over her mouth. She'd never been so embarrassed in her life. "Oh Joe, I didn't mean to..."

"I know." He laced fingers with her, smiling at her with a sweet and lingering tenderness. "It's my fault. I got that train started down the track. I didn't know you didn't have any brakes."

"Joe!"

He laughed. "I'm kidding. Come on. Let's go out on the deck and cool off."

She went with him. The moon was out, the sound of the waves a calming backdrop. She looked into the night sky and sighed. If she hadn't already been pretty sure she was in love with him, she knew for sure now.

Kelly changed her plane reservations in the morning, but could add only one day. There was no getting out of going home on Sunday. After all, her job was worth saving.

Mei was beginning to respond to Joe. It was going to take time for her to be as natural with him as he would like, but it was coming along. They spent Saturday at the beach with her and then took her to a kiddie park where she could play on the equipment. They all three seemed to grow closer every minute they spent together.

Joe couldn't believe how happy it made him just to be with Kelly and Mei. But lurking in the background were the decisions he was going to have to make. Was he really a prince? And if so, was he ready to pick up that mantle?

This was a complicated problem. It wasn't as though there was a nice, placid life waiting for him in Ambria. If he wanted to claim his heritage, he was going to have to fight for it. There was a war waiting to be fought. Was he going to feel strongly enough about all this to be a part of that?

He'd been a fighter all his life. His career was based on the warrior creed. He'd assumed that was the only work he was trained in and the only work he would get. He'd had plenty of offers and he thought he'd take one soon.

But what if he could do something better? Something tied to his own heritage, his own destiny? Getting his country back from the evil clan who'd stolen it, the villains who had murdered his parents, the force that cursed his native land.

Wasn't that what his entire career, his entire life, had prepared him for? If he was a prince—and he was becoming more and more certain that he was—it was his duty, wasn't it?

Kelly seemed to think so.

"I've got my boss setting up some meetings for you," she told him that afternoon. "He'll arrange for your DNA test and—"

"Whoa," Joe said, shocked at how quickly this was coming at him. "I haven't said I would do that yet."

"No." She smiled at him sweetly. "But you will. Won't you?"

He melted. It was that smile that did it. This was not good. She could just about get him to do anything, couldn't she?

"I guess it wouldn't hurt to get the facts," he said grudgingly. "But what are these meetings you're talking about?"

"Different officials will be calling to discuss the possibilities with you." She hesitated, then smiled again, taking his hand in hers. "They'll want you to come to Italy."

"How am I going to do that? I can't leave Mei behind."

"Take her with you, of course. They'll find someone to help with that. Don't worry. Very soon, there will be people popping out of the woodwork to help you with everything. Get ready to feel overwhelmed."

He wasn't sure if he liked that prospect, and his eyes were troubled as he looked down at her. "I haven't said I'd do all this yet, you know," he reminded her.

She nodded. "But you will. You have to."

He had to? His natural sense of rebellion was rising up.

"I don't *have* to do anything," he claimed, feeling grumpy. Reaching out, he brushed back the hair from her face and looked at her lips. "Except kiss you. A lot."

She smiled up at him. "Of course," she murmured. "That goes without saying."

So he did.

On Sunday morning, Kelly was preparing to go, and it broke her heart. How was she going to say goodbye to the child who still clung to her neck every time she got the chance? How many mothers and mother surrogates did this baby have to lose in one lifetime?

And then there was Joe. Kelly couldn't even think about that.

Mei was asleep, and she wasn't going to go in and look at her once more. It was time. She turned to Joe.

He came toward her and pulled her into his arms, rocking her and holding her against him.

"Kelly," he said, his voice rough, "I want you to stay."

She closed her eyes. This was so hard. "Joe, you know I can't. I've thought about it long and hard. But I can't."

"Is it your job?"

She nodded, pulling her head back so she could look in his face. "You are Prince Cassius of Ambria and you have to take your place in that system. No matter how much you try to fight it, you belong there. I don't. I would have no place there, no tie, no claim. And anyway, I would lose my job." She shook her head sadly. "I have to look out for my own future."

He groaned. "If you get on that plane, we'll probably never see each other again."

She knew he was right. But it had to be. She stayed with him until she was already behind schedule, and then she finally tore herself away.

"I don't want you to come to the airport," she told him when he offered.

"Why not?"

She looked at him with tragic eyes. "I need to take my rental car back, anyway. I'd rather cut it off here and try to get back into my normal patterns right away. It'll…it'll be easier if I just…"

Her eyes filled with tears and she turned away. "Goodbye, Joe," she said, her voice choked. "Good luck."

"Kelly, wait."

Shaking her head, she kept walking, fighting back the tears.

She heard him coming up behind her, but she was startled when he put his hand on her elbow, pulled her around and took her into his arms.

"Kelly," he said roughly, looking down into her face. "Don't you know that I love you?"

"Joe…"

His mouth on hers was sweet and urgent all at once. She kissed him back, loving him, longing for him, wishing things were different. But they were what they were.

"Oh, Joe," she said brokenly as she clung to him. "I love you, too. But it doesn't matter. We can't…"

"Why can't we?" he said, wiping away her tears with his finger and gazing at her lovingly. "I don't have to be a prince. I don't even want to be one. I'd rather be with you."

"No." Drawing back, she shook her head. "No, Joe. You have to go to Italy. You have to explore your destiny. I couldn't live with myself if I kept you from that. You know you have to do it."

Reaching up, she pressed her fingertips to his lips in one last gesture of affection. "Goodbye," she whispered again. And she turned and left him there.

He didn't say anything at all as he watched her walk to the car. This wasn't like watching Angie die. Not anything close to that. But it hurt almost as badly.

To be or not to be. A prince, that was.

Did he really want to do this thing? Joe wasn't sure. He had now talked to the liaison people Kelly had set up for him, and they wanted him in Italy right away. They claimed they had accommodations ready for him, including servants and child care for Mei. It sounded kind of cushy—one might almost say royal.

Of course, they were expecting him to take a DNA test first thing. That was only reasonable. And he had no doubt what it would show. He was Prince Cassius. He knew that now.

Prince Cassius of the DeAngelis family who had ruled Ambria for hundreds of years. Wow. That was a real kick in the head.

Did he feel royal? Not really. He felt like the same Army Ranger he'd been since he left school. He'd grown up in a working-class household without any thoughts of privilege, and those early lessons would stay with him all his life. Admittedly, this was going to be quite an adjustment for him. Did he want to make it? Was he sure?

He wasn't sure of much of anything right now. His life was in flux and he was caught in the rapids. But there was one truth that he would never waver on—Mei was going to be with him wherever he went, whatever he did. His first priority would always be her. And Angie would always have a central place in his heart.

But there was something else that was becoming more and more important to him, and it centered around a woman with a mop of curly blonde hair and an irrepressible smile—the very woman who had brought all this royal stuff crashing down on him. Kelly. He missed her every minute. How could you miss someone so much who you hadn't even known two weeks ago? Something about her had worked for him from the very beginning. If he had Kelly with him right now, he'd be a lot more sure of what he was doing.

Was he in love with her? He thought back to how it had been with Angie, how he'd fallen hard from the moment he first saw her, how she'd swept up his life into days of passion, weeks of torture when he was away from her, moments of high drama and the awful, final act of destruction. It had been a wild ride, but—except for the ending—he wouldn't have missed a moment of it. Angie was part of him now, and she had left him with Mei, the best present of his life.

The way he felt about Kelly was different, and yet in some ways it was stronger even and more life-changing. She saw into his soul in ways no one else ever had. She could tell him more with a simple glance than anyone else, as well. In the short time she'd been with him, she'd made a lasting impact on them all. Kelly could have been his angel for the long haul, the center of something big and important. If only they'd had a little longer together…

But life didn't stand still and let you take time with decisions. It came at you quickly and you had to be ready to take it on. They wanted him to be a prince. Okay. He'd give it a try. He'd go to the funeral in Piasa. He'd meet the others and check the lay of the land and decide from there.

There was one missing ingredient, though. Something he was going to have to have. He sat down and looked up some numbers on his cell phone. He had a few people to call.

Kelly had been back to work for three days. California seemed like a dream. Had she really been there? Had she really fallen in love with a prince?

Yes, she had. But it was all over now. She had to get back to real life, even though there was a big, black hole in the middle of her soul.

She'd never been in love before. She hadn't realized

how much it was going to hurt to know she could never have Joe, no matter what she did. For the first two days, she'd felt as though her life was over. She was getting better now. She had finally slept the night before, and was actually able to force down some toast for breakfast before coming in. Now she was just trying to retrain herself to focus on her work and not dream all day about a certain golden surfer who was far, far away.

She was typing up a report when Jim came in waving a piece of paper.

"Guess who's going to the funeral?" he said, looking acerbic.

"Oh. Did you get an assignment?"

"No." He waved the paper at her. "You did."

"What?" She frowned. That couldn't be right.

"It says so right here. Better pack your things. They want you in Italy right away."

"Oh my gosh!"

The whole situation was crazy. How had she been chosen? But she didn't want to ask too many questions. She was afraid someone would say, "Hey, why are we sending her, anyway?" and it would be all over. So she kept her head down and made quick preparations, and before she knew it, she was on the plane to Italy.

And all she could think about was Joe. Would she see him? Would she get a glimpse of Mei? Maybe she'd see them at a fancy restaurant, or maybe there would be a parade and they would be in it. If she waved, would they wave back? How hard would that be—to see them passing and have them look right through her? She didn't know if she would be able to stand it.

But she was going. What would be would be. Piasa wasn't a very big town. Surely she would see them somewhere, at some point.

She landed at the airport and took a five-hour taxi ride into the mountains. The town of Piasa looked as if it belonged in the Swiss Alps. It was very quaint and adorable, with chalets and wildflowers everywhere. She almost expected to see Julie Andrews bursting into song every time she looked at the mountains.

Kelly spent the first day getting acclimatized, checking into her hotel, learning where she needed to go to get information, meeting some of the townsfolk. And asking discreetly if anyone knew anything about the lost princes. No one did.

But all in all, it was pretty exciting meeting Ambrians everywhere. The feeling of kinship was strong and there seemed to be a festive spirit in the air. Something was up, that was for sure.

When she finally got back to her hotel room that first night, there was a message from her home office of the Ambrian News Agency, asking why she hadn't contacted her client yet, and giving a number for doing so.

Client? What client? No one had told her there was a specific client involved. But she supposed that must be why she'd received the last-minute assignment, and no one had completed briefing her on what she was expected to do here.

She looked at the clock. It was too late to do anything about it tonight. She would call the number in the morning. With a sigh, she began to get ready for bed.

And then she heard a strange sound. She stopped, holding her breath. Something brushed against her door, and then there was whispering. And finally, a firm knock.

Her heart began to pound. This was an idyllic, picturesque little town, but she knew behind the pretty pictures lurked a perpetual menace. The Granvillis were behind most of the ugly incidents that happened to expatriot Ambrians. Everywhere she'd gone today, people had warned her to be careful.

She went to the door and listened. There was still whispering, but she couldn't make it out.

"Who is it?" she called.

A voice spoke—what sounded almost like a child's voice.

A child's voice. But it couldn't be….

"Mei?" she said, almost whispering herself. Throwing caution to the wind, she ripped the door open.

"Mei!"

There was the darling little girl, high up in Joe's arms, and now shrieking with laughter and clapping her hands. Kelly was so surprised she stood in shocked paralysis, her mouth open.

"Hey, better let us in," Joe advised, his grin wide and his eyes filled with affection. "You'll have your neighbors up in arms at all the noise soon."

"Joe!" She stepped back and herded them in. "I can't believe this. I was hoping I would find you somewhere, and here you are."

"Darn right," he said. "We've been trying to catch

up with you all afternoon. You were supposed to check in as soon as you got here."

She shook her head. "What are you talking about?"

"Didn't you guess? We're your clients—me and Mei. I got your agency to send you. I told them I needed to hire you as my communications director for awhile."

She stared at him, at a loss. Things were happening too fast.

"Hey." He pointed his thumb at his chest. "Meet the new boss. You're all mine now."

As if she hadn't been all along. Kelly started to laugh, and then she stopped herself, afraid she might lapse into hysteria. This was all so crazy.

Then she took a good look at them. Joe was dressed in a gray sweatshirt with a hood, and so was Mei. They looked like versions of how she'd appeared on the beach when Joe had first noticed her.

"Yeah, we're running around town undercover," he told her cheerfully. "Did you bring your sweats with you? You can join us. That'll keep you incognito as we make our way back to the Marbella House, where we're staying." He glanced at his watch. "Mei is up way past her bedtime, but she wanted to help me find you, so here she is."

Kelly shook her head in wonder. "So you two are okay now?" she asked, though she really didn't have to.

"Sure. Look at this." He set Mei down in a chair and knelt before her.

"Okay, Mei. We need to show Kelly your new talents. Show her. What does the pig say?"

Mei wiggled her nose and made a very cute grunting noise.

"What does the doggie say?"

She scrunched up her face and woofed heartily.

"What does the Mei say?"

She threw her arms out and wrapped them around Joe's neck. "Dada!" she cried happily.

Kelly watched with tears in her eyes. "That is the best present I could ever have," she told Joe, snuffling a bit as he stood and wrapped his arms around her.

"Okay," he said, lifting her chin and dropping a sweet kiss on her lips. "Then I guess I'll have to try to better it."

She blinked up at him. "What do you mean?"

He shrugged. "How would you like a royal wedding?"

"But…I'm not getting married."

He looked surprised. "Oh. Funny. I thought you were."

She was frowning. He was teasing her again, wasn't he? "No, I'm not, and it's not funny at all. In fact, I think you're—"

She stopped dead. He had a diamond ring in his hand. As she gaped at him, he went down on one knee and presented it to her. "Kelly Vrosis, would you be my wife?" he asked, his eyes shining with something that looked very much like love.

"Oh!"

He raised one eyebrow. "I was hoping for a yes."

"But…but—" She was utterly flabbergasted. Never in a million years had she expected anything like this.

"I need you with me, Kelly. Mei needs you, too. And the only way I can guarantee that is to marry you."

She laughed. "So what you're proposing is a marriage of convenience. Your convenience."

"You might say that. I'd rather say we were meant for each other and there is no point in delaying the inevitable."

Her smile could have warmed the room. "I like that kind of talk."

"And your answer is?"

"Yes! Oh, yes!"

"Dada!" Mei chimed in, clapping her hands.

Joe scooped her up and they had a three-way hug, a family at last.

* * * * *

A WINTER PROPOSAL *by Lucy Gordon*

Stockbroker Roscoe is struggling to fight his attraction to his solicitor Pippa. He can't decide whether to kiss her senseless or make a more permanent proposal!

HIS DIAMOND BRIDE *by Lucy Gordon*

Sensible Dee's amazed when pilot Mark pays attention to *her*! He's a risk-taking rogue with a thirst for adventure! But could the kind-hearted girl capture his heart?

SURPRISE: OUTBACK PROPOSAL *by Jennie Adams*

Alex MacKay makes buttoned-up Jane want to drop her professional guard and see where that attraction takes them! Even if he is ten years her junior!

A NATURAL FATHER *by Sarah Mayberry*

Single, pregnant and in need of a business partner is not what Lucy had planned. Still, things start looking up when gorgeous Dominic invests in her company...

BRANDED WITH HIS BABY *by Stella Bagwell*

Nurse Maura had sworn off men—until she was trapped with irresistible Quint during a thunderstorm. One perfect night later, she's pregnant with the rich rancher's baby!

Cherish

Cherish

PRESCRIPTION FOR ROMANCE
by Marie Ferrarella

Paul had a funny feeling about his new PR manager Ramona. Was she a spy trying to uncover his secrets...or a well-intentioned ingénue trying to steal his heart?

LOVE AND THE SINGLE DAD
by Susan Crosby

Donovan's just discovered he's father to a young son. But the newly minted single dad won't be single for long if old flame Laura has anything to say about it.

WEALTHY AUSTRALIAN, SECRET SON
by Margaret Way

Charlotte is shocked when Rohan walks back into her life. Her heart still beats his name. But can she tell him her secret after all the heartbreak of the past?

Cherish™

Three heart-warming stories make Christmas dreams come true...

A VERY *English* Christmas

BETTY NEELS
CAROLINE ANDERSON   SUSANNE JAMES

A WINTER LOVE STORY
by Betty Neels

GIVE ME FOREVER
by Caroline Anderson

JED HUNTER'S RELUCTANT BRIDE
by Susanne James

Available 3rd December 2010

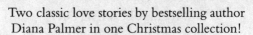

Four fabulous, festive, sparkling romances

SUSAN MEIER
BARBARA WALLACE
PATRICIA THAYER
DONNA ALWARD

Christmas Wishes

& MISTLETOE KISSES

Baby Beneath the Christmas Tree by Susan Meier
Magic Under the Mistletoe by Barbara Wallace
Snowbound Cowboy by Patricia Thayer
A Bride for Rocking H Ranch by Donna Alward

Available 19th November 2010

www.millsandboon.co.uk

M&B

There's nothing more important to a man than family

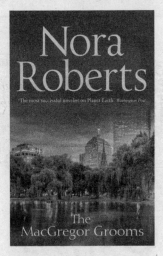

So Daniel MacGregor's found brides for his handsome, eligible grandsons.

DC MacGregor has never met a woman he couldn't forget. Until Layna. Playboy and gambler Duncan Blade is taking the biggest risk of his life—on love. Ian MacGregor is calm and controlled. But Naomi's innocence throws him off balance.

These three gorgeous grooms must say goodbye to their bachelor ways!

Available 7th January 2011

www.millsandboon.co.uk

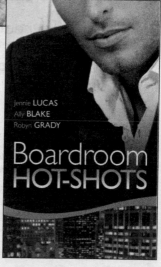

& RIVA™

With This Fling...
by Kelly Hunter

Charlotte Greenstone's convenient, fictional fiancé *inconveniently* resembles sexy stranger Greyson Tyler! Grey agrees to keep Charlotte's secret as long as they enjoy *all* the benefits of a real couple...

Girls' Guide to Flirting with Danger
by Kimberly Lang

When the media discover that marriage counsellor Megan Lowe is the ex-wife of an infamous divorce attorney, Megan has to take the plunge and face her dangerously sexy ex.

Juggling Briefcase & Baby
by Jessica Hart

A weekend working with his ex, Romy, and her baby, Freya, has corporate genius Lex confused. Opposites they may be, but Lex's attraction to happy-go-lucky Romy seems to have grown stronger with the years...

Deserted Island, Dreamy Ex
by Nicola Marsh

Starring in an island-based TV show sounded blissful, until Kristi discovered her Man Friday was her ex, Jared Malone. Of course, she doesn't feel *anything* for him, but can't help hoping he'll like her new bikini...

On sale from 3rd December 2010
Don't miss out!

2 FREE BOOKS
AND A SURPRISE GIFT

We would like to take this opportunity to thank you for reading this Mills & Boon® book by offering you the chance to take TWO more specially selected books from the Cherish™ series absolutely FREE! We're also making this offer to introduce you to the benefits of the Mills & Boon® Book Club™—

- **FREE home delivery**
- **FREE gifts and competitions**
- **FREE monthly Newsletter**
- **Exclusive Mills & Boon Book Club offers**
- **Books available before they're in the shops**

Accepting these FREE books and gift places you under no obligation to buy, you may cancel at any time, even after receiving your free books. Simply complete your details below and return the entire page to the address below. You don't even need a stamp!

YES Please send me 2 free Cherish books and a surprise gift. I understand that unless you hear from me, I will receive 5 superb new stories every month, including two 2-in-1 books priced at £5.30 each, and a single book priced at £3.30, postage and packing free. I am under no obligation to purchase any books and may cancel my subscription at any time. The free books and gift will be mine to keep in any case.

Ms/Mrs/Miss/Mr _____ Initials _____

Surname _____

Address _____

_____ Postcode _____

E-mail _____

Send this whole page to: Mills & Boon Book Club, Free Book Offer, FREEPOST NAT 10298, Richmond, TW9 1BR